TRAINING FREDDIE

The ADVENTURES of the Widow Merle McKinney & her INDOMITABLE SIDEKICK Freddie, the SMARTASS Terrier

CARLITA KOSTY

For June – enjoy the read!
Carlita Kosty
2025

Carlita Kosty
2024

©2024 All rights reserved. No part of this publication may be reproduced, distributed, or transmitted in any form or by any means, including photocopying, recording, or other electronic or mechanical methods, without the prior written permission of the author, except in the case of brief quotations embodied in critical reviews and certain other noncommercial uses permitted by copyright law.

ISBN: 979-8-35094-616-1 paperback
ISBN: 979-8-35094-617-8 ebook

For

Cristina, my mentor

and

Richard, my inspiration

CHAPTER 1

I knew the minute I laid eyes on her she was the sweet sucker for me.

"Well, you're a cute little fella'," she said, leaning over and looking at me sideways through the door of my temporary cage in the puppy pavilion. That was Saturday; I'd been there since Wednesday night, not my first visit. And I'm NOT a puppy!

She had THE KID with her. "Grandma, let's take him out in the play yard and see if he likes us." Really glad to be free at last, I raced around the fence about fifteen times, then stood there, panting, checking them out. Who WERE these people? The Kid was tall and skinny with curly red hair; black jeans fit her long legs like paint. She was all business, asking one question right after another, "Are you sure you don't want a puppy?" "What was this one doing in the puppy room, anyway?" "Before you decide, don't you want to see if there's another one you like better?" Impossible! The Old Lady was all smiles and "Oh, what a sweetie he is!" and "He's so cute, just adorable!" but, she looked like she could use some cheering up. "I can do that. See, I'm already doing it." I sat up, then fell over! She laughed and pointed. Kinda sassy Old Lady, cute grin. I think she liked me.

Merle sat in the office reception area of the animal shelter on Fredericksburg Road, filling out doggie adoption paperwork *(Wow, this is like adopting a child. Wonder if a social worker will make a home visit?)* and discussing possible doggie names with her granddaughter. "The card says his name is 'Lulu.' Didn't they know he's a boy?"

"Well, somebody must have known he was a boy because he's been neutered. Maybe he's 'a lulu of a dog.'" *(hmmm . . . wonder if that really could be it? Flash warning! Naw, he's so cute – and sweet. Bright pink tongue . . .)*

"Grandma, it's a stupid name for a boy dog."

Eventually they settled on "Freddie." Briefly Merle had considered "Asta" because that certainly was who he looked like. But then she thought about years of explaining "Asta" was Nick and Nora Charles' dog in *The Thin Man* movies. (*"Well, yes, a very long time ago, and ... yes, when movies were only in black and white . . ."*) So, in the end they named him for the place they got him, Fredericksburg Road Animal Shelter. Besides, they decided, he looked like a "Freddie," cute and cocky, and all boy.

"Ahhh ... a new name, a new life! Merle, you are one lucky Old Lady. Here comes FREDDIE! ... The Kid's not part of the deal, is she?

Merle had gotten the carpet cleaned in the condo the previous week. She needed to obliterate all traces of the previous dog. The old carpet had certainly seen better days. Each time she had it shampooed, she was sure it was going to disintegrate and was always somewhat astonished to see it not only still whole, but almost clean, except, of course, for a few really bad stains that she tried to cover with area rugs – not expensive orientals, understand, just grandmother hand-me-downs that she had been mending as they unraveled ever since 1985. *(Well, dragging them around to cover doggie spots didn't help, did it?)*

Merle looked at Freddie. Like an old-fashioned stuffed animal, she thought, the stuffed-with-sawdust type, stiff, and just the right size for a footstool. He was mostly tan and white, with a black saddle, coarse kinky hair, stubby lamb's tail, little triangle-shaped floppy ears high on his head, dark brown eyes barely visible above a bottle brush snout, a shiny black nose, and dainty little white feet. She noticed he was in dire need of grooming as his hair was quite long and full which made him seem fat when, in reality, he was quite skinny, and had little tuffs of hair peeking out between his toes like a hobbit.

Merle ratted around in the kitchen while Freddie watched from under the kitchen table where he had planted himself.

"What to eat?" she said aloud. She checked the fridge, then the pantry, then scanned the overflow cabinet shelves, and checked the fridge, again. "Skipped lunch after my workshop this morning so I would have time to go get you, and I'm STARVED! If I were to scramble an egg or two, would you be interested?" She glanced briefly at Freddie who was following her every move, amazed at the sudden flurry of activity. She loaded mayo, eggs, butter, cheese, and Tabasco sauce into her arms and kicked the fridge door shut with a practiced maneuver involving a backward flick of her ankle. Dumped the load on the counter and reached into a lower cabinet to get a frying pan.

"Sure, I'm always up for an egg – or three!"

"I've got to fatten you up! You're nothing but a fuzzball. How about a little grated cheese on that egg?"

"Yeah, yeah. I'd like that a lot."

"I bet you'd like that, wouldn't you, Freddie? I'm probably going to spoil you rotten. And you probably wouldn't mind that, either."

"I'll muster my strength."

Merle cracked five eggs into the old crockery bowl, her grandmother's bowl, the bowl that her 'Buela had used to mix bread and batters and pastry dough in her little house on *la frontera*. (A short dictionary of Spanish Words and Phrases can be found at the end of Chapter 30.) She plopped a generous pat of butter into the old Revere Ware frying pan, the one on which she had replaced the handle, twice. *(Boy, what a pain that was before the Internet! Guess technology is good for some things, after all. Maybe . . .)* As the butter melted and sputtered in the pan, she whipped the eggs with a long-handle whisk and added a splash of milk, salt and pepper, a little dash of garlic powder, and a couple of drops of Tabasco sauce. *(Hope this doesn't offend Freddie's digestion. Well, he's going to have to get used to living with me now.)* She poured the egg mixture into the skillet and looked for the grater. Watching the pale-yellow slivers of Jarlsberg fall directly onto the eggs, she stirred them with a spatula, flipped them over a couple of times, then served about two eggs' worth into Freddie's new bowl and the rest onto her own plate, adding a couple of slices of whole wheat toast for herself. She let Fred's share sit a few minutes on the counter to cool before she gave it to him so he wouldn't burn his mouth. They watched a CNN news update on TV while they enjoyed their treat.

"I think I'm gonna like the food here."

"All my other dogs have always liked this treat. You join a very auspicious line of canines, Fred. Welcome to Merle's house. I think we're going to get along just fine."

Later that evening Merle got out the new red nylon leash she had bought along with some dry dog food at HEB and cut it off its cardboard backing with scissors from the end table in the living room. "Let's see if you're housebroken, Freddie. Maybe I won't have to confine you to the kitchen."

"Broken? What's broken?"

"'Confine' is not a nice word, Merle. I don't like that word. Please don't use it anymore."

"Can you poop and pee outside like a good puppy?"

"I'm NOT a puppy! Of course, I can poop and pee outside. And, I AM a good dog."

"We'll see."

Sunday nite, 9 pm/SA.

Got a new dog yesterday. After my extremely boring workshop, Fay and I went to Fredericksburg Road shelter and picked one out. Not a puppy, though, a two-and-a-half-year-old wire-haired fox terrier. He's a real cutie, but promises to be a handful. The only puppies they had were either too small (like "Chihuahua mix"), that I probably would trip over, or else too large ("German shepherd mix" or "lab mix"), that eventually would be able to knock me over. The little volunteer at the shelter wasn't sure what he was, so I Googled "wire-haired fox terriers" when we got home and up popped photos of doggies that are his spittin' image if he were a little spiffier. He seems well-cared for, even has a microchip, but does need a haircut and nail trim. And he's scratching a lot, so maybe a medicated shampoo? Don't think he has any fleas, but will check again.

Theoretically, he's house trained. So far, so good. I think the carpet cleaners did a pretty good job of removing Babs' legacy. Wish I could afford new carpet, but maybe not such a good idea with a new dog, after all. Wonder why his previous owners brought him back to the shelter? He seems to be a really good dog. Maybe an overseas deployment? SA is, after all, Military City USA.

And entertaining! Freddie plays ball – and actually brings the ball back for me to throw again! Yesterday, when I first brought him home, and was walking him out front, a lady in a black Land Rover drove up and started talking to me about fox terriers. She had had several and gave me all kinds of advice: long walks, lots of attention and affection, etc. But, most pointedly, "Get him some toys. Otherwise, he will surely find some on his own." I did. Went to Petco last night and bought a squishy red squeakyball, rawhide chews and a rope thingie for tug-of-war (after all, he is a terrier, right?). Also bought him a bed. I've never had a dog who slept in a real dog bed, but Fred seems to like it. And he loves the red squeakyball. Makes it sound like he's murdering a mouse.

TRAINING FREDDIE

I've got a ton of papers to grade, but had much rather play with Freddie. I'll be sorry tomorrow. (Unprepared and winging it, as usual. I'm gonna get in trouble one of these days. So far tho', I've got 'em fooled!)

OK, so she was finally gone. Really, I'd never seen anybody make such a fuss over coffee. Guess she didn't want to leave me, huh? Now I had the place to myself. Ahhh … relaxing. I could finally get some sleep. Truth to tell, the puppy pavilion at the animal shelter wasn't exactly quiet like a nursery. Quite the opposite. Just one little bump or burp and EVERYBODY started howling! There was this one little twerp, a Chihuahua I think, maybe a toy poodle, who squeaked non-stop the whole time I was there. "I get it, I get it. You miss your mommy. So, get over it and shut up, already!" (I guess he didn't understand Fox Terrier.) And moving in here with Merle has been somewhat stressful, too, getting used to the new digs and all. She got me a nice plush bed that I knew was going to be great, all wrap-around and cozy. I'd never had a store-bought bed before. All in all, it seemed to be a pretty sweet set-up. At least for an upstairs apartment. I would've liked a yard with some birds to chase and lots of bugs to play with, but maybe we could work that out. She said she was gonna spoil me, right? Boy, was she ever lucky she picked me!

Monday nite, 10:30 pm/SA.

Little stinker peed on the rug today while I was at school! But, really couldn't scold him because (a) it had been several hours since he did it and he wouldn't have understood what he was being punished for, and (b) he was so happy – ecstatic, really – when I got home, my first lengthy absence since I got him, and for almost nine hours. He met me at the door, jumping up (gotta work on THAT, or at least get his nails cut) and licking my face all over when I leaned down. Wouldn't stop. And I was laughing so hard I was crying, really! Felt so good, too, that laugh.

Such a change from poor old Babs. How long did I nurse her? About six weeks, that last time, I think. I should have given up sooner, I guess. After all, she was almost seventeen, deaf, practically blind, and pretty much incontinent. Suffered from respiratory distress (well, they can't breathe very well, can they, bulldogs, with their flattened faces?) and arthritis, and probably several other things. And then she quit eating. Dr. Jennifer was so sweet, made the entire ordeal of having her put down almost bearable. She got down on the floor, with an old brown quilt (how many dogs had died on that same quilt, I wondered?), and held Babs' head in her lap, petted her, and talked softly to her, as the euthanasia drugs took effect. I was so distraught at the time that I just left, running out to the Jeep without even paying the bill, and then bawling my eyes out. But I did write Dr. Jen a nice thank-you later, telling her how much I appreciated her empathy and considerate manner in caring for Babs.

Another connection with John gone. Things just keep slipping away. I can't hold on to them no matter how hard I try. A few days ago Peggy told me that she saved John's last phone message from the hospital on her machine if I wanted to hear it. Do I?

Merle crammed the blue spiral notebook that she used as a journal under a pile of papers in the top cabinet of the living room bookshelf. *(Lord help me if any of the grandkids ever finds this. Only saving grace might be that none of them can read cursive, except Fay of course, because they don't teach handwriting in school anymore.)* She pulled an icy Bohemia out of the fridge and popped the top with the magnetic "church key" she kept stuck to the side of her fridge. Then, she opened the drawer to the old library table in the living room, reached in the back and pulled out a pack of cigarettes, felt around for the lighter, grabbed the red ceramic ashtray and sat down at the coffee table. (*Gotta quit this. Really, really gotta quit! Shit, why am I still doing this? Need a compelling reason to quit. Seems like I'm only able to make changes when I'm on deadline! Story of my life, I guess. Sure hope I don't run out of deadlines!)* Sitting cross-legged on the sofa, she picked up the blue Bicycle cards and began to shuffle. She handled the cards with the ease and efficiency of a long-time player. Feathered each time, then winkled one half-deck into the other, and shuffled, then feathered again. Now she laid out a hand of Solitaire and began to play. Freddie had watched this ritual from under the coffee table; now he jumped up to sit beside Merle.

"I don't have a man, Freddie. You're my main man, now. Can you handle it?"

"I love you, Merle. Can I lick your face?"

CHAPTER 2

San Antonio is an old city, at least by western hemisphere standards. It has all manner of peculiarities: a river that meanders through downtown, streets that disappear and reappear rather whimsically, neighborhoods that have experienced numerous incarnations and multiple revivals. And Spanish, Spanish everywhere! It's entirely possible to spend the whole day in downtown San Antonio and never hear a word of English. Most "Anglo" San Antonians possess at least a rudimentary amount of practical Spanish; can get the jest of advertisements and store signs, and can tell the difference between *chili con queso* and *chili con carne* on a menu.

Merle had grown up speaking Spanish with her mother and the Mexican housekeeper who came once a week. A lot of her classmates at William B. Travis Elementary spoke Spanish at home, but weren't allowed to speak it at school during the 1950s. But, of course, they did. On the playground it was a forbidden pleasure they frequently enjoyed, out of the hearing of the yard-duty teacher, whispering and giggling when they got away with it. She knew all the bad words by the time she was ten. When she took "real" Spanish in junior high, she found it unbelievably easy, but very different from what she and her friends spoke. All of her Spanish teachers were amazed that a little redhead named McKinney had such a dead perfect Spanish accent. Many years later, one of her Hispanic students told her that she was the only white woman he had ever known who could pronounce Spanish. That ranked among the top ten compliments she had collected in her lifetime and that she took out of her memory box and played with sometimes when she needed to cheer herself up.

She was christened Esperanza Merlot McKinney on the Sunday after D-Day, 1944. She had an uncle who insisted on calling her "Hope," but most people, certainly her friends, just called her "Merle." The "Esperanza" part of her name, her mother said, was because she was her mother's great hope during those long months her father was fighting Nazis in Europe. And the "Merlot" was what her parents were drinking the night she was conceived, the night before her father shipped out. Merle didn't meet her father until she was over a year old when she became daddy's girl on the spot.

When she was two, her father bought her a puppy, a Boston bull terrier named Lucky, who somehow survived Merle's terrible twos and became totally attached to the willful toddler. The two of them, Merle and Lucky, pretty much raised each other. Later, she and her dad and Lucky played ball hours-on-end, under the giant pecan trees, in the big backyard of the old house on West Huisache. Lucky even submitted himself to being dressed in doll clothes and having his picture taken. He slept on an old feather pillow covered in faded corduroy, on the floor at the foot of Merle's bed – at least until mom went to sleep. Then he would hop up onto Merle's bed and spend the rest of the night curled around her feet. As soon as the alarm clock went off in the morning, he jumped back down and settled on his pillow again. Mom actually knew the trick; she had come into Merle's room early one morning and felt the warm spot on the bed, looked at Lucky on the floor, and knew. She never said a thing, but she knew.

"Come on, Freddie, please find a place to poop. Now would be a good time. Mommy's really in a hurry this morning – gotta get to school so I can keep you in doggie treats."

"These things can't be rushed, Merle."

Freddie sniffed around on the grass, finally located a spot to his liking, spun around several times, squinched himself up, and pooped.

"There you go – good boy. I knew you could do it."

"A little less commentary would make this a lot easier, you know."

(God, what a day this promises to be! The friggin' STAAR Test, all day locked up with the same thirty anxious kids and the impossible task of keeping them all quiet after everyone is finished; after school my meeting with Dwayne's mom and the VP – that should be fun! Then taking the Jeep to the shop and arranging for transportation tomorrow. Jeez, why is it always the car? It's ALWAYS the car! How much time and anxiety – not to mention money – does a car cost the average American every year? Wonder how that compares with not having a car?)

That thought reminded Merle of John's old red Cherokee. Whenever she saw John in her head he was driving the red Cherokee with a cigarette hanging out of his mouth as he surged through the gears. The car fit him perfectly and he not so much drove it as wore it.

She grabbed her coffee out of the microwave when it beeped, got a granola bar out of the pantry, shouldered her purse and book bag, hung her car keys in the pocket placket of her slacks, changed from her regular inside glasses to her prescription sunglasses, and started down the stairs. . . Freddie was waiting expectantly at the landing, pink tongue hanging out and stubby tail making quick circles.

"No, Fred, you can't go to school with me. No doggies at school. Do you want a 'going away treat'?"

"If that's the best you have to offer, I'll take it."

"Come on, I'll get you a pig's ear."

"Pig's ear! Oh boy, oh boy! . . . Oh itch, oh itch!"

Freddie stopped in his tracks and began to scratch his chin furiously with his left hind leg, closing his eyes tight and making little huffy sounds.

"Oh, dear, Fred. Maybe we need a visit to the vet. You've been scratching ever since I brought you home. And I know you don't have any fleas, so what is the problem?" She put down her purse and book bag and coffee, got a pig's ear strip out of the plastic bag in the pantry and gave it to Freddie. Then, she hoisted her purse and bag again and grabbed the travel mug, "Be a good dog, Fred. Guard the house. Take messages." Freddie watched Merle down the stairs, head cocked and ears rotating.

"When are you coming home? Merle, don't get me wrong, I really like pigs' ears, I really do, but they're a poor substitute."

TRAINING FREDDIE

Thursday nite, 11:35/SA.

Am I ever going to quit crying? It sneaks up on me. I think I'm fine, then I see or hear something that triggers a memory, and I start again. Today it was finding John's porn collection, of all things! A little clutch of color computer printouts stuffed in the bottom drawer of his bathroom cabinet. (I was looking for saddle soap to clean my old navy sandals, and, oops, what's this?) John's been dead over a year – I need to stop this. And my glasses! I get tear spatters on the INSIDE of my glasses! How is that even possible? Do my eyes squirt out tears, or what?

Guess I need to clean out all his stuff, probably should have done it months go – maybe it'll be symbolic and cathartic, a personal cleansing, as it were. I'm putting it on my list for this summer.

Maybe what I really need is a distraction of the male persuasion – other than Freddie, although he is a treat. A human male would be nice. Anyway, I'm going to the cottage next Friday after school just as quick as I can – gotta get the hell outta Dodge! Freddie hasn't been, yet. Wonder how that'll be?

Still smoking! God, please help me find a compelling reason to quit. I know I can do it – I've done it before. I did quit when John was diagnosed, but HE didn't – that was part of the problem. But then when I no longer had John, I started again, for comfort and connection, I guess, thinking I could quit anytime. And I can. I just need a really good reason.

I overheard her tell the story like this. She was on the phone with her friend Doris, explaining why she got the locks changed on our condo.

"It was last Thursday, STAAR week at school, and the Social Studies test on Friday was the last one in the series. My test group had been pretty good all week and, being their history teacher, I wanted to do something special for them on the day of MY test. So, I decided to make some of my famous chocolate candy, the stuff John used to call "chocolate turdettes." I needed to make two batches in order to have enough for each kid to have at least three or four pieces. So, I made one batch Wednesday night and planned to make a second Thursday night. When I got home from school on Thursday afternoon, there was the first batch of candy laid out on the kitchen table just as I had left it, a section of newspaper laid on top with wax paper. If I don't put the newspaper down under the wax paper the heat from the candy makes the wax melt onto the table top and it's the devil to get off! Little chocolate turdettes all lined up in rows of five. Except, seven were missing from one end. All of one row and two from the next. Very neat and clean. No crumbs. No rumpled or torn paper.

"Now, I remembered that I had eaten three pieces the night before. I took one right after I finished them and put the pan in to soak. Went and plopped myself in front of the TV with a mushy, warm wad of chocolate. Then I took another two pieces with me for bedsnack while I read my mystery. That left four pieces unaccounted for. Had I been sleepwalking? Or, more specifically, had I been sleep-eating?

"I looked at Freddie. 'Did you do this?' The four cane-back chairs around the kitchen table were pushed all the way in. Nothing else on the table was disturbed. Two bottles and one vase with clippings I'm rooting in water were still just where I had put them. The basket I use for miscellaneous junk was right where it always was, and with a baggie full of doggie chew-stix right on top, untouched. He couldn't have! Impossible! There was no way he could have jumped up on the table – it's slick, you know, and he's only ten inches tall – and certainly not without knocking something over. And the four missing pieces of candy were in a friggin' row. Right off the end.

"So, I called Peggy, 'Were you over here today?'"

"'No, why?'"

"'Someone ate four pieces of the chocolate candy I made last night and I'm trying to figure out what happened.' After I explained the whole situation to her, I called all the other people who have keys to this place. Unfortunately, but characteristically, I couldn't exactly remember who all that included. We've been here for twenty years, after all. I've probably had a dozen or more extra keys during that time. They all went somewhere. I called the project manager. No, she hadn't been here, nor had there been any workmen. Peggy asked Michael – now, he really loves this candy – but, no. By then I was beginning to get frantic. Who had been in my condo? This was getting really spooky.

"Talked to Peggy again – since I promised her I would get back to her, as concerned as she is about my safety, a real mother hen, she is – and we decided maybe I needed to get the locks changed. OK, maybe so. So, she got Michael to come by Saturday and change out the locks for me. He's a real sweetie, does a lot for Peg. I thanked him both for the locks and for taking care of my baby.

"OK, so that was a week ago. Then yesterday morning, I happened to leave the butter out on the kitchen table instead of putting it back in the fridge like I usually do. On top of that, it was uncovered, no plastic wrap. Last night when I picked it up to use for dinner I noticed little lick marks on it, sort of mushed off one end. Then I checked: both the chairs were pushed all the way in and nothing else was disturbed. Everything just exactly as I had left it that morning. There was even a dirty dinner plate on the table with a little bit of uneaten meatloaf from the night before – still there, undisturbed, no lick marks."

(sigh)

"I haven't told Peg about the butter, yet."

(Chocolate! Mmmm ... my drug of choice).

"Come on, Freddie, let me hook you up. No, you can't take the squeaky-ball on walkies. Here, drop it. That's a good boy, have a treat." Merle always had doggie treats in her pocket to reward Freddie when he did something right. (*One of these days I'm going to forget about these when I do laundry.*)

She unlatched the patio gate and stepped onto the sidewalk, let the knotted red nylon braid leash slide through her hand. The first knot had been accidental, then after she discovered how handy it was for controlling Freddie when he suddenly lurched off in all directions, she put in two more. (*Got to work on leash manners!*)

"Look at that moon, Fred. Almost full. It's going to be really big and fat and gold this weekend at the coast. Wish I had someone to share it with."

"You have me! I like moons."

"I've been thinking about this a lot. I'm really tired of crying all the time and feeling sorry for myself. I want a new sweetie to have some fun with. I'm just not cut out to be a solitary person. And, truth to tell, I miss sex. What I need is a man."

"Now you're hurting my feelings."

"So, I said a little prayer. I promised God that when I find a boyfriend, I'll quit smoking – just as soon as I get laid. How's that?"

"Ah … I don't think this is going to work out, Merle."

CHAPTER 3

"And a little more defined waistline might be appropriate."

Dr. Jennifer had just prescribed a regimen of steroids, antibiotics, and antihistamines for Freddie's itching. "He seems to have gained several pounds since you got him, and rather rapidly, too. *(Oh great! Now I'm going to have to put my dog on a diet, too. He just seemed so pathetically skinny when I got him.)* "Let me know if this ruby-red rash doesn't disappear in a day or two. And keep him on the fish and potato diet – nothing else. We need to see if he has a food allergy we can isolate. So, one protein and one starch, only." Merle paid the two-hundred-dollar-plus bill, asked the vet tech to put the two bags and six cans of special diet in the Jeep, and herded Freddie onto the front seat which she had covered with an old blue bathmat. He had been to visit the groomer the day before, and as they drove down Austin Highway, Merle noted that he looked pretty spiffy riding shotgun, ears flapping in the wind.

They had stopped at the vet's office on her way out of town Friday afternoon. Made it just before they closed, as usual. The little yellow Jeep Liberty knew the way south, surely not as well as John's old red Cherokee, but Merle was on auto-pilot, nevertheless: McAllister Freeway through town, then I-37 south to the US 181 cut-off just outside Loop 410, on to Floresville, Kenedy, Goliad, Refugio and the little bay-side resort village of Copano Beach. One hundred, forty-one miles of south Texas back roads, two-and-a-half hours of south Texas brush country. Until you reach the Gulf of Mexico.

Copano Bay lies in the scruffy backwater of the mid-Texas coast, tucked away in a labyrinth of inlets, lagoons, bayous, tidal pools, and salt flats. It was explored by the Spanish as early as 1519, and, looking at a map or maneuvering a kayak through the narrow and sometimes disappearing waterways, one wonders how they ever found their way out. The bay is very shallow now, after centuries of silting and other natural processes filling it up with debris. Certainly not enough depth today for a Spanish galleon. People say that some years back, when a gulf hurricane hit Rockport on the peninsula to the east, half of that city was literally blown into the bay. According to local lore, there are still cars and trucks and refrigerators and parts of houses underwater just off shore, making the bay even shallower than it was before the storm.

Copano Bay, however, is famous for oysters; the beds are prolific and easily harvested. Merle used her binoculars, or the telescope she set up in the front room of the cottage, to watch the oystermen on their rafts as they worked. Real hunks they were! Fun to watch – boys playing with high-power tools, dangerous equipment, and other big-boy toys, getting all sweaty, dirty, and being totally macho. You could almost smell the testosterone from five miles away.

As late as the 1920s there was actually a real beach at Copano Beach. Merle had seen old, grainy, black and white photographs of men in striped, knee-length trunks and tank tops strutting around while bloomer-clad ladies with ruffled parasols watched over a multitude of blurry children chasing each other, splashing in the surf, or building sand castles. The sand was white, or seemed so, and waves coming in just like on the open Gulf. And a long, wide pier with a handsome bathhouse at the end. But now the beach had totally disappeared. Bay water washed up against bulkheads, a fractured ancient seawall, and into salt-grass tidal ponds. Houses situated near the water's edge were all elevated and a dozen or more wooden piers stretched out into the shallow bay.

Along the rocky coast surrounding the bay there grew native mesquite trees, low scrubby things, but with astonishingly beautiful, fern-like, lacy foliage. Of course, there were the famous Coastal Oaks, the unofficial mascot for this part of the Texas shoreline. To say they were "windswept" was an understatement. Where the wind off the Gulf of Mexico hit them, they were practically horizontal. They looked like they were all pointing in the same direction (inland) and saying, "go that-a-way." Recently, tree scientists have tried to dispel the idea that wind caused the deformity, suggesting that it's really the salt in the Gulf air, more on one side of the tree than the other, that shaped them like that. Merle preferred the wind theory. She considered those wind-blown oaks a visual metaphor for what life can do to us if we don't take shelter.

When they were seven miles north of Copano Beach, Merle turned to Freddie and said, "See that flashing light ahead? That marks the 'tension line.' Anything that's bothering you, just leave it right here, by the side of the road. You can pick it up on the way back. Now, (big mellow sigh as they passed under the traffic light) . . . we're below the tension line. So, relax." A little further on she turned the Jeep off the highway onto the town's main drag, then zigzagged over to the beach road and turned into the narrow driveway of a small Victorian cottage. Its white clapboard walls reflected a pale gold light from the rising moon.

"Is this the coast? Are we here? Something smells different. Something smells funky. OH BOY . . . really, really funky! Lemme out! Lemme out!"

Freddie bounded from one car window to another, back seat, front seat, back seat, sticking his head out and lapping in the salt air. Merle lit a ciggie, hooked up Freddie, and walked him across the street to the little park. She sat atop one of the picnic tables, her feet on the attached bench, looking at the shimmering medallion moon and its reflection on the bay, allowing Freddie to wander and drag his leash behind him. Two shore birds paced back and forth on the concrete retaining wall, peering intently at the black water. The tall, elegant one was a Great Blue Heron (The locals say that if you have to ask, "is it a Great Blue?" then it probably isn't.) and his sidekick a squatty night heron. The night heron trailed along behind Big Blue, pecking at him every so often. They reminded Merle of Humphrey Bogart and Peter Lorre in *Casablanca*. ("Do you still have the papers, Rick?") Merle had looked up Great Blue Heron in her Sibley bird reference guide. It said, "solitary and nocturnal." *(Sounds just like John! I lived with that man almost thirty years and he was just as much a mystery to me on the day he died as he was on the day I met him. "Solitary and nocturnal" indeed!)*

"Yikes! What's THAT? That's a LOT of water. Do I drink it or jump into it?"

Friday nite, late/Copano Beach.

God, I love this place! So quiet, so beautiful. Casa Esperanza – "Hope's house . . . house of hope." It certainly has been that. If I hadn't had this place to run away to, I think I would have gone crazy – truly crazy, more crazy than I am normally, whatever that means.

Freddie seems to enjoy it, too. Lots of new sights, sounds, and smells. He tried to eat a dead fish out on the pier, but I managed to convince him that, although Dr. Jen did prescribe fish for his new diet, the more processed variety was really a much better choice.

Saw a cute guy when I was filling up the Jeep in Goliad. No wedding ring – I'm making a point to notice these things now. Sort of cowboy, but kinda sexy, nevertheless. I think he winked at me – I smiled back, anyway. He tried to pet Freddie thru the open window. Fred growled and almost bit him. Protective little bugger, or just a nasty temper? Either way, not good. Very bad impression. Is this going to be a problem, I wonder? Must have a "talk" with Fred!

Wonder how many people my age are out there alone and lonely and wishing they weren't? Thousands? Hundreds of thousands? Maybe even millions? What a waste! Guess, for now anyway, it's just me and my vibrator. But one can dream . . .

Early Saturday morning Merle sat in the kitchen, an old wooden stool pulled up to the white porcelain-top table, forming little bon-bons in the palms of her hands with yucky brown stuff from a big, blue-rimmed, ceramic mixing bowl. She plopped each mushy little ball on a cookie sheet and mashed it with her thumb to make a tiny patty. The oven was warming. The murmur of morning news came softly from the radio set on the local NPR station out of Corpus Christi. She had mixed two cans of special diet fish and potato canned dog food with one cup of instant mashed potato flakes, squished it through her fingers, then patted it into a lump, washed her hands, and coated them with vegetable oil, before beginning to roll the bon-bons.

She walked over to the front door and, using one clean knuckle of her muck-coated right hand, she pushed back the shade and looked for the soon-to-be sunrise. The sky was still indigo and the bay steel blue, but a tiny line was appearing to separate the two. It looked like a thin strand of neon pink yarn stretched across the horizon with a fuzzy knot in the middle.

"Freddie, I hope you appreciate this. I don't know any other little doggie whose mommy makes him homemade treats. Dr. Jen said fish and potato only, so fish and potato it is. A doggie's got to have treats." *(Lord, this stuff smells just awful!)*

"Whoa………… what is that amazing odor? Treats? Did you say treats? I'm drooling already."

Freddie was trying to sit up cute and straight on the kitchen floor but his front feet kept sliding on the slick surface, so he was continually repositioning one foot, then the other, back-peddling, trying to get a better purchase and push himself upright. It was a losing battle. Just as soon as he pulled one foot in, the other slipped out from under him. But he was determined. If he had been able to get traction, he would have been scooting around the kitchen floor backwards on his butt.

The sun was just beginning to push a tiny edge above the bay, turning the sky mauve with pale gold streaks, and making a skeleton silhouette of the park's pier. Narrow rays of pink-tinged light filtered through the blinds into the kitchen.

Merle placed the cookie sheet of patty treats into the oven to bake. *(This stuff is going to smell even worse once it begins to heat.)*

"Come on, Twinkletoes, let's go walkies. You're in for a show!"

We headed toward the pier. I didn't want to leave that wonderful aroma coming from the kitchen, but Merle seemed to have her heart set on a walk. She hooked me up on the red leash and off we went toward the pier. I had to run to keep up with her. No sniffing!

"Hurry up, Freddie, we don't want to miss this."

The wooden pier planks clattered as we ran over them. Several gulls swooped in to investigate. Two black and white stilts were rooting around in the salt grass, looking like anorexic penguins.

"Hey, guys, hope you find something good."

We were practically flying now, when the sun suddenly popped up over the bay, huge and red-orange.

"Whoa! I need my shades!"

Blinding gold light shot across the water, turning its surface into amber-hued iridescent satin.

"Magic. This is magic! Look, the fish scales are glowing. Look at me, I'm glowing."

They had reached the end of the pier where it widened into a platform with benches all around. Merle spread her arms out and twirled around in the sunlight, shutting her eyes to the glare, but seeing it anyway right through her eyelids. The bay was dead calm, deep blue just a moment before, now shimmering bronze. Tall, puffy pink clouds billowed way overhead, backlit with a pale florescent yellow.

"Sit up, Fred. Give me your little feet. Here . . . up, up! Now, dance with me."

She pulled Fred into a standing position and proceeded to dance him around in a circle, more or less, swinging his front paws back and forth. Reluctant at first, then getting into the spirit, Freddie grinned and tried to figure what she was going to do next, when she began to sing,

" . . . here we go, 'round and 'round we go . . ."

Glorious! The two of them, alone on the pier, a frizzy-haired old lady and her spunky little dog, oblivious in their joy.

Then, in an instant, a micro-breath, the effect was gone. The sun became just the sun again, already heating things up, and the fish scales just made the floor and the benches look dirty. Actually, they were dirty – and a little smelly, too. Freddie and Merle walked slowly back toward the park, passing a father and son with their fishing rods and buckets of bait, heading out for a morning on the pier.

"Well, how'd you like that?" Merle asked Freddie.

"Cool! Can you make it happen again?"

"Come on, let's go check on your treats and get ready to go into town."

CHAPTER 4

In the years immediately following the Civil War, the village of Rockport had been little more than a fishing and shrimping community, and a coastal retreat for the wealthy. In 1886 the railroad came and by the turn of the century, fishing and shipbuilding, plus meat packing and shipping, had become established industries. The shipyards were especially useful in war production for both world wars. It grew popular in the fifties as a low-key, inexpensive holiday destination among the residents of Houston and San Antonio, both within three hours driving time. The creation of Key Alegro and its high-end vacation homes in the mid-sixties began to bring in the more affluent resort-seekers with their sailboats and interior decorators. Art galleries and antique shops sprang up along the main street downtown and seafood restaurants proliferated. But many mom-and-pop motels along Fulton Beach Road, with their rickety piers and rusty porch chairs, remained even into the twenty-first century.

Rockport, and its satellite Fulton, are located on a peninsula between Aransas Bay and Copano Bay, thirty miles up the coast from Corpus Christi, on the "Texas Riviera." Merle could see Rockport from her front porch, only eight miles across the water, but driving there was a different story altogether. The only road skirts the south end of Copano Bay and takes twenty-eight miles to reach downtown

Rockport. Fishing and shrimping are still major industries, but tourism has pretty much taken over.

Merle followed Fulton Beach Road north, passed the cut-off to Key Alegro at the humpback bridge, then turned the Jeep into Fulton Harbor parking lot and eased into the last space available with any shade whatsoever. The bi-monthly Farmers' Market always drew quite a crowd. After lowering all four windows a bit past half-way so Freddie could get air, but not jump out easily, she filled a Styrofoam cup with water from a plastic bottle she kept under her seat and set it in the cup holder between the two front seats. Then she dipped her fingers in the water and dampened Freddie's nose.

"OK, here's water if you want it. Now behave . . . I'll be back in a little bit."

"You're leaving? You're leaving ME ALL ALONE? Merle! Don't you know the National Advisory Board on Pet Safety says NOT to do this? . . . Merle? . . . And I think it's illegal . . ." Merle shut the Jeep door, clicked the lock, and put the keys in her pocket, fob hanging out and flopping against her thigh.

(Cantaloupes, first, then tomatoes . . . onions? maybe some mangos? Oooo, calabaza!) She wandered around a bit, looking at various booths, inspecting the fruits and vegetables, bunches of flowers, and homemade canned goods, all colorful and aromatic. A sudden gust of wind off Aransas Bay almost blew her hat off, so rather than walk around with one hand on her head, she took it off and stuffed it into her string tote

bag, letting the wind whip her hair. *(I'm going to look like I combed my hair with an eggbeater!)* She was paying a young Hispanic vendor for two fat cantaloupes and a bag of yellow onions, when she noticed the tall man standing behind her. He appeared to be mid-sixties, was dressed in khaki shorts with a Texas Tech sweatshirt, and a pony-tail. *(A pony-tail! I love men with pony-tails! Guess it's my inner hippie self.)* She looked up at him, smiled, a front lock of her hair spinning like a pinwheel out of control.

"I'll be finished in a minute, here. I promise," pushing the twirling hair back from her eyes.

"Take your time, little lady. Do you come here often?"

"I try to come whenever I'm down here on the right Saturday."

"Oh? Where are you from?"

"San Antonio – how about you?"

"Me, too! I have an old house over near Jefferson High School, where I graduated, I might add. Same house, too, I inherited it from my parents. I really love living in that historic area, all that great craftsman and art deco architecture."

And so began a casual, friendly conversation that led to a discovery that they knew several people mutually and a comparison of recipes for *calabaza*, the Mexican squash stew which Merle usually served with corn bread instead of tortillas. Then a slow walk along the waterfront and an invitation for coffee at Starbucks when they both were back in San Antonio. *(Wow. Is this how you meet guys? This is easy. And me with eggbeater hair, too!)*

Merle gave the pony-tail guy her San Antonio phone number and finished her shopping. As she paid for a jar of Bluebonnet honey, she glanced back at her recent acquaintance one more time. He towered above the elderly tourists and Hispanic ladies gathered around the watermelons and honeydews, his pale silver hair glinting in the sun.

For some obscure reason Freddie was asleep on the car floor, back of the driver's seat, and stayed there until they were half-way back to the cottage when he crawled sleepily over the console, pawed up the bathmat until he had it just the way he wanted, and curled up again in the front seat. Merle never even realized that she had just been "picked up."

Looking at oneself nude in a mirror with pure, clean coastal sunlight was somewhat of a shock if one isn't accustomed to such clarity. Merle stood in the large old-fashioned bathroom of the cottage, in front of a Victorian cheval mirror that was tilted just right to be full-length for her short frame. With a window to her back, she considered her reflection: clear blue eyes, the color of the bay on a bright June day, lots of laugh lines at the sides, a smattering of freckles across the nose and forehead. *(Well, some are probably age spots, but you can't really tell the difference, can you? They're all brown!)* All her own teeth – more or less. *(Oh dear, need to bleach – sorta let that slide when I started smoking again, figured what's the use?)*

She fluffed up her mop of hair, pulling strands down around her face. Salt-and-cinnamon hair, curly and short, "wash & wear" hair. *(Maybe a few gold highlights would brighten up the face?)* A mouth that used to be full and sensuous in her youth had tightened considerably after forty plus years of teaching school. *(Well, what do you expect? Should wear more pink lipstick – but gotta be careful, pink likes to turn purple on me. Maybe peach? Anyway, this brown stuff has got to go – been wearing it since I was twenty-six! At the time I thought it was my salvation, now it just looks muddy!)* Neck and chest not bad – skin didn't show too much sun damage. Amazing really, considering the number of times she had fried herself when she was a teen. On one particular holiday in the Rio Grande Valley when she was about fourteen, all she remembered was lying on the bed at the motel in the air-conditioning, slathered all over with Noxzema, and reading Seventeen magazine. Didn't even remember how she got the burn.

Upper arms, the universal curse of post-menopausal women, weren't too dangly. Yet . . . but maybe some exercises were in order. Actually, the whole body could use a bit of tightening and toning. Maybe it would help with the morning aches and pains, too. Mom used to say, "aches and pains of which few people die." True, but they certainly make life unpleasant. Still skinny, though. Good advice she had gotten years ago when she twisted her right knee and developed arthritis, "stay active and stay thin," the doctor had said. And she did. Well . . . mostly.

The butt appeared to be somewhat saggy, creased all over with tiny wrinkles, like crepe paper. *(Really ought to try some of that "skin-firming moisturizer," and soon!)* But all in all, not too bad for almost sixty-whatever! She did wish, however, that she would stop shrinking. More exercise? More calcium? She remembered when she was "five foot two, eyes of blue." Now nothing rhymed with "five foot, three-quarters."

She turned around, picked up the old, heavy, beveled hand mirror from the little marble shelf above the sink, and pondered the rear view. Her shoulders and back were broad and smooth and relatively freckle-free. *(How did that happen? Haven't been swimming enough this year. John loved my back, was the one thing about my body that never failed to turn him on. Well, I'm certainly glad something of mine did. God, he was good. Making love with that man was amazing!)* As she stood there, naked in the sunlight, her brain began playing tricks. She could feel John's warm breath on the back of her neck, his tongue tracing little circles down her back. Then, suddenly, she realized she was crying. *(Shit! Here we go again! Will this never stop?)* She dropped onto the little pink painted-wicker chair and pressed the heels of her hands against her eyes, the rose print chintz-covered cushion slick and cold on her bare ass.

That evening around six, an Oakville cheerleader came to the door selling raffle tickets. Copano Beach kids went to school in Oakville, twenty-three miles on the school bus each way. While she and Merle were talking, Freddie seized the opportunity and took off, right from the porch – didn't even bother with the steps. He glanced once over his shoulder at Merle who was shrieking, "No, Freddie, NO!" and leaped into freedom. It might have been the long nap that morning. It might have been that he had been either in the house or on a leash for weeks now. Or it might have been Merle's strange mood since she met Willie, the pony-tail from San Antonio, that morning. But he just had to get loose.

Merle went after him, leaving the little cheerleader flapping her arms and stammering apologies, but he was far too quick for her. He could walk faster than she could run. Little white fuzzy feet went flying. Not a clue where he was going.

Saturday nite, 8 pm/Copano Beach

FRED'S GONE! Took off! Can't find him anywhere. Dammit!

He looked back at me just before he jumped. He made a conscious decision. I could see it in his squinty little eyes, "Fuck you, lady! I'm outta' here!" After I gave up chasing him, I drove around a bit, but never saw him. OK, now what? Am I going to find him in the morning squished on the highway? He wouldn't wander THAT far, would he? Little turd! I'll go out and look again in a few minutes. It's going to be dark soon. If he get's lost . . . ?

He's been acting weird since this morning, since I met Willie Epps. Hmmm . . . Have I been talking about him? Maybe so.

9 pm

I drove six blocks each direction from the cottage – no Freddie. I whistled, I called his name over and over until I'm hoarse and . . . nothing. Not a glimpse. Guess I'll just have to wait for him to come home – if he can come home. Stupid little bugger. The longer he's gone, the more lost he's going to get.

TRAINING FREDDIE

9:30 pm

Dear God, I hope he's OK. Please, please make him be OK. Lord, please don't let me lose Freddie. I don't think I can do this – I've lost so much already, I can't lose Freddie, too. Funny how the little mutt has become so important to me in just a few weeks.

About an hour later, Merle decided to try looking for Freddie one more time, not holding out much hope as it had been almost five hours since he escaped. She drove all the way up Sandpiper until it dead-ended, then over to Surfside and all the way back, staying in first gear and using the heavy blue flashlight to search among the salt cedars and parked cars. The tiny circle of bright light was stark and empty, everything still. No moving parts, until she frightened a grey striped cat that, in turn, knocked over a garbage can, thankfully empty. It was quite dark now, no moon yet. She had just pulled onto Laughing Gull when she saw him. Right in the middle of the street, slowly walking along, headed directly toward the Jeep, headed toward the cottage, and listing to one side like he might have been drunk. *(Well, I'll give him that much, he WAS going home!)* He seemed very pale, a waif, ethereal and skinny, she thought. Spotlit about thirty feet in front of her, he had the proverbial deer-in-the-headlights stare, eyes like saucers. Merle's heart was pounding, *(Thank you, Lord! Thank you!)* she opened the car door and called to him.

"Freddie, COME!" He stopped, cocked his head, and listened, then sprang into a flat-out run, leaped into the car, over Merle's lap, poking her in the stomach with a wet-footed hind leg, and flopped onto the old blue bathmat in the passenger seat. *(Alright, positive reinforcement is what we need here.)*

"Good boy, Freddie. Good doggie. I really missed you. Where'd you go?" Now he was licking her face as she leaned over to hook the leash onto his collar. *(No more runabouts for you, at least not tonight.)*

"I went EVERYWHERE! It was AMAZING! Trash cans, a couple of nice labs two blocks over — we said we'd get back together real soon, they can really run once they get moving — great fire hydrants, telephone poles, and trees, lots and lots of trees. Must've peed eighteen times, and would've done more, but I ran out. Marked from the cottage to the trailer park and back. Ahhh, the trailer park — now that's a really fascinating place. Great crawling-under spaces. Got startled by a couple of big pink birds, thought they were going to eat me, or fly off with me, until I realized they were fake. Really tall, scary, fake pink birds. Imagine that!"

"I worried about you so much, I was really scared you wouldn't come back. Please don't do that again."

"Thanks for coming to get me. I was getting a little tired. I love you, Merle. I didn't mean to worry you."

"I want you to be a good dog for me and not run away."

"I am a good dog, Merle."

Back at the cottage, Merle fixed herself one of her famous grilled cheese sandwiches with broiled tomatoes and parmesan while she gave

Freddie some of the treats she had baked that morning. The house had finally cleared of the baked fish and potato smell after she burned three ginger-scented candles placed strategically in the kitchen and dining room. After eating, she poured herself a mug of freshly-brewed decaf, added a jigger of brandy, some Splenda, and no-fat half-and-half, then went out on the front porch and sat in the swing. The over-full moon was just rising from behind some low, smoky clouds, shooting bronze streaks across the surface of the inky bay. A big gawky pelican sailed by in silhouette against the moon, attempting to look cool. He almost made it until he ran out of lift and started to flap. She finally gave in to Freddie's scratching and whining at the door and brought him out, but on the leash. He sniffed around a little, then hopped up on the swing beside Merle. After a few minutes he snuggled as close as he could get to her thigh and laid his head in her lap.

"You know I can't do without you, don't you, Freddie?" She rubbed his back, patted his little fuzzy head, and played with his floppy ears.

"I'm really sorry I scared you, Merle, but sometimes a doggie just needs to explore — and smell."

"Remember, I told you that you're my main man? Well, that means I need for you to be responsible."

"Right. Responsible. That's me, responsible doggie." He lifted his head and looked her in the eye, expecting her to understand.

The wind had picked up some, so the mosquitoes left them alone.

CHAPTER 5

Merle sat cross-legged on the sofa hunched over the oval-top coffee table and shuffled the blue cards. Smoke rose slowly from her lit cigarette perched on the edge of the red ceramic ashtray. She shuffled, feathered, then shuffled again. Then again. And again. Then she held the deck in her right hand while she took a few cards from the bottom of the deck with her left hand and slid them into the others, dropping and slipping them into the larger portion of the cards, over and over. Then she shuffled and feathered again, taking care not to look at the bottom card.

She began to lay out a hand of Solitaire on the glossy table top. First card up, the ace of hearts. "Ah, a good sign. Power card in hearts. I have the power. I'm the queen of hearts." Count six down, then one up, another five down, one up . . .

"Let's see: some little clubs and spades, and there's the queen of spades, the bitch. Please let me find the king of diamonds quick." She played the ace of hearts, leaving a space with no king to fill it and started through the deck, three at a time, turn them over, deuce of spades. Not much help there. Three more, jack of diamonds, played him on the queen of spades. Three more, king of hearts. She placed him in the vacant space, then looked at the queen of spades sitting there big as life. "Damn! Can't play the bitch on my sweetie." She looked at the picture of the red king with his hair tied back like Willie's ponytail;

then flopped the deck down, scooped up the cards, turning some over, winkled them into a deck and began to shuffle again. "That one didn't count."

"What's the matter, Merle? I thought your phone call made you happy? And by the way, just in case you want to know what would make me happy? Going back to the coast would do the trick. I really like it down there, much better than here, and . . ."

And it had made her happy, the phone call that is. When she and Freddie got back to the condo in San Antonio, there had been a message on Merle's voice mail. Willie Epps wanted her to call him. She did and he asked her out for the following Saturday, dinner at Mi Tierra restaurant, downtown on old Market Square (or "Mi T's" as many locals say), a San Antonio tradition, certainly one of the city's most historic and colorful eating establishments. Merle hadn't been there in years, since before John died, long before. They used to take out-of-towners there all the time, but not in recent years. Merle wondered if the place had changed. Probably not.

Monday nite, 10 pm/SA

OK, what do I have to do to get ready for this DATE? Oh shit, do I even know how to DO this? Gotta fumigate the condo – he doesn't know I smoke as I do it mostly when I'm alone (private sin, private solace?). Maybe he'll be my "reason" to quit! Wouldn't that be a hoot!

What am I going to WEAR? This is important. Want to present the appropriate image. Not too stiff, but not too sexy, either. A nice color. Casual – he seems like a casual sort of guy. So . . . what does a sixty-plus-year-old widow school teacher wear on her first date with an eligible sixty-something-year-old retired . . . what? What did he do? Don't think he told me. Surely, I would have remembered if he had told me. (I'm not that far gone, am I?) Apparently not much now, to judge from all the volunteer and cultural stuff he does. Must have made pretty good money. Well, that would be nice, certainly wouldn't want to take on a charity case.

Been feeling a little out-of-sorts, edgy, the past few days, then realized I hadn't taken my "pussy pills" in a while. That's what John used to call my hormone replacement vaginal suppositories. Dr. Maldonado was so funny when she prescribed them, "Well, 'down there' is where you need them, so makes sense to put them 'down there,' doesn't it?" They sure make a difference. Wouldn't want to be grumpy on my date!

AND I need to NOT talk about John on my date! Wonder if grandkids are appropriate? Maybe, if he has some?

I'm in a state of paralyzed panic: my brain is doing double-time, but my body is doing nothing! And these last few weeks of school are gonna be a bitch!

"I could come by your place around four-thirty on Thursday and meet Freddie. Then we can set up a schedule." Merle had called the dog trainer recommended by her vet's office. Freddie's running off down at the coast had really scared her, so she decided to bite the bullet and get some professional help.

"The main thing I'm concerned about is coming when called."

"Well, we'll probably work on several basic things. That will be part of it."

Merle thought Dr. Gould sounded like an elderly professor. Very calm and soothing. *(Sure hope he can do something with Freddie, quick. I can't be worried about him all the time.)* She and Freddie had watched The Dog Whisperer on TV several times, so she knew that errant doggies could be fixed. And Freddie knew something was afoot, he just wasn't sure what it was.

Freddie sat up on the sofa beside Merle, all prim and proper, little triangle ears cocked toward the sound. When Cesar spoke to the problem-dog-in-question, Freddie paid close attention.

"No, no, no. Don't give in. It's all over, man!"

Freddie's ears swiveled around slowly like those giant radar receivers they used to search outer space for signs of intelligence. He whimpered occasionally and made little sympathetic growling sounds when appropriate. Once or twice he looked over his shoulder at Merle. *(Just checking.)*

From the TV, ". . . and just remember: Exercise, Discipline, Affection."

"No, no, Merle. Don't listen to him. He's got it all wrong. It's 'Exercise, AFFECTION, Affection!' Or maybe it's, 'Exercise, TREATS, Affection!'"

"Freddie, I want to tell you something. I hired a teacher for you today, sort of a doggie professor. He's going to teach us how to get you to behave."

"I don't like the sound of this, Merle. I KNOW how to behave, I just don't want to, sometimes."

"Especially not running off like you did at the coast."

"Ah, yes, the Coast. Now THAT was fun. Honest, Merle, I won't do it again. I PROMISE."

"So, he's coming over to meet you tomorrow. Please be nice."

"I'm a nice dog, Merle."

Saturday morning came a lot quicker than Merle expected. She had tons of stuff to do to get ready for her date with Willie and, as usual, was running out of time. She had gone to the beauty parlor and gotten her hair done early. *(Note to self: never, ever, get a haircut on the day of an important event!)* Now she was sitting on the sofa with her feet propped up on the coffee table, little blue foam dividers between her toes, waiting for the pearly, peachy-pink nail polish to dry and eating a potato and egg breakfast taco from the *taqueria* up the street, sipping rewarmed coffee while she considered her freckled toes. *(Would be nice if I could sneak a nap in this afternoon. Do I have time? Let's see, gotta bathe and shave legs, pluck nose hair, spray apartment, Fabreeze sofas and light candles, walk and feed Fred. Still haven't decided for sure what to wear . . . aghhh! And the kitchen is still a mess!)*

In the end she decided on a peasant skirt, which she rarely wore, because it made her feel girly, and a cotton T-shirt because it was comfortable, soft, and a beautiful shade of aquamarine. Her New Mexican Indian squash blossom necklace would probably have been too much, but a nice folksy strand of Mexican turquoise beads was just perfect. She knew for sure she had made the right choices the minute she saw Willie in his jeans, sandals and *guayabera*. So, they left for dinner looking very San Antonio.

After the *chiles rellenos* and *guacamole*, they had *flan* and *café con leche* for dessert, continuing to talk and only marginally distracted by the twinkle lights and shimmering silver banners overhead. During the course of their dinner conversation, Merle learned that Willie had grown up an only child in San Antonio, had been married briefly when he was in his twenties, managed to avoid the Vietnam War by the skin of his teeth, and loved to cook. He had no children, not even nieces or nephews, and, of course, no grandchildren. She thought he looked sad when he told her that. *(Well, I certainly have enough to go around.)* So, she told him about Fay and Bobby and little Rosie. He seemed genuinely interested, smiled and nodded a lot, asked surprisingly insightful questions. But she resisted the temptation of all grandmothers to get out the snapshots, which was fortunate because John's picture was still prominent in her wallet photo collection.

And they discovered they had a mutual acquaintance, Ellie Mayfield. She and Merle had graduated together from Alamo Heights High School too many years ago to think about, back when Ellie was the token Black in a snooty white neighborhood. The Civil Rights Movement was center stage in everyone's consciousness back then and the student body went all out to make her feel welcome, or at least so it seemed on the surface, anyway. But Ellie wanted to be more than a symbol. She was really smart, really good-looking, and a very talented artist. So she set about creating a persona – and a life – to prove to the world that she was an individual and should be treated as a person, not a people. She studied architecture at UT Austin in order to have a profession to fall back on if needed, but most of her life had made her living as an artist. Now she worked out of a studio in the Blue Star complex just south of downtown San Antonio.

Willie had worked with her several times in community initiatives (which always seemed to involve endless cocktail parties) and cultural projects (more cocktail parties). They shared Ellie stories and discussed how much she loved that *avant guarde* painting she did with the garish colors, but made her living off the post cards printed from her charming miniature water colors of cute little fat Mexican ladies. *(Maybe I'll call Ellie and ask about this guy. Haven't talked to her in at least a year. Should be good for an hour's entertainment – hearing about her adventures, most of them sexual. Not sure how she does it . . . always seems to have some handsome hunk hanging around.)*

When they got back to the condo, Merle asked Willie in and was greatly relieved when she climbed the stairs and noticed not even a trace of cigarette smoke. (*Ah, yes. Let's hear it for modern chemistry!*) Freddie made quite a fuss and Merle tried the new "sit" command the Professor had taught them, but Fred was too excited to listen, so didn't do his part. When he finally calmed down, and they were able to sit down, Merle and Willie shared a dessert wine Merle had in the fridge and talked a bit more.

Willie said he had had a wonderful time and got up to leave, reaching for Merle to give her a hug, when Freddie suddenly appeared between them, sniffed once, and began to pee on Willie's foot. Not just a little tinkle that could be construed as an accident. No, this was an intentional, purposeful, full-stream release, as if from a small garden hose. Urine darkened the bottoms of Willie's jeans and started to run between his toes, making big dark splotches on his leather sandals and turning his toenails a regrettable shade of yellow. It began to puddle around his cuticles and seep under the nails. Merle jumped up aghast, then stood there paralyzed, eyes stuck on wide open, mouth open, too, but nothing coming out, watching as Willie jumped around yelling.

"Gross! Aw . . . Gross!"

"Oh my God! Fred! BAD DOG! BAD, BAD DOG!"

Finally, she moved, ran to the kitchen for a towel.

"Oh, Willie, I am SO SORRY!" as she tried in vain to mop up the wet mess from his foot. Freddie had crawled under a chair to sulk. Willie was trying to be a good sport about it all – don't worry, accidents happen, and all that, but she could tell he was really pissed. (*Well, that would be the appropriate term, wouldn't it?*)

It was a rather awkward end to an otherwise delightful evening, but Merle managed to smile as Willie said he would call her when they parted in the downstairs patio. She went back inside, locked the door, and turned to find Freddie on the stairs, just eye-level, looking straight at her – cold, hard stare from under his long dark lashes. He wasn't smiling.

Merle put her hands on her hips and leaned over until she was nose to nose with Fred.

"You little turd!"

"That guy is trouble, Merle."

"I swear, Freddie, if you scare off my new boyfriend, I'm going to take you back to Fredericksburg Road!"

"Listen to me, Merle. The dude's no good!"

Suddenly Merle felt a sharp pain in her chest, right between her boobs. An old familiar feeling, the bowling ball she had carried around for months and months after John died. Placing her fist right where it hurt, she turned, dropped to the stairs, and dissolved into tears. Freddie began to lick at her cheek.

"Merle, sweetie, please don't do that. Just let's not see that weasel Willie guy again. OK?"

"Oh, don't lick my face! You caused this, you little green-eyed monster! You're not going to lick your way out of this one!"

CHAPTER 6

There are very few professions in which you get to start over once a year. Fortunately for the students involved, teaching is one of them. Otherwise, their teachers would all be insane after five years or less, at least the middle school teachers would. Early adolescence is a difficult experience under the best of circumstances and no less so for the enduring souls who work with those adolescents. The one real perk of the job is that you get to start over every fall with a new set of kids, a new schedule, new challenges, and frequently a new room. Summer vacation is not a perk; it is a necessary mental health recovery period.

But just as a new school year starts every fall, it must end every June. *(Oh my God, will this EVER end?)* Merle was babysitting her fifth period on the penultimate day of classes. Already she had handed out about a zillion history crossword puzzles, geography puzzles, brain teasers, and Highlights magazine line drawing "can you find it?" puzzles. Also several decks of playing cards from her closet. Most of the room was engaged . . . in something. She snagged the idle few to help her unload bookshelves and pack boxes from her closet because she was changing rooms once again. *(OK, tomorrow is all concerts, award assemblies, year books, and flocks of teenage girls crying. I can do it. Just keep smiling. And keep moving.)*

That afternoon as an exhausted Merle unlocked her front door, she heard the phone ringing. She hadn't heard from Willie in four days and she was beginning to get somewhat anxious. So, she ran up the stairs two at a time, Freddie nipping at her legs. Just as she reached for the receiver, it stopped ringing and went to voice mail, or so she thought. While she waited for the caller to record a message, she saw that Freddie had pooped in the living room, between the sofa and the bookcase. Grabbing a couple of Kleenex from a box on the shelf, she scooped up the still-warm pile and headed for the bathroom to flush it, when the phone rang again. This time she reached it on the first ring. Standing, and then eventually sitting, in her office, phone receiver in one hand and a wad of all-too-real dog shit in the other, she talked with Willie for almost an hour. *(Jeez, a cigarette would be nice right now.)* By the time she got off the phone she had heard about several famous scandals in recent San Antonio history, knew Willie's views on the new River Walk extension, and had a second date for Friday night. *(It's a miracle!)*

"Merle, let's go OUTSIDE! Can't you see I'm crossing my legs and trying not to pee? Come on, let's go! Now would be good, please."

"OK, OK, Wiggletail! Let's go walkies."

Freddie ran figure eights on the living room carpet, digging toenails in deep on the turns, gaining speed on the straight-aways. Merle grabbed the leash and they headed downstairs. Now totally hyped, Freddie sailed over the last few steps and then slammed into the opposite wall of the small entry, nose first. "Watch it, Fred!" Merle made a mental note to speak to the Professor about Freddie's house-training, and then she began to hatch a plan for managing his peculiar behavior around Willie on Friday night. *(I'll drug him! I already give him a Benadryl for his allergies, so how about I give him two? If I took twice my normal dose it would put me out of commission for several hours. Hmmm . . . Worth a try?)*

"Now I want to recognize the library staff and their assistants, …" *(oh, let's get ON with it!)* It was already 9:45 on Friday morning as Merle sat in the school cafeteria listening to her principal recognize and praise literally everyone on the faculty and staff, all one hundred and thirteen of them, department by department, and give each one of them a giant chocolate bar with "Lozano Middle School" printed on it.

The morning had started with breakfast tacos, juice, and coffee at 7:30, a friendly, almost giddy, gathering of dead tired, but restless teachers, ready to be free for the summer. Just like the kids had been yesterday. Between the tacos and the formal presentations, there had been some lobbing of taco-wrapper wads of tin foil across the room – first from a select few (mostly the PE Department) and then a general free-for-all.

(I'm not sure having a date – a really important second date, AND me offering to cook – is such a good idea on the day school closes. I've still got to pack and move more boxes, type up my room report, sort and label my keys, turn in my A/V equipment, clear my school email account, contact two parents whose kids were absent yesterday, and get my attendance report verified with the school attendance secretary. What else? I'm sure there must be something else. I'm not going to

get out of here until mid-afternoon, later if this BS lasts much longer. AND I have to go get a few things for dinner at HEB . . . then at least prep to cook . . . and shower . . . walk and feed Freddie. Wonder when would be the best time to give Freddie the extra Benadryl? And why do I suddenly feel like what's-her-name Borgia?)*

Merle wheeled the Jeep into a suddenly vacant space in the HEB parking lot and got out, grabbed a cart, and headed for the fresh produce section. Arroz con pollo, Mexican chicken and rice. She always wondered why you put the chicken first in English, but the rice first in Spanish. Differences in philosophy over the desirable ratio of chicken to rice, or rice to chicken, possibly? *(Let's see . . . tomatoes. Always best with fresh tomatoes. Green bell peppers and sweet red peppers, both. Cilantro, Mexican parsley. Smells so good, fresh and clean. Crush the leaves between your fingers and inhale. And onions, sweet Texas 1015 yellow onions.)* She picked up and put down several onions, holding, feeling them in her hand. *(John used to say the optimum size of an onion was a tennis ball. Don't know how the hell he knew that since he didn't play tennis, nor anything else. For all of his athletic-style, lanky frame, he was lazy as sin.)* She stared at the onion, tears welling up in her eyes. *(oh, sweet John . . . oh shit . . . here it comes again!)* She glanced around to see if anyone was watching. *(Maybe I can blame it on the onions, although these onions aren't stinky at all.)* She bagged several quickly as she felt the tears build pressure and heat behind her eyeballs and they began to leak down the sides of her face. She wiped each cheek with the back of her hand. *(The LIST . . . focus on the damn list! Get the stuff you need and get the hell out of here before you make a total fool of yourself! Grab the chicken breasts and the French bread. Have everything else at home, oh . . . the avocados . . . right. Why am I doing this?)* She jerked the grocery cart into an open line and unloaded onto the conveyor; accepted plastic bags, which she hated, without protest because she didn't trust her own voice if she requested paper like John used to do. She could almost hear him asking the checker for them now, his soothing baritone just the tiniest bit arrogant.

Once in her Jeep cocoon, she let it all go, using her stash of take-out-food napkins which she kept in the console cup holder to mop up her face, dab at her eyelashes and clean her glasses – again.

(Argh! Hair's not dry yet!) Merle reached for the make-up base, shook it fiercely and began to dab spots and smears on her face, using her finger tips to blend them into each other and cover the freckles and the brown "age spots." The bottle was almost empty, so it took considerably longer each time she put her finger over the opening and shook some of the skin-tinted liquid onto her finger tip. *(Now for the eyes. Where is the damn thingie, the Q-tip-like doo-dad, whatever you call it, I can't find it. OK – I'm looking all over the counter, under used tissue, move stuff around . . . Where the hell IS it? OK, use a regular Q-tip . . .)* When she rubbed the Q-tip on the cake of eye-shadow the cotton began to come unwound and turned into a fluff-ball. *(This isn't going to work!)* She tried her finger tip, little finger. *(Not too accurate, but serviceable.)* Leaning toward the mirror to see better – always a problem for near-sighted gals. *(You take your glasses off to put on eye make-up, but then*

you can't see to get it in the right place!) As she straightened up, her elbow hit the cologne bottle and it tumbled to the tile floor, bounced once and then hit the tile again and shattered, releasing a strong wave of eau d'Blue Grass. *(Shit! Good thing I already used it tonight.)* She stepped over the broken glass and evaporating fragrance, *(Lord, I paid a lot of money for that stuff. Dammit!)* and closed the bathroom door so Freddie wouldn't get into it. *(So – it's going to be one of THOSE nights, is it)?*

After sweeping up the glass and dumping the aromatic mess in the kitchen garbage, she returned to the bath. *(OK, mascara. Steady now, or you'll get it all over your face. Maybe the regular strength – that super-thick-n-long stuff is really hard to control, especially with droopy eyelids – well, not exactly droopy, but certainly closer to the lashes than they used to be. This make-up business is taking longer and longer the older I get . . . and with diminishing returns.)*

In the compact condo kitchen Merle began by grabbing pots and lids from the cupboards. The major ingredients were still in their plastic bags on the kitchen table. Stretching to reach the small cabinet above the oven hood, she almost dumped a whole pile of assorted size skillets on her head as she pulled out the largest from the bottom of the stack. After slopping in a generous amount of olive oil, she turned the burner on low so the oil could heat while she prepared the chicken breasts. Already skinless and boneless *(thank heaven for modern packaging!)* the chicken got a liberal salting, peppering and garlic powdering, then was carefully laid in the hot skillet. While the chicken was sizzling, she chopped the veggies into bite-sized pieces and piled them in a bowl; first the onion, then the red bell pepper and the green one. Three Roma tomatoes, in pieces, went into a different bowl. The smoke from the cooking chicken began to permeate the small kitchen and finally overcame the sweet perfume smell escaping from the garbage can.

When the chicken breasts were golden brown on both sides, she used tongs to lift them from the pan onto newspaper, topped with paper towel, to drain. Using another piece of newspaper wadded up, she wiped the skillet clean, put it back on the burner and poured in more olive oil. As that heated, she measured rice and added it to the heating oil. *(This is what gives "Mexican rice" it's unique flavor – the frying of the rice first, before cooking it with liquid. I wonder if that's what the Chinese do, too? Have to check on that . . .)* After dumping in the bowlful of chopped onion and peppers, she stirred the rice and veggie mix with a wooden spatula. As the rice turned an opaque, creamy white, she added more salt and garlic powder, a little chili powder, and a dab of brown sugar – to keep the garlic from tasting bitter, *(probably should be using fresh garlic, but I'm in a hurry, right?)* then added the chopped tomatoes which immediately begin to sizzle and steam. Finally she popped the lid on a can of chicken broth, poured it into the skillet and stired. As the mixture heated, she clipped off several sprigs of the fresh cilantro and cut them into slivers with her orange-handled kitchen scissors. *(Maybe it's time to rotate scissors again: buy a new pair of sewing scissors, move the sewing scissors to the gift-wrap drawer, the gift-wrap scissors to the kitchen, and these to school. School is the graveyard for scissors.)*

"OK, Freddie, time for your treat." *(Alright, he's used to getting his Benadryl at this time, so he shouldn't notice anything different, right? He can't count pills in his mouth, can he?)*

"*Merle, why are you acting so weird?*" Freddie took the canned dog food bonbon from Merle's hand and swallowed so quickly it seemed he inhaled it.

"*What's happening?*"

"There you go. Good dog." *(And I'll put you in the bedroom as soon as Willie arrives – should be a little sleepy by then.)*

"*Are we having company?*"

The doorbell rang, Merle straightened up, startled.

"Early, dammit!" She let herself out onto the balcony and peered over the rail. There was Willie Epps in rough-dried khaki shorts, faded turquoise t-shirt – Merle's absolute favorite color – and flip-flops, his little bald spot shining through the combover in the late afternoon sun. And in his left hand was a somewhat crude bouquet of open pink roses, yellow lilies, some little purple flowers on longish stems, all apparently handpicked from his own yard and all wrapped in a newspaper cone. *(Oh, my God! Flowers! Oh my God!)*

"Hi, Willie, I'll be right down." *(FLOWERS!!! OK, get a grip.)* Back in the kitchen, Freddie stood directly in Merle's path to the stairs and stared at her. She could see a green glint in his eyes, or so she imagined.

"*It's that Willie weasel person, isn't it?*"

CHAPTER 7

"I think you need to get rid of the dog. You've only had him a few months, right?"

"Right."

"He just got really attached to you and now he's jealous of your new man. Face it, honey, interested men aren't that thick on the ground. You need to get rid of the dog." Doris had called Saturday morning early to see if Merle wanted to go hang out at some ice house near San Antonio College and listen to a *conjunto* band she once played drums with, and with whom her first husband still played accordion. Merle wasn't really interested, but she was happy to have someone to talk to about the previous night's disaster. And Doris always had advice – not always good advice, but fresh options, nevertheless.

"I can't do that. He's part of the family already. But I'll tell you what, last night I was ready to chuck him off the balcony! He stood right on Willie's chest like a mountain goat, nose in Willie's face, growling! There was poor Willie terrified, all cringed back, and scared to death. All through dinner Freddie had scratched and whined and barked from behind the bedroom door. Thought he was NEVER going to quit. So finally, when he did, and as things got quiet and we were having after-dinner coffee with brandy in the living room (and I was wishing I had had time to make flan – you know how much I like flan, and most men do, too), and listening to jazz on KRTU, I decided to let Fred out.

BIG MISTAKE. He bee-lined straight for Willie and pinned him to the sofa. I had to pull him off and he snapped at me!"

"Oh no, can't have that, honey. Get rid of the damn dog."

"I have a dog trainer coming this afternoon. He's a retired vet and somewhat of a dog psychologist, according to my Dr. Jen, so I'm counting on him to help me sort this out. I originally asked him to help me train Fred not to run off. Gave me quite a scare down at the coast several weeks ago."

"Well, good luck. Don't expect miracles! . . . So, tell me about Willie . . . he brought flowers?"

"YES, isn't that a hoot? I was SO impressed. I can't tell you how many years . . . and he listens to me go on about Fay and Bobby and Rosie, seems genuinely interested."

"You didn't discuss your GRANDKIDS did you? Honey, we need to have a TALK."

"Yeah, yeah, I know. I don't have this dating thing down good yet. But he really did seem interested, especially in Bobby. Not so much in making doll clothes with Rosie or Fay's drum solos. I think he misses not having a grandson of his own."

"So, no kids. Any wives?"

"One brief wife many years ago. Don't know what happened. He wasn't forthcoming and I certainly didn't want to pry."

"Visible means of support? . . . retired from . . .?"

"Don't know. Doesn't talk about it. He seems to have money, tho'. I think he inherited the house, so it's probably his, free and clear."

"Unless he's borrowed against it to support his lifestyle. Or has one of those tricky reverse mortgages."

"I really doubt that."

Doris hesitated a bit, "Merle, be careful. You're vulnerable, you know that, right? Please remember that. Take care of yourself first . . . and, listen, if this professor doesn't help, get rid of the dog. And soon, honey."

Saturday afternoon/SA.

Well, I certainly made a mess of things! Benadryl had the opposite effect on Freddie – made him more uncontrollable than ever. He did his best to ruin our dinner and then terrorized Willie.

AND I think I did the domestic thing WAY too early. I'm sure he thinks I'm too eager by far!

BUT we have another date – for tomorrow afternoon. AMAZING! This thing is somehow working in spite of a multitude of debacles. Maybe he really likes me? Is that possible? We're going on a picnic, and a walking tour. (Yea, no Freddie to worry about!)

But yesterday I had a scene in the produce dept of HEB! Fell apart right there in the onions. What am I going to do if this happens when I'm with Willie?

The Dog Professor is coming at 4 pm.

"You're going to have to spend a lot of time with him, you know that, don't you?"

"I do now. Well, this is the best time to do it then, since I'm on summer vacation."

"Changing the habits of an adult dog – especially one that you don't have any history on – is not an easy task. It will take patience. And positive reinforcement."

"I'm a middle school teacher. I understand patience and positive reinforcement."

Dr. Gould was tall and thin, full head of white hair and a cute goatee. He was sort of a skinny version of the Kentucky colonel with the fried chicken, dressed in khakis, a yellow polo shirt, and tennies, instead of the white linen suit. Freddie was feigning disinterest, sitting against the wall with one hind leg to the side like a puppy, but taking it all in, nevertheless. They worked on "sit," "stay," and "come." The Professor had a pocketful of treats and gave him one each time he did what was asked. Merle had warned him about Freddie's allergies, so he assured her that they were made of only egg and cheese. Fred seemed to really like them – or really liked pleasing the Professor. Then they went outside to work on leash manners.

"Now, don't let him drag you. Stop, have him sit and give him a treat, then say 'Freddie, free' and go on. Stop every time he tries to pull on the leash." *(at this rate we'll get about twenty feet – this afternoon!)*

"I'm really worried about his not coming to me when he's off the leash," Merle said, hesitantly.

"We need to get the basics down first. Get him used to responding to your commands. *(Coming when called IS basic!)*

Freddie hadn't made up his mind about the Professor yet, but he thought the treats were great.

The Sunday afternoon picnic with Willie was idyllic in every sense of the word. They drove a while through Brackenridge Park, but found most every table occupied and lots of families there with way more *mijitos* and *mijitas* running around than Merle and Willie cared to endure. So, they went over the hill and down into Olmos Park, in Olmos Basin, where there was hardly anyone at all. They found an old moss-encrusted concrete picnic table under a huge live oak tree.

Olmos means oak in Spanish, just like *Alamo* means cottonwood. San Antonio is full of tree names just like every American city, but in Spanish. Olmos Park is a small, rambling campus of scattered tables, old stone bar-b-que pits, and walking paths. Not much else. It floods every time San Antonio gets more than an inch of rain because it's in the lowest spot just above Olmos Dam. The dam was built after a disastrous flood in 1921 had water up to second story windows of office buildings downtown. The dam was supposed to have fixed that problem, but the one time it was to be put to the test, it was so old that the experts decided to open it up and take their chances because they were afraid it would fail. Originally there was a road across the top the dam, but some years back engineers had rerouted the trans-basin traffic to a new road below the dam, for safety one assumes.

Merle missed the old road with its low mossy stone walls and dim lights in squat stone turrets along the top and in little niches through the incredibly serpentine entrance and exit, on both the Olmos Park and Alamo Heights sides of the dam. *(Late at night it was VERY romantic to drive across the dam coming home from a date. The new road has no charm!)* Merle remembered numerous birthday parties here in the park, possibly at this very table. Always with a *piñata*. *(Trees are almost too big now to hang a piñata. Branches are way too high. You'd never get a rope over them.)*

Willie began to unload food and supplies from his truck. Willie drove one of those giant pick-up trucks that are more luxury sedan than utility vehicle. He had thought of EVERYTHING, or so it seemed to Merle. A beautiful platter of boiled shrimp, ruby grapefruit, and avocado slices with fresh dill and lime slices, watermelon and cantaloupe salad, fat little *bolillos*, the hard French rolls favored by both Mexicans and Mexican-Americans, and whose name was also a slang term for an Anglo, sort of the Mexican version of "honky." And soft butter. Cloth table cover and cloth napkins. Real silver – not just good plastic, but actual sterling flatware, as near as she could tell without turning the fork over and looking. (*Silver! Is this guy for real?)* And wine, a Texas-grown blush (Willie said he knew the vintner) in an absolutely lovely shade of burnished pink. They remarked that it tasted pretty good, too. He served it in real wine glasses – old ones, with etched designs in Art Nouveau style. *(Contemporary with his house?)*

They ate slowly, enjoying the cool afternoon breeze and their quiet surroundings, especially magical considering US 281, the McAllister Freeway, that connected downtown San Antonio with the Airport, was less than a hundred yards away. An elevated and sound-proofed highway, it was a marvel of silence underneath, as they were now. After dinner, they lingered over the wine, discussing all sorts of esoteric topics, or nothing at all. Merle thought it was the most fascinating conversation she had ever had. And she knew she was drunk.

After a while they decided that a walking tour, on top of such a fine meal, would be a little much, and why don't they hold that for another day? Then Willie brought forth the most exquisite chocolate torte with little shaved chocolate curls on top. He did admit with a self-conscious smile, that this, at least, came from *La Madeleine* bakery. *(Good taste!)*

Merle had chosen a yellow, flower print pique sundress and white sandals for this occasion. As she and Willie walked hand-in-hand back to his truck, she felt very, very young.

It was already dark when they got back to the condo and entered Merle's patio. As she was getting out her key, Willie suddenly picked her up, hugged her and swung her around in circles. She was startled and unprepared for this outburst of affection and athleticism, but she absolutely loved it. So much fun. It felt so good. And she was so drunk. She laughed out loud as she clung to his neck. And he smelled so good, too. Lavender, she thought.

"Freddie has lost about a pound and a half. Much better. How's the itching? Are you giving him the Benadryl regularly?" Dr. Jennifer was checking Freddie's ears.

"He seems to be holding his own with the itching and scratching. At least he's not making himself raw like he was a few weeks ago. Why doesn't the Benadryl make him sleepy? It sure makes me sleepy, and, at least weight-wise, I seem to be giving him a lot of it. If I had proportionally that amount, I'd be on my ass."

"Different species, different drug reactions." *(Now she tells me!)*

"Ah." Merle nodded.

Yeah! We're going to the coast. We're going to the coast!!

Merle was piling grocery bags, the cooler, her computer, a large tote, all at the top of the stairs where Freddie was spinning in circles, not even pretending to chase his tail, just circles for the sake of circles.

She decided late last night. Unfortunately, we're taking the kid and the other two people puppies. That could pose a problem... but, I'll worry about that later. THE COAST! ADVENTURE, HERE WE COME!

"Slow down, calm down, Freddie. Don't knock things over. Yes, we're going to the coast – and what's even better, we're going to the beach. The real beach, the Gulf of Mexico, not just Copano Bay."

"Beach...?"

Merle loaded all the paraphernalia into the back of the Jeep. *(Wow, this is a LOT of STUFF! When John and I bought the Copano Beach cottage, the goal was to have the place so well stocked and supplied that I would be able to pick up my purse and just go. Ha! That NEVER happened. Why is it that I have to cart around all this STUFF?)* She walked Freddie around the condominium complex quickly, not paying too much attention to his leash manners today as she was in a hurry to be off. Peggy's kids were waiting on her.

"In you go. Good dog." Freddie jumped into the passenger seat and turned around three times while Merle walked to the driver's side. Once she was inside, he jumped into her lap and began to lick her face, eagerly kissing her on the lips.

"I love you, Merle."

"No tongues, Fred."

CHAPTER 8

"So, is this the ferry?" Bobby had his head stuck out the window as they pulled up behind a long line of cars on highway 361, the northern route onto Mustang Island and the resort town of Port Aransas.

"Well, this is the LINE for the ferry." Merle worried about the wisdom of this trip to the beach, the real beach. But the line began to move and continued moving at a fairly steady rate. She looked around at the industrial complex to the south. They were constructing an off-shore drilling platform at one of the plants. She couldn't believe the size of the structure, and she reckoned it must be at least two miles away, across marshes and salt flats. Through the hazy atmosphere the silhouette reminded her of an opening scene from one of the Star Wars movies. She thought it had to be the size of a Houston skyscraper.

"What's that big fancy boat over there?" Bobby asked, nodding toward the other side of the road.

"Oh, that's a gambling boat. They take people out beyond the three-mile limit so they can drink and gamble in international waters where it isn't illegal – to gamble, that is."

"Sounds like fun." Bobby immediately saw himself in an Old West style poker game. *(Not so fast, kid, you're only nine years old!)*

Merle glanced into the back seat. Fay was plugged into her iPod, nodding to an inaudible rhythm, little Rosie was asleep in her car seat, and Freddie was stretched out between them, enjoying the sun, his right hind leg twitching as if in rhythm with Fay's private music.

Finally, they were directed onto one of the five free ferries the State of Texas operated around the clock between Aransas Pass on the mainland and Port Aransas on the island. Merle set the emergency brake and she and Bobby got out of the car to look at ships in the Intercoastal Canal that they were now crossing. Greedy and very plump seagulls cartwheeled and squawked above. Some passengers obliged them by tossing potato chips or taco bits or whatever they had up in the air for the birds to catch. *(You're not going to think they're so cute when one poops on you.)* The passage took all of twelve minutes, but it was enough time to see an Arabian tanker, under a Dutch flag, passing through, and two sailboats just playing around, the larger one with a bright, multi-colored spinnaker.

After exiting the ferry, they drove into Port A and turned south onto the Park Road toward the public beaches which begin about five miles south of town. They had stopped at one of the hundreds of souvenir shops that lined the street to purchase a Beach Permit, Merle having forgotten the one she bought at Spring Break, that she had conveniently placed on the cottage bulletin board so it would be easy for people going to the beach to find, if they remembered to look. Taking Beach Access Road #2, Merle reminded herself how glad she was that the Liberty had four-wheel drive, and recalled a few years back when a group of overly enthusiastic teens on this very beach had offered to help her and John get the old red Cherokee unstuck. John had ventured just a little too far into the dry sand and they were up to the hubcaps in it. The kids, *(probably half drunk – and almost certainly stoned!)*, had towed them out with their monster truck, but had bent the tie-rod in the process. The Cherokee developed a teeth-rattling shimmy and they had had to sacrifice one day of their vacation to sit with it at a repair garage in Rockport.

Merle drove a quarter mile or so down the beach until they found a spot relatively uncrowded and pulled in facing the water. She could smell the ocean strong in her nostrils as she inhaled until her chest hurt. Salty, and funky, and magnetic. Freddie woke up and began barking at the gulls that had accumulated in the air overhead. He jumped out of the car and went straight for the seaweed washed up in piles at the high tide line. Sniffing as though his life depended on finding something, he moved rapidly along the ridge, nose to the ground, tail going in circles, not even noticing the waves coming in. Then suddenly, just as his feet were about to get wet, he looked up at the water not two feet away and stopped, paralyzed.

"Whoa! Is this the BEACH?"

"Look, Freddie, the Gulf of Mexico. Right out there. If you swim straight out and just keep going, you'll end up in Key West, Florida."

"Lady, I ain't swimming anywhere. That looks scary. But this brown stuff smells SO FUNKY ... yummm ... fish in here somewhere?"

Merle left him snuffling around in the seaweed heaps while she went in search of a beer. Fred was off his leash and she wondered if she would regret this. So far, he didn't seem inclined to wander – or swim.

If one were expecting Florida, the Texas coast would probably be a great disappointment. But it did have a sort of rough-around-the-edges charm. The sand wasn't white, but was usually clean and a pleasant medium tan color. The water wasn't particularly clear, but it was usually warm, and the beaches were shallow a long way out on all the barrier islands like Mustang and Padre. Around what they called the Coastal Bend, or the Redneck Riviera, with Corpus Christi in the center, there was a labyrinth of bays and inlets and bayous. Some of this waterfront property was industrial, oil refineries and large-scale construction predominating, some commercial, some stacked with high-rise condos, but some relatively untouched stretches of beach, particularly in the Padre Island National Seashore. Merle marveled at the unexpected majesty of the scene when the clouds were just right, as they were now, and the wind was blowing fiercely, as it was now, and as it did almost all the time. When she looked down the beach, taking in the open water, waves slamming onto shore, wind burning her face, and tall white clouds billowing, it was really quite grand. Felt like looking into eternity.

The sticky black stuff washed up on the beach that they called "tar" was really crude oil inevitably leaked from that off-shore rig just barely visible in the haze over the Gulf. But Merle had found lots of nice shells and sand dollars out here. Only occasionally did she run into a few jellyfish, not that she could have seen them in the murky water. Forget snorkeling – wouldn't be able to see anything. In the nineties, an underwater archaeology team discovered the location of the French explorer LaSalle's ship in Matagorda Bay by mucking around in the mud and finding a seventeenth century French cannon totally by feel. Couldn't see a thing. But the fishing was almost always good and the birds were amazing. Merle especially liked the roseate spoonbills, called them

Texas Flamingos. And there was the comfort dress aspect, too. Merle felt right at home in her old, frayed Levi cut-offs, halter top and flip-flops. Unlike the few times she had been to Florida beaches where she had felt like she needed a designer bikini and a big fancy matching tote bag or she was underdressed. (Sort of like her Sunday School teacher many years ago who had sold her brand-new Ford T-Bird soon after buying it because she had felt like she needed to dress up every time she drove it! The protocol exhausted her.)

Merle settled into one of the low-slung beach chairs and stared out at the horizon. *(How can anyone live landlocked? I would suffocate! I want to never, ever live more than a few hours from the coast. This is so beautiful. Got to have it. Guess I've always been a water baby. Read one of those factoids once that said fifty percent of the American people live within fifty miles of a coast. Duh! No wonder all those pioneer women out on the Great Plains went loony.)* She let her mind drift as the big kids played in the surf on boogie boards and Rosie tried to make a sand castle, but kept losing it to the waves. *(Wish I had a ciggie, but not in front of the kiddies. Damn.)* She leaned her head back. It was hot and very bright, squint-your-eyes bright, aviator Ray Bans notwithstanding.

A tune faintly audible from a neighboring car took her back to another day at the beach; it had been hot and very bright then, too. She had taken off in the old blue Mustang convertible and headed to Galveston, destination Bolivar Point beach. A six-pack of Coors in the cooler, a towel and tube of suntan lotion on the seat beside her. *(We didn't have "sunscreen" back then, only suntan lotion.)* She'd had on her blue polka-dot bikini, wooden-sole Dr. Scholl sandals, and nothing else. Almost like driving barefoot and naked.

(Don't think I'd been on the beach more than fifteen minutes when Archie drove up on his motorcycle. His eyes were so blue they looked like they were lit from behind with one of those high intensity lamps, like sunlight shining through cobalt blue stained glass. Boy, was I ready for him! Lonely, horny, and looking for trouble.)

Six weeks into a six-month trial separation from John, Merle had spent most of that summer in Houston listening to sad love songs, looking at old pictures and feeling sorry for herself. Then, one Saturday morning, she had gotten up, looked in the mirror, and said out loud, "Fuck this shit! I'm going to have some fun." Which she set about doing immediately. Hence the impromptu trip to the beach.

She and Archie had talked for hours, until after sunset, *(what on earth about?),* and drank beer. Then they drove about half a mile down the beach to Archie's place, not much more than an efficiency apartment on stilts. His "fishing camp" he called it. Parked the Mustang and the bike under the house. By this time, they were exceedingly drunk. Then they proceeded to smoke some grass he had, drank a lot of Welch's grape juice, and made love on the floor, burnt-orange shag carpet and all, until they were so hungry they had to go out for burgers in the middle of the night. *(Oh my Lord, did that man know what to do with his tongue! At least I came to my senses long enough to head home after the burgers.)* Merle felt herself flush remembering the sensations Archie had evoked, then she quickly glanced around to see if anyone had been watching.

Later that night, and with a chilled glass of Moscato, Merle sat at the dining room table playing Solitaire while Bobby played some obscure card game of his own devising. Fay had a date with a boy from Rockport she had met at Spring Break, and Rosie was asleep on the futon. Everybody freshly showered, shampooed, and fed, although there were still piles of shells on the front porch and miniature sand dunes in the bathroom.

"Why don't you play that queen of diamonds on the king of clubs?"

"Can't."

"Why?"

"Special rules."

"What special rules?"

"Blue cards."

"Grandma, you're weird." *(Probably so.)*

Thursday nite: late, tired, and sunburned/Copano Beach

We had just gotten back from Port A, unloading, everything a mess, sand everywhere, everybody exhausted and sunburned – well, I was exhausted, the kids had a nap on the way home. Rosie knocked the lighthouse magnet off the fridge door as she was putting the unused drinks back in the fridge to cool. Freddie grabbed it and disappeared under the bed. It was the one I got on our New England trip years ago, the Newport Rhode Island lighthouse molded in white, semi-flexible plastic and fused to a magnetic bottom layer. Chewed it right up and downed it, he did. Then, just a few minutes later, I walked out on the front porch to supervise the rinsing-off of beach toys before they came inside, and arrived just in time to see a toy salamander's tail disappear into Fred's mouth, slurped up like a string of spaghetti, didn't even bother to chew. Straight down the gullet. It had been a fluorescent pink creature, floppy, almost translucent plastic with glitter bits suspended in it.

Do you think he needs dinner?

Merle loved early summer in south Texas when the grass was still green and the breezes still cool. It just smelled so good, full of promise. The honey mesquite trees produced little pale green caterpillar-like things that the humming birds and the butterflies found irresistible. Individually identifiable bird songs and insect noises filled the humid air. Of course, the mosquitoes were the size of dragon flies because of recent rain, and cricket season was just beginning, but she had long since accepted the fact that living with bugs was part of the overall coast experience. *(Except for roaches. I don't do roaches! No way, no how!)* So, when the weather was pretty, she took every opportunity to get out into it. Freddie agreed with this philosophy completely.

The Kid had been bugging Merle to teach her how to drive stick-shift, like our little Jeep. So, we went out in the country toward the cemetery. I didn't know about the driving lesson part until after we were on our way. They traded places, the Kid driving. We did some stops and starts, mostly driving very, very, very slow. Parked and turned around several times. I had settled nicely into the back seat, when we turned rather suddenly into the entrance of the old cemetery. It had been raining a lot that week and the grass was thick and wet. Well, just as the Kid turned in, the Jeep slid off the road to the right, then she panicked and gunned the engine as she popped the clutch. The car spun totally around so we ended up on the road, FACING THE OTHER WAY! Wow, and was it quick! And exciting!

After the mud had settled, so to speak, Merle said to the Kid,

"It's OK. You did fine. People pay good money to learn to do what you just did. Only, next time take it a little slower."

"Freddie fell in the trash bag."

Man, I wish she would wrap her gum in something before she throws it away.

Merle had almost succeeded in doing what she came to the coast to do, and that was to put Willie at a distance for a bit while she tried to figure out what was going on, and what she wanted her part to be. But he kept creeping back into her brain and she couldn't keep him out. All she wanted to do was think about him. She hadn't told anybody except Doris about Willie yet. Was she afraid of questions? Scrutiny? Of sounding like a lovesick teenager? Did she have any idea what she was doing?

On the way back to San Antonio, she checked her phone messages and found that Willie had called. Several times. She smiled.

"Well, you look pleased with yourself."

"Freddie, I want to have a serious talk with you about Willie."

"Uh—oh. Not that slimy creep again. I thought we'd forgotten about him. Merle, really... there's nothing to talk about here."

"I don't know what you don't like about him. I think the problem is you're jealous."

"He's never played ball with me. Never even tried!"

CHAPTER 9

Texans have been visiting back and forth across the Mexican border ever since there was a border. Growing up in San Antonio, day trips to Nuevo Laredo were a frequent thing for Merle. She and her mom, or she and her friends, went two or three times a year, almost always a few weeks before Christmas to go gift shopping and to buy baking staples like raw sugar and strong Mexican vanilla. And, of course, to buy booze. Merle laughed when she remembered the time her mother and some friends got busted by customs agents when they tried to bring back more rum and tequila than the law allowed. Imagine four little old blue-haired ladies being interrogated in the DEA office like suspected drug smugglers.

Any traveler would agree that border towns were nothing like the interior of Mexico, their attention focused almost entirely on pleasing tourists. They were a great place to shop, and eat. Unfortunately, recent paranoia over terrorists and drug wars has severely reduced that type of commerce. Even Marti's, the high-end souvenir, clothing, and folk-art store that was always a must-shop, across-the-border destination for many wealthy San Antonians, has moved its main store north to San Antonio, near the touristy River Walk. And the legendary Cadillac Bar closed its doors after eighty-plus years of serving authentic Mexican cuisine and lots of booze to Norteamericanos.

"We'll leave early Saturday morning and have lunch in Ciudad Acuña. Then drive down to a little village I know where some friends of mine support an orphanage run by a bunch of destitute nuns. You'll like it. It's in an old abandoned hacienda, like a little oasis in the middle of nowhere. And the kids are cute. You can talk Spanish with them. Then we can spend the night in Piedras Negras and come back on Sunday morning."

Merle had returned Willie's call when she got back from delivering Peggy's kids and all their beach paraphernalia to their house. Now she was listening as he described his plan, elaborating on his invitation to take a trip to Mexico the following weekend. *(Is this a PROPOSITION? I did hear "spend the night," didn't I?)* She felt her heart begin to race. *(OK, Merle, this is it! Decide RIGHT NOW if you want to sleep with this guy!)*

"Yes, that sounds like fun, Willie. What time do you want to leave?"

And that was it. They were going on a trip to romantic Mexico and spending the night in a motel. Just like that. *(Wow! What just happened?)* Merle got her ciggies and the little red ceramic ashtray out of the library table drawer and plopped down on the sofa. She put her head back, inhaled, then exhaled slowly, watching the smoke rise. *(Well, well, WELL, . . . maybe my smoking days will soon be over. Hee hee!)* Merle opened a small wood box on the coffee table and took out the blue Bicycle cards. She shuffled, then began to lay out a hand of Solitaire.

"Whaddaya' think, Fred? Is it time for me to quit smoking?"

"I think there's something you're not telling me, here, Merle."

(I don't think I'll tell him just yet about his upcoming overnight at the doggie motel.)

Merle and Willie left San Antonio at six on Saturday morning and had crossed the border at Del Rio to Ciudad Acuña by noon. They ate lunch at a Mexican bar/restaurant, a *cantina*, in Acuña, an old stone building, luxuriant bougainvillea hanging over the patio, nice and cool even though it was hot and dry outside. Walking across the polished tile floor echoed softly in the quiet interior. Interesting old *Revolución* posters on the walls. They drank Mexican beer and ate *tortas*, a sort of Mexican version of the po'boy, with fried potatoes. Merle had been happy to show off her Spanish. Now they were on their way to the ranch where the sisters ran the orphanage. Willie said there were about fifty-five children and only about six adults, depending on who you counted. Willie had packed several containers of school supplies and other assorted items for the kids, in addition to large packages of T-shirts and jeans. Merle contributed a dozen boxes of pencils and another ten boxes of map colors she had bought on sale at Walmart and had been saving for her classes.

After passing through several dusty little villages on the highway, they turned off onto an unmarked dirt road, straight and flat, into nowhere, just a narrow path over scrub-brush prairie. *(Maybe I should have called Ellie about this guy before coming on this adventure. I haven't even Goggled him yet! Probably a no-no for modern daters.)* After about eight miles of kicking up dust, they began to see a low structure rise out of the haze over the horizon. A large, rambling house from a previous era, and a quaint little church off to one side. Several smallish out-buildings, adobe walls and red tile roofs. Classic. It looked like a movie set *(possibly for Ramona? Or Zorro?)* except for the satellite dish and the well-worn blue Ford pick-up under a corrugated steel shed. As they got closer, Merle noticed that the buildings were in poor repair, but the yard was full of roses and some other bright flowers she didn't recognize. A number of mesquite trees cast a lacy shade over the courtyard. *(Charming, even if a little decrepit around the edges, but still . . . absolutely simpático!)*

The children seemed to be engaged in a variety of activities, mostly outside. A few were working in what appeared to be a vegetable garden. At one end of the long veranda several girls were shucking corn, while some of the older boys were repairing the door to a small barn. A group of younger children were playing a game involving standing in a circle and running around. Merle looked for the nuns, expecting traditional habits, but saw none. A middle-aged Mexican woman in jeans and T-shirt, short cropped hair, motioned them to the entry.

"Come on, let's go meet the staff." Willie got out of the truck and trotted off toward the main door in the middle of the veranda. *(Cute ass!)* As soon as it became apparent, he wasn't going to open the truck door for her and help her down, as had been his habit, she jumped down and followed him into the hacienda. Soon she found herself in a cool tiled entryway, potted hibiscus along one side, patterned blue and yellow tile on the walls, and a wrought iron chandelier hanging from the high arched ceiling. She could see into the patio, in the middle of the big house, and the *sala*, off to the left.

"Merle, this is Sister Corazón." The lady in jeans and T-shirt stuck out her hand. *(Wow. Things sure have changed.)* "She's in charge . . . Sister, this is my friend Merle McKinney from San Antonio. We've brought a load of goodies for the kids."

By this time a number of children had gathered on the veranda and around the door, not quite entering, but certainly growing in both number and interest level. They knew that Willie always brought gifts from the United States when he visited and were eager to see what he had this time. Sister Corazón had just ushered Merle and Willie into the *sala*, a large comfortable living room, when a young woman with an apron over her jeans and T-shirt, entered, wiping her hands. On her heels came a barrel-shaped person, dressed in what can only be described as a "Mumu," with a pitcher of rosy-colored *aguas frescas*.

"Ah, here we come. Meet Sisters Adela and Luz. Sister Adela is named for the *Adelitas* who fought in the Revolution. Her grandmother was with Zapata's forces in Torreón." *(Peculiar namesake for a nun.)*

They visited with the sisters for a few minutes, then Willie excused himself while he and Sister Corazón went off to her office. Sister Luz took Merle on a short walking tour of the grounds and they talked with some of the children. They thought her Spanish was funny in spots, but were eager to talk to the *huera,* nevertheless. Judging from their names, as well as their complexions, she assumed most of them were Indian. All bright black eyes and white teeth, glossy black hair. Later, some of the older boys unloaded the boxes and packages from Willie's truck, then they said their good-byes and left. On the drive to Piedras Negras, Merle mentally reviewed the interlude and discovered that she had gained a new respect for Willie. *(What a guy!)*

After the requisite *cabrito* dinner and a nice bottle of red wine at Moderno's Restaurant and Bar. *(Well, they're all "and Bar," aren't they? Mexican entrepreneurs certainly know what the Norteamericanos want.)* A stroll around the plaza, and they were back at their motel. The room was decorated in typical Mexican tourist style, lots of wrought iron, bright colors and patterned tile, and large paintings of quaint Mexican villages. Good air conditioner *(thank heavens!)*. Rustic table and chairs, big TV, and two double beds. Merle decided she needed a shower.

The water pressure was paltry and even that was tepid, at best. But it gave her a few minutes respite to prepare herself both emotionally and physically for what was to come. *(Wonder when it's appropriate to ask about "safe sex"? Last time I was dating, that phrase meant something entirely different!)* All lotioned, deodorized, and flossed, she emerged from the bath in her yellow cotton knit nightshirt with a turquoise silk wrap-robe over. *(I match the décor.)* Willie was propped up in one of the beds, lamp on, reading *Sports Illustrated.* He smiled when he saw her. His silver hair, now out of the ponytail, was loose around his shoulders. Merle almost swooned. He took off his reading glasses.

"Feel better? Ready for bed?"

She nodded. *(OK, what's next? Somebody give me a program, please!)*

"You want to get settled in before I turn out the light?"

Confused now, Merle looked at the other bed and considered the fact that Willie wasn't moving over, and before she could stop herself, she had blurted out,

"I really rather not sleep alone."

"Oh, . . . OK. Here, you can bunk in with me," turning the covers back for her and scooting over to the other side of his bed. After he had punched the pillow a couple of times, and gotten his head comfortable, he said, "You can turn off the light. Night."

Merle took off her robe and laid it on the unoccupied bed. Then she turned off the lamp and lay down on her back in the space Willie had vacated, staring at the ceiling, her brain a whirl of conflict. As Willie began to snore, all she could think about was that scene in *The Way We Were* where Barbara Streisand slips into bed with a passed-out Robert Redford, and nothing happens.

Next thing she knew Willie was waking her up to tell her that he was going swimming. *(Good God, what time is it?)* Merle pulled herself out of bed and rummaged through her suitcase for morning clothes. With a somewhat abbreviated toilette and fresh undies, she felt much better. Now in the motel coffee shop, she was having *pan dulce,* the Mexican sweetbread that isn't really sweet, but really yummy with whipped butter, and *café con leche,* while she read the Sunday morning paper. She especially liked to read the society columns in Mexican papers, the language was always so arch and effusive, with abundant adjectives, and decorative phrases. Very vocabulary enhancing. This one was *El Mañana* from Nuevo Laredo, but she wasn't paying much attention to what she was reading, just passing her eyes over the words, not registering anything. *(Did that really happen last night? Or NOT happen, would be more appropriate. What the hell is going on here? Am I an idiot? Probably so!)* In a few minutes Willie came in, cheerful and invigorated from his swim, and joined her for breakfast, opting for *huevos rancheros* and refried beans with fresh corn tortillas. Merle smiled. *(He's really cute, regardless . . .)*

They managed to cross the border in good order without too much delay, and the drive back to San Antonio on highway 57 and I-35 was quiet and uneventful. The towns in those parts were pretty spread out. Willie had big band music on his fancy stereo system, and it sounded like all forty musicians were in the cab with them, but it didn't exactly match Merle's funky mood. *(Well, this certainly gives a whole new perspective to the age-old question, "Are you sleeping with him?")*

"What are you looking for? Can I help? Here, let me lick your face."

Freddie gingerly stepped over one of several piles of books on the bedroom floor, trying not to knock them over, as he attempted to reach Merle's lap, but she was not to be distracted from her mission. She had pulled a bunch of boxes out from under her bed, had all of them open, and was frantically going through titles, leaving little stacks hither and yon. She distractedly picked him up and set him to one side. *(Small hardback, blue cloth binding, silver lettering . . . where IS it?)* She sat up on her heels, looked around, then pulled out another box and opened it.

"Ah, ha! Here it is. *The Sensuous Woman* by "J." Well, it was good advice in 1969, it should still be good advice today." She had read a few years ago that it had been written by a man. *(So what? Gives it more authority, in my opinion.)* She had fixated on it for weeks when she first read it soon after it came out, even trying some of the outlandish exercises and activities. *(John was thrilled out of his mind! God, men are so easy. At least that one was. What IS the deal with Willie?)* Now she took the little book into the living room and stretched out on the sofa, bare feet on the armrest, head propped up on a throw pillow. The book's binding creaked when she opened it.

"Merle, you're acting really weird."

Freddie tried to get her attention to play ball. She had been in another world ever since they came home. And he hadn't liked the doggie motel one bit. He picked up the red squeakyball and nudged it gently onto her tummy. Absently, she put the ball on the floor and pushed him away.

Much later, after Freddie had totally destroyed a bone-shaped chew toy and eaten most of it, he discovered she was asleep. He hopped up on the sofa beside her, lay down, and rested his chin on her shoulder, his nose in her ear. He shut his eyes really tight and snuggled in with a little wiggle, and a sigh.

"I love you, Merle."

CHAPTER 10

Merle's face began to burn.

"Girl, he's a real sleaze. Stay away from him."

She had finally called her friend Ellie Mayfield whom Willie had mentioned knowing on their first date. She had meant to do this weeks ago, before she got emotionally involved. *(Too late for that now.)* But she didn't have a real reason to talk to Ellie other than to inquire about Willie. So, she just kept putting it off until she found a legitimate, if not plausible, excuse to call, so it wouldn't seem that she was calling just to check up on him. She wanted to be able to say, just incidentally, very casually, "Oh, by the way, do you know a guy named Willie Epps?" So, she had done that. Talked for about twenty minutes with Ellie about the art show opening at the Blue Star that she had read about in the morning *Express-News*. Then she mentioned Willie's name, and now she was getting an earful she never expected.

What had she expected? Maybe, "sweet guy, a little old for you, isn't he?" or "a little odd, but interesting," or possibly, "a funny old fart" – anything but this. She was starting to get that hot-all-over feeling that she got whenever she experienced a really unpleasant surprise, somewhere between exploding and throwing up.

"Where did you meet him?"

"At the farmers' market in Rockport."

"Oh my God, girl, what have you been doing? Didn't your mama tell you not to pick up strangers? That is especially important when you're away from home."

"He seemed nice."

"Oh yeah, he's all the gentleman at first. Then he gets possessive and controlling. But mostly it's that there's something creepy about him. Not that he's bad in bed, actually, he's fantastic. *(well . . . I wouldn't know, would I? All he did with me was snore!)* But there is something I can't quite describe – just creepy."

Ellie had been the only person-of-color in Merle's graduating class at Alamo Heights High School. Actually, she was what would be called mixed-race, or biracial, in later years, after the Civil Rights Movement taught us that vocabulary matters. The tacky term in those years was "high yellow." *(Well, we were all racists back then, weren't we? We never would have admitted it, of course, but the language we used said otherwise.)* She was smart, talented, edgy, and had spent most of her youth proving that she wasn't a token anything.

Merle decided not to share her embarrassing episode in Mexico with Ellie just yet.

So, later that evening Merle sat on her balcony and pondered "creepy." She watched the young people park their cars along side streets and flock to the clutch of clubs that had sprouted up along Broadway. Smoking, of course, cigarette after cigarette. Freddie had stretched out on the cool concrete beside her chair. Sitting in the dark, feet propped up on the railing, porch chair leaned back, still processing what Ellie had said. Willie hadn't told her that he had dated Ellie, just that he knew her. Wonder why he left that part out? *(Surely he could assume I'd call her sooner or later.)* Was there something "creepy" about him that she had missed in her rush to find a man? Ellie had made her promise never to mention their conversation to Willie, but to think seriously about never seeing him again.

Well, Freddie HAD peed on him, after all, hadn't he? What did Freddie know?

And Ellie had been quite insistent about his sleaziness, even more so than her normal hyperbolic self. Or . . . just possibly . . . was Ellie suffering from a latent case of sour grapes? She didn't mention how they broke up, did she? Finally, after running in mental circles for quite a while, Merle decided that she should consider the uncertainty of intent in Ellie's comments and not worry too much about what she had said. But, still . . .

"Get off my chest, Freddie! You scared me to death." Merle pushed him off the bed. Then, groggily, "No doggies in the bed. I am NOT going to be one of those peculiar old ladies who sleep with their dogs." *(Although, it's usually a Chihuahua.)*

"Come on, Merle, wake up. I gotta pee! Like NOW."

"OK, OK. I know you've probably gotta pee. Stop jumping around, please. Stop. STOP! Oh . . . right, SIT. There, good dog." She looked around frantically for where his treats were – oh, yes, in her pants pocket. "Just let me wake up, here, and I'll find some clothes . . . take you outside."

She looked at herself in the bathroom mirror and was horrified to see matching pimples, twins as it were, nestled into the smile lines on either side of her mouth. *(WHAT IS THIS? Not only am I acting like a teenager about Willie, now I'm getting pimples – and in my WRINKLES! God, this just isn't fair!)* As she walked Freddie, she decided that maybe it was time for a personal inventory. Figure out what the hell she was doing.

Wednesday nite/SA

Took Freddie out to Olmos Park (yes, where Willie and I had our picnic – guess I was feeling sentimental) and had a training session. Went fairly well, I think. Until he discovered the snake. Not much of a snake. Nevertheless, Fred had to do his monster-slayer act. I had to get the red leash and haul him back to the Jeep. I'm walking along, pulling him, when I looked back and he had the snake in his mouth. Took about five minutes to get him to drop it. And it was very dead, chewed completely thru. Sharp little teeth Fred has.

July 4th coming up next week. Good Lord, how did that happen? That's the middle of the summer, already! Where did it go? I do this every year dammit! I think summer has just started and then July 4th creeps up on me and surprises me. Life really does speed up, the older you get.

Willie called this afternoon. Wants to take me and Bobby to a Missions game on Friday nite. How about that!! Not sure what the message is here, not sure there is one, but I like it. I always get patriotic this time of year and what's more American than a baseball game on a Friday nite? Of course, nothing romantic about having Bobby along, but it's sweet. As I've thought before, maybe Willie misses having a family, especially a grandson. Well, Bobby's about as special as they come. Straight out of central casting for a 1950s sitcom. Sandy hair, freckles, collects frogs and bugs and other icky things, hates to take a bath, and lives on peanut butter and jelly sandwiches. I think he and Willie will get on famously.

Let's see, after the game we can drop Bobby at home and come back here. Maybe I can try some of the SENSUOUS WOMAN suggestions. Better pass on wrapping myself in cling wrap. At my age that would probably frighten him more than excite him. Need to review the other ideas in "J"'s advice. (I keep remembering when "she" appeared on a TV interview show after the book was published and became oh-so-popular. She wore a mask! So, now I guess that must have been an actress? I sorta wondered about that at the time.)

Rain was coming down in sheets! You could hardly see across the street. It was going to flood as only San Antonio can flood. Olmos Park would be under eight feet of water soon. The flood gage on Devine Road would disappear completely. *(Wasn't it just a couple of weeks ago we were in drought mode, Stage Two water rationing?)*

Merle sat at the kitchen table and stared out the sliding glass door as she drank her third cup of coffee and smoked a cigarette. *(The baseball field is going to be a lake!)* She knew Willie would be calling any minute to change plans for tonight.

"*Merle, honey, I really gotta go pee . . . like soon, please.*" Freddie was spinning in circles at Merle's feet.

"OK, OK. I have to get dressed for the deluge. This may take a few minutes." She headed toward the bath to get out of her nightie and into some real clothes. "Why don't you sit down and chew on something?"

"*If I sit down, I relax, and then . . . ooops. So, hurry up, please.*"

It didn't look like it was going to let up anytime soon, so Merle put on the big OD plastic poncho she had bought years ago at an Army/Navy surplus store and her rubber boots.

"Alright, little Puddleduck, let's go for a swim." She hooked him up on the red knotted leash and they headed downstairs just as the phone began to ring. Freddie was tugging anxiously on the leash.

"Well, of course! Aw, shit! Let it ring, dammit! Come on, let's go, Fred." They stepped out into the downpour. The sidewalk was already a river. Merle watched leaves wash over her boots as Freddie searched in vain for a dry patch of grass on which to pee.

When they came back inside Freddie was completely soaked. Merle got an old bath towel to dry him with and the terrier in him came out immediately. He growled and snapped at the new toy, then shook so violently that toward the end of the spasm his hind legs cleared the floor completely and he fell over. He wanted to play much more than he wanted to get dry, enjoying himself so much and making Merle laugh so much that she almost forgot to check her phone message. As she suspected, it was Willie wanting to change plans.

"OK, one hard-boiled egg for each broiled chicken breast. Check. Half a package of shell macaroni, cooked and cooled. Check. Chopped fresh cilantro. Check. Chopped celery. Check. Mayo. Check." Merle was standing at the kitchen table, a glass of white wine in her hand. She preferred a sweet white, in spite of her name. *(And I ALWAYS cook better with wine! Even in the morning – well, almost noon.)* The ingredients for chicken salad covered the table surface with a very large, and very old, ochre-colored pottery mixing bowl in the center. The bowl was so old that the glaze was faded to a rosy tan and was completely crazed in a spider web of tiny cracks. Merle loved using old kitchen things, and she had quite a collection. This bowl had been her grandmother's when she was a bride on *la frontera* in the Texas border town of Eagle Pass. There was no bridge across the Rio Grande then and she was one of only about a dozen white women in the mostly Mexican village. Merle imagined her kneading bread dough in this very bowl as she stood at a kitchen table, not unlike the one Merle was using now, in her little turn-of-the-century frame house with no yard, just packed dirt, a white-painted fence, and a few roses. Merle had a scrapbook full of small black-and-white photographs of that house and of her grandparents when they lived there, before they moved to San Antonio to open a hardware store in 1916.

Willie had, of course, cancelled on the Missions game, but hadn't offered an alternative, either. So, after sulking around all day Saturday, Merle had skipped church this morning *(Again! God, I'm such a heathen!)* and packed for the coast.

Now she was cooking and getting the Casa fortified for the onslaught. Fourth of July festivities in Copano Beach were coming up on Thursday and all of Peggy's family would be down. She really needed to get the cottage settled and have a few minutes to herself before they all piled in, dogs included. *(Hmmm . . . Wonder how Fred will get along with Pip?)* She always thought of Pip as plural – he was certainly big enough to be two dogs. (Fay had been reading *Great Expectations* when they got the twelve-pound puppy.) And he certainly got into enough trouble for two dogs, maybe three.

Merle was determined to get Willie out of her head. Thinking about him made her crazy. But he wouldn't stay out. Had there been something in her voice on the phone that put him off? Could he tell that she knew something and wasn't telling? This was the first time she had talked to him since she endured Ellie's lecture. Now she thought about that again. Was there something creepy about him after all? Or did Ellie just have bad memories? And what about this apparent lack of physical attraction? Is he just shy? Had she been too brazen when she invited herself into his bed in Mexico? What on earth was going on?

Freddie came into the kitchen and licked his empty food bowl a few times, then shoved it over to Merle's feet and sat down by it. Cocked his head to one side and glared at her.

"Hi there, sleepyhead. Are you hungry now? Must be me cooking got you interested. Thought you were going to sleep all day!" She scooped some of Freddie's hypo-allergenic kibble into his dish and put it back in its place on the floor below the pantry, next to his giant water bowl.

"*Merle, you've been acting pretty strange. Are you thinking about that weasel person problem?*"

"Here, have some of your grub. You've certainly been keeping a low profile recently."

"*He's no good, honey. I've got a nasty feeling about that dude.*" Freddie noticed his bowl was full and dug in.

The fog makes everything weird. You see things that aren't there and you don't see things that you know must be there. It makes everything soft-focus, lights with haloes, and the bay invisible past the grass in the park.

It was way past midnight when Merle and Freddie finished watching Jimmy Stewart in *Harvey* (Merle's favorite feel-good movie) and went out for their final walk of the evening. Coastal fog had moved in and obliterated everything past a few yards. The overhead lights in the park were useless. Actually, they seemed to distort images.

Freddie stopped, tense, alert, growled at … nothing.

"It's OK, Fred. It's just the fog."

"*No. It's not OK, Merle. It's plain spooky.*"

"I know it feels spooky, but it's just water hanging in the air. Mother Nature can't decide what to do with it."

"*I want to go back in the house.*" Freddie began pulling Merle around, pawing at the grass and straining on his leash.

"Get your business done and we'll go back in the house, if you're scared."

The only way she knew the pier was there was the blurry light at the end. (*No walking out on the pier for me, tonite. That looks to be the stuff nightmares are made of.*) Then she thought she saw something moving on the pier, under one of the lights. Not large enough to be a person. A child, maybe? As she got closer she thought she could make out the shape of a large bird, a large skinny bird, almost visible through the fog. All the while, Freddie was desperately trying to pull her the other way.

The Ghost Heron. That's what she'd come to think of him as. A Great Blue, to be sure, but pale, almost silver. He'd been around a lot in the weeks following John's death, walking the wave break almost every night. Then he disappeared for a while. Recently he had returned for sporadic appearances, usually at oddly opportune times. (*Solitary and nocturnal! Wonder why he's back now? Should I talk to him? What should I say? OK, wait, Merle. Snap out of it! It's just a bird . . . a strange bird, but still a bird. This fog has you jumpy – and weird.*)

Freddie finished up in no time and they hurried back to the cottage, Merle still a little surprised at herself. (*Must have been the fog.*) She almost never got scared in Copano Beach. Well, she really didn't get scared much at all, not that kind of scared. Maybe a little in San Antonio, but never at the coast. Truth to tell, there were only three things that frightened Merle McKinney: pain, Alzheimer's, and being lonely in her old age. That third fear, loneliness, of course, had only been added to her list after John died. Most of her life she only had to worry about two.

"And that's why I adopted this cute little fat doggie!" Merle was laughing and playing with Freddie on the big, overstuffed chintz sofa in the living room, rubbing his fuzzy tummy and teasing his paws. He was lapping up the attention and the affection.

"This adoption thing, Merle, it doesn't go just one way, you know. I adopted you, too."

CHAPTER 11

Tuesday nite/Copano Beach

Forgot my toothbrush in San Antonio and couldn't find the one I usually leave down here, so John's old one was still in the bath and I used it. Didn't feel that strange AND I didn't fall apart thinking about him. Progress? All my thoughts focused on Willie now? Current uncertainty and frustration edged out exhausting grief? Well, however that works out, it's really nice to be obsessed with a real living, breathing person, rather than someone who's been dead for sixteen months! (Then why am I still counting?)

The FAMILY arrived tonight. It's been all backpacks and tote bags and dogs everywhere, ever since. The whole town is gearing up for Thursday's Fourth of July celebration – tents already pitched in the park for the food tables. Local sandwich shop has been selling T-shirts for weeks. Bobby is going to decorate my bicycle and intends to ride it in the parade, red-white-and-blue crepe paper woven into the wheels and streamers from the handlebars. It being a "girl's bike" doesn't seem to faze him. Classic.

Decided NOT to listen to John's last phone message, after all. Peg said there was nothing important in it, he just couldn't find his call button, or something, and was pretty much out-of-it. I think I did the right thing.

Freddie and Pip seem to be making friends, playing like old buds. Really good for old Fred.

Michael had the kids fishing out on the pier. Rosie proudly carried her Disney Princess fishing pole as she followed Daddy and Bobby. Freddie wanted to go too, but Merle convinced him to stay at the cottage and play with the squeakyball while she tidied away the kitchen. (*Gotta keep up with this hourly or it will get totally out of control!*) Merle was indulging in her fantasy about someday – after she retired, that mythical someday – when she would have an authentic "grandma's kitchen" complete with a fresh-baked fruit pie sitting on the white enamel table, covered with a blue and white checkered dishtowel, and the red-topped glass Tom's jar would be full of oatmeal raisin cookies. And, of course, everything else would be spotless, shiny, and in place, unlike now with dog bowls strewn everywhere, dirty dishes squeezed between shopping totes and brown paper bags (*well....at least they're environmentally conscious! The only place they litter is my kitchen!*) of miscellaneous extra food Peg and Michael had brought, plus a bartender's collection of booze and wine bottles. The beer was already in the fridge.

"MOM?" Merle snapped out of her reverie when Bobby came barreling through the front door, hitting the streetcar dinger that served as a doorbell on the heavy oak door, and setting the dogs off. "MOM? FAY? SOMEBODY? DAD NEEDS YOU!"

Peg and Fay came in from the living room where they had been watching a movie. "What's going on . . .?"

"There's a turtle in the bay, near the pier. It's dying . . . we think. Dad wants to get it out and see if we can help it."

Peggy, ever the organizer, sprang into action. "Mom, go online, please, and look up "the turtle man" in Port A. Get a phone number. I think his place is called the ARC." She was already in the utility room ratting around trying to find the old rubber waders she and the kids used when gigging flounder. After she got the heavy overalls on, she chose a large, beat-up Styrofoam cooler from a shelf filled with an assortment of coolers of various sizes and conditions. (*At a beach house you just never know when you're going to need another cooler!*) This one had a heavy red plastic handle which would make carrying a sea turtle much easier.

Merle's Google search for "turtle man, Port Aransas TX" yielded a whole slew of articles about Dr. Tony Amos, originally from London, educated in Bermuda, director of the Animal Rescue Keep, and a Coastal Bend sea turtle guru. Photos showed a tall, thin man with white Andrew Jackson hair and a full white beard, tinted glasses. But she also discovered that he had died several years before, a tragic loss, but that his organization was still very active. She copied down the emergency phone number.

A few minutes later, Peg arrived on the front porch, followed noisily by Rosie and Bobby, Michael bringing up the rear, and the equipment. Merle watched her set down the sloshing cooler and peel off her awkward outfit. The turtle had three oysters attached, cemented, to its back.

After talking to an ARC turtle caretaker for several minutes, and determining that their turtle was a female, Peggy made plans to meet him at the Aransas Pass/Port Aransas Ferry. Fay and Peggy named the turtle Sweetpea and took her in the car to the ferry parking lot on the Aransas Pass side, parked and rode the ferry as pedestrians with the turtle cooler in tow. A pleasant young man in cut-offs and an ARC T-shirt met them in the parking lot on the other side, quite enthusiastic to get a female and assuring them that Sweetpea would be fine once the oysters were removed – a delicate, but usually successful process – and she had her equilibrium back. The oysters apparently had attached themselves to her shell when they were tiny, then as they grew, she had more and more difficulty swimming, carrying the extra weight.

Peg and Fay were back in Copano Beach in less than three hours, not bad considering the holiday traffic. If they had tried to take the car over to the island, they probably would have waited at least two hours in line to get onto one of the five ferries operating today. In fact, there were constantly-updated, lighted signs posted along highway 361 leading to the ferry dock that told drivers how long the wait was from their locations. Drivers could decide if they wanted to wait or turn around, go back to Aransas Pass, and make a fifty-mile southern loop through Corpus Christi and over the JFK causeway to Mustang Island – about an hour's drive on a good day.

That evening they all ate boiled shrimp around the dining room table. Large bowls had been placed conveniently in several places to collect shrimp shells and trash. The dogs had positioned themselves strategically to catch any morsel that might fall their way. Even though the shrimp was the main event, there was no shortage of accessories: hot garlic butter, cocktail sauce, creamy horseradish, curry-and-mustard-in-mayo, all for dipping warm peeled shrimp. There was also Cole slaw, boiled red potatoes, corn-on-the-cob, and hot, crusty French bread. Fay had made fresh *guacamole* in the three-footed Mexican lava-stone bowl, quartered tomatoes on the side. It was a messy, greasy, rowdy, fabulous feast. Merle's favorite Linda Ronstadt CD was playing softly on the box as the kids mellowed out, focused on eating, and the adults mellowed out, focused on the wine – and the shrimp, of course. Merle was convinced that shrimp was one of the major food groups.

After dinner, and Blue Bell ice cream all around, the kitchen was whipped into a semblance of order to be ready for breakfast. They had decided to play Sequence, and Fay got out the homemade game board that her great-grandfather had designed and constructed out of plywood years ago. She wiped off the table and set up the game. Peggy and Michael were partners, Fay and Bobby paired up and Rosie agreed to play as long as Grandma was her partner and would help her, "a little."

It was only after she was in bed, and reading her new Kellerman mystery, that Merle realized she hadn't thought about Willie all day.

Her eyes felt like sandpaper, her face a disaster. Merle leaned closer to the mirror as she pulled out her lower lids and plopped in some Visine drops. (*Eeek! A little too late last nite. A little too much Sequence . . . and wine, well maybe a lot too much wine. But it was really nice – like old times, like before John died.*) She moistened the side of her index finger on her tongue and drug it across the skin under each eye to erase the mascara smudges from sleeping with her face in the pillow. Merle had never cultivated the habit of removing her make-up at night, so she always woke up with raccoon eyes. Sometimes on rushed mornings, or really casual days, like today, she just touched up and went. (*A little make-up base can hide a multitude of sins! Just pile it on. No wonder I'm still getting zits!*) Then some natural pink lipstick. (*Looks good, very just-woke-up pretty. That's a cute trick! Good luck.*) Maybe the eyelash curler?

Smell of potatoes boiling on the stove, patriotic music on the classical FM station, kids and dogs running everywhere, doors open and air-conditioning flowing freely into the ninety-degree-plus atmosphere outside, two frosty beers on the table, Merle and Peggy were in the kitchen making their contributions for the town picnic in the park which would come after the parade.

"Mom, you are the only person I know who uses sweet pickle relish in potato salad. It's all either dill – or mustard. Your's is so different – and good."

"I really prefer India relish, when I can find it. For some reason it's increasingly difficult to find." Merle poked one of the boiling potatoes with a long fork, then picked up the large pot with the blue terrycloth potholders and carried it across the kitchen to the old porcelain sink. Rising steam fogged Merle's glasses and the short hair around her face began to curl up into tiny ringlets.

"How do you get your boiled eggs to peel so neat? These are going to look just awful." Peggy was struggling with shards and flakes of shell.

"Use old eggs. But don't worry, you're going to cut those up, anyway, so it really doesn't matter what they look like."

"But isn't there something about the way you cool them?"

"Yes, you let them sit in the hot water after you turn it off about five minutes, then douse them in cold running water. As they cool, reach in and crack them good, all over, but leave them in the water, maybe even add some ice. Let them sit thirty minutes or so, but run the water every now and then to keep it cold. The secret is to change the temperature suddenly and to never let them dry out. If the eggs are also old, the shells will just slide off."

"Ah, yes, now I remember . . . ah . . . what's going on with you and Willie?"

"I don't know." *(Where did THAT come from?)*

"I thought you liked him?" Head down, concentrating on her egg project. *(And I don't want to talk about it. Is she smiling?)*

"I thought I did, too." *(God, this is uncomfortable! Why is this so uncomfortable for me?)* Merle sat down at the other end of the table and began squashing the potatoes with a large metal spoon, skins and all, salting and peppering, stabbing at them perhaps a little too vigorously. Suddenly a very agitated child burst through the door.

"Pip has Mr. Fairchild's weenies! He got them off the grill and he and Freddie are EATING them! Mr. Fairchild is really mad!" *(Yes! Saved by the kid!)* Rosie was all out of breath from running, face as red as her hair, sweat droplets on top of the freckles.

"Good grief, how did that happen?" Peggy grabbed Pip's horse halter leash, and Merle grabbed the knotted red one as they flew out the front door to stop the destruction and assess the mayhem. Arriving in their neighbor's driveway, they found Owen Fairchild standing in front of an empty grill, with his tongs still in his hand, watching Pip and Freddie fight over the hot dogs – not only the ones that had been cooking, but several previously unopened packages they were tugging and tearing apart, pausing only to gulp down great chunks of meat without bothering to chew or worry about the plastic wrappers. Mr. Fairchild's usually immaculate and manicured lawn was a total wreck. *(Yeah, he's pissed!)*

After no small amount of chasing and grabbing, Merle and Peggy got the two dogs hooked up and sent Fay and Bobby back to the house with the errant animals. They stammered apologies to the Fairchilds and their guests, hoping at least to neutralize the situation. *(These people are NOT amused!)* Then Merle hopped in the Jeep and went to the corner store for replacement weenies while Peggy sent Rosie for a plastic garbage bag and then enlisted her help picking up the debris. Except for the places where Pip's enormous paws had dug into the turf, kicking up tuffs of grass and dirt like a clumsy golfer, the Fairchilds' yard looked almost like it had before the weenie disaster.

Merle quickly delivered the bag of hotdogs to Mr. Fairchild, offered yet another apology, then walked back to the cottage.

"Will people PLEASE keep the front door closed?!"

About four o'clock that afternoon sirens began to blare and people began to assemble on their front porches, with lawn chairs augmenting porch furniture in order to provide seating for guests, all along the parade route which was mostly Bayshore Drive and Plummer Avenue.

As Merle's family settled onto the swing and into the chairs, drinks in hand, the leaders came into view and everybody stood up for the flags, both United States and Texas, of course. The Color Guard was a Oakville Boy Scout Troop which was followed immediately by all the emergency vehicles making a huge annoying racket and flashing their lights – the fire truck from the Copano Beach Volunteer Fire Department, Sheriff's cars from Refugio County, EMS from Refugio ... others from surrounding counties and towns. Freddie's ears couldn't take the loud noises, so Merle put him inside for the duration.

Peggy had mixed patriotic tri-color Margaritas for the event: frozen margarita with fresh raspberries for the red, regular frozen margarita for the white (even if it was a little bit green), and regular frozen margarita with blue food coloring for the blue, all layered into champagne flutes. When served on the tray, the effect was very Coastal Living magazine. In fact, the whole front porch and parade scene at Casa Esperanza had taken on a Norman Rockwell appearance. Except maybe for the margaritas.

Merle looked up to see Lady Liberty and Uncle Sam strolling hand-in-hand (actually Mr. and Mrs. Mayor of Copano Beach – a largely ceremonial position), followed by more scouts, this time the girls. Soon came the floats, some built on flatbed dollies – a fisherman in a rowboat, another Lady Liberty portrayed as a mermaid pushed by assistants in fish costumes. Some were decorated cars or pick-up trucks, some were flatbed wagons pulled by tractors, several quite elaborate. (*Well, not quite like the Fiesta parades in San Antonio, but still...*) There were entries from area churches, or their Vacation Bible Schools with bunches of cute kids onboard, and representative civic and social organizations from Refugio, Aransas, and San Patricio Counties. Finally came the obligatory elected officials in shiny convertibles decorated with red, white, and blue streamers. One beautiful, bright blue, classic Corvette. (*Wow! Love that car! Want to DRIVE that car!*) They were followed by a herd of kids on bikes bringing up the rear. There was Bobby on Merle's bicycle. He had added red and orange and yellow streamers to his helmet so that, with the wind blowing like it was, he looked like his head was on fire. (*He'll be thrilled to know how badass that looks! Must remember to tell him.*) Rosie was on her Big Wheel as she wasn't able to navigate a two-wheeler yet. She was meandering, ... far left curve, then far right curve, then back left . . . (*She must have learned that maneuver from the Shriners on their tiny motorcycles* in the San Antonio Fiesta parades.) Everybody else stayed out of her way so that she had about thirty feet leeway at any one time. She peddled as fast as she could, racing really, making great arcs, big smile plastered on her red-white-and-blue painted face.

As soon as the parade ended, and all the grown-ups were pleasantly buzzed, they walked over to Pineda Park for the picnic. The Red Pelican Sandwich Shop was serving free hot dogs and all the trimmings at one tent. Merle and Fay carried containers with contributions from Casa Esperanza. Merle put her potato salad on a table under the side-dish tent (*did I remember to put my name on both the bowl and the spoon?*) She held the container up over her head and checked. *(. . . ah, yes. OK, then.)* and Fay put her mother's peach cobbler with the desserts.

The park had filled with people within about fifteen minutes. Already there were lines at the food tents. You could hear a country band off in the distance – probably at the pavilion (*or on someone's front porch*). Colored tents everywhere – red, blue, green, turquoise. People sitting in lawn chairs or on oversized coolers, fighting the wind for their paper plates. More than one toddler had hot dog mess all down his front from having his plate blown into him. Seemed like a lot of people in wheelchairs, a few with caretakers. Some were old or disabled, more were wounded warriors. A group of teens were pitching horseshoes and several kids were twirling hula-hoops. (*Wow. I remember when I was really good at that. I picked up "The Twist" easily, too. Guess the skills are related.*) All the while Copano Bay formed a backdrop for this scene of small town Texana. The wind was kicking up whitecaps on the aquamarine water; they marched slowly across the bay, as far as the eye could see. The wind was hot and smelled of salt. Overhead fat gulls screeched, "caw . . . caw."

"Granma, I want a BLUE *raspa*. They make your tongue blue. I want to have a blue tongue." Rosie tugged at Merle's hand, pulling her toward the *raspa* cart that the Baptist Church had parked at the edge of the street. "They're only a dollar." *Raspas* are South Texas snow cones, literally flavored shaved ice, but Merle wondered about the cultural authenticity of Baptist *raspas*.

Later that night Michael and Peggy decided to take the kids into Rockport to watch the fireworks along the beach, close-up. Merle said she'd just as soon watch them from her front porch, even if she had to use binoculars. They took Pip, so she and Freddie were alone in the suddenly, strangely silent house.

"Want to go to the park and watch the fireworks?"

"*I don't think I know what fireworks are.*"

"You probably don't even know what fireworks are, and won't be able to see them, anyway." Merle picked up her binoculars from the hall tree and placed the strap around her neck.

"Come keep me company and I'll watch the fireworks." She hooked Freddie onto the red knotted leash, but didn't bother with mosquito spray since the wind was still fierce.

"We need to talk about that little escapade with the weenies this afternoon."

"*I was led astray.*"

They sat on top of one of the picnic tables close to the water, Merle with her feet on the bench (*well, I would sit cross-legged, except it doesn't feel that great anymore*). Freddie was sitting up straight next to her, his whiskers blowing in the wind and his ears flapping. Great multi-colored flares and swirls had already begun to light up the sky over Rockport, eight miles across Copano Bay. Merle was totally enchanted, even at that distance. She had always loved fireworks, but never liked the noise. This was just perfect. Even the heat which was so intense earlier had abated.

She really had meant to chastise Freddie for his behavior with Pip, but never quite worked up to it. What came out was, "Well, that certainly was a memorable Fourth of July, wasn't it, Freddie? Possibly a few too many harrowing experiences for my taste."

"*Ah, the Great Fourth of July Weenie Heist! Already a legend.*"

CHAPTER 12

The TV crackled a bit, then sound came up on cue, *". . . KSAT TV News at Ten: William Russell Epps, longtime San Antonio resident and community volunteer, was arrested this afternoon on charges of distributing child pornography. Neither Mr. Epps nor his attorney, local civil rights lawyer Rufus Stein, were available for comment . . ."*

Merle had arrived home late and just dumped the stuff from the car at the top of the stairs, grabbing the TV remote and heading to the kitchen with the cooler. *(I'll unpack in the morning. Gotta walk Fred and go to bed.)* She automatically punched the power button and grabbed a frosty Bohemia out of the fridge, then almost dropped the beer when she heard the headlines. "What the HELL?"

Stunned, Merle decided she'd better check her phone messages. Sure enough, first one, Alamo Heights police lieutenant asking her to please call regarding a current investigation, and leaving both his office and cell phone numbers. Merle sat down hard in the chair by the phone and chug-a-lugged the Bohemia before she picked up the phone again.

"This is Merle McKinney returning your call."

"Yes, ma'am. Thank you so much for calling. We are investigating one William Epps whom I believe you know. We found your name and contact information a number of times in his residence and on his electronic devices. *(Oh my God, they've searched his house! SHIT! Have I left anything over there?)*

"Yes, I know him. I just heard the TV news headline about his arrest. What's going on?"

"That's what we're trying to find that out. How long have you known him?"

"About three months."

"How would you characterize your relationship with him?"

"I met him in Rockport and I've been dating him, somewhat casually, I suppose you'd say." Merle's face was burning. She felt hot all over and she had that awful, unpleasant, I'm-going-to-throw-up-any-minute feeling again. *(This is happening all too often of late!)*

"And did you have any reason to suspect that he was doing anything illegal?"

"NO, of course not."

"Do you know what he does for a living?"

"I believe he's retired, but I don't know exactly from what. He never shared that with me. He talked mostly about his volunteer activities and charity interests."

"And what would those be?"

"The Little Church of La Villita, Friends of the Public Library, Boysville, the Historic Preservation Committee, I think one of the sub-committees of the Fiesta Commission, and . . . oh yes, he sponsors an orphanage in Mexico."

"I see. Do you know if he has direct contact with children in any of these activities?"

"Not for certain, but he probably could if he wanted to."

"What do you know about this Mexican orphanage?" *(Do they know I've BEEN there?)*

"It's just across the border a few miles, near Piedras Negras. Very isolated, but a charming location nevertheless. It's run by a group of nuns."

"So, you've been there?"

"Ah . . . yes. A few weeks ago I accompanied Willie . . . ah, Mr. Epps, when he delivered some clothes and supplies to them."

"Interesting. Do you think you could possibly come by the station and look at some of these pictures to see if maybe you recognize any of the subjects?" *(oh, no . . .aw, shit!)*

The next afternoon Merle sat in the Alamo Heights Police station waiting area, dreading what she was about to see. *(What the HELL am I doing here? How did my life come to this? John, how dare you die and leave me to get all tangled up in this friggin' mess!)*

"Ms. McKinney?"

"Ah . . . Yessir. Right here."

The Alamo Heights Police Department was once housed in an old bungalow behind the Alamo Heights Fire Department on Broadway, the sign so hidden one would have thought nobody ever actually needed to find it. But a few years back the municipality had razed the old buildings and built a glass and stone state-of-the-art facility, complete with atrium, that any small city could be proud of, even if it didn't exactly fit in with the twenties and thirties era architectural style of the neighborhood. The huge new complex, which sat beneath two water towers, housed the Fire Department and City Hall as well as the Police – around back, as before.

Merle parked her little Jeep in one of the spaces labeled Visitor, in the newly paved parking lot, under a live oak tree, grabbed her purse and headed inside. The door was marked by an old-style neon sign. *(Probably the only item saved from the old structure.)* The new offices were open and light, the main entry three stories tall, with a wood picnic table and benches in the enclosed patio. Merle noticed the ATM machine in the hallway. *(Well, that's convenient! Ah . . . duh! That's the point, I guess.)*

Ushered to a white-washed brick interview room, she now sat at a fold-down redwood table across from an extremely large Hispanic man in a very starched and very tight dark blue uniform. *(Wow. I wonder if his wife does his shirts? Probably not. Nobody irons like that anymore. Looks more like a pro job. Would probably stand up by itself.)* Lt. Ibrahim Espinoza was elaborating on what he had told her the night before.

"Yes, ma'am, we believe he was distributing to a large number of dealers in several states. We'll probably have the FBI in here soon. So far, we've found over twenty-eight thousand images on his hard drive and a large collection of memory devices. He even had them organized into "suites" as he called them, hundreds of photos in each, for sales purposes no doubt. One titled "Spanish Angels," after the Willie Nelson song I suppose, is all Hispanic children – most of them in some sort of church, looks old . . . and Mexican. So, when you told me about the orphanage you visited, I thought maybe you should come down and see if you can help us. Actually, these children do look more Indian than Hispanic, now that I think about it." *(Uh – oh.)*

Lt. Espinoza produced a fat folder with computer print-out photos on regular printer paper and handed it over to Merle. She opened it and examined each picture carefully. The photography was exquisite, the images angelic, soft focus black and white, the old mission church in all it's charming decay was the setting for young brown bodies. It could easily have been considered high art except that all the children were naked. She stopped and pointed at the picture of an Indian boy sitting demurely at the feet of a *santo*, face upturned as if in prayer. *(Oh, my God!)*

"His name is Emilio. I talked with him at the orphanage."

"Dammit, Ellie, he USED ME AS COVER when he visited that . . . that . . . that . . . PLACE in Mexico where he keeps the children! Those probably aren't even real nuns! I thought at the time that they were a little hinky."

"Need I say, 'I told you so?'"

"And BOBBY, for christssake! The only reason we didn't go with Willie on an outing was that the Missions game got rained out!" *(And then, of course, he got arrested!)*

Ellie was sympathetic, but Merle didn't feel it. Ellie just let her vent.

Saturday nite/SA

Guess I owe Freddie an apology. Apparently, Willie really is a creep – and a criminal – and a PERVERT! AND OUTTA MY LIFE! How in God's name did I miss it? Well, that adventure in Mexico WAS more than a little ODD, to say the least.

I've been interrogated by the AH police, I-told-you-so'ed by Ellie, and scrutinized by Freddie. Haven't heard a word from Peg. Surely she's heard the news by now, seems to be everywhere – or am I looking for it? Guess she's waiting for me to call her. What do I say? Well, this makes our almost conversation down at the cottage irrelevant now! And why do I feel like I'll be reporting to my mother?

Got all kinds of stuff to do, errands to run . . . but can't focus on anything. This mess is really making me crazy! Can't seem to wrap my brain around it.

Maybe I'll go to church in the morning. Haven't been in quite a while. Could really use some solace right now. Hmmm . . . Is there anybody at church who knows I know Willie Epps? Maybe I'll skip coffee hour.

The American Episcopal Church is a direct descendant of the Church of England, that being the official religion of the first English colonists in the Americas. Merle thought everything about it was historical and traditional. She loved the form and ritual that sometimes put her into a semi-trance during services. *(Well, Christianity has a long history of mysticism, doesn't it?)*

    She'd had a religious epiphany, more of a season than an event, when she was about thirteen, and before she discovered boys. One night she watched *The White Sister* with Lillian Gish on late night TV, and then a few months later read *The Nun's Story*, which would soon be made into a movie starring her favorite actress, Audrey Hepburn. After a lot of soul-searching and day-dreaming about pristine white habits and pastoral mission stations in Africa, she came to the conclusion that she should become a nun. But she was faced with a logistic dilemma as she was Protestant, specifically, a Methodist, at that time. Then, while researching convents and religious orders in the library at school, she discovered Anglican nuns! *(That's Episcopal! They're Protestant, right?)* The future history teacher knew the story of Henry VIII and Anne Boleyn and how England became Protestant. That was IT! The answer to her prayers – and her dreams. She began cultivating Episcopalian friends at school so she could go to church with them and her parents wouldn't think she was being weird. In the end, it all turned out to be teenage hormonal angst, but her love for the Episcopal Church endured. She considered herself a cradle Christian, so not exactly a convert, but drawn nevertheless to the beautiful, ancient ritual and rites practiced by the high church.

Merle slid into a pew and opened the bulletin to find the processional hymn, but the choir began before she could find the page.

"Dear Lord and Father of mankind, forgive our foolish ways; reclothe us in our rightful mind, ..." The organ rumbled mellow and low. *(Oh crap, so it's going to be like this, is it? Good one, God! Can't wait for the Lessons of the Day!)*

She did almost skip coffee hour, but as she was heading toward the parking lot, Alpha Ann, one of Fay's close friends, called out to her.

"Fay's grandmother . . . ah, Ms. McKinney. Wait up, please. Are you leaving? I wanted to talk to you."

"What is it, sweetie?"

"Fay told me about your teaching her to drive stick-shift. *(Well, that's stretching it a bit.)* And, I was wondering – well – could you teach me, too? I promise I'll be real careful with your Jeep."

"I think I could manage that, but not here in town. You'd need to come down to the cottage with Fay sometime and we'll do it on the back roads there at the coast."

"Yea! Oh, THANK YOU!" She hugged Merle, then backed off. "Could you come talk to my mom?"

So, Merle went to the parish hall for coffee, after all, but spent most of her time talking with Alpha Ann's parents and setting a tentative date for her visit with Fay. Not a word from anybody about Willie. *(Whew!)*

"Food, I need food! What's that AA reminder, "HALT"? Never allow yourself to become too Hungary, Angry, Lonely, or Tired. OK, so let's start with the hungry and let the other parts take care of themselves for a while. One thing at a time, right, Freddie? Never was much good at multi-tasking. Hmmm … eggs sound nice. Boiled eggs with butter n' pepper? Wait, no, I want Mexican – Taquitos? Too much trouble. Pinto beans? Not enough time. And I sure don't want to go out by myself … not now … Ah, ha! What I need is scrambled eggs and chili." Merle was banging around in the kitchen; Freddie had taken refuge under the kitchen table.

"Sure hope WE get over this soon. Weirdo Willie sure isn't worth all this fuss."

TRAINING FREDDIE

I was really starting to get worried about ole Merle. She had been in a major funk all day now. She hadn't even played ball with me, not once. And she knows I love to play ball.

"Freddie, I'm going to tell you something really strange." She got the eggs out of the fridge and broke three into a bowl, and found the wire whisk. From the pantry she pulled out a can of Wolf brand chili with beans, opened it, and plopped the dog-food colored mass into a saucepan to heat. (*for something that tastes so good, it sure looks yucky to start ...*)

"So, there was a news article in this morning's paper about Willie. Complete with a photograph, one he probably uses – ah, make that used – for his charity and civic promotions … God, what a jerk! How could I have been so stupid! . . . Anyway, I read the whole thing. Morbid curiosity, I guess. And I may have to testify at his trial. (*eek!*) He was a very busy boy. And a very naughty boy. And I think I know his lawyer. I went to Travis Elementary with him – many, many years ago." (*Wow. Too many years ago. Sixty, maybe?*) She poured the scrambled eggs into the skillet where butter was already bubbling. On the counter she had a small plastic cutting board with a little pile of chopped onion and an open plastic bag of grated cheddar cheese.

"OK, you're eating. That's good. Eating is always good. Can I have some cheese?"

Merle scraped the eggs into a cereal bowl, ladled on hot chili, then sprinkled minced onion and grated cheese on top. Before she put the cheese bag back in the fridge, she wadded up a bit in her hand.

"Here, Fred. Have some cheese." After he snarfed it out of her palm, she grabbed a spoon, a Bohemia, and a napkin and went to the living room where she settled in on the sofa. Freddie followed, but was somewhat put off by the aroma of the chili, full of cumin, coriander and garlic.

"So, I'm looking at Willie's picture – there he was, ponytail, shit-eating grin and all – and he WINKED at me. I swear, that same Clark Gable wink as on our first date, when he said goodnight to me down in the patio." (*And I swooned.*)

"See! He's still messing with you. Even from jail. He's a rat, Merle. Trust me.

Can I have some more cheese? Please?"

Sunday afternoon/SA.

OK, so Peggy called and I HAD to talk to her. She already knew the basics. She kept saying, "Mom, I'm so sorry" over and over. Why did I keep hearing, "How could you have been so stupid?" It was, thankfully, a short conversation because she had to take Bobby to a birthday party. (Fay was at North Star Mall with some friends, or she would have been glad to drive him to his event.) Not quite as bad as I had feared – well, almost. What role reversal! Don't think I like it much.

She wanted to know what I'm going to do now.

What AM I going to do now?

She suggested one of the online dating sites, says several of her friends have used them to good result. Hmmm . . . not sure I'm ready for that, yet. Sounds dicey.

Late that night Merle sat at the coffee table with the pack of blue Bicycle cards in her hands, searching frantically through the deck.

"Here you are, you bastard!" She slapped the king of hearts down on the tabletop, then took a black permanent marker and X-ed out the royal face. "I'm gonna put a target on you and pin you up on the fence out back and get out granny's old pearl-handled pistol!" But when she found the gun, there were no bullets for it, which was probably just as well since she didn't have a permit for it either. *(Do you even need a permit now in Texas?)*

She had been stomping around the apartment for hours in a state of hysterical fury. Freddie retreated to his bed, curled up, but was wide awake, watching Merle, his little triangle ears constantly alert, eyes following her every distracted move.

"Merle, your visit to church this morning doesn't seem to have helped you much."

"Freddie, if you knew then what I know now, why the hell didn't you bite him in the balls instead of just peeing on his foot?"

"Do you know what happens to doggies who do that sort of thing?"

"My God, what a stupid, stupid little twit I was!"

"Gloating is beneath me, Merle. But I'm really glad you finally got the picture, honey. We deserve better."

Merle pulled the new pack of cigarettes from the back of the library table drawer, snatching them open. She had already gone through one pack and was starting on her second. She plopped down on the sofa with her feet up on one arm, head down flat, and smoked, reaching over to the red ceramic ashtray when necessary, missing as often as she got the ash in. She was starting to relax a bit – maybe it was the three glasses of Barefoot Moscato she'd had – but her brain and her gut were still struggling for control. She looked at the ciggie in her fingers.

"Good Lord, at this rate I'm gonna get lung cancer before I get laid!"

"Come on, Merle. Are you still on that? Isn't trying to get laid what got you into this pickle?

"What am I going to do, Freddie?" He jumped up and stood on her chest, one dainty paw poking her left boob.

"Here, let me lick your face!"

CHAPTER 13

"OK, now we're getting to it! Enough about me, on to the important part – what I want. Let's see … 'Rate by importance the following attributes you would like in a partner.' Alrighty, then …" Merle was hunched over her laptop as she read aloud, as she had been doing for several hours, all but ignoring an absolutely gorgeous Chamber of Commerce day on Copano Bay.

"Here we go . . . 'Number one. Level of Education.' VERY important. Please no dummies. Ten.

"'Sense of Humor.' Absolutely essential. Ten.

"'Financial Stability.' Sure don't need a charity case. I'll barely be able to take care of myself once I retire. Definitely important. Ten.

"'Loyalty.' Goes without saying. Ten.

"'Personal hygiene.' Eeek! Ten.

"'Likes Animals.' A must. And I'll make a point of including a photo of me with Freddie so there will be no doubt that I have an actual animal in my life. Ten.

"'Non-Smoker.' Of course. Don't want a smoker. No, no. Nasty, unhealthy habit. Whole house smells like an ashtray all the time.' (After all, I'm quitting as soon as – you know …) Ten.

"'Honesty.' Well, I should certainly hope so! Ten.

"'Height.' Hmmm. I'm not really prejudiced against short guys; it's just that I'd rather be with a tall one. And I don't want Peggy to think about us as, 'my parents, the munchkins.' So ... maybe seven? No, ... Eight.

"'Tolerance and Open-Mindedness.' Better be, with my family and friends. And my politics, and religion, and opinions, and habits ... Ten, definitely ten.

"'Belief in God.' Oh, dear. Atheists are just a little too cocky for me. *(I mean really, how can any sane person believe he can make it all on his own?)* So, guess this one's a Ten, too.

"'Physical Intimacy.' You betcha! TEN."

Merle leaned back, stretched, popped her neck, stretched some more, and looked over her answers. "Ten ... Ten ... Ten ... Ten ... Ten ... Ten ... Well, this certainly should give them something to work on. If I'm going to order one up, I might as well ask for what I want, right?"

Maybe I want to rethink this whole adoption business. I didn't sign up for this. Merle has been awful to live with the past few weeks. I mean awful ... just AWFUL! Wicked-witch-of-the-west awful! She hasn't played ball with me, she hasn't talked to me when we walked — except to bitch about that whacko Willie — and she hasn't laughed at me, not once. How can that be? I'm SO CUTE! She used to tell me so all the time. Now, she's not even looking. All she's done is sit around and smoke cigarettes and play cards. And eat. She's into the fridge about every fifteen minutes. Yikes, I hope I'm not losing my charm? Naw ... Impossible! But still, it isn't working on ole Grumpy.

She said she had to get out of San Antonio because everything she looked at reminded her of Willie and that made her want to throw up. And Willie never came to the coast house. It's "clean" — no Willie cooties. I was real glad, too. At least here I can chase birds and bunnies — that is, if she lets me off the leash. (Which won't happen more than once, so I'd better enjoy it ... if I get the chance? Maybe the RV park again?)

Now she's had her nose in that computer for the past two hours. Says she's looking for an electronic boyfriend. Considering her recent track record, maybe an electronic boyfriend is the way to go. Wonder how that works ... ?

"Chocolate! I need chocolate!"

"*Did I hear someone say 'chocolate'?*" Freddie's ears perked up as he trotted after Merle into the kitchen, nails clicking a staccato on the hardwood floor.

"I need a major infusion of chocolate. Ice cream and frozen snack size Milky Ways aren't doing it for me anymore," Merle said aloud as she rummaged through the shelves of the open kitchen pantry, checking expiration dates on boxes and cans. "A little over two years expired looks to be the freshest I've got. Really need to update the food supply down here." She opened a box of Betty Crocker chocolate cake mix and turned on the oven as she began to read the instructions.

"Three eggs! I don't want to waste three eggs on this mess if it turns into a disaster . . . no, wait . . . it won't be a disaster … it'll be fine. Maybe just a little flat? Chocolate flatcake!." She thought about the tub of Cool Whip she had thawed in the fridge. It was "lite" Cool Whip, too. Or maybe the whipped Philly cream cheese? "Which would be best on warm chocolate cake, with no-sugar Hershey's syrup drizzled over it?" (*Oh, dear Lord, bedsnack heaven!*) She lifted the mixer from a cabinet under the counter and snapped the beaters into place.

Freddie smiled. "Chocolate, the food of the gods."

Saturday afternoon/Copano Beach (waiting for my chocolate flatcake to bake).

Arrrgh. Got on the scales this am. Big mistake. 121 lbs. 120 lbs. USED TO BE my set-point – when I was 5'2", before I shrank! John always said he could tell my emotional state by my weight. Guess I'm officially depressed. And officially fat. Or is it that I'm fat because I'm depressed – or am I depressed because I'm fat? And my knee hurts, dammit. Actually, everything hurts. Need to exercise. Maybe I'll get out the bike. (Yeah, right. I need to get off the sofa, first.) You have to exercise everything to keep it from hurting – and to keep it working. (hmmm . . . there are several parts I would like a chance to exercise . . .)

DAMMIT! I'll have to start school this year in my FAT clothes! Shit! School! I had almost forgotten. Temporarily blocked it out. Living like there was no end to summer.

Wonder how soon I can retire? Gotta check on that. Working interferes with my life – yeah, right, what life?

Who was it that said you only have yourself to blame if you're not happy? Oh yes, that was me. How could

I have been so glib? Well, I suppose if you're not sad some of the time, you can't really appreciate being happy, now can you?

Spent my entire morning setting up an account and "profile" on eHarmony. Decided to try this online dating thing. Can't hurt, right? What's the worst that can happen? Nobody is interested in me? (Well, that's what I have now!) Daunting project. Choosing photos was really the most difficult part. Well, yes, and writing the profile. Seriously, what do you say? Considering how I want to present myself and then finding pix that show that side me was pretty tricky. Of course, I included Freddie – the one on the front porch swing. He looks so spiffy. And the one from Galveston several years ago – my hair looks great in that one. Also the snapshot from Thanksgiving at Peggy's house last year – that black suit makes me look wonderfully thin. And the champagne glass in my hand makes me look really elegant. (Ha!) Still need something tomboyish to balance those out. How about drinking beer on the beach? (Possibly too much alcohol?) Maybe one from a crabbing expedition with Michael and the kids. And possibly one from a school event? But don't want to post too many; that would make me seem conceited – or too busy for a relationship.

Wonder how long it will take before I start seeing "matches"?

Fay and Alpha Ann are coming down tomorrow – with Bobby and Rosie in tow. It was supposed to be just the two girls driving down by themselves – and a promised driving lesson on stick-shift for Alpha Ann. But, no, Peggy insisted that the two little ones come, too.

"What! You can't just take SOME of my children. If you take one, you take them all – so I can have a holiday, too," was what she said. I'm surprised she didn't insist on me inviting Michael, too! So . . . here they come.

Merle woke up with a start at the sound of the garbage truck emptying the blue plastic bins she had put out the night before. She raised the shade in the living room just as the truck passed and stared astonished at the park beyond. White stars were scattered all over the light brown thatch of the park's grass. August and September are hard on South Texas. Inland, temperatures frequently top a hundred for days on end. Along the coast the heat is somewhat modulated by prevailing winds off the Gulf, keeping the temperature five to ten degrees lower. However, the lack of rain usually turns everything brown by mid-July, even if the spring has been wet and wildflowers prolific. Usually, the last anybody sees of a green lawn until Thanksgiving is at their Fourth of July barbeque. Watering doesn't help. It only brings out the dandelions and crabgrass.

Merle put the coffee on and retrieved her glasses from the bedroom. The park was amazingly and totally abloom with rain lilies. Small white flowers on delicate, slender stems had literally popped up overnight. (*Guess it must have rained last night. I didn't hear anything.*) The whole scene looked like the movie set for *Camelot*, or some fantasy flick. Both eerie and ethereal. Merle quickly changed into pull-on linen pants and a T-shirt, plus sandals, and hooked Freddie on the leash to go check out the situation.

"Come on, Fred. We gotta see this!"

Freddie was mesmerized by the flowers. He wanted to eat them, but the wind wouldn't leave them still for him to bite (*probably just as well, don't know if they would make him sick or not*). He snapped and missed, snapped and missed again, … all the while, the white stars were bending and bobbing in the wind. The whole top layer of the park lawn was moving.

"What ARE these things? This is impossible. Yikes, they're magic. What am I doing trying to eat magic?" Merle just laughed at me. OK, so that's an improvement.

"These will be gone by this afternoon, Freddie. Unless we get some more rain. The sun will kill them."

Right then the early morning sun was just high enough to shine through the translucent lily petals making them seem lit from within. Fairy lights.

Freddie began to roll in the lilies; wiggled around on his back, snapped at a few. (*Looks like fun!*)

"Is that fun, Freddie?"

"A little squishy, but satisfying." He pranced off, lifting his little hobbit feet high in the air like a baby Clydesdale.

Later that afternoon, Merle was playing Sol at the dining room table, waiting for the kids to arrive. (*If Bobby were a little older, we could teach him Bridge.*) She knew Fay played Bridge and was pretty sure about Alpha Ann. (*Good preparation for sorority life at college.*) Merle had learned to play Bridge when she was in high school. She and three friends, one of whom had an older brother who was a fraternity card shark at UT Austin. He was a scholarship student who earned his spending money playing Bridge with his frat brothers and relieving them of their excessive allowances. The four girls met frequently at one of their homes for a Saturday night slumber party and Bridge lesson. The home most often chosen was the one where the parents were out of town or at a party. If circumstances permitted, the evening's activities usually included a clandestine visit to the family liquor cabinet. That's when Merle learned to appreciate a Cuba Libre. When "Cuba Libre" actually meant something, before Cuba self-destructed, in the post-Batista glory days, before Fidel Castro announced, "Oh, by the way, I'm a communist." Merle remembered the furor that had caused in her house. Her father had contributed fifty dollars to the Castro campaign when they were fund-raising in Mexico, and he was livid. Wouldn't talk about it for days, just got all red when Cuba was mentioned and grunted a lot.

She and John had played Gin for hours on end. Seems the card game was the backdrop for almost every serious discussion they had during thirty-five years of marriage. But Gin is not a game played alone, so after John died she took up Solitaire. Now she was pretty much addicted to it, often interpreting the outcomes of her games to tell her fortune. She shuffled and was laying out another hand when she heard a car door slam, and then the kids began spilling into the house.

This new kid is quite the looker. At least, if I was a teenage boy I'd be looking. She's almost as tall as Fay, but rounder, and blonde. And she talks with her hands a lot, and with her eyes. She and Fay and Merle and I were in our Jeep driving on back roads near the water, north of town. The ride was kinda bumpy. When we got to the cemetery, Merle let Alpha Ann drive and I realized I was in for another driving lesson. Of course, nobody warned me this time either.

"Yikes, everybody hold on, Annie's at the wheel!"

We chugged along, Merle calmly telling Alpha Ann what to do. Which she didn't do. She didn't slow down. She didn't get the clutch all the way in. She didn't give it gas when she let the clutch out. And she didn't stay on the road.

We practiced backing up and turning around in the gravel parking lot at the cemetery for a long time, and she got pretty good at that part. I was in the back seat with Fay, sort of bouncing around.

"OK, left foot on the clutch, right foot on the brake. Now, push the gear shift down and far right. Got it?"

"Yes."

"Take your right foot off the brake and give it just a little gas while you slowly let the clutch out."

Chug ... chug ... chug. And we backed up. Over and over and over ...

Finally, Merle asked Alpha Ann if she wanted to drive home.

"Sure, if you think I'm ready."

"You had a slow start, but I think you have the hang of it now."

"Which way do I go? It's kinda confusing out here, all flat ... and all."

"Well, you'll have to find a place to turn around; I don't know myself where this road ends up."

Alpha Ann immediately swerved to the right and swung the car around to the left to make a U-turn, only she didn't downshift and the road wasn't quite wide enough for that sort of move. So, halfway down the opposite shoulder, headed toward a ditch, the Jeep's engine stalled out. Annie did manage to find the brake just before we rolled all the way into the water. When we stopped, we were tilted dramatically forward.

"Oh my gosh, Ms. McKinney, I am SO SORRY. Wow, ah … what do I do NOW?" She was sort of shaking and starting to whimper just a little.

"First, calm down and take a deep breath. Here, let's set the emergency brake before your knee starts to shake." Merle pulled up the handle and patted Alpha Ann's thigh.

"OK, you have two choices. You get out and let me drive. Or we can try baptism by fire, and I'll teach you – talk you through, that is – a rather tricky maneuver for you to get us out. What do you think?"

"I'm better now. I want to try it. At least then I'll know what to do and not be scared. Need to be prepared for emergencies, right? Oh … what happens if I screw it up and we wind up in the ditch?"

"That's what I have AAA for." Merle looked into the back seat. "Fay, do you have bars on your phone? Just in case. Ha, ha." Fay pulled her iPhone out of her pocket and nodded. "Alrighty, then, let's do this."

"Bring it on!" Alpha Ann looked as brave as a frightened sixteen-year-old could. She was biting her lip to keep the tears back.

"First you have to start the car. The emergency brake is on, so you won't roll. Push the clutch in and take it out of gear, into neutral. Leave your left foot on the clutch, right foot on the gas, and start the engine. OK, now here's the tricky part. You've had ballet, so you will probably be good at this. Put your right heel on the gas pedal and your right toe on the brake. Yes, like that, with your foot turned in. You want a balance halfway between stopping and going. You're going to shift into reverse, then slowly … slowly and very carefully, let the clutch out. You really need three feet for this operation, but your right foot multi-tasking can work. Your knees aren't shaking, are they?"

"No, they're fine now. That's a LOT to remember. I hope I can do this."

"There's a first time for everything, Alpha Ann. If you're going to drive a stick-shift you need to learn how to do this."

To everyone's astonishment, she made it! There were several false starts where she killed the engine again and had to start over. And it took a while for her foot to learn what Merle meant by "balance," and it was pretty jerky, but we made it back onto the pavement. We had all been holding our collective breath while Alpha Ann struggled. Now we all cheered. I was jumping all over the back seat, from window to window, in and out of Fay's lap, and when the Jeep surged backwards, I toppled into the trash bag.

"Grams, Freddie's in the trash again!"

"Gum. Gotta watch for gum."

After turkey sandwiches and chips all around, they each had a bowl of watermelon cubes, slurping as they ate. Merle always cut the melon up and kept it in a big plastic bin in the fridge so her family would eat it. If they had to deal with rinds and seeds and mess, it would sit in the fridge and rot. *(Are these people really kin to me?)* They cleared the table, loaded the dishwasher *(thank God for the dishwasher – it makes having guests so much nicer.)* and each went off to do their own things – mostly read or nap. The two little ones were watching a movie in the living room, but were using ear buds. It was hot as hell outside, so everyone was enjoying the miracle of air-conditioning. Merle was listening to classical music on the NPR station out of Corpus Christi. She always felt self-righteous when she listened to classical music, like she was improving herself. After a few minutes Merle decided to check her email to see if she had gotten any responses from eHarmony.

"First, I need a drink," as she shuffled into the kitchen. "Oh, hi Fuzzyface! Are you hungry?" Freddie was pushing around his empty food bowl with his nose.

"*If you please.*" He sat and looked at her, right ear flopped.

After filling his bowl with kibble, she poured herself a glass of Moscato, then gathered her cigarettes, ashtray and lighter from the sideboard and flopped in front of the computer. In a few minutes Freddie slowly sauntered in and curled up on top of her left foot, then burped.

"Were you scared this afternoon when Alpha Ann was trying to get the Jeep out of the ditch? I bet you were, I was a little, too. Maybe I shouldn't be doing that sort of thing with the girls?"

"*Well, she finally got it, didn't she? That was the point, wasn't it? You worry too much, Merle.*"

"Oh, I think she learned a good skill – don't know where she'll practice it – but really didn't intend to scare the daylights out of my doggie. You've probably had your fill of driving lessons for a while."

"Oh, I'm getting to be an old hand at automotive adventures. Not to worry, Merle, I can take it all in stride. But I really wish you'd wrap your gum in something."

CHAPTER 14

"Good Lord!" she said out loud. Her inbox was all match responses. Filled the screen. "Wow. I had no idea!" *(And they give the guy's first name. Well, that's cool. Hmmm . . . six feet two, retired engineer, age sixty-eight, oh . . . but he lives in Houston. Too far. Let's see . . . six feet, salesman . . . maybe not . . . oh, OK, here we go ... six feet one, retired history professor, age seventy. Cool. Cute, too. Nice smile. Let's see what he says about himself . . .)* Merle continued to look through the matches' profiles and photos, totally immersed and absolutely captivated. *(So, what do I do now? I think all these guys got my information, too, at the same time I got theirs. I think that's the way it works. Do I wait for one of them to contact me? I think so. Is there a handbook for online dating protocol? I need it, now.)* She hadn't heard Fay get up from her nap and nearly jumped out of her skin at the voice from behind her right ear.

"Way to go, Grams!" Fay leaned over her shoulder reading the computer screen.

"Aw, shit! I was trying to do this on the QT, so don't tell your mother, OK? PLEASE?" *(DAMMIT! Gotta be discreet about this. Just what I need – romantic advice from my sixteen-year-old granddaughter.)*

"I think it's great. You deserve a good guy after that pervert you got mixed up with. Let me know when you pick one out. I want to see." Still only half awake, Fay shuffled off to the kitchen and poured herself a glass of chilled sun tea. Merle shut down and put away her laptop, then cleared the table for Solitaire and got a refill on her wine.

Bobby and Rosie were begging Merle to take them crabbing. She finally gave in, even though she had never been crabbing without Michael. Michael was the consummate fisherman. He could catch anything – and they had eaten a lot of what he caught through the years. Crabs were special. They tasted even better than shrimp, but were a lot more difficult and complicated to get at – both in the catching and in the picking. Merle took a plastic baggie full of trash chicken parts out of the freezer and put it in the drainer to thaw.

"OK, if we're going crabbing, we need to get organized. Then we'll go about half an hour before sunset. Dusk is usually the time when the crabs are hungry. Besides, it'll be cooler then, too." *(Of course, the mosquitoes will be out in full force, unless the wind picks up.)* "Don't forget the bug spray!"

"I know what we need, Grandma. I'll get the stuff." Off Bobby went to the storage shed in the back yard. A few minutes later, "Grandma … Rosie? Come help please." He was lugging multiple buckets and nets, one dragging on the ground, and his hands were full of fishing lines on spools. His face was all red and little beads of perspiration had formed all over his forehead and on his freckled nose. He dumped everything on the back porch. Merle went out to check, followed by Rosie.

"I thought we used string." Rosie scrutinized the rolls and tangles of fishing line in a heap on the porch floor.

"Yes, we do. Bobby just forgot. Why don't you go get it out of the top drawer of the sideboard in the dining room?" Merle wanted to avoid as much bickering between the siblings as possible. "And we're going to need a large, old cooler. Big enough for ice and whatever we catch. Bobby, can you find one in the utility room? Let me know if you need for me to reach it for you."

They finally got everything assembled on the front porch, in the shade. "Small bucket for bait *(Don't forget to put the thawed chicken in before we leave.)*, plastic bag with string, scissors, and tongs, two long-handled nets, beat-up old Styrofoam cooler for ice and crabs. "Everyone have their aqua-slippers? Don't want to slip, and don't want a crab to get your toe." Merle looked at disappointed faces. "Yes, shoes. No whining."

"But the mud feels so good between my toes," Bobby offered, hopefully.

"It won't feel so good when you're sitting in it. Or flopping around on it trying to get out of the pond."

They drove the eight plus miles to where the far western end of Copano Bay spreads out into salt flats and sloughs. Fay and Alpha Ann opted for a vampire movie back at the cottage, so Bobby rode shotgun for Merle and little sister Rosie was in her booster car seat in the back with Freddie, who was actively trying to lick her face. *(Start 'em young, I say!)* When they crossed the second small bridge, she turned the Jeep onto the shoulder, checked her rearview mirror, then quickly drove across the highway and down a crushed shell path on the other side which led to a flat area almost under the bridge. *(Oh, good. No one else here.)* There was a sign posted by the Texas Parks and Wildlife Department. Merle wanted to read it aloud to Bobby and Rosie, but she couldn't get close enough to see it clearly, what with the reflection of the setting sun glaring at her off the Lucite cover.

"That sign says we can only keep the boy crabs because the girl crabs make baby crabs. Eventually, that will mean more for us to eat."

"So, how do we tell the boy crabs from the girl crabs?" Rosie wanted to know.

"Dad showed us, remember? They look different on the underneath. The boy crabs are all sealed up and have a shell piece that looks like a pull-tab." *(Or a penis, depending on one's point of view. Please, Lord, no anatomy questions today.)*

"Here, guys, let's you tie some bait on lines and I'll go get Freddie." Merle walked back to the car and hooked Freddie onto the leash, then found a metal ring to hook him to under the bridge where he could see what was happening, but wouldn't be underfoot. By the time she was done, the kids had five lines ready to throw in, and Rosie had chicken mess smeared all over the front of her pink T-shirt. Merle checked for aqua-shoes, and sprayed both kids with mosquito repellant, then told them to go ahead.

They tossed the chicken necks, or wings, or whatever, as far out into the pond as they could, then secured the other end of each line with a rock. And they waited. And waited … Meanwhile, the sun had just set and the sky was ablaze with red and gold swirls. Merle looked up at the flashy display around her. All the little tidal pools, and the big bay beyond, reflected the exploding sky in unbelievable hues and tones. Several water birds added motion to the landscape ... cranes, egrets, herons ... moving in slow silhouette against the sunset. *(John and I used to come here just to watch this . . . we'd sit on the hood of the car and . . .)*

"GRANDMA!" Merle was startled out of her reverie by Rosie's shrill voice. "Bobby's gonna fall in!" She quickly ascertained that nothing had changed during her trip down memory lane except that Bobby had moved closer to the water, actually into the shallows, and was leaning over trying to see into the depths below.

"I thought I saw a crab," he explained, just as Freddie came bounding down the embankment, pink tongue flapping, and jumped up on Bobby, shoving him into the water. Splash! Gurgle! Splash, splutter ... and much yelling. Rosie and Merle finally got hold of his arms and he was able to climb up the steep, slippery bank. *(No, Merle, no, no. You are NOT going to say "I told you so.")*

By the time they got Bobby dried off, and most of the mud and swamp grass removed, it was already dark. Apparently the crabs weren't hungry. So, they packed up their gear, put Fred and their stuff in the Jeep and headed home, Merle still wondering how on earth Freddie could have gotten loose.

"Well, boys are braver. I was taking a chance – that's what brave people do. They take risks."

"You weren't brave, you were stupid. Girls are smarter. I was the one who DIDN'T fall in!"

Merle turned into the driveway. "Nobody goes in empty-handed." She looked at her granddaughter waking up in the back seat, "Aw jeez,

Rosie, didn't you wipe off your feet before you got in the car? Yuk, what a mess! And, you have mud up to your knees!"

"I was rescuing Bobby."

Some comfort food was in order after their ordeal. Tuna noodle casserole sounded good, "Merle style." The kids loved it and Merle found it addictive to the point of embarrassment. While the children were showering and getting every towel in the house wet, Merle got the carton of sliced fresh mushrooms out of the fridge and plopped them into a skillet to sauté with some butter, salt, pepper, and garlic powder. Then she put water on to boil for the noodles, plenty of salt. From the crisper drawer in the fridge she took two skinny green onions which she sliced fine on the diagonal so they wouldn't roll off the board. Those she added to the mushrooms in the frying pan. From the open cupboard behind the back door she gathered a large can of albacore tuna in water, a glass jar of Alfredo sauce, and a small can of baby green peas, all of which she opened, draining the tuna and the peas. After the noodles were cooked *al dente,* and drained, she mixed everything in 'Buela's large crockery bowl. She had greased the Pyrex casserole dish with butter, using her bare fingers, squishing the butter around generously. Now the tuna noodle mixture was patted into the dish evenly. Then she sprinkled grated Parmesan cheese over the top and dotted it with blobs of butter.

"About thirty or forty minutes at three hundred fifty degrees and I'll have a bunch of happy campers!" Her project started to smell good almost immediately. In all the excitement Merle hadn't realized how hungry she was.

Late that night, when all the children were safely asleep, Merle checked her emails again. Wonder of wonders, there were three messages from matches who wanted to begin correspondence with her. *(Wow! I was hoping for maybe one – in a few days. Now, what? Guess I better see who these guys are.)* She read and re-read each profile and looked at each set of photos about six times. Suddenly realizing she had spent over an hour at this, she decided to wait until morning to continue. Freddie watched as she put away the computer and got ready for bed, following her from room to room. In the kitchen she poured herself a small glass of fizzy water to take to bed. Just about to lock the front door, she noticed the moon was rising, just past full.

"Freddie, want to go look at the moon?" She hooked him on the red leash and they went onto the front porch. The rising moon was a gold disc across the bay, a rippled path of amber light made it's way to the shore below the park across the street. As they settled on the swing, the hoot of a barred owl pierced Merle's consciousness and she smiled. *(God, I LOVE this place!)*

Freddie considered the June bug flopping around on the deck under the swing. (I wonder if I can get to that buzzy bug without getting tangled up in the leash? I wonder what he tastes like? Fritos, I bet. I like Fritos. I like this place, too. It has Frito bugs, and big fake pink birds, and fish-smelly piers, and frog patties in the street. The big city doesn't have any of that. And bunnies – lots of bunnies. I love bunnies. I wonder what bunnies taste like? If I could only catch one ... those are fast little suckers! That Beep Beep roadrunner's got nothin' on bunnies. And there was that baby one we found in the park. We thought it was dead until Merle poked it with her finger and it jumped about three feet then disappeared down a hole – a rabbit hole, I guess. Just dove into nothing – and gone. Poof! Imagine that! Freaky, it was.) Freddie was leaning his head over the edge of the swing further and further, totally engrossed in his bug. Merle leaned back and gazed at the moon, a wistful, slightly hopeful expression on her face, as relaxed and peaceful as she had been in quite a while. All of a sudden, Freddie slipped off the swing, nose first, onto the deck and the bug. Bug flew up Merle's pants leg in its frantic effort to get away from falling Freddie, and clung there, as June bugs like to do. No matter how she jiggled and danced and shook, the June bug wouldn't budge. Finally, she went inside to the bath and took the pants off, grabbing the bug in a paper towel. She threw on her robe and went back to Freddie on the porch, who was nursing his crunched nose. She tried to release the bug, but now it clung to the paper towel. At last she was able to shake it free and it flew off quite noisily in that erratic way of June bugs, bumping into things.

"Freddie, I got messages from electronic boyfriends tonight. How about that?"

"I was wondering how that project was working out for you."

"I just want to find someone to have fun with – and … well, you know… play with."

"Back to that, are we? Merle, I've heard that getting laid isn't all it's cracked up to be."

"Well, I guess you wouldn't know about getting laid, would you? You're fixed."

"I've heard rumors."

CHAPTER 15

What would the fashion industry call that peculiar season of the year from the last week of August until mid-October when students, as well as many teachers, are in full fall fashion inside the air-conditioning, but outside it's still summer? School starts a week or two before Labor Day, in the absolutely hottest month in South Texas. *(Well, it's a toss-up between August and September, isn't it?)* A few years ago on September thirteenth it was one hundred and thirteen degrees at four-thirty in the afternoon. Merle had a clear memory of that afternoon, not only because it had two thirteens in it, but because as she walked out the school library door that day, and into the school parking lot, she was blasted with hot air so extreme that it literally knocked her backward several steps. A few minutes later, when she was in her car, she was quite relieved to hear the temperature announced on the radio because she had thought she was having a stroke. *(Is this where we're headed on climate change? Oh, dear Lord!)*

Teenagers all want to wear their new "fall" school clothes, which are quite appropriate for the temperature in the classroom, usually around sixty-eight degrees, but the minute the bell rings in the afternoon, they start peeling things off. Some of them even carry shorts, tee-shirts and flip-flops in their backpacks to wear home on the bus, which is not air-conditioned. Imagine what the girls' restroom is like during the ten minutes between the end of eighth period and when the busses leave campus.

Where fashion truly challenges reality, however, is at the Friday night football games. Teen girls have a universal and burning desire to show off their new duds, so they come dressed like they live in Wisconsin when the temperature is still ninety-five degrees at ten o'clock at night in Texas. This phenomenon is enthusiastically and shamelessly encouraged by *Seventeen* magazine's humongous Back-to-School issue each August. Actually, the Back-to-School issue has been a revered ritual among teenage girls for more than four generations. Merle remembered them well.

Merle was all wound up when she pulled the Jeep into the parking lot at Lozano Middle School. She hadn't been able to sleep since three-thirty that morning, her brain doing double-time, and now she was on her fourth cup of coffee since she'd finally gotten out of bed at five-thirty. She had "dressed up" for the first day of school – that is to say, she added a jacket (with her National History Day pin in the lapel, of course) to her usual long-sleeved, cotton T-shirt and linen slacks. She traded her super comfortable SAS sandals for leather flats and knee-hi hose, and put on a nice strand of beads. Later, in a few weeks, when she became accustomed to the intense air-conditioning, and she had established with her classes who was in charge, she would transition to slightly more casual outfits. She was a great believer in being comfortable in the classroom and really couldn't understand those women who taught all day in girdle-tight dresses and five inch heels. *(Or platforms, for heaven's sake!)*

Of course, the real break-through for comfort in the classroom was air-conditioning. It seems that schools were just about the last public places in the South to benefit from this technological miracle. Probably, the assumption was that children didn't complain and they couldn't vote. It wasn't until the 1980s, when data began to come in that showed test scores dramatically and consistently improved when students were in air-conditioned test venues, that public school districts in South Texas made a serious effort to air-condition their schools. Merle had never attended an air-conditioned school, not even college, and she taught more than fifteen years before she had an air-conditioned classroom of her own. *(But the principal's office always had A/C!)*

She remembered her own struggle with fashion versus reality in high school, during her junior year. That was the Golden Age of the Petticoat, cotton gauze or net, in ruffled tiers, and super-starched so that, if done-up properly, the petticoat could stand up on its own. She wore several such garments at a time, making her skirt flare out about three feet from her legs. While quite attractive and mostly comfortable when walking or standing, sitting in this get-up was tricky, at best. And sitting in school desks was almost impossible. She had to turn sideways, mash the sides of her skirt down, sit, then mash her lap down so it would fit under the desk top, and swivel around to sit correctly. When both the temperature and the humidity hovered around one hundred, like in early September, her thighs sweated and the starched crinoline stuck to her skin. After class was over, she would have to peel the fabric off her thighs before she could move.

Ah, yes, School Days. Reading, writing, and arithmetic . . . and registration cards, and shot records, and class counts, and seating charts, and bulletin boards, and department meetings, and lesson plans … Her head was abuzz with the long list of chores and errands she still had to do as she unlocked her classroom door and flipped on the lights. It was so cold in the room that the windows were all fogged up.

"This is probably the only day this year I'll be early, so I'd better use it well. Copies . . . I need copies. Where's that stack of stuff I had Friday?"

The copy room was humming with both machines going flat out and a handful of teachers gathered around, drinking coffee from the teachers' lounge next door, and making small talk over the din. Merle got in queue. *(Let's see, a hundred and sixty copies each of the parent letter, the supply list and class rules, but only ninety-five copies of the History Fair information sheet because that's just for Honors.)* She checked the list she had made on a sticky-note last thing before she left on Friday.

The stacks of papers still warm in her hands, she stopped by the cafeteria to say "*hola*" and ask "*¿qué pasa?*" to the food service staff and to get one of their delicious homemade sweet rolls. *(Yeah, these are great for my diet! But I do need sugar to keep up with the kids today.)* She had never seen such a hyped-up crowd. The noise level was at critical. *(oh, boy!)* A group of about twenty-five seventh and eighth graders were checking the computer lists posted on the floor-to-ceiling windows on the far side of the cafeteria to see where they were supposed to go first period, having left their schedules that came in the mail at home. The sixth graders were all sitting in one area, looking scared to death.

Back in her room, she used the last few minutes before the first bell to write *(Print, Merle, print. You know kids can't read cursive these days.)* her name, room number, and schedule on the whiteboard. Then, right in the middle, she wrote in large, brilliant purple letters *(Love these fancy colored markers! They are so cool . . . and . . . useful!)* "ARE YOU IN THE RIGHT CLASS?" with a big arrow pointing at her schedule. She hated the fact that they didn't teach kids to write in longhand anymore. *(No time – too many standardized tests. No child left untested, etc.)* Thirty years she spent perfecting her blackboard script and now she couldn't use it anymore.

The eight-thirty go-to-class bell rang. Merle collected her roll sheets from the lectern, her neon pink highlighter from her desk, checked her pockets for jumbo paper clips, pen in hand, and went to the hall to stand by her classroom door.

"Show Time!"

(What a long day. What a long, boring, stupid day. Where IS Merle? This is worse than having her grumpy all the time – having her gone all the time. I want to play ball, I want to cuddle, I want to lick face. How can I be cute if I don't have an audience? And I need to pee, too. Soon.)

Freddie was stretched out on the landing, head resting on his paws, ears twitching. With eyes keenly focused on the front door, he was waiting expectantly for it to open and for his misery to end. The very second he heard the patio gate open, he was down the stairs, jumping up on the door, scratching and squealing and wiggling. Merle had to push him back to get the door open.

"Oh my God, Freddie. I forgot all about you. Oh, you poor baby. You must need to pee something awful. Here, let me get the leash. Stay still, will you?"

Freddie was all over Merle so that when she sat down on the bottom step to hook the leash, he licked all over her face, her ears, her neck, and wouldn't stop. She laughed until she got the crying giggles. She hugged him, he wiggled out and started licking her all over again.

"Merle, I am SO GLAD to see you. I missed you SO MUCH!"

"OK, OK. I can tell you missed me." She finally stood up, Fred still jumping at her legs, and tried to get him out the door. "Come on, Wiggletail. Let's go."

That evening after supper, Merle sat on the sofa in the living room, watching junk TV, and worked on her new seating charts. She took small sticky-notes, cut them in half lengthwise, and placed them in rows on colored cardstock sheets in which she had punched three holes. *(Six across and five deep, that's thirty. And I can put two desks between the windows if I have to. Largest class today was thirty-one. If that holds, I'll only need one extra desk. Hmm . . . "isolation booth"? I already have a few candidates.)* Then she pulled out her computer-printed roll sheets on which she had made notations – names, nicknames, Spec.Ed, ESL, etc. – and highlighted in bright pink those who had been present in class the first day. Keeping them in alphabetical order, and leaving extra desks in the back in her smaller classes – everyone needs to be up front if possible – she carefully copied names, first then last, in her neatest printing, and with her black ink fountain pen. Merle loved using an old-fashioned fountain pen because it felt balanced in her hand and because it's slight scratch on the paper vibrated from her fingers up into her hand and let her know she was writing something important. She wrote small so there was space for future notes on the bottom half of the half sticky-note, things like dates of phone calls to mama. Most of these "seats" would last through May. She would just move them around each six weeks or so when students changed seats – or when she changed their seats for them.

Although fox terriers are famously inventive, Freddie had not yet mastered the trick of throwing the ball and catching it himself. He still needed a partner to play ball. So, he was carrying the red squeakyball around in his mouth and looking wistfully at Merle who was engrossed in her school project. Finally, he took the ball over to the sofa, laid it down beside her and nudged it in her direction with his nose so that it came to rest against her thigh.

"Oh dear, Freddie. I've really ignored you, haven't I? OK, I'll put this stuff away and play ball with you."

"Hi, Merle. Remember me? Your Cutie Pie?" Freddie ran to the other side of the living room, at the top of the stairs, to wait for her to toss the ball to him so he could catch it. They played with a soft, textured red rubber ball and Merle threw it very carefully so as not to hit a lamp or vase. *(Softball training pays off!)* Occasionally, Freddie decided to play soccer, hitting the ball with his nose and bouncing it way up high. That's when they would have to quit.

"Here, Fred. Catch." And he did. "Good Boy. That's one."

"Please let's not count. Let's just play. Give me a hard one."

"Maybe you don't want to count. Huh? OK, here's a hard one." She lobbed the ball over the railing and down the stairs. Freddie had seen what she was aiming at and was at the bottom entranceway before the ball hit. He loped up the stairs, ball in his teeth.

"Wow. You're really good tonight."

"HA! Thought you had me there, didn't you?" He put the ball down, panting, pink tongue hanging out.

Monday nite/SA

FIRST DAY OF SCHOOL! Survived lost schedules, lost boyfriends, lost football pads, lost ESL kids, and sixth graders who couldn't open their lockers. No matter what the current innovations and technology, the first day of school is always the same. That moment just before the first bell when the class is still empty, pristine, all the bulletin boards neat and unmarred, all the bookcases tidy, handout papers in neat stacks. Full of potential, full of mystery, full of promise. Then, in they come, the thundering herd. And loud! (Maybe I should have had an extra sweet roll this morning – they were WAY ahead of me on sugar.)

But it seems strange this year, distant, like I'm just watching myself go through the motions. What's the matter with me? I need to find some enthusiasm. Focus on the kids. Remember, always, that I may be the only person a kid can talk to – or ask for help. Need to at least appear open to that. And possibly teach them some history along the way. If I'm lucky.

This is almost as bad as last year right after John died. Remember, concentrate on the kids. That's what I did then and it was a good year, all things considered. Well, at least I'm not crying all the time. And I do have a sweet little doggie waiting for me at home. I feel so bad about leaving him home alone so much. Seems unfair after all summer with me all day, every day. Going to check on retirement options soon. (Wow – How's that for an optimistic way to start the new school year!)

Obviously, my mind is NOT on school.

What I want is a man!

All during the teacher work week before the first day of school, and over the weekend before the big day, Merle had been checking her eHarmony responses carefully. A few she had shut down immediately, like an eighty-six-year-old retired insurance salesman. He had absolutely nothing going for him, and he didn't look too healthy, either. *(His profile sounded like he was looking for a nurse. All I need is another sick old man to take care of.)* Some she shut down after reading their "must haves" and "can't stands." Some would say she was being picky, but she believed picky was the way to go right now, in view of recent disasters. She did, however, find about five who seemed to be reasonably suited to her criteria and now she was trying to carry on a correspondence, within the eHarmony structure and guidelines, with all five of them. And she was finding this very difficult to keep track of. She couldn't remember what she had told to whom or who had told her what, and she even created a chart to keep the details straight. Finally, she decided that this was unnecessarily complicated, that what she needed to do was choose one and let the others ride for now. So, she did. His name was Chuck.

"Guess what, Freddie, I decided on an electronic boyfriend. We're getting acquainted online now."

"As long as he stays in the computer!"

"We'll email back and forth for a while, then maybe we will meet face-to-face. Then, if we like each other, we might date and you can meet him."

"Uh-oh! I knew there had to be a catch to this electronic boyfriend routine."

CHAPTER 16

Merle remembered the exact day her boobs fell. She was sitting in the bathtub at the house in Terrell Hills. That was the year Peggy was in ninth grade at Alamo Heights High School. Merle remembered because they had gone to a Band competition later that afternoon and she had been quite self-conscious, positive that people were staring at her. It was a Saturday morning, a bright, lazy Saturday morning. John was puttering around in the kitchen. This development was not a gradual process. It had happened literally overnight. Just the evening before she had noticed briefly that her boobs still stood up straight, nipples pointed forward, like they had been when she was in high school. Quite a marvel indeed after those years of her Hippie Period that she spent going without a bra altogether, except, of course, at school. A weekend Hippie she had been – far too old for the real thing, already employed, married, and a mother. In high school her friends had frequently remarked on the outstanding posture of her tits. Small, but upright. She never wore a padded or uplift bra and was thrilled out of her mind in the seventies when someone invented the "no-bra." Maybe it was all those ballet classes when she was a child, maybe it was her genes, maybe it was the swimming, or the softball, maybe it was just luck, but she had every reason to be proud of her front. She eventually changed to an underwire hook-in-front bra, a reluctant concession to the few extra pounds she had carried around in her thirties and forties.

She looked at the girls now. Pointed straight down. *(Well, at least I have mine. Not every gal my age can say that.)*

Merle continued her nightly routine of generous bath powder in all the appropriate places, brush and floss teeth, spritz cologne, and comfy cotton nightie. She considered her toenails and decided to put an oil treatment on them. Now she was sitting sideways on the sofa, bare feet on the cushion next to her, writing in her journal which was propped up on her knees. Freddie had positioned himself Sphinx-like on the other side of her feet, busily licking the oil off her toes.

Thursday nite, late/SA

What a week! I'm exhausted. Open House was tonite for seventh and eighth graders. Got the room all ready, spruced myself up a bit, and walked over to the teachers' lounge where the PTA had dinner for us. Baked potatoes with all the trimmings and a nice salad, assortment of dressings. Hot crusty French bread, but notably not garlic butter. They let the parents in at 6:30. Had ten minutes with each class – not enough time, and some of them wouldn't leave. A few good prospects for History Fair. The Honors classes are hyper; so are their parents. Driving home I got kinda maudlin. How many years have I been doing this? I think this is forty. I remember the first: I was working on the bulletin board (some things never change) after school before Open House and a daddy stopped by my classroom, stuck his head in and asked, "Where's your teacher?" (I did look very young, just out of college and all.) I replied, "She went down the hall." Oh boy, was he surprised later when he showed up in one of my classes. By then

I had my shoes on and I was standing in front of the class, not on top of a student desk. He apologized later, and I laughed.

Well, I'm going to meet Chuck. I gave him my phone number a couple of days ago and he called me last nite. We talked about twenty minutes – not sure what about. History, I guess, he's a classicist, Greeks and Romans and all that. I suppose that's marginally better than a Civil War buff, but still not my fave. Anyway, he seems nice and jolly. And substantial. If his photos are to be believed, he's shaped kinda like a fire hydrant, but a tall fire hydrant – six feet. (I sorta favor substantial these days, John was so frail that last year . . . well, would be nice to have something to hold onto.) He spent some time as headmaster at a military boys' school somewhere in the Midwest, not sure what else he's done. And he lives in Kerrville – I think – not completely clear on that part.

So, we're meeting Saturday nite at this barbeque joint in northwest Bexar County that he likes. What am I going to wear?

Merle had always loved Audrey Hepburn. Ever since she was a teenager. Actually, she had wanted to BE Audrey Hepburn. A red-headed, freckled Audrey Hepburn. That would have worked, wouldn't it? Well, she had the eyes for it, didn't she? Big, wide, innocent eyes, ingénue eyes. And she loved the clothes! Right now she was sitting cross-legged on the sofa watching *Funny Face,* one of her all-time favorites, on a home-made video tape (*If this old VCR ever conks out, I'm in real trouble!).* Freddie curled up beside her and went to sleep, not being particularly interested in nineteen-fifties fashion – or in Audrey Hepburn. She cried every time she saw the wedding dress scene. Today was no exception. But the balloon sequence was to die for. She rewound and watched it twice. Feeling a little cramped, she unfolded her legs and repositioned her weight on the sofa. (*Ooh, that hurts the knee. Dammit!*) Then was amazed once again at how *chic* Hepburn looked in the skinny black pants, black turtleneck, and white sox with black loafers. (*If I tried that now I'd look like a bag lady! But in nineteen-sixty . . .*)

She decided her toenails could use a coat of polish, she stopped the tape and went to fetch the equipment which she kept in a plastic basket in the bathroom. Sitting back down on the sofa and propping one foot at a time up on the coffee table, she removed the old polish which had all but disappeared, it being so long since she had done this project last. She was very careful with the polish remover (*John used to say it was the universal solvent!*), making sure it was in a coaster and there were plenty of paper towels handy.

"Yuk. That stuff smells awful, Merle. Burns my nose. I'm very sensitive, you know. Cut it out." Freddie hopped to the floor and curled up on the other side of the room.

"Can't take the smell? Sorry, Freddie. I'll be through in just a minute."

She started the video tape again, and continued with her pedicure, choosing a pretty, pearly peach shellac to finish off (*well, it goes nicely with the freckles, don't you think?*), and daydreaming about wearing the outfits Hepburn was showing off in the movie.

Friday nite, late/SA

Freddie doesn't like nail polish remover. Surprise, surprise. And my knee hurts. Thought I was over that! It's the old soft-ball thing from when I was in seventh grade, I guess. Tore some cartilage around the right knee while sliding into first base. Really didn't enjoy much of the rest of the season that year, although our church team won the city trophy. Without me. I couldn't run. Had a lot of trouble with it when I was pregnant with Peggy. Hurt like hell. Doctor said it was the beginning of arthritis and had happened because of the sudden weight gain. Suggested I stay skinny (yeah, right, when I'm pregnant!) and active the rest of my life to avoid problems. Guess this is what he was talking about.

Going to meet Chuck tomorrow nite. I'm "cautiously hopeful", as the politicians say. He sounds like a good ole' boy, but pleasant enough, and maybe fun and interesting, if I'm lucky. We'll see. At least this is a start. My first "electronic boyfriend."

Finally deciding on tan silk jeans that made her thighs look thin, with a V-neck cotton T-shirt in a soft ocean blue that matched her eyes, Merle opted for dressy sandals rather than boots. *(Too hot! It's August in South Texas, for christssake.)* And the pearl-drop shell necklace John had bought from some hippie vendor at a music festival back in the seventies. She took extra time and care with her make-up, hoping as always for improved results. The pouches below her eyes were a little less obvious than a few minutes before she applied eye cream. *(Ah, the magic of modern chemistry.)* After the make-up base, a natural-toned eye shadow and plain black mascara. She positioned the eyelash curler around her upper lashes and squeezed hard, with both hands, counted to twenty, and released. Then feathered out the little globs left behind and wiped off the apparatus with a Kleenex before putting it away, not wanting to leave such an obscene-looking tool out for public view, even in her bathroom. She considered her choices for lipstick. All her life she had been looking for the perfect lipstick color that would change her life. For a while, in the late sixties, she found it. Charles of the Ritz came out with their Brandywine, the first of the "brown lipsticks." It was heaven. Pleasing, flattering rosy color without any red or purple tones. She had loved it. It made her look lovely and healthy, and natural. But now she needed more color, specifically more pink. She had resolved several years ago to wear more pink in order to look cheery and younger. Finally, she chose a light peachy pink and added a generous dusting of rich rose blush that made her look lightly sunburned.

The Lone Star Junction Bar and Grill was a hellava place to find, maps and phone instructions notwithstanding. It was WAY off the proverbial beaten path. *(God, I hope I can find my way home. And I hope my headlights are working.)* At last she saw the blinking green neon sign, "BAR-B-Q." She pulled into the gravel parking lot and saw him right off, standing beside his enormous maroon Suburban. All the other cars in the lot were trucks, most with gun racks and "God Bless America" bumper stickers. He had on khaki walking shorts, like a British colonial army officer, and white stockings. Maybe Teddy Roosevelt, all he needed was a monocle and a swagger stick. But when she got closer she saw that he was wearing white elastic support hose that barely constrained his swollen legs. *(You know, if my legs looked like that, I think I would wear long pants. Especially for a first date! Hmmm . . .)*

They introduced themselves, and he put his arm around her waist as they walked inside. The waitress, bouffant hair, gum, and all, showed them to a booth with tall wooden benches, and handed them barbecue sauce-stained menus. They ordered beer, Bud Light for him and Coors for her. *(Don't think they have Bohemia here, probably can't even pronounce it.)* Merle had seen roadhouses before, but this topped anything she had ever experienced, this was the ultimate Texas Redneck Roadhouse. It had all the requisite paraphernalia out front – Texas Lone Star flag, Confederate battle flag, and the Texas Revolutionary "Come and Take It!" flag with the canon on it. A disparaging cartoon of the president facing yet another dilemma was posted on an easel by the entrance where most restaurants would have listed the day's specials. Chuck assured her that the best thing on the menu was ribs, so they both ordered the ribs with coleslaw, potato salad and beans. The waitress brought them a plastic basket with sliced white sandwich bread in it. *(OMG, this place is a classic!)*

Chuck told her about his ranch in Kerrville and his hunting hounds, some kind of blue-tick special. Merle told him about teaching history to middle schoolers and about Freddie. Several hunting anecdotes later, she was beginning to wonder what on earth had "matched" her with this guy when their food arrived. Chuck smiled real big, and said,

"God bless the Second Amendment. Amen. Let's eat."

Not knowing quite how to respond to the invocation, she decided to stick to food as a topic of conversation. Food seemed safe.

"This looks delicious."

"Damn right!"

Chuck clearly enjoyed his ribs. And his beer. At some point, after the plates were cleared, hands and faces wiped, and Merle had a cup of coffee in front of her, they began to talk about his son who was serving on an aircraft carrier in the Mediterranean, or the Persian Gulf, or somewhere over there, and the conversation started to morph. Chuck was getting all worked up about immigration, illegal immigrants and how they were ruining the economy, the shoddy job the feds were doing at patrolling the border, etc., etc., etc. Then he whipped out his smartphone and showed her a picture of an aircraft carrier runway painted with life-size silhouettes of a family as though they were running across the landing surface. Explaining to her that this, of course, was a family of illegals trying to cross the border. He had a jolly laugh, thinking the photo hilarious. *(My God, this guy is a caricature of a bigot! That pic has to be photo-shopped. Doesn't it? They couldn't really do that, could they? The Navy wouldn't let them!)* Suddenly, Merle felt an unexpected wave of sadness, remembering several of her Hispanic students who had joined the Navy, two wanting to serve on aircraft carriers. She dearly hoped they didn't face this kind of raw racism wherever they were now.

Not wanting to continue the conversation on the topics Chuck seemed determined to enjoy, and seeing that Chuck had had perhaps a few too many Bud Lights, Merle hurried up with her coffee, made her excuses, however insincere they were, and left. She wanted to run to the Jeep, but was afraid her dressy sandals wouldn't make it on the gravel. *(And to think I got all dressed up for that jerk!)*

"Talk to me, Merle." Freddie was pulling at the leash so that he almost choked himself with each labored step. Merle, forgetting all about the Professor's instructions, just pulled back. Several times she was glad for the knots in the leash as Freddie tried to bolt off in unanticipated directions.

"Hold on tight, sweetie. I'm counting on you to balance me out, here. When I'm tripod, you're supposed to pull, OK?"

"I blew it again, Freddie. Chuck turned out to be a Hill Country jackass," Merle said as she tightened her hold on the leash.

"I take it things didn't go well with the electronic boyfriend?"

"He certainly didn't meet the 'tolerance and open-mindedness' criteria."

"Can't you just pick another one?"

"Don't know if I want to try again. That's two bummers in a row."

"I grant your record isn't great, but maybe with practice ..."

"Maybe I'm too old for this."

"I don't think you're old, Merle. I mean, not OLD old."

"I'm an old, old lady, Fred."

"You're not an OLD, old lady! You're a NEW old lady."

CHAPTER 17

This is the thing about The Leash. Taking care of someone like Merle could be quite the burden for a less mature doggie. It's a huge responsibility. You gotta be sensitive to her moods — and needs. And you gotta make her laugh. She can be a little ditzy sometimes. Well, a lot of the time, actually. Not the most stable table in the room, my Merle. So, she really, really needs me. She needs me to be there at her fingertips, in touch at all times, so to speak. Stalwart, that's me. Having her on the leash makes her feel secure. That's why I put up with it, even tho' I'd rather run free and do my own thing. Truth to tell, she pretty much comes with me wherever I want to go, even if a little slower than I would like. I mean, what if someone attacked her? I'd be right there to defend her, right? Or what if she fell and hurt herself? She is a little wobbly now and then. I'd have to run for help, wouldn't I? Or what if she had a breakdown? I'd have to lick her face real quick. And besides, being a self-disciplined, well-mannered, responsible, grown-up doggie makes me more attractive, don't you think?

Freddie sat up a little straighter and considered himself.

And she's needed the leash quite a lot lately. We've been going out for walkies five and six times a day. I know she's a little agitated right now, but I don't always need to pee that often.

"Hey, Twinkletoes, want to go walkies?"

Here we go again.

They were walking down Lawndale, near Broadway, when they found the wallet. Freddie turned it over in the gutter with his nose and was starting to chew on it when Merle noticed what he had. It was Sunday morning, eleven-ish, and it had rained rather heavily overnight. She heard the bells from St. Anthony of Padua begin to toll for eleven o'clock mass. (*Dear Lord, once again I didn't make it to church – I'm such an awful heathen!*) Merle had stayed up really late the night before reading her mystery novel and was still groggy even at this hour, and after two cups of coffee, number three in her hand.

"Here, let me see what you have there. Give it to me."

"I found it; I want to chew it."

"Here, Freddie. Drop it."

"Don't want to drop it, Merle. It's nasty and smells funky. You wouldn't like it."

"Come on, Freddie. Drop it, NOW!" Merle was beginning to get frustrated, still a little afraid of actually taking something away from Fred, something he possibly perceived as food. She glared at him, her schoolteacher look. They stood eyes locked while Merle waited, and waited, and waited . . . finally, slowly, reluctantly, Freddie let the folded leather slip from his teeth and worked his jaws like he was trying to compose himself. He sat and stared down at it, ears cocked.

"OK, already. Here, I was gonna give it to you, anyway, just wanted a little chew, first. Don't get your panties all bunched up. Yikes!"

Merle unfolded the soggy wallet and examined the contents. It was thin, dark brown leather, even darker now from being soaked, not much inside, no photos. One hundred eighty-five dollars in cash. A Texas driver's license, a San Antonio College ID card, and a slip from the Bexar County Adult Probation Department *(Uh-oh. He was probably violating his probation by going to one of the clubs on Broadway last night where alcohol is served. Let's see how old he is . . . ah, twenty-one, just barely.)* She closed it up and put it in her pocket to call about later, when she was back inside. It felt heavy and damp against her thigh. Freddie had lost interest, having found a little pile of soggy French fries someone had tossed into the ditch last night.

"OK, I'm hungry! And I gotta wake up. That was a really good Kellerman I finished last night, but I'm trashed today. What can I eat . . .?" Merle began ratting around in the pantry and fridge – going back and forth from one to the other. "Arrgh! And I have grades to work on. How can it be almost mid-term, already? We just started this year, didn't we? I don't even know all their names, yet." She put her third cup of coffee into the microwave to reheat as she wondered, once again, how many hours, days or weeks even, of a person's life are spent waiting in front of a microwave? Just waiting.

"How about an egg sandwich? Quick and easy and comforting." She got butter, eggs, mayonnaise, onion and cheese out of the fridge and placed them on the counter.

"Yes, thank you, I'd like one very much. No onion on mine, please."

"I'll even scramble an egg for you, Freddie. How's that?"

"I'd really prefer the whole thing, but scrambled egg will do. Could you maybe put a little cheese on it?"

"Maybe I'll sprinkle a little grated cheddar on it for you."

"Hot damn! Gourmet snack time."

"I'm calling Angel de la Rosa. Does he live here?"

After she had gobbled up a huge sandwich and Freddie foundered himself on eggs and cheese, Merle sat at her desk and picked up the phone. She had looked up "de la Rosa" in the San Antonio phone book, but found no Angel. She did, however, locate another de la Rosa, one Mariana, at the same address as Angel had on his driver's license. She tried the number.

"That's my son. He's not here right now," the lady answered in Spanish-accented, but perfectly clear, English. "May I take a message?" Merle left her name and number and said she had his wallet and for him to call as soon as possible.

While she was waiting for Angel to call, and to avoid doing her grades, she sat down at her computer and checked her eHarmony account to see what was happening. She was quite amazed at herself for getting back on the horse so soon after the unfortunate Chuck episode. One would think such a disaster would warn one off, at least for a while. But hope springs eternal, it seems, and she decided to try again. (*Good for me!*) Immediately there popped up a message saying that a match had requested Fast Track. *(What the hell is that?)* She clicked on the information balloon and read the fine print. Apparently, this person wanted to meet her pronto, skipping all the guided questions that eHarmony suggested. *(Well, that's a first. Hmmm . . . Let's take a look at him . . . He certainly is direct! And, WOW, he really is a looker, too!)*

So, his name was Phil, a retired language teacher, five feet eleven inches tall, age seventy-one. Very handsome. *(Hey, cutie! Where've YOU been all my life?)* Lots of sports pictures. (*Good Lord, is there anything he doesn't play – or ride?)* There was something distantly familiar about him that she couldn't for the for the life of her place in memory. And he had a dog. An absolutely adorable mutt, medium sized, wiry salt and pepper hair, cocky face with perky little ears. Too cute, by far!

What to do? What to do? Surely, she was flattered that someone, especially someone like this guy seemed to be (*well . . . that was the operative term, wasn't it? "Seemed to be"),* liked her profile enough to want to meet her immediately. But somehow it felt off, too good to be true. Or was she being overly cautious because of recent events? Wasn't she due something exceptional after recent disappointments? Maybe Mr. Wonderful really did exist. *(But the reason I joined eHarmony instead of one of those "meat market" dating sites was to get the extra screening and this guy is avoiding that part. Hmmm.)*

She decided she needed to call Doris Luna. Doris was always ready with advice, though her own personal life was perpetually in turmoil. Maybe she could talk Merle through this one – help her see options and other viewpoints. A little upbeat chit-chat from Doris would do her good.

"Want me to ask Alex to shadow you at whatever restaurant you decide on? He's home on break, working on a project. I'm sure he'd be glad to help out his Aunt Merle." Doris had insisted on coming over rather than just talking on the phone. Now they were sitting on Merle's balcony, with their feet propped up on the railing, watching the cars go by on Broadway and drinking the margaritas which Merle had whipped up in her blender. Chips and *queso* were in two bowls on the little white table between the two rattan chairs. Not real margaritas, just frozen limeade, tequila – lots of tequila – and ice. Not authentic, but serviceable nonetheless.

Alex Luna was Doris' son, an architecture student at Rice University in Houston. Really cute kid, heartbreakingly handsome, and smart, just like his father, Doris' ex-husband number one. Doris had been married twice more since Javier Luna, but she kept the Luna name for Alex's sake. Javier had grown up with a different last name than his mother and had loathed it! Said it "scarred him for life" (a little over dramatic, Merle had always thought). But Doris had agreed, encouraged by the generous trust fund Javier made available as long as she remained Doris Luna. And, although his mother was obviously Anglo with her blue eyes and freckled skin, with a name like Alejandro Estéban García Luna, Alex couldn't ever deny his Hispanic-ness.

Doris was trying to convince Merle to see this Phil guy, and to accept his Fast Track invitation.

"Look, sweetie, he might be just exactly what you want. Nothing ventured, nothing gained."

"What do you think would happen if I decline the Fast Track and insist he follow the rules?"

"He might think you're a prude. And I know you're not. You want to get laid, right?"

"Not to put too fine a point on it."

While she was outside with Doris, Angel de la Rosa had called and left a message with a cell phone number. Now she called him back.

"Ms. McKinney, my mom said you found my wallet?"

"Yes, I've got it. It was in a drainage ditch on Lawndale, just off Broadway. It's in pretty bad shape, quite wet from the rain, and my dog tried to eat it. Were you at one of the Broadway clubs recently?"

"Yes, last night. Ah . . . what was in the wallet?

"Your IDs and cash – about a hundred and eighty-five dollars."

"Oh – great." She could hear sincere relief in his voice. "I was really worried . . . about my money. Could I come over and get it, please?"

"Sure. Right now?"

"Yes, please, if you don't mind." Merle gave him the address and instructions for finding her condo. "I'll be there in about thirty minutes."

And so he was. Angel de la Rosa arrived in a metallic purple, custom-painted, 1958 Cadillac Deville convertible, with the top down. (*Oh, my God! I did NOT expect this!*)

The tall, well-built young Hispanic man opened the patio gate and smiled at Merle. "Are you my guardian angel?" Merle laughed.

"No, I'm not Angel's angel! Your fairy godmother, perhaps – *tu hada madrina*?" Angel laughed, too. Sort of swaggered into the patio, but seemed slightly uncomfortable in obviously fresh-pressed clothes – jeans and a starched, bright red poplin long-sleeve shirt, but old and worn tennies and a Spurs gimmie cap. (*His mother must have made him clean up.*)

"That's quite a car you've got there! Do you ever take it down to the Pig Stand on Friday nights?"

"Yeah . . . yes, I do. Do you know about that?"

"Sure, my husband was a classic car buff. We would have dinner down there every now and then on Fridays and spend an hour or so looking at the cars in the parking lot and talking with the guys and gals."

As Merle handed the sodden wallet to Angel, she noticed what she thought were gang tattoos on the back and between the fingers of his left hand. Crosses and stars and crescent moons. (*Uh-oh. Better not invite him inside.*)

"Listen, *muchísimas gracias* for this, *madrina*! I can't tell you how much I appreciate your kindness. If there's ever anything I can do for you, please don't think twice about calling me. Do you still have my cell number?"

"Yes, I think so. And you are very welcome, but I don't think I need anything right now. Thank you just the same."

"I mean it, really. Anything. Anytime. Keep my number in your cell phone, OK? I've got your back, *madrina*." And she believed he really did mean it.

Freddie hadn't gotten a good look at Angel, but he did get a good smell. Angel smelled dangerous.

"Well, that was a little scary. Not to mention bizarre." she said with a frown on her face as she shut and bolted the front door, not quite sure what to make of what had just happened.

Sunday nite/SA

Busy Sunday, even without church. (God forgive me for things done and things left undone.) Mexican gang-banger kid lost his wallet. I wonder why it wasn't one of those portfolio style bill-folds that the vatos carry chained to their belts? Maybe because he still lives with his mother? Freddie found it in the ditch down the block a way. The kid came and got it OK, but it was a rather unnerving experience, to say the least. But his car was something else! Straight off the Friday nite extravaganza at Mary Ann's Pig Stand down on Broadway. John and I used to really enjoy that scene. But I don't remember ever seeing a metallic purple Cadillac convertible!

I've pretty much decided to go ahead with the Fast Track that my new eH match Phil wants. This might be a mistake, but Doris talked me into it, and she's going to arrange for Alex to have my back during the first date, if I want. Maybe so. Just in case things turn weird. As Doris reminded me, I do need to be careful.

Especially after recent events. She didn't say that, but I heard it nevertheless.

I'm really tired, seems like all the time. And my knee hurts. Maybe I need to go to a gym. Think I have a free membership with my school district group health insurance. That's probably a very good idea. Where do I find the time? I'm not getting enough sleep as it is. But, maybe . . . maybe I can actually get into a program this time. I keep thinking about that documentary I saw years ago where a group of elderly retired ballerinas, mostly in their mid-eighties, met at seven every morning to "take a class." That's the term they used for working out – "take a class." Those old gals were amazing – all of them so lithe and limber, even if wrinkled and gray. Their gracefulness made them seem much younger. I wonder how badly their joints hurt? But it never showed either in their posture or on their faces. My God, if I had that kind of fortitude, I'd be unstoppable!

Maybe I need a weekend at the coast. Maybe I need to retire. And go to Casa Esperanza permanently.

"Let's go walkies, Freddie." He presented himself straightaway at the top of the stairs where Merle stood with the red leash in her hand, fingering the knots.

"I thought you'd forgotten about me, lost in a reverie you were. What are you so unsettled about, Merle?"

"Sorry, I almost forgot about you. I've been distracted." (*In spades!*)

They ambled around the paths and sidewalks of the condominium complex, hardly noticing where they were walking. Merle immersed in her own thoughts and Freddie chasing bugs.

"So, Freddie, I'm thinking we might go to the coast soon. I need a break. Things are getting too complicated here – and school is crazy, crazy hard. I'm not liking it much right now."

"The coast? Did you say the COAST? Oh boy, oh boy, oh boy, oh BOY… ahhhh… Frito bugs and gecko tails on the porch… and fish head jerky on the pier… and grasshoppers in the park… and turtle patties in the street…"

"Life just seems simpler at the coast."

"And the snacks are better, too,"

CHAPTER 18

"OK, here's the drill, Alex. We're meeting at Hsiu Yu Thursday night at seven. You want to get there a little before then, stay in the parking lot, then follow me in after a few minutes and get a table where you can see me. I'll pay for your dinner, of course."

"Not a chance. This is mom's treat! She insisted; you know how she is when she gets started on a project. She thinks it's a hoot! I think it's going to be exciting, spying as it were. I'll take a textbook and pretend to study. I'll be real casual, Aunt Merle. Don't you worry about a thing."

"Alright, so hang around 'til you know I'm back home – alone. I'll text you."

"You got it. You want to decide on some emergency signal in case you want me to step in?" Merle laughed.

"No, I don't think we'll need that extreme. Thanks, anyway." Alex promised to fill his mother in on the plans and hung up.

Merle had called Phil on Monday night after she accepted the Fast Track and he sent her his phone number. They were to meet for the first time at a Chinese restaurant up the street on Broadway. She had been somewhat embarrassed because she was flustered and stuttered some on the phone, but she thought his voice felt like rubbing velvet over her cheek. (*Maybe he has that effect on all the girls?*) So now she was obsessed with what to wear. She had about eight pair of slacks and at least a dozen tops strewn about on her bed. Shoes scattered around, plus a few scarves and several strands of beads, making quite the colorful mosaic, if one stood back and considered the mess as art. Rather than being a cacophony, it was predominately blues, blue being Merle's favorite color. She dearly loved all the shades, from periwinkle to aqua and everything in between, from midnight and navy to peacock teal to robin's egg or pale ice blue. Her wedding had been blue, four bridesmaids in pale blue chiffon with matching blue pill-box hats and blue veils studded with baby pearls. Very nineteen-sixties. Very summer. She thought the dresses were beautiful (*doesn't every bride?)* and were of a style that could be "worn again," as they say. But in retrospect, she had to admit that most of them probably went straight to the back of the closet never to be seen – or worn – again. She and John had married in a sunset service at a chapel in the Texas Hill Country. Instead of the anticipated cool evening breeze, there had been a late summer thunderstorm, a real gully-washer it had been, and the fading rays of the sun she had expected to be shining through the stained-glass windows during the service turned out to be lightning bolts. At the time she had been quite concerned that it was an omen. But now, of course, that idea seemed silly.

"Something sophisticated, but casual and classic. Something that makes me look thin." She rummaged through the piles and pulled out a pair of navy silk twill slacks, almost like chino, but lighter weight and with that slight sheen, and a soft, drapey hand. She had gotten them at a thrift store in Houston several years ago. A real find they had been, Ann

Taylor Petite. Fit like a dream. Then she ratted around in her closet and located a soft gauzy shell top in a swirly pattern of turquoise and cobalt.

"Gorgeous! Makes my eyes look intense. Do I dare try blue eye shadow? Maybe not on the first date. Maybe not at all. I did that thirty years ago." A long rope of funky navy blue and evergreen painted wooden beads would keep the outfit from looking dressy, and she had some comfortable navy SAS sandals that would be perfect. (*Matchy, matchy! Do I need to do the toenails again?*) She checked her feet and decided it wouldn't be a bad idea to redo the polish if she had time. She considered the possibility that doing her nails or toes was one of those coping rituals – things she did to calm herself down in times of stress or crisis. She knew shampooing her hair was, had been since she was a teenager. When life got intense, she ALWAYS washed her hair.

Tuesday nite/SA

OK, so I'm all set for my date with Fast Track Phil Thursday evening. Got the clothes. Got the bodyguard. Got the guardian comadre waiting in the wings and demanding full disclosure. Will work on the hair and nails and toes tomorrow when I get home from my after-school department meeting.

Fay left a message while I was talking to Alex (Is there a rule somewhere that says all calls of any importance come at the same time? I swear, I go days with no calls at all, then two or three or more all at the same time!) And I didn't retrieve it until after it was too late to call her back. Said she wanted to talk to me, had a favor to ask. Hmmm . . . Wonder what she wants to talk about?

Or needs? Well . . . Peggy is pretty busy with the little ones right now; maybe Fay just wants someone to talk to. Or – oh heavens – maybe she wants someone to "talk" to? Uh-oh! Well, she is sixteen, after all. I was wallowing in teenage angst when I was her age, but maybe I'm not the best example. Maybe she just has boyfriend problems. (I hope.) Or maybe she has sex questions – can I handle that? Yeah, I think so, as long as she doesn't get personal – which she will, of course, almost certainly do! I better decide now how much I'm prepared to share.

Good Lord, what if she asks about drugs? Peg will kill me if I tell her the truth – that I used to smoke dope.

So, something else to worry about.

The next evening Merle was slouched on the sofa with a beer and a cigarette, waiting for her toenails to dry.

"I thought that department meeting would NEVER end! Here it is almost nine o'clock and I haven't even eaten dinner."

"Dinner? Did I hear someone say, 'dinner'?" Freddie trotted into the living room, his nails clicking on the kitchen floor until he hit the carpet.

"I have a date with my new electronic boyfriend tomorrow night, Fred."

"I knew it! I knew you were exceptionally distracted about something and wondered if that might be it."

Merle picked up the blue Bicycle cards and shuffled, feathered, and shuffled again. "His name is Phil and he has a dog named Perkins. Maybe if this works out, you can meet Perkins."

Well — that's a good sign. That he has a dog. Not sure about the name, tho'... 'Perkins'? Sounds like something you'd take for a tummy ache.

"Yes, I think having a dog makes him more promising." She held out her hand and looked at the ciggie, "Maybe soon I won't be doing this anymore. Seems like all I do these days is sit around playing Sol and smoking. And talking to you."

Yes, let's not forget about the therapeutic benefits of talking things out with me.

"Maybe Phil is The One. I sure hope so. I need a success experience for a change."

I'm reserving judgment, sweetie. Take it slow, OK? Your track record ain't so good in this area!

As always, there were cut flowers on the countertop as she entered Hsiu Yu Chinese Restaurant, making the entry-way smell fresh and clean before the food smells took over. A tall cylindrical vase of them, red carnations, orange gladiolas, bright yellow day lilies, and a number of blooms that Merle couldn't identify. She glanced across the dining room and spotted Phil immediately. He had a booth on the other side of the room, sort of in a corner, and he stood up when he saw her enter. Casual preppy – a polo shirt without logo, so faded it had a patina (*Maybe it's his good luck shirt?*) and khakis worn to soft. Tassel loafers, no socks. He waved and motioned her over. Phil seemed quite tall, but slender and graceful in the style of athletes or dancers. He was balding on top, but what hair he did have curled around his ears in salt and pepper ringlets. He smiled. *(Oh, my God, he has dimples! Or . . . a dimple? Yes, that's it. He has one dimple. How cute!)* And the eyes! Well . . . Merle hadn't seen eyes like Phil's since . . . well, since high school. *(What WAS that guy's name? Could have drowned in those eyes!)* Phil's were big, chestnut brown, puppy-dog eyes that crinkled at the corners when he smiled. And *(OMG!)* long, black, curly eyelashes. WAY over the top in the looks department! A matinee idol, an eleven on a scale of one to ten.

Just then Merle noticed Alex coming into the restaurant and indicating to the hostess where he wanted to sit, holding up his book as though to explain that he needed good light and that table right there would do fine.

"You must be Merle. Have a seat, be comfortable."

"Yes, I must be, mustn't I? And you're Phil. Nice to meet you. What's new with you, Phil?" She had little trouble focusing on her date and forgot about Alex altogether. She did, however, give him a thumbs-up behind her back as she and Phil left, much later. Alex paid his bill and got himself out of the restaurant just in time to catch a scene he found so touching he almost cried. Rather than waiting for her to text him to make sure she was home safe and sound, he followed her back home in his little red Miata, pulled in behind her in the parking lot, and proceeded to kid her mercilessly about what he had just seen.

"But, actually, Aunt Merle, I think I know that guy. He's a foreign language teacher, right?"

"Yes, retired from St. Mary's Hall. How did you know? You didn't go to St. Mary's Hall, you went to TMI."

"He tutored my step-sister in Italian several years ago. He's real good. She made a B, and that was a miracle, trust me. Bianca has trouble speaking English, much less Italian! Although, his looks might have encouraged her a bit, if you know what I mean? For an old guy he really is a handsome devil!" Merle knew exactly what Alex meant.

"Well, he certainly is charming, Freddie. And interesting. And sweet. He said he was shy, but he kissed me on the cheek when we said goodbye in the parking lot. ON THE CHEEK! Can you believe it? So tender and old-fashioned. Maybe he is shy, after all."

"What's the big deal? I kiss you on the cheek everyday!" And the nose, and the ears, and..."

"Don't eat that stuff, Fred, it's yucky."

Freddie was engrossed in the acorn dust spread all over the parking lot. October is Acorn Month in San Antonio. Acorns fall off all the live oak trees; not the leaves, just the acorns. And they were getting an early start this year. Dogs eat them, squirrels bury them, and kids chuck them at each other. This year there was an abundant crop since the spring had been so wet. Merle's condo grounds had a great number of live oaks and there were piles of acorns everywhere. Cars driving over them in the parking lot smushed them into the powder Freddie was now eagerly licking off the asphalt.

"OK, OK. I know I didn't tell you, but we're going to the coast. Right NOW! I decided just about the time school was out and I got a parent phone call I'd rather forget about altogether. I gotta get out of here. This city makes me crazy. I gotta figure out my friggin' life!"

"YES! The COAST! Can I help us pack? Here's my red squeakyball, and my rawhide chew." Freddie nosed his toys to the top of the stairs.

Merle had no idea she could pack so fast. They were on the freeway within thirty minutes from the time she opened the front door. Freddie's walk had been abbreviated, to say the least. She couldn't explain the sudden urge to get the hell out of town even to herself. But she just had to go someplace calm and quiet and get her head straight. She was already smitten with Phil and didn't know if that was bad or good. Or what to do about it. He had followed up their date with clever and engaging emails, and now they had a date for the coming Friday night's Alamo Heights football game. And she got tingly every time she thought about it. The drive south was easier than usual, maybe because she was earlier than usual. And there were only a few more potholes between Kenedy and Refugio, near the oilfields. Oilfields were terrible on Texas highways.

Friday nite/Copano Beach

Arrived early for once. Fred didn't know what to make of my urgency, but he was all for it. Gotta use this weekend to figure out what's going on. Fast Track Phil is making me crazy. And all sorts of weird things keep running thru my brain . . .

Why are men's genitalia attached in the front, as though God had left them out of the original model and just stuck them on at the last minute? They dangle there in the open, completely exposed. Totally unprotected by nature. For all to view and critique, at least in our primitive, pre-clothing days. Why would God do that? Is there something primal here that we are missing today in our civilized "modern" age? Is that why guys seem so obsessed with their arrangements – because they're looking at them all the time? Did the poor babies evolve that way for a reason? Mating? (Eveready, the cave man!) Macho prowess based on – what else? – size. ("See, mine's bigger than yours." "No way!" Some things never change.) Hierarchy? How on earth would you judge that one? Oldest? Maybe God put their privates on the outside to remind the suckers that they're vulnerable.

And then there's the whole issue of codpieces on guys, but fig leaves on art, during the Renaissance, and the legend that Elvis regularly put a coke bottle down his pants leg during his concerts. What's that all about? And what lengths they go to to protect the boys. All those accessories necessary for sports or combat or even day-to-day activity. (Did those Greeks REALLY compete at the Olympics totally naked? How did that work out for them? Certainly the ladies loved it! There were ladies among the coliseum spectators, yes? If there weren't, that's a tragedy!)

And what a fuss men make when the equipment doesn't work right! Note the abundance of performance enhancing pharmaceuticals advertised on TV. Is there anyone in America who hasn't seen a Viagra or Cialis ad? (Does that hapless couple ever get out of their individual tubs? How do parents of small children explain all this? Which is more difficult – explaining ED drugs, or ads for feminine sanitary products?) Does anybody get embarrassed by anything anymore?

And why am I thinking about all this?

Am I going to retire this year or not? I'm going to have to decide in the next few months.

"Well, at least they can see what they're doing!" Merle was in the bathroom, just out of the shower, still naked and a little damp, trying to see her twat with a hand mirror. (*God, this is awkward – maybe hidden away isn't the right place for genitals, after all. Makes it extremely difficult to self-service the parts.*) She thought she had a sore spot and was looking to see if it was red, but couldn't see anything. Decided to slather herself with Neosporin, anyway, and continued getting dressed. Jean Naté bath powder in the armpits, under the boobs, butt, and feet. Then undies, pull-on linen pants, balancing herself with one hand on the countertop (*I used to be able to do this one-leg-at-a-time routine standing in the middle of the room, balanced. When did that end?*), and a pale blue, long sleeve, cotton T-shirt. She spritzed on some Blue Grass – quite a lot of Blue Grass, actually, and started on the face.

"Bye, Freddie." She picked up the Jeep keys, her purse, and her hat.

"I wanna go! I wanna go! Please, please." He was jumping around like a dervish.

"No, sorry, you can't go this time. It would be really boring in the car. And hot. Maybe too hot for you. Please stay out of the trash. Here's a treat for you. Guard the house, please, and take messages."

"Are you trying to bribe me? What kind of treat?"

"Yes. I'm trying to bribe you. Here, take this nice pig's ear." Freddie sat watching her leave with the treat in his teeth and his head cocked.

"Saturday morning, beautiful day, nice sleep, off to a Thrift Store Adventure!" Merle's love affair with thrift stores started many years earlier when she and John were first married, with very little money, and then when there were children, and even less money. She had begun shopping in thrift stores and at garage sales for household items, and later some clothes, to stretch the budget. Then it became a form of recreation, a treasure hunt, and hobby. Now, whenever she went into a conventional dress shop or department store, she suffered severe sticker-shock. She had, through the years, upgraded occasionally to resale consignment stores for special things, but even those establishments only charge about a quarter of retail. There were several choice, classic items in Merle's closet now that she had scored at resale stores. And, if nothing else, it was a fun way to indulge one's love of fashion without going bankrupt in the process. But mostly, the hunt was just plain fun.

The ultimate adventure, of course, was to shop at a thrift store in a foreign, preferably exotic, place – like Hawaii or Las Vegas, both of which Merle had done. However, her most interesting experience had to have been a Jewish charities store in Miami that featured a whole wall of used menorahs. (*Imagine that! I had no idea there were so many styles! Gentiles never consider these things, I guess.*)

Merle was on her way to Castaways in Rockport, a venerable establishment and one of the best kept secrets of the Texas Coastal Bend. After all, who goes to a thrift store on vacation? (*I do! Every chance I get!*) She began going to Castaways back in the seventies when she and John had first started visiting Rockport for long weekends or vacations. She had discovered it quite by accident. Nor was John immune to treasure hunt fever. He had a favorite junk yard on Hwy 35 north of the causeway to Lamar, so he would leave Merle at Castaways while he did his pickers thing, and return for her about three hours later. Then they would go back to their vacation condo and show off their prizes over a bottle of wine. Merle made a point of taking a trip to Castaways whenever she was in Rockport.

The drive from Copano Beach to Rockport took thirty to forty-five minutes, depending on how many birds you stop and look at. Cranes, egrets, and herons seemed to love fishing on the salt flats at the south end of the bay. And there were gulls or pelicans atop every visible post or branch sticking up out of the water. Occasionally, one saw roseatte spoonbills, those large, lanky, pink-feathered, prehistoric-looking members of the ibis family. They were her favorites. But Merle left the binoculars in the glove compartment today; she was on a mission.

She pulled the Jeep into the parking lot. (*Wow, this new building was worth the move just for the parking lot! This one's got real parking spaces, actually marked off with paint. And curbs. And landscaping. Big change from the horrible situation over on Church Street where the old building was, especially on Saturday mornings. Had to park in people's front yards. I'm sure the old neighbors are really glad they've moved.*) Automatically, she checked that she had her tape measure, her Visa card, and her phone in her pockets and her inside glasses hanging from the neck of her T-shirt; then she stashed her purse under the front seat. Took off her jacket and hat, left them on the car seat, locked the door and put the keys in her pocket. This was standard operating procedure for thrift store shopping. She needed her hands free, and she protected herself from purse grabbers, too. After all, thrift shop shoppers neeed to concentrate on the hunt – no distractions.

Castaways was an ecumenical endeavor by a coalition of Rockport churches. Profits benefited both the community at large and the individual congregations. Rockport was an especially lucrative place to shop because it was pretty much ground zero for the Texas Riviera, lots of high-end vacation homes – and high-end vacation wardrobes. All the items for sale at Castaways carried price tags with a code for the church which would receive the profit. "E" was for Episcopal, "L" for Lutheran, "M" for Methodist, and so on. An "S" meant Shop – for those donors who wanted to get rid of their junk for a good cause, but who were unwilling to commit to a specific denomination. Those funds were used to keep the utilities on and pay the administrative costs associated with running a non-profit business. All the workers were volunteers from the participating churches, scheduled in on respective days of the week, one day per church. Merle frequently thought about volunteering for the Episcopal Church so she could check out the new stuff as it came in.

After a nap, Merle tried on all her new fashions, making three piles: keep and wash, take to cleaners or alter, and recycle. Then she and Freddie finished off the barbeque she had brought back from Rockport. Freddie really enjoyed the ribs, made a performance of it, complete with loud gnawing noises. Now they were on the front porch swing admiring the moon on the water. *(Has it really been a month since I was here last?)*

"You know, Freddie, I haven't done any of the things I told myself I was coming down here to do – to think, to get caught up with my homework – but I feel great, anyway. Today was fun. I feel much more relaxed. I'll think tomorrow."

"Well . . . I didn't have that great a time since you left me here by myself all morning, but I will admit those ribs almost made up for the neglect." He ooched a little closer.

Merle looked at the lighted pier on Copano Bay and the city lights of Rockport off in the distance. Freddie stared at a big brown bunny now statue-still on the front lawn, looking like dinner. Three white egrets flew silently by.

"On the cheek, huh? Come ON, Merle! Really?"

CHAPTER 19

Merle sat on the park bench, Freddie perched on the table behind her, as she tried to see Rockport across the Bay. A front had moved in overnight making the sky so overcast that it was impossible to discern the horizon. Only the huge white tent-building of the fish hatchery was visible. *(But that's closer, on Swan Lake, maybe five miles closer. I'll have to get out the atlas.)* The temperature had dropped, too. It had begun to drizzle, and she noticed the wind had increased some and was kicking up whitecaps on the battleship gray water. She picked up the blue-tinted aluminum travel mug that held her third cup of coffee.

"How many Sundays in a row is this now that I haven't made it to church? Maybe I could read Morning Prayer? I think I've got a BCP, The Book of Common Prayer, someplace in the cottage."

The storm came up rapidly. Merle and Freddie had to run back to the cottage to keep from getting soaked. Settled in the dining room now, all dried off, she laid out a hand of Solitaire and thought about what to eat for breakfast. Freddie was already into his breakfast, loud snaffling noises echoing from the kitchen.

Just then one of the shutters slammed closed and scared the daylights out of both of them. Freddie jumped straight up and barked. The loose shutter immediately cut the daylight coming through the dining room window in half. Then it started to flap back and forth, and bang. It was horridly loud and extremely annoying.

"Crap! Now I've got to go out in that mess and latch the friggin' shutter!" Merle exclaimed as she stuffed herself into her old navy poplin rain jacket with the drawstring hood and stashed a pair of pliers from the utility room tool chest in into her pocket. The heavy front door proved extremely difficult to open, and the stinging wind and rain in her face almost drove her back inside, but she soldiered on. (*Really wish I'd changed into my Wellies, too! Sandals are getting all muddy.*) Using a small plastic stool to stand on so she could reach the shutter latch, she managed to get it fastened without too much trouble, and without breaking a fingernail or two, as usually happened in this operation. (*OK, that's fixed. But for how long? And what happened to that serenity I was almost feeling just a few minutes ago? Shit!*)

As soon as there was a lull in the storm, Merle decided to make a run for it. Packed up her stuff, put the dog and the cooler in the car, and headed up the highway. *(I didn't even touch those seventh grade projects. Just lugged them down here and now I'm lugging them back. Guess that's what I'm working on tonight. Hope I can get through all eighty-seven of them . . . coffee, lots of coffee.)* Merle wasn't particularly thrilled with the idea of a Sunday evening of homework, but it had to be done.

"That's how I keep you in treats, Freddie."

"Acknowledged and appreciated, Merle."

About eight miles southwest of Copano Beach, at the intersection of two country roads, a veggie and fruit stand was a perennial attraction. Merle stopped, parked on the shoulder, and walked to the pick-up truck that served as anchor for various awnings and assorted display arrangements that made up the mobile green grocer store. She wanted to get a watermelon for her downstairs neighbor and, of course, for herself. *(This will probably be the last one of the season. Hope they're still good.)*

Many years earlier, soon after she moved into the condo, she had begun taking cut-up watermelon to her downstairs neighbor Olivia whenever she fixed some for her own family. At first she was hesitant because Olivia was Black and Merle didn't want to appear the clueless honky feeding into stereotypes. But it turned out that Olivia really loved watermelon and was most grateful. Usually, Merle's plastic containers that she used for the melon chunks were returned with cookies or some other baked treat in them.

(Sweet Olivia. Taught me how to be a widow. I guess I'm still learning. Held me and let me cry my eyes out many a time during those early, ugly months. What a good friend – need to take care of our friends. Someday they'll probably be all we have. Maybe that's all any of us have, anyway.)

"OK, Grams, I'll see you about five on Wednesday, right? That's tomorrow. If I'm running late, I'll text you."

Merle had completely forgotten about Fay and her problem – or question – or whatever. So, she worried about it all day at school, trying to think of every possible scenario – and what she might say in response.

Now Fay was at her door, knocking, then opening . . . up she came, notebook in hand. *(What's this?)*

"Hi, Grams, I just have a few minutes, but wanted to talk to you about a BIG favor." She plopped down in one of the blue club chairs, tucked her feet up under her. *(hmmm . . . wonder where she got that move?)* "So I was talking to my new boyfriend Justin the other night and he told me he just loves Mexican flan, and I know you make the best flan in the world, so . . . could you please, please teach me how to make it? I know it's a lot of trouble, and I know you're busy, but I would really, really love it if you could . . .?" Fay smiled at her with that adorable grin that had charmed grandma ever since the kid was in diapers.

"Sure, sweetie. But mine is actually Cuban. From the Columbia Restaurant in Tampa, Florida. It's a little different from Mexican. Has anisette in it, licorice liqueur." *(This is IT? This is the big "problem"? WOW! . . . Well, OK . . . I can do this. God, this girl is well put-together! What an amazing job Peggy and Michael have done. She's so . . . so . . . so . . . NORMAL! Can you even say that about a teenager these days? Are any of them truly "normal"? Really don't think so. That's what makes them so interesting to teach, I guess.)*

"Oh. Didn't realize that. Yours does taste different from what I get in Mexican restaurants. All I know is that it's heaven. Really rich and yummy. Well, maybe it does have a slight licorice flavor, now that I think about it."

"So, when do you want to do this?"

"I was thinking maybe Saturday afternoon? Is that possible?"

"Sure."

"OK, so what ingredients do I need to get?" Fay extracted a ballpoint pen from her voluminous hobo bag, pulled the top off with her teeth, then opened her little spiral notebook.

"We'll need a dozen eggs, a quart of whole milk, and a small bag of sugar – four or five cups, depending on how much of that gooey caramel sauce you want. I've got everything else here – the seasonings, that is. It's mostly milk and sugar and eggs. Oh, and bring all your mom's little Pyrex custard cups. My recipe makes about eighteen to twenty individual puds."

"Guess I should bring something to carry them home in, too, huh?"

"You can leave a few for me, you know. I can put my diet on hold for a few days."

"Grams, you don't need to diet. You look great! Hope I look this good when I'm your age . . . OK, then. I'll see you Saturday – maybe two-ish? I'll bring all the stuff. Sure you don't mind?"

"Not a bit. We'll have a good time." *(Boy, I sure squeaked by that one! Slicker than owl shit! Thank you, Lord.)*

"SQUEEK! SQUAWK!" The high-pitched noise so startled Merle as she stumbled through the dark living room that she almost dropped her glasses which she still had in her hand rather than on her face.

"DAMMIT! Oh . . . Freddie's ball . . . and here he is!" Freddie had magically appeared at her feet, seated expectantly, tail wagging, in the dark, only the night light from the oven in the kitchen lending some small illumination. Merle was pretty sure he was smiling, maybe even laughing.

"You left this here on purpose, didn't you, you little turd? Scared me to death!"

"Let's play! You know you want to play."

TRAINING FREDDIE

"No, Fred. I don't want to play. My God, what time is it? . . . Ayiii, two-thirty! . . . Orange juice. I need orange juice . . . and tinkle . . . and bed . . . Oh shit, I have a date TONIGHT with PHIL! Football game, home game . . . I need SLEEP."

"OK, be that way. Your opportunity loss. I've been practicing. I can push the ball off the top step, now, and catch it before it hits the bottom. Cool, right?"

"Back to bed, Fred."

(Not too much Blue Grass! I'm probably so immune to it that I can't really tell how strong it is. The heavy duty mascara? Yes, I think so. With the eyelash curler . . . ah, the magical eyelash curler!) Merle had chosen natural linen jeans that made her butt look cute and a black rayon, long-sleeve aviator shirt, tail out, little side vents, and brown leather SAS sandals. (*Yes, it's football season, but it's only October and that's still summer in SA. Strange customs we have here in Texas – all the trappings and festivities of fall, but the weather is from hell!*) Very casual, but very classy. And comfortable – always a bonus. Not "tacky old" at all, she thought.

Phil arrived exactly on time. (*That's three times in a row for him. Maybe his military family background? Wonder if being late pisses him off? Guess I'd rather not find out!*) Merle went downstairs to let him in, Freddie on her heels.

"Hi Phil. Meet Freddie." She had picked up the wiggletail and was holding him tightly. Phil let him sniff and lick his hand before petting his head and rubbing him behind the ears. She followed Phil up the stairs to the living room. (*Nice butt!*) Phil wore faded levis and a royal blue polo shirt with an Alamo Heights High School logo. And tennies. Expensive tennies, but lived in. Certainly not dress tennis. She thought they might be New Balance from the store in the Quarry one of her classmates owned.

"He's very energetic, isn't he? Does he like to play ball?"

"YES, I DO!" Freddie trotted off to find his red squeakyball.

"My dog Perkins loves his ball, but I think Freddie just might rival him." Freddie had brought the ball into the living room and put it in Phil's hand. (*Uh-oh. I think Phil has a friend. I'm in trouble.*) "Can I throw it for him in here?" (*Well, that was sweet of him to ask.*)

"Sure. Just keep it near the floor. Try not to knock anything over. Occasionally he decides to play soccer, starts hitting it with his nose and tossing it up in the air. Then we have to stop."

Merle went around the apartment turning off lights, then set the wooden broom handle that she used as a "lock" in the balcony sliding glass door. She checked her purse, thought a minute, and went to look for her Mexican noise-maker and her cowbell. Phil and Freddie had bonded over a red rubber ball.

As they walked into the Alamo Heights stadium Merle felt like she was back in high school, on a date with a big senior. All she needed was one of those gigantic, gaudy, mum corsages like the cheerleaders had on now, that were already losing their petals as they bounced around on the girls' ample and shapely chests. (*They're clones! Some things never change. The high school football scene is immortal!*) They found seats about half-way up the stands, near the center and next to the band. Merle looked for Fay but couldn't spot her. They said hi to several people they thought they recognized, and settled in. Although the lights were on full, it was still quite light at seven-thirty in the evening. The super-illuminated field gave the feeling of a movie set, sort of glittery and surreal. Merle pulled the noise-makers out of her purse.

Turned out that Phil was quite an enthusiastic fan even though he had never played football himself. He was a swimmer, and a cyclist, and a tennis player. Merle had looked him up in her Olmos from her freshman year when Phil had been a senior. All the preppy sports, plus National Honor Society, and a bunch of service organizations, activities, and awards. It said he was going to Southern Methodist University, and indeed he did. (*I gotta find someone who was at SMU with him. Soon!*) He seemed to know so many people at the game that Merle wondered just how active he was in alumni and booster organizations – or how much money he gave. And she felt ashamed of herself. In a good year she made one, possibly two, games to see Fay march in the band, plus the compulsory Christmas concert, and maybe attended the senior play. That was pretty much her involvement with her alma mater. *(Well . . . I've bought a lot of fundraiser crap over the years, too!)* This was home turf and she felt like a visitor. But all that suddenly changed when, against all odds, Heights scored at the last minute and won the game. The crowd erupted, everyone was ecstatic, people yelling and horns blaring, lights flashing in the parking lot. The confusion spilled onto Broadway with a parade of celebratory demonstrations and antics so typical of the American teenager after a varsity victory. Merle and

Phil stopped for pizza on the way home, along with about a thousand kids from the game.

Phil could NOT get the cork out of the wine bottle! He was sitting on the kitchen floor struggling with the corkscrew, the chilled Riesling between his knees. Freddie assumed this was all for his benefit, so was enthusiastically licking Phil's face.

"Merle! Help! Get this dog off me, please." Phil was laughing so hard he had tears on his cheeks and would have been doubled over if he hadn't fallen over. That did it, the cork popped.

They set up dinner in the living room, on the coffee table, and tuned the Bose to classical FM. Merle sat in "John's place" and Phil sat in "Merle's place" on the love seat sofas. Freddie curled up on the floor with his chin comfortably resting on top of one of Phil's sneakers which were parked at the top of the stairs. Phil had taken off his shoes almost immediately upon arriving and was now padding around in his socks. (*Glad he feels at home!*) They were starving, so the pizza was fabulous. The wine was cool and clear and deliciously light. And the conversation was witty and engaging. Who knows what they talked about? Merle certainly couldn't remember the next day. They finished off three-fourths of a large pizza and the entire bottle of vino.

At some point the dishes got cleared and coffee got made. Merle ratted around in the cupboard and found a bit of brandy to put in it, just to make things perfect. Now with Mozart on the box, they were enjoying their after-dinner drinks, still talking about something or other, when Merle suddenly became aware that Phil had shifted to her sofa, no longer opposite her, but sitting beside her, and really quite close. (*Ah-ha! Wonder what he has in mind . . . ?*) They played with each other's hands for a few minutes, in silence, then he slipped his arm behind her and gently pulled her toward him. She felt all tingly and magical, and just a tiny bit apprehensive.

"Sounds like the festivities have died down outside," she managed, somewhat breathlessly.

"Well, let's see if we can't start some of our own." He turned her head toward him and kissed her. Soft and tender at first, then full-tongue, deep and intense, holding her head with one hand and pressing her body against him with the other. Merle swore later that she had felt it all the way to her toes.

Totally oblivious to time, they continued to explore and enjoy each other in this activity formerly known as "petting." Long, luxurious caresses and embraces punctuated by eager kisses and shy smiles. So, could two old people enjoy making-out? You betcha! And how! Actually, they just might have enjoyed fondling and groping more than youngsters because, for the superannuated, it was so totally unexpected.

During a lull, Merle got up and went into the kitchen, stepping over Freddie on the way. Phil followed her in, close on her heels, grabbed her around the waist, and kissed the back of her neck while she tried unsuccessfully to pour coffee. When they were in the living room again, she noticed that he had taken off his watch and had laid it on the coffee table. (*So as not to scratch me? How thoughtful – and sweet! . . . And sexy! What's he going to do?*) She noticed that she had a warm, skittery sensation all over, like fairy dust in her veins. Then he had his hand under her shirt and she felt him touch a nipple. Her response was so immediate that he kept doing it. *(Can I have an orgasm like this? I think maybe so . . .)*

Finally, they sat up, almost like waking up, astonished and surprised at what they had just been doing, and how much fun they were having doing it. What an amazing thing all this was! They laughed a little, then laughed a lot, and decided maybe it was time for Phil to go home.

Both Merle and Phil were more than a little mussed up, not unlike teenagers coming in from a date that had ended with that activity formerly known as "parking," except they hadn't been in a car. Phil tucked in his shirt, laced up his shoes and then threw the ball for Freddie a couple of times. Freddie, now alert, joyfully raced up and down the stairs retrieving his toy, happy to be noticed again at last.

Another long kiss and a big bear hug in the patio, and he was gone. Merle floated back inside, sat down on the bottom step, and hugged Freddie.

"Alrighty, then. That was a success. That was FANTASTIC! Totally over the top! I had no idea." She couldn't keep from smiling; both because of her euphoric state and because Freddie was squirming so vigorously and was happily slobbering all over her ear.

"He certainly seems to like you, Merle."

"Think he likes me, Fred? Yes, I think so, too. I sure as hell like him!"

"I could sorta tell that, sweetie. You couldn't keep your hands off him. Kinda like when you play with me on the sofa, rubbing my tummy, and I bliss out."

"Yeah, I guess you picked up on that."

"So . . . what comes next? Sniffing butts?"

CHAPTER 20

"Merle, honey, be careful. You've been without a man for a while now, and you just might be a little too eager." Winnie Maverick had called early Saturday and asked Merle to join her on a thrift store adventure. So they were in Winnie's little baby blue Subaru on their way to the Boysville Auxiliary store on west Olmos Drive.

"Yes, I probably am. And I have absolutely no resistance to this guy! None. Zip. Zero. Nada. But it feels fantastic! Last night he could have had me on the floor, right there in the living room. Wasn't me that stopped him."

"Sounds dangerous to me. Is he that sexy?"

"Oh my God, Winnie. He is truly over the top on sex appeal. I can't imagine what he sees in dull, dumpy me."

"How about a roll in the hay?"

"That'll be fine with me. I'm ready."

They pulled into the parking lot and managed to find a place under a mesquite tree that provided some minimal shade. The temp was already in the low nineties, full sun. Another hot and sticky day in south Texas. *("It's not the heat, it's the stupidity." Isn't that what John used to say?)* Merle put her tape measure and her VISA card in her pocket and her purse under the seat while Winnie spread the foldable sun reflector over the dashboard and folded down the two window shades to hold it in place against the windshield. Winnie's platinum white pageboy swung forward, completely hiding her face as she stretched to reach the passenger side. Her oversize sunglasses concealed her chocolate doe-eyes. She was pretty in the classical sense, with pink lips, white teeth, rosy cheeks, perfectly shaped brows, beautifully French-manicured nails and toes, like little pearls; and she was Merle's one friend who, at barely five feet, was as short as Merle herself. Throughout her thirty-five years teaching elementary school her first graders had adopted her as their goddess – and just their size! *(Wonder if SHE has shrunk? Seems to be about the same ratio to me as she has always been, so if I've shrunk . . .)*

"So, what do you know about this guy?"

"Well . . . he's a Heights graduate, and SMU. A foreign language teacher at St. Mary's Hall. Retired now, although I get the impression that he never really had to work at all, if you know what I mean – old family money . . . probably, not sure. But his dad was in the military – Army colonel, I think, fought in WWII like my daddy. Has three sisters, all older and all professionals, one's an attorney. Very accomplished family, and very athletic. They have what he calls a *ranchito* up in the Hill Country someplace, maybe near Vanderpool or Leakey, close to the Frio River."

A pleasant-looking elderly Black man held the door for them as they entered the brightly lit and well air-conditioned, cement block building.

"Pleasant shopping, ladies. Hope you find the bargains you're looking for."

"Thank you kindly, sir," Winnie answered and Merle smiled. *(A kindred spirit!)*

Two Latinas rushed to enter in front of them (*busy day!*). The store was quite spacious, like a small supermarket, but crammed with stuff – lots and lots of stuff. Winnie wandered off to the books and CDs; Merle zeroed in on the petite size clothing. She zipped through the hangers, looking for colors and styles she liked, stopping occasionally to check a size or measure a waistline and inseam. (*Don't want to have to alter something if I can avoid it. . . oh boy, here're some Ann Taylor slacks. Nice mocha brown twill, and probably fit, too. But, wish they were blue. Maybe I'll buy them, anyway.*) Merle took the pants off the rack and slung them over her shoulder, hanger and all, while she continued to peruse her options.

"So, has this guy ever been married?" Winnie had abandoned the books and CDs and joined Merle at the petites rack.

"Yes, I think so. He was a little vague about that and I didn't want to scare him off by pumping him for details." Merle grabbed a pretty little turquoise gauzy top and added it to the growing pile on her shoulder. Oh, and a really cute pinstripe vest. (*I can be Annie Hall again! Loved that look! Wonder if it will come back in style before I'm too old to enjoy it again?*)

"OK, another topic, how's school?"

"I'm thinking about retiring this year."

"That bad, huh? You really need to retire while you still like the little buggers. I don't miss it a bit. So, so glad I got out when I did."

"Right now all I want to do is bop them on the head!"

"My point, exactly!"

Freddie was pacing. And growling. He was pretty sure there was someone strange in the patio, but he couldn't see anybody from the balcony. Merle had left the sliding glass door ajar so he could come and go, get some sunshine and fresh air. He really liked that, but it wasn't solving his current problem. He nosed around and finally found the red squeakyball and began to chew on it. Chewing helped him think.

OK, so I sorta recognize the smell, but can't place it. The condo yard workers out by the sidewalk are confusing me. How can I isolate the odor that doesn't belong? And why can't I place it? Come on, Fred, think... uh-oh, someone unlocking the front door...

"Grams? Grams, are you here? . . . Guess not. Hi, Freddie. Here, bring the ball. Let's play 'til Grams gets home."

"SURE! I'm ALWAYS up for playing ball. Your grandma has been a little distracted of late. But that new fella', Phil, he's quite the ball player. Have I mentioned that I like him? Seems Merle's taste in electronic boyfriends is improving."

"This ball has seen some use . . . and some teeth!" Fay rolled the tattered rubber toy around in her long fingers. "Here, catch!"

Freddie, missed the catch, but bounced the ball off his nose and down the stairs. Just then the front door opened and Merle came in, perfectly in time to catch the ball, almost as if she had practiced it, except for the startled look on her face.

"What's this, Freddie?" She started up the stairs. "Oh, dear Lord, Fay! You startled me." Merle almost dropped her thrift store bag. "Dammit! I completely forgot you were coming, sweetie. Good thing Winnie had orchestra practice back in Castroville this afternoon, or you'd be waiting a very long time. We were on a roll. Sorry!"

"It's OK. You're here. Let's get started. I brought all the stuff you told me to, plus a big, flat box top to take home *flanes*. Justin's gonna be blown away!"

The kid wasn't the person I had smelled. But by then I had lost the scent...

Twenty minutes later both Merle and Fay had donned full length, wrap-around tie aprons – Fay in the almost white canvas one with the Tabasco label print and Merle in her favorite, the oilcloth Virgin of Guadalupe print that she had purchased at an *Hecho a Mano* Christmas bazaar several years ago. The electric mixer was whirring away on low as it smoothed together milk and eggs and sugar. Two large shallow baking pans were set out on the counter, each filled with Pyrex custard cups set in rows. Some were antique, etched or scalloped, and of remarkably thin glass; others were new, utilitarian, and thick-sided. One of the things Merle always checked for at thrift stores was custard cups since her supply seemed to be constantly dwindling without explanation. A large kettle on the stovetop emitted puffs of steam occasionally, but never quite whistled. The kitchen smelled strongly of burned sugar as grandmother and granddaughter prepared the caramel sauce they now poured into the bottoms of the cups.

"So, Grams, how is the eHarmony project going?"

"Be really careful with that, sweetie. It's ridiculously hot! Burn you bad, in a nanosec." Merle watched tensely as Fay tilted the copper-bottomed sauce pan to distribute the bubbly amber liquid evenly among the custard cups, leaving tiny strings of hardened sugar as she moved from one cup to the next. She was mentally scrambling to process Fay's question. *(Where did THAT come from? This is an ambush! Wonder if Peggy put her up to it?)* "I found a few prospects. I'm in the process of checking them out."

"Alex said he played bodyguard for you last week. As if Alex would be any threat to anybody – except maybe all the females who fall in love with him." Fay finished with the last of the cups and put the pan in the sink to soak.

"Shit! I should have told Alex to put a sock in it! Yes, his mother insisted – after my notorious track record with 'nice' elderly gentlemen!" *(Note to self: Wring Alex's handsome neck next time I see him!)*

"So . . . who is this guy, Grams?"

"He's a retired teacher, like I want to be, and he seems really nice." *(Don't panic. She can smell panic.)*

". . . and? . . . and? . . . a few more details, please. Have you seen him again?"

"Ah . . . here, we need to get this pudding underway. Check and make sure the stuff in the mixer is ready. I'll get spices. And the anisette."

As they were ladling the thin milk and egg mixture into the custard cups, trying not to spill, Fay tried again.

"So . . . have you seen – what is his name, anyway?"

"Phil. Phillip O'Conner Mathis. And, yes, actually. We went to the Heights game last night. Tried to see you, but never found you." *(Is there ANY way I can change the subject?)*

"Oh, they had me sitting in a different place last night. Something about keeping my eye on a freshman drummer who thinks he's Charlie Watts. So . . . how was the date?"

"Are you reporting back to your mother?"

"NO, . . . no. I swear, not a word! I just heard it from Alex when I saw him at the bike shop. Mom is not in the loop. No mom, no, no." Fay crossed her heart with the almost empty ladle, a few drops of the sticky liquid running down her wrist to her arm. Merle opened the oven, pulled out the top rack using an oven mitt and positioned one of the large baking pans containing about a dozen custards. She took the kettle from the stove top and very, very carefully poured boiling water into the pan until it was about an inch deep around the custards. Then, just as carefully, she pushed the rack back into place. Fay repeated the procedure on the bottom rack.

"What's this cooking-in-water drill called? Some funny French name, isn't it?"

"*Bain Marie*. Means Marie's bath."

"I think Marie got her tush scalded!" Fay closed the oven door and pulled out her phone to set the timer. "How long?"

"We'll check at fifty minutes to see if the custard is set."

"Got it. Okay, now . . . what about last night's date with . . . Phil?"

"I had a really good time." *(Well . . . I did! Boy, did I ever!)*

"Grams, you're blushing. Oh, my God, my granny is BLUSHING!" *(I don't suppose she'd believe it was the heat from the oven, would she?)*

Saturday afternoon, late/SA

Things have changed! And that black rayon aviator shirt I wore to the game last nite was absolutely inspired! Fast Track Phil came on strong. And I loved it! What a deal! He's got the magic touch – and I want more of it! (Who's that character in Oklahoma *who sings, "I'm just a girl who can't say no"?)*

So – in his own way – he was all the gentleman. Hands totally above the waist – but, WOW, did he make good use of the territory he limited himself to!

Wonder what he's doing tonite? Processing what happened last nite, I hope. Maybe he's at the gym working out. He's in GREAT shape. All I can say is WOW!

Freddie was acting really strange when I came home from shopping this afternoon. Wonder what's up with him?

Fay was here this afternoon to make flan and she grilled me about eHarmony and Phil. Not a good scene. Really don't want a rerun on that one!

I think I detected a very slight, elusive chill in the air when I walked Freddie this am. Maybe, just maybe, this awful heat is waning. What is it that excites us about the changing season? When we're at the end of a exhausting summer of drought and heat or a depressing winter of drizzly cold? I know I'll be just as optimistic when signs of spring appear in February. (after the January doldrums – and semester exams . . .) But right now, I'm hopeful for cool fronts, homemade soup, and turtle neck sweaters instead of T-shirts and flip-flops. God help me if I ever lose my enthusiasm for the new weather in fall and spring – that's probably a sign it's all over!

I bought the fall fashion issue of Seventeen *magazine today when I refilled my pussy pill Rx at Walgreens, ostensibly to take to school for my advisory eighth grade girls to look at. But, truthfully, more for me. The fall fashion issue, now about two inches thick, has been one of my secret pleasures since I was fourteen! I get lost in it – takes me back! Also got some new nail polish in a shimmery frosted peach for my toes. Complements the freckles.*

Merle pulled the Jeep over onto the shoulder of Contour Drive in Olmos Park, one of San Antonio's most prestigious addresses in an old, elite part of town; a quiet, sedate, winding road with Olmos Basin Park on one side and a string of enormous mansions on the other, most of them hidden behind walls or thick hedges. She checked the street number with what she had found on her Google search, and stared at the ornate wrought iron gate and driveway beyond. Lush foliage and large, ancient trees, several pecans, and a cottonwood. A simple brass plate above the mailbox on the gate announced the address. (*Well, all I can say is, "HOLY SHIT!" . . . just like Ali McGraw in Love Story when she got her first look at Ryan O'Neal's family estate. Phil certainly didn't get THAT on a teacher's salary!*) She could almost see the house beyond the drive, a two-story Austin stone structure, classic lines, dark teal shutters, and a candy-apple red front door. At least two seemingly functional chimneys, so the house was probably built in the nineteen-twenties or thirties when this area was first developed. Merle drove several blocks down Contour, then whipped the Jeep around *(Love the tight turning radius on this baby! It's almost worth the extra gas she guzzles.)* and came back by Phil's house, checking it out again as she drove slowly by, hoping there weren't any surveillance cameras around. (*Well – that's pretty amazing. 'Buela always said it's just as easy to fall in love with a rich man as a poor man. Maybe I did it right this time.)*

Deciding she needed to rush the season a bit, and cheer herself up in the process, and it not being quite late enough weather-wise to clean out her closet and organize her fall wardrobe, Merle had chosen to turn down the air-conditioning temp to sixty-eight degrees and make herself a cup of hot chocolate, complete with mini-marshmallows and a shot of Kahlua. Willie Nelson was playing on the box with Merle singing along as she laid out a hand of Sol on the coffee table. *(I guess Phil will have to be the King of Diamonds, in light of recent discoveries.)*

"OK, here we go . . . Ah, little clubs, jack of diamonds, some middle hearts and spades. No aces." Merle sat back and considered the hand she had just laid out as she lit a cigarette, took several puffs, then placed it in the red ceramic ashtray as she began to play. She counted off the first three cards in the deck and turned them over on the table.

"Ah-ha, the ace of clubs, and here is the deuce. Turn it over and get . . . get . . . the four of clubs. Now I need the trey. So, Freddie, what have you been so antsy about lately?"

"Sorry I've been distracted, Merle. There was somebody hanging around outside that … "

"Actually, I think I've caught the antsies from you. I've had a creepy feeling someone's watching me. Silly, I guess."

"No, sweetie, not silly. There is someone, I just wish I knew who."

"Could it be Phil? Is he checking me out like I checked him out? Following me – or something?"

"No, definitely not Phil. Phil is a good guy. Phil plays ball. And rubs my tummy. And he smells like rawhide and grass and bacon. This guy smells sinister, like gasoline and nervous sweat."

"You don't suppose it's Angel de la Rosa, do you? That gangbanger kid who lost his wallet?"

"No … not Angel, but … a lot LIKE Angel. Has the same flavors as Angel, I think, now that you mention him."

"It better not be Angel! If I keep feeling this way, I can always call his mother."

"Probably not a good idea."

"Well, I'm going to be extra vigilant for a while, anyway."

"That's a very good plan, sweetie."

"It couldn't be anything to do with Willie, could it?" Merle allowed herself a momentary lapse into a very uncomfortable place in her head, then quickly snapped out of it.

"No, I really think he's gone, hopefully for good. Out of my life." *(Thank you, Lord!)* She tried to relax her jaw which had begun to twitch. "So . . . what are we going to have for dinner, Fred?"

"I thought you'd never ask. Food is always a comforting and elevating topic. How about something with cheese?"

"I think we'll do toasted cheese sandwiches. How's that? A little stretchy melted Swiss on your kibble?"

"*My favorite!*"

CHAPTER 21

"Shit! What's THIS?" Merle was staring into her bathroom vanity mirror at the puffy red spot below and to the left of her nose, sort of nestled into the diagonal crease line above the corner of her mouth. She very gingerly patted it with the tip of her finger. It was marginally tender and hurt a bit when she pressed on it.

"It's a friggin' PIMPLE, that's what it is, dammit! What, am I SIXTEEN again?" She took a cotton ball from the apothecary jar on the countertop and dampened it with Sea Breeze astringent, carefully wiped the offending spot, then ratted around in the drawer for her Neutrogena zit-zapper cream.

"This thing just popped up overnight. It's going to need some concealer before I go out in public. As soon as the cream dries. Dammit! Maybe I can head it off at the pass; make it just go away, not come to an ugly head. Wonder if my kids will notice? Well, of course they will! Eighth graders notice everything. Some of the snippy girls comment sarcastically when I wear the same pair of shoes two days in a row. Are these eruptions caused by hormones? Figures. I'm a hormonal basket case! Well, at least I'm not crying all the time." Merle cringed a little at the prospect of a day at school with a zit rising on her face like a volcano." *(Teaching is a damn difficult, stressful job, holidays and summers notwithstanding!)*

Having finally networked herself to a friend-of-a-friend who had known Phillip Mathis when he was at SMU in the sixties, Merle was on the phone with Cassie Camargo, Doris Luna's former sister-in-law, from when Doris had been married to Alex's father, Javier. Now Merle was listening to Cassie's recollections – in great detail.

"Remember that line from *The Way We Were* when they were talking about the Robert Redford character, that 'Things came easy to him'? Well, that was Phil, exactly. He made the Dean's List every semester, and not on easy stuff, either. He was a modern languages major. Really good at linguistics. Spent a year in Spain perfecting his Spanish. Wasn't bad looking, either. He was a Homecoming Court muckety-muck of some title one year. And he did sports, too – tennis and swimming, and baseball some, I think. Not much for football, though. Not bulky enough – or stupid enough. He's quite sharp and creative, you know."

"Did he have a college sweetheart that you knew of?"

"Oh, he was very much the ladies' man! He dated every beauty on campus at some time or another. Even me – except I wasn't a beauty. *(Now we're getting somewhere.)* But I was a Tri-Delt. I guess that counted. You know how things were in the "bad old days." *(Do I ever! Wow, this is good stuff to know. Maybe I should be taking notes?)* "But no, no one special that I can remember. I heard that he married soon after graduation, but it didn't last long. I don't know any details, or names, or anything. Last I knew he was teaching French and Italian at St. Mary's Hall. Can you imagine? The girls must have been falling all over themselves!"

"He's retired now."

"I bet he's just as busy as ever, involved in all sorts of community and civic projects. He couldn't stay idle – or still."

"I've noticed that."

"He likes things his way, though. A bit spoiled like that. But he has such an engaging and endearing manner, you want to give in just to please him. Then he smiles at you with that one dimple of his, and it's all over." *(Oh, boy. I know what that feels like! She's good.)*

"Then, afterward, when you have time to think about what happened, you get so frustrated you want to choke him." *(OK, haven't gotten to that part, yet.)*

"How do his sisters react to his behavior?" Cassie laughed.

"Oh, my God. They fawn over him like you wouldn't believe. Especially Amanda, the oldest one, the dermatologist." *(Good to know. Noted: don't want to cross Amanda.)* Cassie took a sip of something that rattled ice, then continued, "Overall, he was sorta quiet and externally gentle, but you knew – or maybe you just felt – that there was something more there. But he played it very close. Never opened up to me, or even acted like he might want to." *(Difficult men. My specialty. Lived with one for over thirty years.)*

They moved on to other topics, mostly centered around Alex, evidently the pride and joy of the entire Luna *familia*. Merle agreed with enthusiasm that Alex was handsome, and talented, and a sweetie pie. She thanked Cassie profusely and signed off, pondering the intelligence she had just gained. Were new strategies or attitudes in order?

"Hi, Freddie. You look saggy, like Eeyore. What's wrong? Have I been ignoring you again?" Never one to pass on an opportunity to leverage guilt, Freddie picked up the red squeakyball and brought it to Merle who was curled up on the sofa, cell phone still in her hand.

"Strange things are happening around here, lady. Watch your back. I can't watch it for you all the time."

"Fred, you look so serious. Let's play catch, cheer you up." She tossed the ball over the railing into the stairwell. Freddie bounded after it, all his forebodings forgotten. A wonderful thing for dogs, play is, and for their humans, too.

It happened unexpectedly late Saturday afternoon. They were scheduled to go to an early movie and dinner. *(And then . . .?)* Phil came to pick Merle up at the condo a little after six. Late sun was filtering through the Balfour Aurelia in the window seat, illuminating about a million dust particles in the circulating air, and lending the old oriental rug a distinguished patina. At the sound of the doorbell, she ran down the stairs to open the door for him. In one smooth motion he grabbed her around the waist with his right arm as he closed and locked the door behind him with his left. Then immediately enveloped her and pulled her so close she couldn't breathe. Caught completely off-guard, she resisted at first, then semi-resisted, sorta resisted, maybe three or four seconds, and then melted into him. (*What the hell is going on here? Is this for real?*) He put his hand on her lower back and pulled her even closer. Then came the now-legendary tongue with a long, deep, slow kiss. Like the first one a week ago that she had been fantasizing about every night. Had it only been a week? Seemed a whole lifetime. They kissed each other's faces, and necks, and ears. Then, desperately they found mouths again. (*Good Lord, thought I'd forgotten how to do this!*)

She had been playing a favorite CD of Mexican composer Augustín Lara's love songs, hoping Phil would notice her sophisticated and urbane taste in music. Now the plaintive melodies continued, lovely, but unheeded. *"Amor, de mis amores . . ."* filtered thru her brain as her ears began to ring, droning out the words and music, everything, totally focused on him, this beautiful, vibrant man who, evidently, wanted her intensely, and right now! She caught her breath and pushed him away just a bit.

"Oh my, I missed you, too." She stepped up the stairs behind her one step so as to be more level with him, given the disparity in their heights. She touched his face, ran fingers into his curls, then gently, and softly, slowly kissed him, just lips at first, then a shy, hesitant, exploring tongue, her tongue this time. It felt so nice, so familiar, so perfect. Suddenly she became aware of him hard against her thigh. (*Talk about feeling like a teenager! Now what?*)

". . . te quiero como a nadie quiero . . ."

He pressed her into him so there was no doubt about what he felt. She managed, just barely, to say, "We're going to be late for the movie."

"What movie?" he answered in a tone that indicated this was all there was to be said about the movie topic, as he took her hand and led her upstairs. *(Well, Rhett Butler would have picked me up and carried me to the bedroom! But then, Rhett Butler wasn't seventy-plus, either!)*

Fred was quietly observing this scene from the top of the stairs where he had retreated when the fireworks started.

"Yikes! What happened? I didn't expect that! That was faster than a Copano cottontail. He's just TOO smooth! Come on, Merle, get a grip!"

(*Oh shit! The heating pad is still under my pillow, from the other night when my knee was hurting so bad... and he's going to find it. Now won't that be romantic?... Not to mention the vibrator under the bed.*)

"... Santa. Santa mía..."

Merle was in free-fall! No alcohol, no drugs, just pure hormonal high. Absolutely dying to get her hands on him, to touch and feel that amazing body under the soft linen *guayabera* which had miraculously become unbuttoned. (*Oh, this is fun. This is REALLY FUN. This is wonderful, magnificent!*) She couldn't stop smiling, almost giggling. Her skin was tingling as she finished undoing his shirt and helped him slip it off and lay it on the wingback chair. Her breath was coming short now, in little gasps. He pulled her T-shirt over her head and gently dropped it beside him, then began unbuckling his belt and unbuttoning his levis *(yes, classic Levis – what else?).* Before she knew what had happened, Phil was standing naked before her, washed in the soft, rosy light from the bedside lamp, feet slightly apart, arms resting at his sides with palms up, smiling at her with his one dimple and his bedroom eyes, as though he were posing for Leonardo's Vitruvian Man. (*My God, he's gorgeous! I can't believe this is actually happening – I'm gonna just die – right now, Lord. Truly, I'll be happy. This is it. Take me home to Jesus.*)

Very gently, Phil pushed her onto the bed, as he began fumbling with the waistband of her slacks. (*Are his hands trembling?... Oh my God, WHAT is he doing?*) He was, in fact, kissing her breasts, teasing the nipples with his tongue. What had happened to her bra? She couldn't remember. He finally got her unbuttoned and negotiated the zipper, then peeled her pants down, as they rolled back and forth on the bed. Underneath he discovered plain, nude-tone bikini panties. (*And mother told me to always wear clean panties in case of an accident! Is this what she meant?*)

"Leave the light on. I want to see you."

"*Eres el razón de mi existe , , ,*"

He knelt on the bed above her now and she saw that he was more than ready to take her. She didn't even mind – hardly even noticed – when he paused and asked, "Sweetheart, do you have any baby oil… or perhaps some Vaseline?"

After some scrambling and fumbling around in the bathroom, she watched him apply the baby oil, strangely fixated on the process. Then, suddenly, he was on top of her, again. She felt his warm skin against her own, plastered together as they were, from neck to toes, and she knew she had the fairy dust in her veins again. Gently, she wrapped her legs around him and pulled him into her.

"*Arráncame la vida . . .*"

Freddie sat in the bedroom doorway, intent on the activity atop the big bed. His antennae ears rotated one direction, then the other, as he cocked his head to focus more carefully.

"Wow … she only lets me lick her face."

"OK, OK, Freddie. I'm awake, already. Stop scratching, please. I'll take you out just as soon as I . . . as I . . . get untangled here." Merle sat up and looked at the bedside clock. It glowed eight forty-seven. She began unwrapping twisted sheets and pulling her legs free, trying not to wake Phil who was snoring, face down, spread-eagle, swaddled in the green velour blanket. *(WOW! What a night, ALL night! Absolutely amazing. Can I even move?)*

Phil twitched a bit, then moaned and rolled over, almost choking himself on the blanket. Neither one of them had on a stitch of clothes. *(Well, there hardly seemed any point, after all that.)*

"I need to walk Fred. I'll be right back, OK? Please let me know you hear me." Phil mumbled an affirmative and Merle left him in the bed while she found sweats to pull on, and some flip-flops, no underwear. She couldn't find either part. Freddie was anxious and skittery, but Merle was gliding on afterglow. Outside she discovered an absolutely magnificent fall day, slight chill and bright sun *(maybe it IS time to reorganize the closet!),* scent of acorns mashed on the driveway and in the street. They performed a short, perfunctory walk, Merle on auto-pilot, then came back to the condo. Inside the patio Merle picked up the fat Sunday paper and dangled it's shiny plastic bag from her fingers. She could see there was some sort of advertising give-away attached, maybe a new cereal sample? As she opened the door they were immediately overcome by the celestial aroma of brewing coffee. *(Oh my God, he MAKES COFFEE! . . . This truly is heaven. It's like I ordered him up from a catalog, fully-loaded, all the options. This is scary!)*

Phil had showered, dressed, and was now standing in the kitchen with his head inside the fridge, looking for half-and-half. *(Men are amazing! How can they be so quick getting showered and dressed? He was practically comatose when I left.)*

"I didn't tell you that I have to go to church this morning. *(CHURCH!)* Sorry, but I'm going to have to leave *muy pronto*. Have to be at St. Mark's at ten." (*He's going to CHURCH? Well, that certainly is different.*) Merle's incredulity must have been obvious on her face because he continued, "My nephew Trey, Amanda's eldest grandson, is being confirmed, the bishop and all the smells and bells, at St. Mark's church downtown on Travis Park. Sort of a command appearance, orders from the family, if you know what I mean." *(Ah-ha! He's an Episcopalian – or at least his sister is.)* And he smiled, with his one dimple. Merle virtually melted, knees all mooshy, and almost dropped her coffee; decided she'd better sit down. *(OK, so THAT'S what Cassie was talking about!)*

Phil sat with her at the round kitchen table, drinking coffee and playing with her hands. "Listen, about last night . . ."

"Yes . . . ?"

"We can't tell anybody about it, you know. Nobody would believe us."

"It was pretty damn phenomenal, you know. I had a hellava good time, regardless of how I feel this morning. Did you get any sleep?"

"Not much. What time did we get up and have supper – or breakfast – or whatever that was? What it was, by the way, was very, very good."

"You were just very, very hungry. I think it was about two-thirty or so."

"OK, so I wasn't dreaming. We really did make love all night?" Merle thought he looked like he was about ten years old. *(Aw, shucks . . . See what I did?)*

"Yes, indeed we did, lover boy. You were absolutely amazing. I don't think I've ever been so deliciously ravished." Phil laughed at this, then bowed his head a bit and turned just the slightest shade of pink. *(Adorable! Oh, my God, I could eat you up in a minute!)*

Suddenly Phil popped up, placed his coffee cup on the counter, gave her a quick, chaste peck on the cheek and was gone. "I'll call you later," as he loped down the stairs.

Merle finished her coffee in a daze, put both cups in the sink, then walked slowly back to her bedroom. The bedclothes were still all a jumble, and, in the clear morning light, she could see some small smudges here and there, the tells of what had happened in this place last night – and in her life. She flopped forward onto the mattress and inhaled deeply, breathing him in, then buried her face in his pillow, where she stayed a long, long while, almost drifting off before she struggled up again, disoriented and fuzzy.

"OK, that's enough wallowing in euphoria. I'm starving. FOOD! I need food. Now! And a ciggie. I need chocolate." Very slowly becoming more alert, she stumbled into the living room, automatically pulled her cigarettes and lighter out of the library table drawer, lit up, and continued into the kitchen where she began browsing the pantry, then the fridge. Delighted when she discovered the Blue Bell double chocolate delight ice cream in the freezer, she got one of the big bowls out of the cupboard and scooped quite a generous serving of the frozen treat into it. Freddie had heard the sound of chocolate ice cream falling into a bowl and appeared noiselessly, magically, at Merle's feet, hoping a mishap might fall his way.

"Oh . . . Freddie. You scared me. How do you do that?"

"Chocolate. My favorite!"

"I wonder if he would come to the coast with me for Columbus Day weekend? I get Monday off. He could bring his dog, Freddie. You and Perkins could play together."

"Perkins? Really? His name is Perkins? What kind of a prissy-ass name is Perkins? Yikes!"

"Probably he'd think my little Victorian cottage that I love so much is nothing but a fishing shack! Probably he's accustomed to staying in one of those glitzy condos in Rockport or Port A. With a boat slip, a designer swimming pool, and an on-site, state-of-the-art gym. And a catamaran in storage. Or maybe a jet ski. I'd prefer the catamaran, thank you; jet skis are too noisy."

Merle stepped out onto the balcony, her hands full, then suddenly she stopped and stared at the ashtray and her burning, half-smoked cigarette.

"Well, damn! So much for quitting smoking when I got laid. That didn't work out so well, did it?"

"It's a sign, Merle."

CHAPTER 22

Merle sat on the sofa with her coffee and her cigarette, leafing through the front section of the Sunday *San Antonio Express-News*. *(They never have those beautiful fashion illustrations anymore. Wonder what happened? I miss them!)* Next to *Seventeen* magazine, Merle had loved looking at the old Frost Bros. newspaper advertising with their artist-drawn depictions of the newest chic arrivals in ladies ready-to-wear. In the nineteen-fifties Frost's was San Antonio's answer to Neiman Marcus, the Dallas-based luxury department store. And Merle had been lucky enough to have purchased her wedding dress at Frost's. It came complete with a very helpful and enthusiastic bridal consultant. *(Wonder if anybody does that anymore? Surely so! But so many custom services seem to have disappeared in our modern world of outlets and discount stores. She even came to the church and pushed me down the aisle!)* Frost's hand-sketched ads had favored willowy models wearing lovely frocks or graceful suits or sporty slacks with sweaters, all in classic poses. One could assemble a very classy seasonal wardrobe from the clippings. *(I bet Phil grew up in a world of women dressed like Frost Bros. ads.)* Joske's, another iconic San Antonio retailer ("Joske's of Texas, by the Alamo, San Antonio"), advertised in the newspaper, too, but their illustrations were much more realistic and rather pedestrian, Merle had thought. She preferred the romantic, somewhat ethereal style that the Frost Bros. artists employed and she could easily visualize herself in roles wearing the garments they featured. She thought there was still a box full of examples she had clipped and saved all those years ago somewhere in the dark, mysterious depths of the living room closet. Someday she would make a scrapbook. *(How many scrapbooks and photo albums does that make now, that I'm going to make? Someday.)*

(I used to modify those designs using Vogue Patterns and make my own original outfits in high school and college. Actually, I used to sew a lot! Teaching takes up so much damn time now, I just don't – except for alterations, and I HATE alterations! Haven't done much of anything since Peggy's wedding dress, except some super easy little shifts for Fay when she was a toddler, with colorful rick-rack and cute appliqués. Rosie wore them, too. They were fun – oh, and the Barbie clothes. Really never liked making Barbie clothes much. She was so ridiculously hard to fit, all out of proportion as she was. If you fit her waist and hips, then you couldn't possibly get the dress or blouse over her enormous boobs. Wonder if I'll ever make another wedding dress? Fay's? Rosie's? Mine?)

All this thinking about style and fashion dressmaking had put Merle in a mood to visit a fabric store. After thrift stores, her favorite. She could waste hours and hours in JoAnn's, not to mention lots of money. *(But, they offer GOOD coupons!)* Although she had pretty much given up making clothes for herself from scratch, she still collected the material for future fantasies. There were at least six extra-large plastic storage bins in the guest room closet holding her current supply. This included fifty or more years of acquired piece goods and trim of various types, even a few items inherited from her grandmother, another world-class fabric collector *(Is it genetic?),* as well as her recent purchases, and dozens of rolled-up scrap bundles, the leftovers from things she had made through the years. *(Another scrapbook to be made.)* Overflow filled assorted drawers and shelves and chests and cabinets. *(Oh, yes, and the unfinished projects, a venerable assemblage to be sure.)*

"Speaking of unfinished projects, I gotta get my grades done – TODAY! Everything's due tomorrow morning by eight. Shit! I was all ready for a fabric store adventure."

"Does that mean you're going to be here today? And tonight?" Freddie had joined Merle on the sofa and was trying ineffectively to lick her face, hopping around on the newspaper which was still open on her lap, making a great crinkling noise, and ripping little gashes in the newsprint with his unclipped nails.

"Yes, yes, Freddie. I'm going to be home tonight. We'll play some. OK?"

Later Sunday evening Merle sat in front of her computer entering grades and test scores from a huge stack of papers she had graded that afternoon. They were sorted into classes – seven piles spread out on the sofa and the coffee table. Her brain was numb as she now punched in the numbers for the last class.

"God, I hate doing this! This is the one thing I really, really abhor about teaching. Well . . . this and calling parents with bad news. And discipline. Don't like discipline at all, I'm no good at it. And worrying about it gives me a headache! I want the little stinkers to be so enthralled with the subject matter and my vast knowledge and wisdom, that they are mesmerized, not talking to each other or playing with their phones and ignoring me. Things certainly have changed in the forty years I've been teaching! Believe it or not, there once was a time when you could actually get a middle schooler's full, focused attention – for up to fifteen or twenty minutes at a time."

Another forty-five minutes of checking averages to make sure nobody failed that she didn't want to fail, tinkering with several numbers, and entering a few comments here and there, she clicked the Submit button, then stacked up the piles, cris-crossed by class, and stuffed them into her big khaki canvas school bag.

"Lord, I remember all too well when we had to do all the math ourselves, and then complete giant computer bubble sheets. Really cumbersome and time-consuming. Used White Out when I made a mistake that wouldn't erase. But it seemed that no matter how careful I was, I always got back error print-outs. The counselors must have hated me. What a project that was!" Actually, Merle preferred letter grades to number grades. Numbers were too precise. "Nothing in history is ever precise, so why should grades in history class be precise?"

"Yes, Freddie, we're going outside. I know it's late, really late, but I'm DONE!" Freddie had been pacing for the last fifteen or twenty minutes. Merle folded a plastic doggie poop bag into her pocket, picked up her keys, put them in her other pocket, grabbed the red knotted leash off the banister where it lived when not in use, and hooked Freddie up. She stood and thought a second, then quickly found her small LED flashlight, just in case. *(Condo grounds are dark at night, sometimes even a little spooky. Everything looks so different in the dark. Shadows deceive.)*

"Merle, sweetie, you work too much! You need to play more. You need to play with ME more."

"I know, I know. I work too much. Don't seem to be able to cut it down – not and do a decent job. Teaching is a greedy profession – it takes over your life." *(Already I miss summer. Wouldn't it be nice if we were going for our walk in Pineda Park, with the sea spray blowing up into our faces from waves hitting the breaker wall? Of course, the hair would be a disaster – kink up tighter than a corkscrew – but it wouldn't matter because I wouldn't be going to school the next morning. Ah-ha!)* This retirement concept was starting to take hold in Merle's consciousness.

Freddie scurried along the narrow sidewalk, nose to the ground, sniffing as fast as he could sniff, sort of weaving from side to side. Merle tried desperately to avoid the uneven cracks in the cement, not wanting to fall in the dark. *(Falling and breaking something is a real possibility at my age. Gotta be careful. That would truly fuck up my life, now wouldn't it?)*

"Slow down, Fred. What's gotten into you? Stop darting off in all directions, please."

"That's the smell! He's here. Or he's been here. Gotta figure it out... Gotta figure it out! ..."

Merle tried to pull Freddie into the lighted portions of the condo grounds, but he would have none of it. He practically dragged her into the tree-covered walks and corners, where there was practically no light, where her diminutive pen light hardly penetrated the intense darkness. Suddenly he twirled around three times, squinched up, and pooped. Right on the sidewalk.

"Freddie! What's the deal here? You NEVER do that! Where are your manners?" She picked up the pile with her hand inside the plastic bag, using it as a mitten, turned it inside-out, then twisted the open end around her finger and continued walking, Freddie straining on the lead. Just as she turned a blind corner, under a giant split-leaf philodendron that almost blocked the passage with its huge leaves, she felt something grab her shoulder.

"WHAT . . .?" She spun around, dropped the leash and screeched.

"Shut up, old lady." The skinny Hispanic kid lunged at her, grabbing for her neck. She felt for the warm, bulging baggie in her hand, palmed the mushy end, and smashed the wad into his face, rubbing his eyes and nose as hard as she could in the split second she had to make contact. He froze and screamed and sputtered, desperately trying to wipe his face.

"*Chinga!* What did you do to me, bitch?" He backed off, pivoted and ran off around the corner of the closest building. Merle sat down abruptly on the retaining wall of a raised flower bed, her knees and hands shaking uncontrollably. Then she suddenly became aware of Freddie barking his brains out and looked for the leash.

"Here, Fred. Where are you? No, DON'T chase him. Come to me. NOW!" She glimpsed the red nylon loop dragging on the ground and grabbed for it. "Come on, we gotta get out of here!" She pulled Fred along as she ran through the maze of buildings and gardens and patios.

"No, not to the house! . . . to the Jeep." She pulled him toward the parking lot, finding the keys in her pocket and pulling them out as she ran. *(Thank you God for remote car locks. Don't think I could negotiate a key into an actual lock right now! Just hope I can get it in the ignition!)*

About three minutes later she was at the corner Seven-Eleven all-night convenience store on Broadway. Slamming the car door, she rushed in and asked to use their phone to call 911, explaining in rapid, erratic phrases that she had been attacked, didn't have her purse or her cell phone, and didn't dare go home because the guy might still be there.

"Slow down, little lady, settle a bit. Here, I'll call for you." The elderly store clerk tried unsuccessfully to calm Merle down. But he did manage to connect with the Alamo Heights Police Department and attempted to explain the situation. A squad car arrived in about ten minutes. By that time the clerk had given Merle an A&W root beer, and found a folding chair for her to sit on.

In the Jeep Freddie was frantic. He switched from one side of the front seat to the other, hopping over the console, trying to see something out the windows, leaving little snuffle smudges on the glass, then pausing to look out the front, paws on the dash. He quickly spun around and jumped into the back. Again and again. There were now three police cruisers in the parking lot, red and blue lights flashing and whirling everywhere. The strobe effect was making him crazy.

"What's going on in there? Where's Merle? What are all these policemen doing? Who's in trouble? I can't see anything and nobody seems to remember about the doggie locked in the car! I

was in danger, too, you know. Dude could've killed both of us! He was a bad-looking hombre. Real evil. But I chased him off. Bet they won't be able to find a trace of him. He's gone. Gone."

Just then the door clicked open and Merle stuck her head in. "Freddie, here's some water for you." She put the Styrofoam cup with tap water into the console holder. Freddie tried it out. "The police searched the condo and the property and found nothing. They say it's safe for us to go home. I just have a few more things to ask the officers, then we'll leave." *(Why am I explaining this to a dog?)*

"See? He's gone, Merle. I scared him off. He's afraid of me … ah, us. He's afraid of us. Let's go home, sweetie. I'll protect you. You can count on Freddie. Here, let me lick your face."

"No, Freddie, not now." Laughing out loud, Merle stuffed the wiggling dog back into the car as she closed the door. *(OK, so that feels a little better. And I'm not shaking anymore, either.)*

Merle swung the Jeep into her covered parking place and set the brake.

"Have you had enough walkies for tonight, Fred?"

"Maybe I'll just tinkle on that big tree right outside our gate. Real convenient, if you know what I mean."

"How about you check out those trees over there and we skip the scenic route, OK?" She pulled her keys out of her pocket, then noticed that her patio light was off. She always left both the patio and the balcony lights on all night, and knew they had been on when she set out on her walk with Freddie.

"What . . .? I guess one of the police officers must have turned it out. I wonder why? Well, that's a pain, can't see anything. Let me find my little pen light. Oh, oops, I don't have my purse. Oh, no . . . it was in my pocket. Damn, must have dropped it in the melee earlier. Shit! OK, Fred, let's go." She opened the tall wooden gate, allowing a sliver of light from the street to fall on the walkway to the front door.

"Man, you are some kind of *chingona*!" A very large shadow suddenly appeared in front of her. The male voice chuckled.

"OH, MY GOD!" Merle stumbled back and almost fell on her ass, scraping her arm on the rough wood of the gate as she flailed about for balance.

"That *pendejo* is still cursing you, *chica*!"

"Is that you . . . ANGEL? Christ, you scared me! What are you doing here?" She was beginning to be able to see just a little bit in the darkness. Angel's mother had definitely not supervised his wardrobe this evening. *(What the hell is going on here?)*

"I'm just checking on you, making sure you're alright. I waited 'til all the cops were gone"

"You KNEW about this? I thought you had my back?"

"I was watching. Saw the whole thing. You didn't need any help. I don't think he'll be back. Better he doesn't know I was here. He'll be washing his face for days trying to get the dog *caca* off!" Angel crossed his arms across his chest and leaned against the front door frame.

"So, what did he want? Do you know who he is?" Merle stood up straight, a little surer of herself now. *(This is really, really bizarre!)*

"To get back at me, I think. For . . . whatever. Yeah, I know him, but I don't talk to him. I made sure he left. He probably would have slapped you around to scare you some and jerked those gold earrings out."

Instinctively Merle grabbed her earlobes, exceedingly thankful to find them intact and still wearing the little gold loops John had given her many years before. She had witnessed a girl fight one time at a middle school in south San Antonio, where she had substituted briefly, when a seventh grader yanked the earrings out of another girl's ears. It was a bloody mess. *(Girl fights are the worst! And that one was spectacular!)* She was beginning to understand how lucky she had been tonight.

"What now?"

"You still have my cell number?"

"Yeah, but . . . do you think I'll need it?"

"I hope not. Probably not – not after the way tonight went down!" Angel smiled and pushed himself free of the wall, reached up into the light fixture over the door and screwed the bulb in. Then he shuffled toward the gate, his diamond ear stud glinting gold in the yellow bug-lite.

"Tén cuidado, madrina chingona. Hasta la vista." He chuckled again and disappeared.

"Hasta la vista, Angel." (*"Hasta la vista,"* indeed! I sure hope I don't see you again!)

"Ouch! Oh, ouch, ouch!" Merle was examining the gash in the underside of her left arm, dabbing at it with a cotton ball soaked in hydrogen peroxide.

"Damn, I'm bleeding all over everything." She grabbed a washcloth off the towel rack, dampened it under the tap and patted a couple of blood spots on her grey heather sweats, making a smudged mess.

"I seem to bleed more easily these days. What's up with that?" After the bleeding stopped, she slathered on Neosporin and covered the wound with three giant band-aids. She noticed that her hands were still a tad shaky – well, no wonder. It had been quite a remarkable night. And morning.

"What time is it? . . . Good Lord, ten after three. And there's no way I'm gonna get to sleep anytime soon. I'll be a zombie if I try to go to school in the morning. Might as well take the day off, don't you think? Monday's lesson is all ready – made sure of that before I left on Friday, knew I'd be working on grades all weekend. And my grades are finalized and submitted . . . So, the kids can wait until Tuesday to complain." Merle kicked off her walking sandals and wiggled into her flip-flops, walked into the living room, sat down at her computer, and pulled up the find-a-substitute website.

"Sounds like a plan to me."

"No, NO! Don't hibernate! Dammit!" Merle rapidly clicked and punched to no avail. Her computer insisted on hibernating in spite of her efforts. She silently counted to ten and pushed the power button. As she waited for it to reboot, she went to the kitchen and got a cold Bohemia out of the fridge.

"Are we gonna eat anything, Merle?"

"I'm starving, Fred. As soon as I finish here, and have a sub for tomorrow, we'll find some dinner – or breakfast – or whatever . . ."

Freddie was parked under the kitchen table intently watching every move Merle made. She browsed the fridge, opened the veggie drawer, examined several plastic containers.

"OK, I have some leftover chicken . . . and some pretty peppers. Do I have any tortillas?" She poked around some more. " . . . yes, indeed, I do have tortillas. Yea, TACOS!" She unloaded an armful of stuff from the refrigerator onto the kitchen counter. "Now a skillet and some olive oil." She chopped up some onion and two colors of sweet peppers into rough chunks and plopped them into the sizzling oil. Then she sliced a cold chicken breast and added it to the peppers and onions. She seasoned the mixture with salt, pepper, garlic powder, and Tabasco. The kitchen was beginning to smell delicious.

"Yes, Freddie, I'm saving some of the chicken just for you." She put aside some chicken skin and scraps.

"You spoil me, Merle."

"Too bad I don't have any fresh cilantro, dried will have to do." She pulled two tortillas out of the plastic bag and lit the closest large stovetop burner, flame medium high. Using a pair of tongs, she flambéed the tortillas one at a time, flipping them over often, moving them around quickly on the flames, allowing them to burn just slightly and become a little crusty on the outside, warm and pliable in the middle. She flopped them on the plate and filled them with the chicken and peppers mix from the skillet, gave Freddie his chicken treat in his bowl, grabbed her beer and nestled into the living room sofa. Freddie enjoyed his snack loudly and enthusiastically.

When she finished eating, and Fred had cuddled up with his head in her lap, and it was almost four o'clock Monday morning, she finally began to unwind and think about what had happened.

"Wow, Freddie, that was some scary evening. Huh? And that Angel character. What do you make of him?"

"I think he likes you."

"Apparently, from what I can sorta figure out, I've come under the protection of a gang, Angel's gang. I suppose it's because I helped him with his wallet, gave it back with all his cash, etc. Seems silly, but maybe he's not used to people treating him honestly. Sad. Seems like basically a nice kid. So, now I'm gonna have a reputation – for being a *chingona*! Me, a badass!" *(hmmm . . . I wonder if he'd have a chat with some of my bullies at school. . . No, no, Merle. Bad idea.)*

"You go, girl! You're gonna be a legend! They're gonna write a corrida about you, like the ones they sing about Mexican drug lords and narco-terrorists."

"And I seem to have acquired a guardian angel – so to speak – whether I like it or not." Merle was beginning to fade. She put her dishes in the sink, turned out all the inside lights, unplugged the phone, and instructed Freddie.

"We sleep til noon. Got that, buster? No standing on my chest and licking my face as soon as the sun comes up. *(Which is in about two hours, I think.)* Then I'm going to Jo-Ann fabrics and play a while before I have to show up at the Alamo Heights Police Department to make a formal statement about tonight – or this morning. You know, as nice as it is, I'm getting really tired of that place! And, I guess I'd better not mention anything about Angel, huh?"

Freddie was all atwit, sitting at the foot of the Merle's bed, fairly quaking. He picked up one front paw, then the other, alternating back and forth, making tiny squeaking sounds, his triangular ears swiveling on his little head. Merle laughed.

"Would you like to sleep on the bed with me tonight? To keep me safe?"

"*Well, yes. I would very much like that. To keep you safe, that is.*"

"OK, just this once. Don't get the idea that this can be a regular thing," she warned as she patted a spot next to her, then laid back to think about Phil a bit before picking up her book.

"*Never crossed my mind, Merle.*" Freddie hopped up on the bed, twirled around three times, and snuggled in, just as close to Merle as he could possibly get.

CHAPTER 23

Monday nite/SA

OK, well . . . this has been a VERY busy weekend. And my life has gotten VERY complicated! At least today was a lot of fun. Played hooky and went to Jo-Ann fabrics for about three hours. Creative relaxing, looking at all the wonderful things I could make if I ever have time to sew again. But then, (Dragnet theme, please) . . . went to the AHPD offices to do the official stuff on last nite's disaster – without mentioning Angel, of course. Who would have thought a Westside gang-banger would crumple at the sight of a little dog poop? What a wimp! Didn't see Lt. Espinoza from the Willie catastrophe.

And Phil! OMG, Phil!! Am I in heaven, or what! ALL NIGHT! I can't process this – me, sixty-plus-year-old lady, frizzy-haired me! We took a break in the wee morning hours to scramble eggs. Ate ravishingly, like starving orphans – we'd missed dinner, you see. (Hmm . . . he still owes me dinner, . . . and a movie.) Then went back to it with renewed enthusiasm. Sunday morning was quite the exciting shock – waking up with a beautiful naked man next to me. Yes, I'm smiling even as I write. I'll take that kind of a shock any day of the week. Every day of the week.

Then he rushed off to church. To friggin' church, for christssake! Well, I hope it's for Christ's sake, and not just for his sister. Church doesn't do you much good if you don't have the right attitude. I should know. And, gotta remember: sister Amanda. She can make him twitch.

I told Phil about my scare Sunday nite (without the Angel part – haven't told him about Angel at all.) He didn't seem that concerned. Oh, he sympathized with me and all, but he wasn't exactly rushing to offer help or comfort! Guess I'm a little pissed. Just a little.

So, he called tonite and we have another date for Friday. A concert, of sorts. Some jazz combo at a local ice house that I sorta know. But he wants to take me to ChrisPark downtown first – never heard of it. Ah, an adventure. I LOVE adventures!

I'm already thinking about inviting him down to the cottage for the Columbus Day weekend – Good Lord, that's only two weeks from now. Maybe I'll mention it to him next time he calls . . .

After putting her journal in the bookshelf hidey-hole, Merle shuffled off to the kitchen for some fizzy water to take to bed. She grabbed a small clean glass out of the dishwasher and filled it with Topo Chico. *(Looks like it's getting time to load the dishwasher again. About half empty. And the sink is filling up, too.)* For some unexplainable reason, Merle hated emptying the clean dishes from the machine and putting them away. Somehow, the act of loading the machine and turning it on made her feel accomplished, but the follow-through not so much. She subscribed to the theory that if you use the clean ones out of the dishwasher, instead of out of the cabinet, by the time you have to empty it to make room for the dirties that are taking over the sink, there will be very few, if any, clean ones to put away. Ideally, it would be none, although she never seemed to reach that ideal. And besides, she had a clever little magnet thingie that turned from "clean" to "dirty" settings. So, she used it. It stayed on "clean" most of the time.

What to wear Friday night? (*This sounds like a very casual sort of date.*) What's the weather going to do? Still hot enough for sandals and linen pants – or move on to loafers and jeans? Time to break out the lacy underwear? *(Do I even have any lacy underwear?)*

"What do you think Freddie? Some tight sexy jeans – the faded ones that show off my tush – and a long sleeve T-shirt, maybe black?"

"*I think you're focused on the wrong questions, here.*"

"Maybe I need to think about the big picture. Like, is Phil The One? Unequivocally, YES! Yes. Yes. Yes." Merle leaned over and looked Fred in the eyes.

"*Merle, sweetie, we've only known him for three weeks, right? (Although one might find that hard to believe considering how you were behaving last time he was here!) Isn't it a little soon to make such a dramatic decision?*"

"OK, I figure I'm due. I spent thirty years of my life catering to one of the most difficult men in the history of the world. I've paid my dues. Now it's time for some payback. I deserve a sweetie in my life for a change." *(Well . . . John really could be very sweet – when he wanted to be, but he could be really cantankerous, too!)* "Someone to take care of me, instead of the other way around."

"If you say so. I don't think it works that way."

Freddie was sitting on the sofa watching Merle paint her toes. Thursday night, papers to grade stacked up on the coffee table, sticky-notes denoting class periods. Freddie wondered why Merle was bothering with the pedicure if she was going to wear the closed-toe loafers she had laid out?

"Should I mention exclusivity to Phil, Fred? And invite him to the coast for Columbus Day weekend? Or the other way around? See if he accepts the coast invitation first, then ask about commitment?" In her state of free-floating euphoria, which had endured despite recent traumatic events, Merle had completely overlooked the more practical points of beginning an intimate physical relationship. *(Oh my God, this is modern dating! What a pain in the ass!)* What she really wanted was for Phil to volunteer a promise to see only her. Should she wait for that to happen? Or would he lose respect for her if she didn't say something? *(This is starting to sound like an advice column in Seventeen magazine!)* Is setting boundaries, as it were, the role of the woman under the new rules of engagement? She had a queasy suspicion it was. So now she was trying to figure out exactly how to do that without upsetting the blissed-out feeling she got every time she thought about Phil.

ChrisPark was the project of Linda Pace, heiress to the Pace hot sauce empire. She created an urban retreat in memory of her son who died of a drug overdose. Wedged into a neighborhood of light industry, wholesale outlets, warehouses, and parking lots, it was one of the best kept secrets in downtown San Antonio. It occupied barely a city block of land on a side street off South Flores, practically underneath the Pan Am Expressway. A privately maintained park offering a secluded place to play or meditate or pray. The thick, tall stands of bamboo completely blocked out the surrounding buildings and traffic noise. The abundance and variety of plants inside were a treat to see and smell, deceiving the visitor as to the actual small footprint of the park, so beautifully landscaped it was. Shady nooks, wandering paths, small vibrant gardens, tiny hidden ponds with crystal water. *(My Lord, how many full-time gardeners does the Pace Foundation employ?)* Phil and Merle arrived in the late afternoon, still hot on the street, but dramatically cooler as they entered the shade of the park.

"Oh, cool. Those little holes are fountains, aren't they?" Merle was looking down at her feet.

"Yes, and something triggers them. I don't know what. Maybe they're on a timer. So, be careful. You might get wet." Phil was standing to the side of the open entrance space, nervously watching Merle.

Merle considered the recessed spouts she was standing on. The tableau brought to mind the classic Marilyn Monroe pose over a New York City sidewalk air vent – in the white pleated-skirt dress, of course. She tried to imagine the same scene with water squirting up underneath Marilyn, instead of air. Not a pretty picture. She scurried off the fountain entryway as quickly as she could.

"Aw, shucks. I was hoping you'd get wet." Big grin, so engaging with his one dimple.

They began to explore one of the paths that led to hidden places tucked away from the main open area. Damp shade closed in. Cicadas that weren't audible just a few steps back droned full orchestra in the late afternoon air. The couple chose a moss-covered, concrete bench under a huge *esperanza* bush, yellow flowers littering the moist ground below. Phil brushed off the debris and the two of them sat down with a big sigh, then a simultaneous giggle. (Soft focus, romantic music . . .)

"I had no idea this place existed, Phil. Thank you so much for showing it to me. It's absolutely gorgeous."

"Yeah, it's pretty special to me. I wanted to share it with you – see what you think."

(OK, this seems to be as good an opening as I might get . . .)

"Thanks. ah, . . . I'd like to share my special place with you, too. How would you like to come for a visit to my cottage in Copano Beach? We have a long holiday weekend coming up, and I thought we might take advantage of it to show you my little piece of the Texas coast." Merle looked him straight in the eyes – and smiled, big smile, tiny laugh lines crinkling up at the edges of her freckled face, now additionally dappled with slanting leaf shadows. *(Should I bat my eyelashes – or would that be too much? Men are notoriously dense when it comes to picking up clues.)*

His head popped up and he smiled again, with his one dimple. *(swoon)*

"Outstanding idea. Sounds like great fun. I think I can do that. I'll check with the family and make sure, but I think so." *(Check with Amanda?)*

"Want to drive down on Friday after school and come back Monday? We can go to the beach, if you want, in Port A. Although it's gonna be crowded, you know, especially the ferry."

"Sure. Sounds like a plan. I'll bring the beer. Plenty of Bohemia for you. I know a really good place to get shrimp in Rockport."

(OK, Merle, you're on a roll – go for it!) "While we're talking future plans, I hope you're not planning on seeing anyone else for awhile, are you?" Merle's head was about to explode. But there, she'd said it . . .

"Oh, I've already suspended my eHarmony account." He nodded as he lowered his head and stared into the clutch of chrysanthemums and daisies so casually assembled at the edge of the small clearing in which they sat. He looked appropriately serious, as if pondering the weight of what he had just said.

"Well, I guess I'd better do the same, huh?" *(Wow. THAT was easy. What was I all worked up over? He really is a sweetie! Oh Jesus, I sure hope he's for real!)*

"I'd appreciate the gesture." He smiled and looked at her again. "Can I bring Perkins? Think Freddie would mind?"

"Of course, bring him. Freddie will love having a playmate." Merle said, confidently.

The combo, *Moco Loco*, proved to be surprisingly good, in spite of the tacky name. Cool jazz with a decidedly Latin flavor. And the beef *fajitas* were delicious, the beer icy cold, the crowd only a little bit raucous. They talked with several of Phil's friends and one teacher Merle knew from school. *(Wow, I had no idea she was into jazz! You never think of these things when you work with people, do you? Like I didn't know until last year that Joanna in the English department worked for twenty years as a private detective, excellent training for a middle school teacher, I would think.)* It was a laid-back, let-it-all-hang-out kind of night when random tablemates became good buddies within fifteen minutes. Merle finished off three Bohemias and enjoyed herself greatly, relieved as she was about her "issues" with Phil. It was probably a good thing that Phil suggested they leave the musical festivities to the younger crowd and go back to Merle's place before they were too wasted to enjoy the remainder of the evening.

And the remainder of the evening had been truly delightful. Not quite the sustained ecstasy she had experienced that first night, but undoubtedly superior to anything she had enjoyed in the past twenty-five years. At least. Maybe thirty. Such enthusiasm! And stamina! And creativity!

"You've WHAT? You've invited ANOTHER DOG to the coast? No, no, no. NO! How could you do this to me, Merle?"

"OK, so Freddie, here's the deal: Phil and Perkins will go down to the cottage with us in about ten days. You'll have fun playing with another dog. I know you will."

"I like Phil, he plays ball with me. That's the POINT – he plays ball with ME!"

"Maybe we'll go to the beach."

"Now don't try to distract me with promises about the beach. Freddie doesn't share. It's bad enough that I share you with Phil now, but not gonna share with some prissy little cur. I'm the one who catches the ball. I'm the one who lays in the sunshine and gets my tummy rubbed. I'm the one that enjoys the street snacks – and Frito bugs. (ah ... yes, Frito bugs ...)

A few days later Merle stood in her bedroom in front of the open clothes closet. Enormous piles of garments, most still on their hangers, covered the bed. She was busily sorting the fall/winter items from the spring/summer ones. Her clipboard and fountain pen were squeezed into the tiny space available between the heaps of clothing. Wardrobe lists – to make mornings easier – were in progress. And she was trying to decide what to wear at the coast Columbus Day weekend with Phil.

"OK, so I checked the weather website and it's gonna be cool, maybe a little wet. So, . . . cuddly clothes. Yes, maybe even a turtleneck if it gets cold enough, or we go to the beach. I'll take the black one, it makes me look skinny. And it's classic." She thought about Jackie Kennedy, but passed on the iconic white poplin slacks, selecting soft tan twill jeans instead. *(If it's wet, it'll be muddy, so no white pants this trip.)* And her taupe suede desert boots. "If it's not cool enough for the turtle, I need some long-sleeved T-shirts in pretty colors. Let's see . . ." She ratted through her drawer and pulled out an indigo blue "South by Southwest" T-shirt with a surreal-looking rabbit in neon blue printed on the front. She had gotten it when she (unwisely, as it turned out) went to the music festival in Austin several years ago. She'd hardly worn it because it was too long for her, needed to be hemmed up – like almost every piece of clothing she had ever bought, but she never got around to shortening it. *(I seem to have several of those. I'm not too good at doing alterations. I hate alterations!)* Then she discovered the dark teal Margaritaville shirt that a friend had brought her from Key West. It had a splashy tropical illustration on the back, perfect for a coastal interlude. "But this one needs shortening, too. Well . . . I have time." She put the two T-shirts in yet another pile on the bed and began gathering up some of the hangers to replace them on the rack. After an hour or so she had the spring/summer things in the spare closet and the fall/winter items organized into tops and bottoms in her main closet, plus an outline of what she had, and what went with what, and what she needed to look for the next time she went shopping. Maybe not at Castaways this coming trip. She wasn't sure how Phil would react to her secret wardrobe source.

Before she sorted out and disposed of the leftovers, she considered a pile of several things to try on before deciding their disposition. First, she pulled on a pair of black, pinwale corduroy pants. *(Hmmm . . . a little snug around the middle. Damn! I like these cords. They go nicely with a lot of stuff.)* Next, she slipped a flouncy, crimson-red chiffon dress over her head, the only shade of red she could wear with her hair. *(I love this dress. It's wonderful at Christmas! And it just floats down, skims the body . . . oops, what's this.)* Merle looked to see why the dress wasn't sliding easily over her torso as was its custom. Then she tugged a bit. *(It's HANGING on my TUMMY! Oh, crap! This is NOT good!*

OK, that's it! It's off to the gym for me. Just as soon as I . . . as I . . . just as soon as I catch up on my grades!)

Disgruntled now, she headed to the kitchen in search of solace. "PBJ! I need a peanut-butter-and-jelly sandwich. Right now!" She grabbed the Jiffy super-smooth out of the pantry and the apricot jam out of the fridge. Then she tried to find space on the counter to put them, plus the plate she slid out of the half-open dishwasher. "Shit! This kitchen is a disaster. How did this happen? I've made a colossal mess again, dammit! And Phil will be here tomorrow night." Merle began to pick up food items that belonged in the pantry, the fridge, or the garbage, and disposed of them in their appropriate locations. *(Good thing I have a small kitchen. This would take forever in the big kitchen down at the cottage. Need to remember that when I'm thinking retirement – and idyllic grandma kitchens.)* Then she gathered the tools that didn't need washing and put them away. Next, she focused on the dishwasher, while running hot water in the sink to rinse off the dirties piled up there. It wasn't that she didn't know how to clean up, or was no good at it, in fact she was rather efficient. She just plain didn't like it. Back in the early seventies, during the golden age of the Women's Movement, she had bought – and displayed, albeit in the back of her walk-in pantry – a huge poster that said FUCK HOUSEWORK. In enormous, but friendly, psychedelic neon letters on a black matte background. She still smiled when she thought about that poster. Sometimes she wished she still had it. Her tribute to feminism. That and encouraging the hell out of every bright, capable, independent girl that came her way during her forty plus years teaching. A few of them still kept in touch.

Freddie jumped up on the open dishwasher door when Merle began loading in the dirty plates. He licked furiously, scooting over a bit each time she added another one. His toenails scratched and clicked on the brushed stainless steel and his long pink tongue plastered itself on each dish and slid over the surface like a snail foot.

"Be careful you don't lick the soap container. You wouldn't like that." She tried to shoo Fred off his platform, but he insisted, now going for the silverware and knives. "You could cut your tongue, you know that?" (*Guess I'd better use the 'sanitize' option for this load.*) She finished fitting all the little pieces into the racks, laid the big things on top, filled both soap containers, closed the door, without Fred, and punched the button.

"Now for that PBJ!"

Etta James belted out, "At last, my love . . ." as Merle curled up on the sofa with a glass of cold, sweet Riesling. *(Goes down smooth after peanut-butter-and-jelly!)* Freddie jumped into her lap without invitation. She sat absently rubbing Freddie's left ear as she thought about Phil.

"I hope I'm not putting too much importance on this visit to the coast, Freddie. I'm trying not to let my expectations get ahead of reality, as seems to happen with me sometimes. I just want to have a fun, relaxing weekend, and get to know Phil better." *(And have lots of fabulous sex.)*

"*I hope you don't expect me to buddy-up with this interloper you've invited.*"

"Don't you worry about being left out; you'll have Perkins to play with."

"*I'm not playing with anything named Perkins!*" Freddie's little neck muscles seemed to clench under Merle's fingers.

"Relax, Freddie. It's going to be alright. Really, I promise. I worry about you sometimes."

Freddie sighed, settled, and snuggled his nose between Merle's boobs. "*I worry about you, too, Merle.*"

CHAPTER 24

"I want to go dancing, Fred. I want Phil to take me dancing."

"I can dance with you. Remember when we danced on the pier down at the coast? You know I can dance. I'm a dancing fool!" Freddie stood up on his hind legs and turned around several times, indeed rather awkwardly, but enthusiastic and without mishap, nonetheless.

"I swear, Fred, sometimes I think you understand exactly what I'm saying! *(Actually, it's kinda spooky.)* Yes, dancing! Here, let's dance." Merle was a little wobbly after two glasses of white Zinfandel on an empty stomach. In her eagerness to accompany Freddie, she dumped part of the third glass onto the old oriental rug that had taken so many abuses since it came into her possession. She could almost hear it sigh as it absorbed one more alien liquid.

"Watch it, Merle. You're not walking too straight."

"Uh-oh. Guess I need a refill." And off to the kitchen she tottered.

Now, curled up on the sofa with Freddie snuggled beside her, Merle was defenselessly allowing all manner of memories to invade her consciousness . . .

One early fall Sunday she and John had gone to Christ Church Cathedral, a high church extravaganza with a huge crowd in attendance, then afterward found a little place to drink Bloody Marys in downtown Houston. *(What was it? La Carafe? French torch songs on the juke box*.) Back home at their funky nineteen-twenties apartment with the hardwood floors and arched doorways, they scrambled up an omelet and then made slow, lazy love all afternoon. She remembered leafy sunlight filtered through the branches of the ancient pecan tree in the back yard and fell on their naked bodies, softened only slightly by the window screen. Just a whisper of a breeze. Merle smiled.

"Dancing. I was thinking about dancing." An Emmylou Harris CD was playing on the box and Merle was getting more and more nostalgic as unfiltered memories crowded into her brain. There was that time at Floore's Country Store when she and John and some friends *(who was that? . . . was it somebody's birthday?)* had gone to see Augie Meyers. Floore's was quite the place in the seventies when Texas "outlaw country" music was the big thing. The movement's undisputed star Willie Nelson was just getting started good. The indoor/outdoor dancehall in the small town of Helotes, northwest of San Antonio, consisted of a ramshackle collection of clapboard buildings and other structures casually arranged around a large cement slab. Dozens of large picnic tables were placed in rows at the perimeter, with the outdoor stage making up one side. Old-fashioned Christmas lights were strung haphazardly above the area in a crisscross pattern, adding a soft glow to the festivities below. It was a busy night, so the lines of people waiting to buy beer at the outside bar overflowed onto the dance floor. Longnecks abounded, as did cowboy boots, belt buckles the size of dinner plates, bell-bottom jeans, and dangly feather earrings. The occasional whiff of marijuana wasn't a surprise to anybody. There had been two largish dogs, maybe a lab and a border collie, presumably family pets, crouched under a picnic table and looking extremely bored. As always, the music was loud, causing people who tried to have a conversation to have to shout at each other. Nobody really understood what anyone else was saying, but that was OK. The atmosphere was what counted. Pure Texas.

She remembered what it was like to dance with John that night. He had held her tightly to him so that it was easy for her to follow his lead, to anticipate his moves. He was smooth – and so very sensual in his tall, lanky way – his right thigh casually slipping between her thighs every few beats as they moved to the music of a Texas two-step. She remembered pressing her face into his chest and inhaling the aroma of freshly-laundered cotton.

"OK. I'm thinking about John – and me WITH John – and I'm NOT crying. I'm smiling, even. Wow, Fred, I'm really smiling about it – instead of getting all maudlin." Merle put out her cigarette in the red ceramic ashtray and looked down at her doggie, now in her lap. "This is progress, right?" But Freddie was asleep. "Well, I was going to talk with you about our upcoming picnic with Phil and Perkins, but guess not tonight. Let's go to bed, Fred."

Saturday afternoon Phil came to pick Merle up for their picnic and field trip to Espada Mission and *Asequia* southeast of town. Merle had made chicken salad sandwiches and packed them in a soft-sided, rolling cooler along with a fresh avocado, a container of pickled mushrooms, baby onions, and olives, some chocolate brownies, and the bottle of Moscato Phil brought. They loaded everything into the trunk of his venerable cream-colored Mercedes. *(This car must be at least twenty-five years old. Shouldn't he have a classic car license plate – or a medal, or something?)*

"Phil, this car is a beauty! Do you keep it shrink-wrapped when not in use?" Merle ran her fingers over the butterscotch tan leather seats and the polished walnut dashboard. Freddie hopped into the back seat.

Phil chuckled. "No, but I do keep it in the garage most of the time."

"Where's Perkins? I thought this was the big day for my play date with Perkins."

"I decided to leave Perkins at home today. He had a touch of asthma and I didn't think an afternoon in the woods would be a good thing."

"Asthma? Really? What kind of a candy-ass complaint is that?"

About forty-five minutes later they pulled into the gravel parking lot at Mission Espada, the smallest and most frequently forgotten of the five San Antonio missions which were built in the 1700s, the Spanish colonial era in Texas. The distinctive façade of the chapel, with its three bells in two open tiers, was often seen in tourist literature, but seldom identified. Local history buffs knew it for its historic *asequia*, or aqueduct. Most people think of Spanish missions as churches, and maybe schools. But they were, in fact, complete self-sufficient communities, some with hundreds of inhabitants. Although, Espada had obviously never had a large population because the chapel was tiny. Daily mass would have been mandatory for both priests and the Indian residents.

Merle picked up Freddie and held him under her left arm while she and Phil entered the empty chapel. *(Nothing says we can't take dogs in. And nobody's around to tell us not to. Besides, God loves animals.)* The ancient stone walls were plastered white inside, small oval-topped windows contained hand-laid glass panes which lent the sunlight a wavy, intoxicated quality as it struggled to brighten the low-ceiling, dim interior. The dark, carved wood pews looked more like straight-back chairs. Each row of four had a fold-out kneeler covered in a bright serape stripe of hand-woven wool. Merle's sneakers were silent on the uneven red tiles as she approached the altar. Slowly she sat down on the front pew, placing Freddie across her lap, front legs hanging to her right and hind legs dangling free on her left. He was straining his nose toward the floor, sniffing loudly, trying in vain to examine some micro-speck only he saw.

Merle sat quietly for some minutes considering the *santos* around the altar and trying to figure out who they were by looking for symbols incorporated into each statue as decoration. She knew that the scallop shell was the sign of St. James, and the lion was St. Jerome, but there were several others she couldn't identify. *(Catholicism is so complicated. How do they remember all that stuff? Did the Indians who sat here three hundred years ago even care?)*

After their quiet time in the chapel, they went in search of a picnic spot.

"Something for us to sit on." Phil pulled a huge bundle out of the trunk of his car. All Merle could see was the quilt's muslin backing, which she noticed was hand stitched in a leaf pattern.

"That's old, isn't it? Sure you want to put it on the ground?"

"Not old. But it is Amish. My parents bought it on one of their road trips a few years ago. It's quite sturdy – and it's king size, so we can spread out." *(OMG! He keeps his old Mercedes in the garage all the time, but he uses an Amish quilt as a tarp. Is he crazy? Or just inexplicably unfocused?)* "Let's try this path. Looks like it might go up on that little rise after this bit of underbrush."

Phil led the way, the quilt rolled up under his left arm and pulling the cooler behind him with his right. Merle followed with Freddie on the leash. Fred, of course, had to smell, and pee on, every sprig and twig along the way.

The smell of cedar and moldering leaves thickened the late afternoon air. *(In February that cedar will mean Cedar Fever for half the state! The Hill Country Revenge! The bane of all allergic central Texans.)* The pungent aroma tickled her nostrils and brought to Merle's mind her cherished Robert Oppenheimer fantasy: In the early eighties she had watched the PBS series featuring Sam Waterston as the iconic atomic bomb scientist, already one of Merle's heroes. Somehow she had become obsessed for several weeks with an imagined love scene between Oppenheimer and his girlfriend, set amongst the Ponderosa pines in the mountains of New Mexico. She looked at Phil ahead of her now on the trail. His broad shoulders muscular under a green plaid flannel shirt much like the one Oppenheimer-Waterston wore in her daydream. Suddenly she felt tingly all over and a little bit lightheaded. She inhaled deeply, unconsciously trying not to disturb the still, quiet atmosphere.

When they reached a small clearing, partially hidden behind thick bushes, Phil dumped the quilt and parked the cooler. She dropped the leash and Freddie wandered several yards away, sat down and waited to see what would happen. The little secluded arbor of live oaks and mesquite featured one especially venerable old tree that had twisted low branches extending over and around their chosen spot. Merle busied herself unpacking the picnic basket while Phil was spreading out the quilt. When she stood up, she barely missed bumping her head on a tree limb, and her hat fell off. Phil grabbed her from behind, flipped her around to face him, and shoved her up against the tree where she had just almost hit her head, her cotton T-shirt little protection from the rough bark. She gasped as he pressed himself against her. His hands were everywhere – all the right places – and suddenly she felt all warm and runny. (*Surprise is quite an aphrodisiac*!)

"Ah, Phil, I think they only do this in the movies. . . Standing up, I mean." He was breathing heavy on her neck now and her sunglasses started to fog.

"Well, I guess we'll find out soon . . ." as he unbuttoned her jeans and nibbled on her neck. Somehow, he had already gotten his own jeans undone and down to his knees.

Freddie, alarmed at Phil's sudden aggressive behavior, began pawing around their feet and making shrill whiney noises. Just then he jumped up, landing both feet on the back of Merle's knees, her legs gave way and down she went, pulling Phil on top of her.

It took several minutes to untangle arms and legs and clothing. Merle, unable to stop giggling once she caught her breath, and Phil practically panting. But soon hormones prevailed and Merle began to feel tingly again. Phil adapted quickly, and it could have been an idyllic moment of absolute rapture except for Freddie's persistent licking of every accessible patch of bare skin. They were almost able to ignore him.

Phil flopped over on his back and sighed, looking up into the lacy leaves of the mesquite. "I wish girls would go back to wearing skirts." Merle grinned.

"Aw . . . just a sweet old-fashioned boy" as she patted his cheek. Merle closed her eyes and breathed in the scent of cedar . . . and Phil.

Freddie lay on the far corner of the quilt, his nose between his paws.

"Sorry. Was I inappropriate? I was just trying to get into the spirit of things."

A few minutes later Phil was picking dead leaves off Merle's naked cheekies, when they noticed simultaneously that Freddie was busy having dinner – their dinner!

"Fred, NO!" Merle hopped around fastening her jeans while Phil grabbed for Freddie who was hurriedly devouring one of the chicken salad sandwiches, complete with cling wrap. "You're gonna choke! Drop it!" The lump went down in one gulp.

"I got bored. I wanted to play ball, but I didn't think you two were in the mood right now."

"At least he didn't get into the brownies. Chocolate is a big no, no for dogs." Phil smoothed out the quilt, a geometric pattern of wine, mustard, and teal solids, and extracted the bottle of wine, plus two glasses, from the cooler. "But most dogs love chocolate"

"Don't I know it!"

Merle was impressed that Phil's first thought was for Freddie's safety. Then she tried to figure out what had just happened . . . under that tree . . . over there . . . *(Ravished again! Oh, boy! I could get used to this.)*

After a delicious, albeit diminished, picnic dinner of chicken salad with all the trimmings, and an entire bottle of the sweet white wine Merle liked so much, they lay on their backs atop the colorful quilt. As it turned out Freddie had only eaten one of the sandwiches, so there had been plenty of food – for everybody. Merle floated in a haze, giddy, and limp like a wildflower picked yesterday. As the long rays of the setting sun covered them in pale gold light, they talked quietly about absolutely nothing, and began to touch each other. First hands and arms, then faces and hair, then they began loosening clothing again. Phil unbuttoned Merle's shirt and was massaging her breasts, with occasional tweaks on her nipples.

"You know you have a direct link between here . . ." He kissed a nipple. ". . . and here." He patted her pubic bump. "Don't you?"

"I sorta suspected it. How'd you figure it out?"

"Research."

Merle laughed. She unbuttoned Phil's levis, pushed them down a bit and began stroking his bare skin. He turned onto his side, propping his head up with one arm, as she ran her finger slowly over his hip and into the small of his back – so smooth to the touch and so firm underneath . . .

"AH – RURRRAH!!!" Freddie erupted in a piercing howl. He had become hopelessly tangled in underbrush, but that wasn't the reason for his outburst. There were children advancing on the trail. Several children. Loud children.

"Here . . . quick!" Phil grabbed the far edge of the quilt and furled it over the two of them, effectively covering them up to their chins. "Stop laughing . . . and be still."

"I'm trying. Stop tickling me." They pulled the cover to their noses and lay very still.

It was well into dusk. Little feet in big tennis shoes crunched the leaves and twigs as they entered the clearing.

"Can you see what's back here?"

"That dog sure is mad."

"Don't do that! Leave me alone!"

"Oh . . . it's just two old people taking a nap."

Phil stuck his hand out from under the cover and shooed them away.

"What the hell was that?! What are kids doing here at this hour?"

"Surely, they have keepers back in the park somewhere. They just got loose." Merle was arranging her clothes and trying to find her shoes. "I need to get Freddie untangled. We should thank him for warning us, you know." Phil helped Merle stand up. "I'm still a little shaky – that could have been . . . ah . . . embarrassing, to say the least."

Later that evening Merle sat propped up on the sofa with an ice pack on her knee, classical FM on the box, glass of wine on the coffee table and a cigarette in her hand. Freddie was asleep on his back, spread-eagle, not a care in the world, snoring loudly. Every now and then one of his paws twitched, straightened out in a perfect ballet pointe for a moment, then flopped back down, totally relaxed. Merle had her journal in her lap and her fountain pen ready, but not yet employed. She pondered the day's developments.

"Damn, my knee hurts. Shouldn't think that little bit of hiking would have affected it so much. Sure wish that Tylenol would kick in." She thought about what her arthritis doctor told her years ago – to stay skinny and stay active. "Gotta exercise more. Does sex count?"

Freddie heard her talking to no one in particular and forced himself awake. He rolled over and shook, then jumped up with Merle and wedged himself between the pillow she had under her knee and the back of the sofa. He laid his chin on top of his front paws and looked up at her from under shaggy brows and long curly eyelashes, trying to get some hint about her mood. *(An emotional girl, our Merle is.)*

"Wow. Today was totally amazing. I don't think I've ever been that excited, or that turned on. Not even when I was a teenager. *(If I can even remember that long ago!)* Maybe it was being outdoors? Maybe it was Phil? *(He is about the sexiest thing I've seen up close in a very long time!)* My God, it was fantastically beautiful – my Oppenheimer fantasy come to life! He couldn't wait to get his hands on me, all over me."

"I was going to mention something about that…"

"Oh, Freddie, I think I really like this guy. Really, REALLY like him!"

"I like him, too, sweetie. He plays ball with me. Although not so much today."

"Oh dear, we sorta left you out of the afternoon's recreational activities, didn't we?" A secret smile tugged at the corners of Merle's mouth. She began to play with Fred's ears.

"Thank heavens for that. I would've been smushed." He screwed his head around and licked her palm, trying to imagine himself in the middle of the melee he had witnessed that afternoon on the quilt, little rabbit legs kicking out from between naked human bodies.

"Getting your leash caught up in the bushes couldn't have been much fun, either. There might have been snakes." Merle wiped her hand against her grey sweatpants. Freddie's attentions had left it wet and itchy.

"Well — for all that — I might have had a better time if Perkins had come, after all!"

"Guess what? Phil is coming tomorrow afternoon and we're going to Beto's for a beer. I think they allow doggies on the patio, so maybe Perkins can come, too."

"Yikes. I'd better be careful what I ask for."

Merle picked up her pen and wrote one line in her journal. *"Dorothy Parker was right: 'There's nothing quite as much fun as a man.'"*

CHAPTER 25

"I don't know why she thought she needed to cheat. I know her, she's NOT a cheater!"

"Parental pressure, maybe? Both her parents are brilliant college professors."

"Yeah, but Alpha Ann isn't mathematical OR scientific. And they're both. They don't get it, Grams!" Fay flopped down on the sofa opposite Merle.

"How'd she get into the AP Algebra class?"

"Well, she didn't do too good on the entrance exam, so her mom waived her in." *(Uh-oh, one of those.)*

"I see."

"She's artistic and creative – she's an absolute genius with color. Much better than I am. But she doesn't even like math. She totally misses the beauty of it – the symmetry, the logic, the joy of working things out. It's all fog to her."

"So, how's she been passing all these weeks?"

"Her brother does her homework for her, then Mr. Zobrinski lets her correct her tests to raise her grade to passing." *(Wonderful! New practices in education win again!)*

"Apparently, she's not learning – even with all that help."

"What can we do? I have to try to help her. She's so embarrassed and upset."

"Well, we can't do anything about whatever the school decides to do as punishment. That's between her, her parents and the principal – and her teacher, I suppose. But you can help her get caught up, and maybe even pass the next test on her own."

"Whatever I can do."

"Will she talk to me?"

"Yes, I think she'd rather talk to you than talk to her parents, if you know what I mean." Merle knew exactly what she meant. Fay stood up, anxiously. "She's in the car now. Shall I go see if she will come in?"

"Oh, good grief! Yes, go get her!"

After more than forty-five minutes of tears and hiccups, Alpha Ann finally admitted she needed a long-term solution and started listening to what Merle and Fay proposed. Their plan was that Annie's brother Lewis would not do her homework for her, even though it was quicker for him, but instead he would work through the practice problems with her, explaining as they went. Fay would help her study for tests, and Annie would see her teacher and apologize, then explain how she intended to remedy the situation. *(Certainly, he'll see the benefit in this arrangement – especially since he's partially responsible for such a mess. He should have noticed something was askew when her homework was all hundreds and her tests were so awful. Well – maybe I shouldn't be too hard on him. He probably has a hundred and fifty or more students. And all of them with hyper-active parents, "helicopter parents.")* Merle also suggested that she have a serious talk with her parents, at an appropriate time, no rush.

"Make an appointment if you need to. Just make sure you have their undivided attention." and discuss her preferences in academic subjects, her talents, and her discomfort at being forced into high-performance math classes. Merle hoped they would see the light. She told Annie to tell them to call her if they wanted to discuss the situation with someone objective and experienced.

Fay left with a smile and a hug and a "You're the best, Grams!"

Alpha Ann had stopped crying. She hugged Merle, sniffled, and said, "Thanks, Ms. McKinney. You've been a big help."

(OMG! You just never know what's coming, do you?)

"This really isn't what I expected today." Merle was sitting across from Phil at a corner table in Beto's Cantina on Broadway. They didn't bring the dogs and they didn't sit outside because it was pouring down rain and had turned cold. *(Well . . . I'm glad this front didn't come yesterday while we were at Espada!)* Both the music and the young crowd were loud and the atmosphere was swampy in the restaurant.

"At least the beer is cold. Let's finish these and go back to your place for a while. OK?"

"Sure." Merle was already thinking ahead. *(Cool! Maybe some soup and a "quiet evening" at home? I've got chicken broth in the freezer . . . and some fresh cilantro . . .)*

Phil paid the tab, left an overly generous cash tip on the table, and they drove back to Merle's condo just a few blocks away.

"Want some of my famous homemade chicken soup tonight? I've got some knockout chicken broth in the freezer and could do it in an hour or less. Perfect evening for soup. I could even whip up a batch of cornbread, if you're real sweet to me." *(Am I being too domestic? Naw... food is always good, right?)* Merle turned on classical FM and hung both her raincoat and Phil's jacket on the backs of the kitchen chairs. They dripped onto the linoleum floor where Freddie was licking up the puddles.

"Freddie, don't do that. You have fresh water in your bowl."

"*I know, but this tastes better. More flavor.*"

"It's like licking the bottom of people's shoes! Don't do it."

"*I haven't tried that. Yet.*"

Phil sat at the kitchen table, took off his wet shoes and put them on a stack of newspapers on the floor. Then he fiddled with the bright-colored, hard rubber coasters, standing them on edge, trying to balance one upright, then spinning one like a top. Merle tinkered in the pantry and fridge looking for soup ingredients. She felt a sudden chill as he spoke.

"Sit down, please. I need to talk to you." *(Uh-oh, I know THAT tone. Every wife and lover in the world knows THAT tone!)* Merle closed the pantry door carefully and sat down across the table from Phil, reluctantly recognizing a rising dread of what was about to come.

"So, what's on your mind?"

"I've been thinking ... about us ..."

"Yes?"

"I think I should be using a condom." *(WHAT! Is this New Age dating? What the hell is this all about? Does he think I might get pregnant, for christssake? Or that he might catch something from me?)*

Phil's surprise announcement suddenly angered Merle to the point that she could barely control her words.

"I'd rather you didn't. I don't like condoms." *(no, no, AND NO!)*

"Why so?" Phil started twirling one of the coasters again.

"Truth to tell?"

"Yes, of course." He looked up at her, expectantly.

"I dislike condoms on principle because it seems like you're protecting me from something distasteful or harmful, and that is just the opposite of what I feel. I want lovemaking to be natural and spontaneous. This is just as much for me as it is for you. And I don't want it calculated or structured." Merle's voice became increasingly passionate as she warmed to her topic. "I want for us both to feel everything – real, and bare, and raw." Conscious now of what she was doing, she paused, took a deep breath, lowered her voice to a soft alto with a slower cadence, the voice she used when she had a come-to-Jesus discussion with a wayward student, and looked Phil directly in the eyes. "I want to bury my face in you. I want to kiss you from your bum to your belly button. And when I take you in my mouth, I don't want to be chewing on latex! *(There! Think I got my point over?)* Actually, Merle was quite astonished at her own audacity.

"OK, I guess that's a no on the condom." Phil appeared perplexed. "I only ask this because I got a call from my ex . . . *(Ex? Who's this "ex" person? He left something out along the way.)* . . . she told me that she had tested positive for papilloma and she said she could only have gotten it from me."

"I thought only teenage girls got that? Didn't we just have some brouhaha over mandatory vaccinations?"

"Apparently not. Men are carriers only. I went to my GP and got tested. It was inconclusive, but still . . . "

Merle didn't know what to say. Her head was exploding, her face burned and she had that hot-all-over feeling again, something between fainting and puking. Phil didn't look so great either. And there they sat for some minutes with the condom issue undecided and more than the tabletop distance between them. Finally, Merle stood up.

". . . ah . . . how about I make some soup for us? We can curl up in front of the tele while it's cooking."

"I have some things I really need to do tonight. Raincheck?" And he smiled at Merle, with his one dimple. "One favor before I go?"

"Sure."

"Could I borrow your copy of *Love in the Time of Cholera*? When we were talking about it the other day I remembered I always wanted to read it. I think I have the Spanish version somewhere *(Of course, you do!)* but that takes a lot of effort that I never got around to putting forth."

Merle laughed. "I can understand that. I'll get it." Merle knew exactly where it was because she had reread some parts after she and Phil had discussed it. She handed the paperback to him. He put on his wet shoes and his jacket, put the book inside as he zipped the front, kissed her on the cheek, and was gone. *(Poof! Just like that! Again.)*

"I'm telling you, Ellie, I looked it up. On Wikipedia. There is no test for boys for papilloma. So that part of his story doesn't jive." Merle had desperately needed to talk to somebody after Phil left – but this was a rather delicate topic, to say the least. She was afraid earth-mother Doris would have a fit, so she had called Ellie Mayfield. Anyway, Ellie was more "with it," being in the art scene and all. She ran with an eclectic crowd and she had dated a number of rather questionable guys, in Merle's estimation, during her romantic career. Merle hadn't talked with Ellie since the whole Willie Epps debacle, remembering that Ellie was the first one to mention that Willie might be just a little bit creepy. (Except, of course, for Freddie.) Maybe Merle could benefit from her extensive experience with men.

"You got into bed with him too soon."

"I wondered about that. Not at the time – it was amazing at the time. Completely over-the-top. But, later. After the euphoria faded."

"You let him sweep you off your feet and now he's having doubts."

"So, what do I do now?"

"Back off."

Merle hadn't told Ellie about her other discovery. While she was online looking up papilloma, she had checked eHarmony. Phil's profile was still up and active. *(Dammit!)*

The TV was on CNN, but with no sound, just animated wallpaper, and classical FM playing softly from the Bose. Merle sat on the sofa surrounded by sewing paraphernalia and the two T-shirts she needed to hem before taking them to the coast for the holiday weekend. She measured twice before she cut the cotton jersey *(just like a carpenter)* and pinned up a one inch hem with the extra-long, glass-headed silk pins that she preferred. *(Knit fabric is weird – the way it curls along the raw edge and doesn't ravel.)* Sewing usually calmed Merle's nerves, but not tonight. She was still in a funk, even after talking to Ellie.

As her expert fingers worked the material, she began to relax a bit and think about garments she had made over the years. Of course, the masterpiece of her dressmaking career had been Peggy's wedding dress. *(That was when I realized that I really can do anything I put my mind to. What a project it was, too – trying to keep school going while I spent every waking minute not in class working on The Dress! Several hundred hours, at least.)* The Vogue pattern she used had twenty-six individual pieces and the design required nine yards of the soft ivory brocade. There were about a hundred tiny buttons down the back and on the insides of the long, fitted sleeves. The deeply cut neckline showed off Peg's beautiful neck and shoulders perfectly. And the color gave her skin a luminous glow. *(Well . . . she was pregnant, so that might have had something to do with the glow part.)* She had looked like a medieval princess in the candlelight at St. David's Episcopal Church. Merle wondered again if there was another wedding dress yet to be made? *(Maybe not as soon as I had hoped. Mr. Phillip O'Conner Mathis is turning out to be not entirely as advertised.)* Merle considered the smoldering cigarette she held loosely between her long, graceful fingers. She flicked ash into the red ceramic ashtray, then wedged the ciggie into the groove on the side and watched the slender, feathery pillar of smoke rise slowly in waves, drawn by the central heating circulation system.

"Guess this is what happens when you renege on a promise to God."

Disgusted with herself now, she pushed the pile of sewing away and stormed into the kitchen.

"Food. I need food! ... chocolate ... beer ... ice cream ... salted almonds ... chips and salsa ... argh!" She dithered around aimlessly, picking things up and putting them back down. Finally, she settled on a big bag of sour cream and onion potato chips, grabbed a cold Bohemia from the fridge, and retreated to the balcony. There she sat for a very long time – in the dark, with her feet propped up on the railing, drinking beer and stuffing herself with chips. After draining the second cold one, she tried to get up and found that she had become painfully stiff and her knee was acting hinky again. *(Shit! Bugger! Damn! Is EVERYTHING falling apart?)*

"Come on Freddie, want to go walkies!"

"Sure. But this is the sixth time today. Are you OK?"

"I need to get outside and think. Things are sorta confused right now. My head isn't straight." *(Hell, my LIFE isn't straight!)*

Once in the patio, Freddie seized on a faint, but familiar odor. Nose to the ground now, he was rapidly weaving back and forth, completely captured by the scent.

"Quit jerking the leash, Fred. What are you doing? Let's GO!"

"That Angel person has been here again."

CHAPTER 26

"Hi, Phil, what's up?" Merle was driving home from school on Loop 410 when her cell phone rang. She had been reluctant to answer it even when she saw Phil's name pop up on the ID screen; it being illegal to talk while driving and traffic was crazy.

"Listen, Merle, I need to talk to you about this weekend."

"Yes?" She was about to tell him that she was in traffic and would call him after she got back home, when she recognized that tone in his voice again, the you're-not-gonna-like-this tone. The tone he had used when he started the condom discussion. *(Arrgh! OK, so what? Don't care if a cop stops me. What else could go wrong?)* Merle's face began to flush and she felt like her head was building pressure, already. Trying to negotiate rush hour madness through the red haze she was seeing, she focused only partially on Phil's words.

"I discovered I have a previous commitment on Sunday evening. Somehow I forgot about it, but I really need to be here in San Antonio. Would you be willing to come back early?" *(What the hell? NO! NO WAY!)*

"Well, . . . ah . . . Phil, having the long weekend was really a major part of this plan. Would you consider coming down in two cars? I really don't want to cut my visit short." Merle was astonished that those words managed to make it out of her mouth.

"Hmmm . . . that might get a little too complicated for me. I think I'd better just stay here. You go have a nice vacation with Freddie. And I'll see you when you get back." *(DAMMIT!)*

"OK, I guess, if that's the way you want to play it."

Merle didn't even remember the rest of her commute. Suddenly she found herself in the middle of her kitchen with Freddie jumping and twirling around her feet. Dumping the mail she had picked up on her way in, along with her keys, on the kitchen table, and her book bag in the chair, she grabbed the red knotted leash and hooked it to Freddie's collar.

"Come on Twinkletoes, let's go walkies."

"Bad day at school? You seem really stressed."

"Maybe a walk in the fresh fall air will help me think straight about what just happened."

"And then I can lick your face! That helps everything."

Headed south now, on Friday afternoon, Merle maneuvered the little Jeep through the twists and turns of the McAllister Freeway – over Olmos Basin, through Incarnate Word College, skirting Brackenridge Park and the zoo, then over the Japanese Tea Garden, past Trinity University and Alamo Stadium, around The Pearl complex, and on into downtown. In the rain. Lots and lots of rain. The cold would come tomorrow. *(This is going to be perfect weather for cuddling, and home-made soup, and cuddling, and hot chocolate, and cuddling . . . and watching old movies, and cuddling . . . if I had someone to cuddle with! DAMMIT! What the hell happened? Shit! Bugger! Fuck!)*

"Well, Freddie, here we are, just you and me on our way to the coast, again. Seems I'll have lots of time to play with you, and go on long walks. I didn't bring any homework, either. And no computer."

"Sounds good, Merle, but you don't. You need me to cheer you up?"

"Really hope you can keep me from thinking too much about Phil – Fast Track Phil, indeed! I'm fast becoming disillusioned, and depressed. Maybe you can cheer me up."

"Sure thing, sweetie. Leave it up to Freddie!"

The drive south was slow and tedious. Considering the weather, she decided to stay on the Interstate to Mathis, where she got off to find some hot coffee and pick up the back road to the cottage. Now, after the drive-thru at Whataburger, she had a large, fragrant Styrofoam cup in the console beside her.

"Sit down, Freddie. Stop jumping around."

"Gotta see that Lab in the truck over there. Did you see that? He licked the window at me! He can't do that!" Fred was pacing, practically prancing, back and forth from the passenger window to trying to get into Merle's lap to look out her window. A white pick-up, with a very large yellow dog sporting a bandana in the passenger seat, had pulled out ahead of them. All a-twit with indignation, Fred was inconsolable.

"Aw . . . jeez, Freddie! Watch the coffee!"

"Oops. OUCH! That's HOT!" Freddie's hind leg had collapsed the thin plastic top and he was up to his knee in the steaming black liquid.

He jerked his foot free and shook it furiously, splashing coffee droplets all over Merle, who was already soaked to her bare butt with the slosh-over from Fred's accident.

"Yeah! It's hot. And I'm sitting in it! Oh, great . . . now I have wet pants and a coffee-stained car seat. You're quite the Destructo Derby, you know that?"

"Sorry, Merle. I panicked. I didn't mean to panic."

Disgruntled and uncomfortable, Merle tried to concentrate on the road, at times invisible through the rain, and shift herself into a coastal mindset as she followed the white stripes on dark pavement to Copano Beach. She slid an Etta James CD into the car stereo player. That helped.

I have to tell you; this wasn't our most pleasant visit to the coast. The weather was awful and Merle was worse. All she did was listen to sad love songs and cry. Then she played with the blue cards and smoked cigarettes, and cried. Once she got mad at absolutely nothing and started throwing things around the house. I hid in the closet after I almost got hit by a ricocheted wooden spoon. We watched a nice old movie on the tele, but she cried after that, too! We even walked out on the pier, which I normally like very much, but her gloomy-bitchy mood pretty much ruined it. She seemed to be absolutely immune to all my ministrations. I got so frustrated I thought I might need a respite — and soon. Don't get me wrong, I was enjoying the Copano cottontails, and the street snacks, and the birds, but my Merle was bringing me down.

Merle stood in front of the pantry looking for something to cook. Preferably something chocolate. She really, really needed chocolate. Still baffled by what she had learned, she wanted solace. And a clear mind. Olivia, her downstairs neighbor in San Antonio, had called to tell her that Phil ("that nice young man you been keepin' company with.") had been ratting around in her patio – and maybe upstairs in her condo, too. Olivia wasn't sure, but she thought she had heard footsteps overhead. And she was certain that nothing was amiss, but she wanted Merle to know, anyway. So, now Merle knew and the knowing unsettled her greatly.

"There it is! That's what I want. Chocolate pudding! Hope I brought enough milk." Merle grabbed the box of Jello cook-and-serve chocolate pudding mix off the open pantry shelf and headed to the fridge.

> *Sunday morning, early/Copano Beach.*
>
> *What the hell was Phil doing at my condo? And why didn't he say anything about it? Did he lose something? Something he doesn't want me to see? This is sooo . . . strange, even spooky.*
>
> *The weather here is just terrible! Water over the roads in a lot of places. Thought about going home, but I told Phil I wanted the long weekend, so have determined to stay til Monday noon, earliest.*
>
> *And this situation is terrible. Haven't heard a peep from Phil. So, what did I expect? I'm sure I sounded pissed at the end of that Twilight Zone phone conversation we had on the freeway. I have this yucky feeling that I am at a turning point, headed downhill from here. What do*

I do? NOTHING! Because I don't have a freakin' clue what's going on!

I am so very tired of being lonesome. I can taste it, like salt. It weasels into my brain and drains energy; blocks the day-to-day joy that used to keep me going.

Dear God, my life is changing too quickly. I can't grab hold of it. Time really does speed up as you get older. Seasons change more rapidly, babies are born more often, people I know die more frequently. Just please don't let me become one of those old ladies who lives in the past. If I can't live in the present, and enjoy what I'm doing in the present, and dream and plan for tomorrow, then I might as well be dead! But, please don't let me die before I'm tired of living.

And please help me have a better attitude today than I had yesterday.

A real sunrise would be nice, too.

Merle peeked under the roll-up shade to see if the sun had appeared yet.

"Don't think there's going to be much of a sunrise this morning, but let's go walkies anyway. It's quit raining right now." She picked up the leash, opened the front door, and waited for Freddie to come get hooked up. He came trotting in – and went right through the door, leaped off the porch, and ran down the street.

"Well . . . there you go! You little shit!" She stood on the front porch with her mouth open and the knotted red leash dangling from her hand, not really believing what she had just seen. "I thought we were over that." Then she found her car keys and her cell phone, and headed for the Jeep. It had started to rain again.

Merle drove up and down all the cross-streets – Spoonbill, Snowy Egret, Pelican, Sandhill, and the others, back and forth from Bayview Blvd. to the highway. *(Oh, dear. The HIGHWAY! Freddie, please, please, please, stay away from the highway! You don't know anything about the highway.)* The rain was fairly pouring now. As they say in west Texas, "like a cow pissing on a flat rock." Windshield wipers strained to control the flood. Merle could barely see. The inside defogger was working overtime. She tried opening the car window to call Fred, but got soaked. *(Wish I had brought my ciggies.)* After twenty minutes or so of this futile activity, seeing not a sign of Freddie anywhere, she headed to Copano Corners drive-in grocery to buy a Sunday paper and a pack of cigarettes. Then she remembered that she hadn't brought her wallet, turned the Jeep around in the parking lot, managed to find most of the potholes now filled with pale tan caliche mud, and went home. *(OK, now what?)* She put a fresh pot of coffee on to brew. *(This may be a very long day!)*

Merle's cell phone chirped. She checked the screen and found it was a text from Fay.

"Mr. Zobrinski just posted grades from Friday's Algebra test. Alpha Ann made an 80! All by herself! Thanks, Grams. She's so happy!" *(Excellent! That worked. At least something is working! Thank heaven for small favors.)*

"Well, this was really stupid! What was I thinking?" Freddie sat under a palm tree, a venerable old sago, water pouring down in sheets all around him, contemplating his situation.

"I just had to get out, didn't I?" He finally admitted to himself that, somehow despite all odds, him being such a smart little fox terrier, he had become hopelessly lost. And the temperature was plummeting. Drenched to the skin, rain droplets hanging from his mustache, beard, and droopy ears, Freddie had begun to quake.

"Yikes! I'm freezing and I can't see ANYTHING!" As he stuck his head out from under the sagging palm fronds, he caught the faint whiff of something interesting – and delicious – in the wet air. Carefully and laboriously stepping around huge puddles that had formed both in the street and along the grassy shoulder, he followed the enticing aroma. It led him through three back yards, around a parked sailboat, across a patio full of garden gnomes peeking out from under enormous pot plants, over a ditch flowing with muddy water, and finally to the crushed shell driveway of a small blue cottage with black plantation shutters and a wrap-around porch. He trotted up the steps, shook himself vigorously, and sat down by the front door, savoring the fragrant air and welcoming the comfort of a dry corner to curl up in.

"It's fish – no, shrimp . . . no, it's sausage. And maybe some shrimp . . . or possibly crab . . ."

"Yes, I have a dog named Freddie." Merle looked at the unfamiliar three-six-one area code number that appeared on her cell phone.

"This is Roy, Leroy Adler. I live at the south end of Bayview, where it turns to dead-end, and I have your dog. I found him on my front porch a few minutes ago when I got back from church. I got your number off his name tag." Merle recognized the Cajun accent immediately. *(What's he doing in Copano Beach? He should be in Houma or New Iberia!)*

With a great sigh of relief, she answered, "Oh, THANK YOU! What's your address? I'll come get him right now."

Carrying a folded doggie towel under her arm, and her umbrella overhead, Merle mounted the steps to the little frame cottage. *(Ouch, knee, again! Dammit!)* Roy already had the door open and was unlatching the screen. She could see behind him into a warmly-lit, old-fashioned living room. Then the aroma that had so enticed Freddie earlier hit her full-on as she stepped inside.

"You're cooking gumbo, aren't you?"

"Yes, ma'am, I sure am. My favorite for weather like this. Hey, thanks for coming so quick. I'm afraid my big 'ole hound wants to eat your little terrier for dinner." And, indeed, Merle could hear scratching behind a door somewhere off to her left. She imagined what a gigantic paw was doing to the already flaking paint, and grimaced.

Roy seemed moderately tall, possibly five-ten or more *(Well, everyone's tall to me.)*, wiry, and very tan. He had wavy gunmetal hair and clear, pale grey eyes. His whole face crinkled and lit up when he smiled – a somewhat cock-eyed grin. *(Sorta like Robin Williams, God bless his soul.)* Merle learned that he had recently retired to Copano Beach after almost fifty years in the oil patch of southern Louisiana, a petroleum engineer. When he was a kid he had spent his summers here, in this cottage with his grandma, and loved every memory of it. He had fished off the pier and gone crabbing down on the salt flats. *(Just like I do now with Bobby and Rosie. How cool!)* He had inherited the house some years earlier, then last year decided to make it his retirement home. He liked to talk. He loved being retired. And he loved to fish. Not necessarily in that order.

Merle bundled her still wet and shaking doggie into the towel, thanked Roy again, and left. As she put her key into the ignition, she paused. "OMG! I didn't even check to see if he was wearing a wedding ring. What's the matter with me?"

Freddie stayed out of sight the rest of the day. Merle read the comics and worked the puzzles in the Sunday *Corpus Christi Caller-Times*, then she ordered an egg sandwich from the Pelican Sandwich Shop. Freddie enjoyed the leftovers. Later, she took a long nap, cuddled in her grandmother's old pink and purple quilt, enjoying half a chapter of her current Elizabeth George novel and several snack-size Milky Ways before she dozed off. By evening the clouds had cleared as the front moved through, and stars sparkled in a rosy-periwinkle sky.

Monday morning, she felt better. So did Fred, although he couldn't shake off a twinge of remorse lurking somewhere in his karma. His spontaneous adventure the day before had been an unmitigated disaster.

"Merle, I'm sorry I ran off yesterday. It was pretty dumb. Don't know what got into me." He jumped into her lap as she sat cross-legged on the white porch swing, drinking coffee from a blue mug and smoking a cigarette, trying not to think about the pain in her knee. With the appearance of the sun, the ground had begun to steam, and eager, enthusiastic mosquitoes were emerging in visible swarms to hunt human blood. Merle swatted at one on her arm, then on her neck.

"I think it's time for us to go in, Fred. I'm getting eaten up – and you will be, too – soon." She wasn't sure how susceptible dogs were to mosquito bites, but she guessed that, at least on the close-clipped areas of his body, he was vulnerable to attack.

Merle had to smile when she remembered the day she and John had visited the Aransas Wildlife Refuge, the same place where oil-covered birds, especially white pelicans, were relocated to recover after the BP oil spill in the Gulf of Mexico. John parked in the visitors' center lot, got out of the car, and was immediately inundated by a swarm of ravenous mosquitoes. They counted seventeen at one time on his leg. He remarked, "At least the wildlife is friendly." Unfortunately, the mosquitoes turned out to be the only wildlife they encountered that day. No armadillos, no alligators, no raccoons, no egrets or cranes. Not even a turkey in sight. And there were always turkeys! But there were exceptionally fine specimens of the coastal blood-suckers in abundant supply.

"You know, you really had me worried. I don't like it when you run off. It scares me."

"And I don't like making you unhappy, sweetie. Anyway, it was a pretty crappy runaround. But that old fisherman was nice, wasn't he?"

"At least your little adventure took my mind off ole Fast-Track Phil! Actually, I almost forgot about him – for a while, anyway." *(Wonder what he's doing? And do I really want to know? Do I care?)*

"Always ready to please, Merle." Freddie smiled.

CHAPTER 27

"Ms. McKinney, can I finish this assignment for homework? I didn't have enough time in class – that is, after I figured out what I was supposed to do." *(If you'd paid attention to instructions instead of texting your boyfriend, you might have caught on sooner!)*

"Sure, Tiffy. Do you have a textbook at home?"

"No, but I have the Internet." *(Will wonders never cease!)*

"Well, OK, but stay away from Wikipedia. Stick with sites that have a dot-edu after their name."

"Yes, ma'am. Thanks." *(That one is doing everything she can to look like the Barbie she was playing with just a couple of years ago! Tiffany Sifuentes, she likes to go by "Tiffy," but the eighth grade boys call her "Tits." Usually behind her back, but even if she heard it, she's just dense enough to think it's a compliment.)* Merle watched Tiffy make her way down the hall, boobs in the lead.

"Ah, a little peace and quiet, at last." Merle walked back inside her first floor classroom, closing the door behind her. "Jeez, last period is always such a struggle. Even if their bodies are in my room, their brains have already gone home – or at least to the bus, their phones, or the Dairy Queen around the corner." The overhead florescent lights, in combination with west sun streaming through the high windows, super-illuminated her workspace. Merle believed light was a metaphor for learning and she liked a lot of it. She really couldn't understand the new-wave practice, popular especially in the Reading and English departments, of having students work in dark classrooms. She knew colleagues who not only closed the blinds, they turned off the overhead lights for their afternoon classes. *(How do the kids even see the printed page? Something rather essential for a Language Arts lesson, I would think. But what do I know? Maybe they do it differently now. They do a lot of things differently now . . . and how would you know if a kid dozes off – unless he snores . . . ?)*

The trailing branches of an enormous split-leaf philodendron cascaded over a tall bookcase at the back of the room, its large shiny leaves reflecting the sunlight like automobile chrome. She began her afterschool straightening ritual – roll up all the maps, pick textbooks up off the floor and slide them back in the racks under the student desks, erase the whiteboard and write tomorrow's date, *(Love this new turquoise marker! Some kid will probably walk off with it soon.),* sort out the papers in the red wire basket on her desk and clip them by class period, attach sticky-notes, check her email *(argh! Ms. Treviño, Jason's mother, again. She can wait. I just gave her an update two days ago.),* turn off her computer, pack her book bag, move the trash can from under her desk to just inside the door (where the afternoon custodian would either trip over it or empty it – she counted on the latter), turn off the lights, and lock the door.

Once in her Jeep, she turned on her cell phone and checked for messages. Doris' name popped up. She put her key into the ignition while she waited for her friend to answer.

"Hi sweetie, got your message. What are you doing? I thought you were with that delegation from Peru, doing your Chamber of Commerce interpreter's gig."

"Oh, I had a short break, and I knew you would be out of class soon, so thought I would check on you. Haven't heard much lately. Are you doing OK?"

"Yeah, well . . . I've been a little distracted."

"I hope it was by a man."

"Pretty much, yes." *(Now is NOT the time I want to talk about this.)*

"You sound tired, honey. Kids give you a hard time today?"

"Let's just say retirement is looking better and better all the time. How long is it until Thanksgiving?"

"Hey, let's do dinner tonight. Can you? I should be finished here in an hour or so. I'll send these *Limeños* off to wreak havoc on the River Walk and we can retreat to a margarita at Los Barrios."

"Wonderful idea. I could really benefit from a margarita. To hell with my homework, there's always tomorrow, right? Say about two hours? I'll meet you there. That'll give me time to walk Freddie and take a shower. A shower and a margarita sounds really good right now."

On her way home Merle pondered her situation with Phil and thanked her lucky stars, once again, that she had chosen a profession which demanded total presence from its practitioners. She hadn't thought about Phil even once since she unlocked her classroom door that morning and turned on the lights. Work had been her salvation during times of marital and parental crisis in the past, and it was saving her again.

(Keeps me from going totally crazy! That having to be entirely focused on what I'm doing right now. Absolutely no time to brood about my love life – or lack thereof.)

Dinner at Los Barrios was a delight anytime, but an unexpected dinner out at this venerable San Antonio eatery in the middle of the week was a special treat, indeed. And Los B made the best margaritas in town! Merle in her little yellow Jeep and Doris in her black Lexus SUV *(My God, she looks like a drug dealer! And how does she keep that sucker cool in August?)* drove into the restaurant parking lot almost at the same time. They hugged a few minutes, then walked inside, and were seated at one of the booths in the old section of the rambling building.

The aroma of tostados, chilies, and garlic drenched the air. Paintings by local Hispanic artists were casually displayed on the walls, the focus being a bigger than life size portrait of Elvira Barrios, the restaurant's founder, dominating one end of the dining room. The atmosphere was unusually cheerful as most of the customers seemed to be on their second, or possibly their third, drink of the evening. Empty Mexican beer bottles littered the tabletops along with empty margarita glasses and salsa bowls.

After a margarita and a half, each, and a lot of nonsense conversation, Doris got serious.

"So, honey, what has you so upset?" She pinned Merle with her *comadre* stare. The same stare Merle used on students when she wanted them to confess to something.

"A man, of course." Merle sighed and slumped on the bench as she played absentmindedly with unruly curls which had invaded her face space. Suddenly the tequila kicked in and Merle began to unload all her agonies and anxieties from the last week. Doris sat sipping her frozen drink, licking salt off her lips and the edge of her glass, nodding, and making an occasional funny, but concerned, face to keep Merle going.

They – mostly Merle – talked all through the *flautas* and the *chalupas*, and several coffees afterwards. Merle shed a few tears and Doris made soothing noises in response. Now they were once again in the parking lot.

"I guess I really needed to talk to somebody. Thanks for suggesting this, sweetie. I feel much better."

"You know, no matter how good the sex is, at the end of the day you have to trust the guy. Seems to me that's not happening right now."

"Yeah, you got that right."

"And the whole purpose of intimate personal relationships is to make your life fuller and happier. This one appears to be somewhat counter-productive."

"Relationships! I really hate that word. But, listen, thanks for hearing me. You're a really good friend. And thanks for the advice – seems I need to do some thinking about this, huh?"

Doris nodded. They hugged again, got into their respective vehicles, and went home their separate ways; Merle east on Basse Road to Alamo Heights and Doris south on Blanco to Monte Vista.

Now temporarily relieved of her emotional burden, humming softly to herself, and more than just a little bit tipsy, Merle had some difficulty finding the right key for her front door. *(Shit! And I forgot to turn on the patio light, again, too. Dammit! I have too many keys. Hmmm . . . retirement would eliminate, ah, let's see . . . three, four . . . and if I moved to the coast . . . well, a whole damn bunch of them . . .)*

"You need some help there, *chica*?" A deep, amused voice came out of the dark. Merle jumped straight up; her keyring clattering onto the concrete pavers beneath her feet.

"Jesus God, Angel, I wish you'd stop scaring me like this!" Angel picked up her keys and handed them to her. Now, she knew why the porch light was out. *(Guess I ought to start expecting these impromptu visitations.)*

He chuckled. "I need to talk to you about that guy you've been seeing." *(Uh-oh. What now?)*

"Phil Mathis."

"Yeah. That's him. That dude's got another *chica*."

Merle opened and closed her mouth twice before she answered, stumbled, cleared her throat, and tried again. "And you know this because . . .?"

"I've sorta been keeping tabs on him."

"I see." Merle knew the color had drained out of her face. She felt it go. But she hoped Angel couldn't see that in the dark.

"Want me to take care of him for you?" Merle was afraid to imagine what "take care of him" meant in Angel's lexicon.

"Ah . . . no, I don't think so, Angel. I'll do the taking care of, thanks."

"OK. I 'spose. But you be careful. I want my *madrina chingona* to be happy and that *pendejo* isn't gonna do it for you. Don't trust him." *(Where have I heard that before?)*

"I appreciate your concern. I'll . . . ah, take that advice under advisement – and in the spirit in which it's offered."

"I hope so, *chica*. You still have my phone number?"

"Yes, Angel, in my cell phone."

"OK, then. *Buena suerte, viejita!*" He screwed the lightbulb back into the overhead fixture and was gone, an apparition quickly dissolved in the cool evening air.

Merle remembered a teacher friend of hers who had gone through an unusually nasty divorce. One day an eighth-grade gangbanger, one of her scariest students, the type teachers have nightmares about, offered, in all seriousness, to "take care" of her soon-to-be-ex-husband. It was pretty clear what he had meant. The friend, of course, was horrified. But, what really had concerned her most was that the kid actually believed she might agree to that kind of permanent solution.

"Gotta keep my wits about me! My life is becoming exceedingly weird!"

For the first time Merle seriously considered ending it with Phil, regardless of how much she dreaded a confrontation – and the loss of her fantasies. The uncertainty and unpredictability of Phil's attraction was making her crazy. Of course, Doris had been right, "at the end of the day you have to trust the guy." And she didn't. Not anymore. So . . . what to do? She thought maybe she should let all the recent input stew a while before she decided on anything drastic. *(And why haven't I heard from him? I've been home three days, now.)* But she also knew that the old sleep-on-it method of problem resolution probably wouldn't work too well this time because she invariably dreamed about Phil – wonderful erotic dreams that left her tingly and damp when she awoke.

Two days later she decided it really was over. Tears slowly leaking into her wrinkles and down her face, a smoking cigarette pinched tightly between her fingers and strewing ashes onto the keyboard, she composed a tortured email explaining her decision. *(Why do I have to fucking EXPLAIN?)* She left it in her drafts folder for another twenty-four hours, then pushed send. A response came almost immediately. "I understand how you feel." was all he said.

"And to think I'm doing this on the word of a Westside gangbanger! Have I totally lost my mind?" The relief she thought she'd feel turned out to be elusive, at best.

"Freddie, I think I'll lay off electronic boyfriends for a while." *(Maybe even men, in general – and on principle! Things don't seem to be working out so well between me and the opposite sex!)*

"Hope that means you'll have more time to play with me."

"Maybe I'll have more time to play with you. Where's your red squeakyball?"

"Oh boy, oh boy. We haven't played ball in a long time. You've been really distracted, you know?" Freddie ran off, nose to the ground, little fuzzy feet moving so fast it was impossible to discern individual steps. (Red squeakyball... I know it's here – somewhere... red squeakyball... where are you?)

"I know I've been distracted lately. I've really neglected my favorite little doggie."

Fred nosed the errant ball from behind Merle's bedroom door, picked it up and brought it to Merle in the living room. She threw it over the banister and down the stairwell. Freddie bounded after it, ears erect and lamb's tail twirling as he went.

"You know, Fred, men are jerks – and bullies."

"Hey, watch it with the gender bashing! I'm your main man, remember?"

Saturday was Halloween and Peggy had a party planned for neighborhood kids after they finished their trick-or-treating. Merle promised to come over early to take pictures of costumes and to help with logistics. Freddie insisted on accompanying her to the festivities because he had an uneasy feeling about staying in the condo by himself. *(Something facetious is afoot tonight!)* Merle arranged a basket of snack size Milky Ways and Snickers on the low, white wrought-iron table by the front door, taping above it a note that read,

"Please take only two. Thanks. The Wicked Witch who lives here appreciates your cooperation. Boo to you! And Happy Halloween! P.S. Please don't leave the wrappers on the ground. There's a trash can in the corner."

Merle had been working on her own costume all day. She loved Halloween – and costumes. Often over the years she had worn something completely outrageous to school, reinforcing the perception among the student body that she really was a crazy old lady. Once she had been called in by the principal because her costume was "just a bit too realistic." *(But it would have won first place at the Zombie Jamboree!)* Seemed she was scaring the sixth graders.

That morning she had hauled the costume box down from the top shelf of her closet and found the old long, black gaberdine skirt with the uneven hem. Then, choosing a black turtleneck *(It's going to be cool-ish, isn't it? That is, below eighty degrees.)* from her everyday wardrobe, she completed the outfit with a truly disgusting, ratty old grey shawl with moth-eaten fringe. She added black and red striped leggings and her hiking boots.

"OK, looks good." Merle appraised herself in the full-length mirror on the back of her bedroom door. "Now for accessories and make-up!"

Rummaging through her jewelry box she located a marcasite and ebony spider broach. The sparkly arachnid was mounted on its clasp with a spring that allowed it to float and move as the wearer walked or moved. She pinned it to the fold-over on her turtleneck sweater, on the left side, just under her chin. *(Hee, hee.)* Using a long metal chain belt she had actually worn in the sixties, she fashioned a medieval chatelaine, like the mistress of the manor might have worn. From it she hung an old, rusty, wind-up clock missing its hands, a small hand bell, a pair of clunky schoolroom scissors with only half a blade on one side, several skeleton keys, and an old ornate fountain pen. Tying on a "pocket," that is, a small drawstring cloth bag, she filled it with foil-wrapped Hershey's kisses. She clanked, and rustled, and jingled whenever she moved. Next, she took a pair of dark green clip-on sun shades and cut one of the lenses in a jagged edge, as though it had broken off diagonally. Then she attached the shades to her regular wire-rim glasses and checked her reflection. *(Wow. That's a great effect! Have to remember this one!)* Finally, she ratted her hair, sprayed it good, applied green eyeshadow both over and beneath her eyes, and black lipstick. *(Damn, I forgot to get black nail polish!)*

"Perfect!" Merle turned this way and that, checking herself out in the mirror. Freddie looked up and growled.

Once at Peggy's house, Freddie ran off to find Pip, Peg's pony-impersonating dog and Freddie's partner in crime. They got on famously, even though Pip outweighed Freddie by at least eighty pounds. Fred was faster. The grass in the backyard would need several weeks to recover after tonight.

"Eeek! Is that you, Grams?" Fay squinted at Merle as she came out the front door. Fay was dressed in a Wonder Woman outfit *(and filled it out quite nicely!),* her hands full of black plastic garbage bags and masking tape.

"Going to help with the decorations?"

"Yeah, I'm making buzzards out of pink plastic yard flamingos. Mom has a dozen of them in the garage. Big ones."

"Vultures. You're making turkey vultures!" Peggy yelled from the kitchen. "They're the ones with the red heads."

"Whatever. They look real in the dark. Check 'em out in a few minutes." Fay went off to her project.

It was crazy busy inside Peggy's house, as usual. *(Three kids plus Halloween, what do you expect?)* But, also as usual, Peg had things firmly under control. It just looked chaotic. Merle took several cute costume pictures *(Rosie's Tinkerbelle was the best!)*, then shared a pre-party beer with her daughter while the little ones were out trick-or-treating. Neither had eaten dinner, so they sat on barstools at the kitchen counter and sampled the party snacks.

Some while later, Merle went out to the front porch and sat down on the steps to get some fresh air and to look at Fay's vultures, now artfully scattered about the front yard. *(Yes, they do look quite real. And they're HUGE!.)* Two little girls, almost identically small and skinny, dressed in Disney Princess costumes, and dwarfed even further by the giant plastic birds, began walking very gingerly up the sidewalk from the street, then stopped and peered at the vultures, tightly clutching their orange plastic jack-o-lanterns, and visibly gathering courage to proceed. Regrettably, Merle wasn't up to speed on Disney Princesses, so she didn't know what names to call them. *(An unforgivable deficit for the grandmother of a six-year-old girl! How could I be so out of touch?)*

"Good evening, ladies." She said in her best witchy voice. "Are you looking for a treat?"

The princesses looked up simultaneously, focused just a second on Merle, then began to scream, hugging each other desperately.

"Oh, no. Don't be afraid. I didn't mean to frighten you." Merle got up and started toward them. The girls cringed. *(Wow, this get-up is better than I thought.)* "Now, none of that! Come, come!" Merle grabbed one hand each and practically drug them to the porch. "Here, have a seat on the steps while I find a treat for you." Merle untied her "pocket" with the chocolate kisses and gave one to each girl. *(They can't eat chocolate and screech at the same time, can they?)* Finally, a princess spoke.

"Are you a real witch?"

"I am tonight. But, I'm a good witch. Like Glenda in the *Wizard of Oz.*" *(They do still watch the* Wizard of Oz, *right?)*

"Well, you don't look much like a good witch."

"Yeah, you're really ugly." The second princess nodded her head enthusiastically as she chimed in. ". . . ah . . . I mean, that's a GREAT costume . . . just not for a GOOD witch." She fidgeted with the colorful, sparkly trim on her skirt.

"You could comb your hair nice." The first princess offered her advice.

"Yeah, and maybe get some new glasses." Warming to the subject, princess number two added, "Maybe you could get sparkly frames?"

For several minutes during this exchange Merle had been feeling a certain undercurrent of déjà vu as the girls talked, then it hit her, this was the newspaper story she had read and loved so many years ago. She remembered it, clearly now, as both poignant and funny – and quite endearing. One Halloween, Rene Carpenter, the astronaut's wife who did a regular column in the *Houston Chronicle*, wrote about a distraught witch who was consoled by a group of neighborhood girls. The memory made Merle smile. *(ah . . . the bad old days!)* She had read Rene's columns faithfully and treasured the wisdom and insight in each. Life was difficult – and often confusing – for a young professional woman trying to balance career and motherhood in the sixties. Rene understood that and her words had helped Merle find her way. *(My God, that was the Dark Ages, wasn't it?)*

Since they had calmed down somewhat, Merle sent the princesses on their way. *(Well, the good thing about dressing up as an ugly old witch when you're my age is that you don't have to fake the old part! And those two cutie-pies were doing their best to get me to work on the ugly part.)* Just as she was getting up to go inside, Pip, with Freddie hot on his heels, came rushing through the front door. Freddie skidded to a reckless stop, just microns from the edge of the porch, almost toppling over and tumbling down the steps. He took one frantic look at the monsters on the front lawn, began to growl, then threw his head back, nose in the air, and let out an impressively chilling howl. Sounded like the great hound of the Baskervilles, it did. Truly blood-curdling, especially coming from such a little doggie.

"HUSH, Freddie. Stop that bellowing! Stop it right now!"

"Merle, hurry, get inside! We're being invaded! I'll try to hold 'em off." Freddie was twirling in tight little circles, like he did when he wanted to poop. And poop, he did. Right there on Peggy's front porch.

"FREDDIE! For heaven's sake, what's gotten into you? They're PLASTIC, you dummy! They're plastic flamingos with garbage sacks on them. Calm down now, will you?" Merle leaned over, scooped up Fred, and carried him directly to the Jeep.

A few minutes later they were driving home, Freddie now subdued. Actually, he was mortified at his earlier lack of perception and total failure to behave appropriately in a crisis. And he wanted to forget the whole thing, please.

"That was a really nasty trick to pull on such a sweet little doggie, Fred. I'm sorry you got scared." *(Literally scared the shit out of you!)*

Merle reached over to the passenger seat and rubbed behind Fred's ear, then patted his back. Instantly and gratefully comforted, Freddie sat up.

"I love you so much, Merle! Can I lick your face?" He stood up, put one paw on Merle's shoulder, and started with her ear, licking furiously with his ridiculously long pink tongue.

"Stop it, stop it now!" Merle giggled, laughed out loud, wiggled and shrugged, trying to get Freddie off of her. "You'll make me have a wreck. Stop it. DOWN!"

"OK! OK! I'm down. But it's nice to hear you laugh!" (And NOT hear about that Phil person.)

"I know you love me. I love you, too." *(And it did feel good to laugh so hard. And to not think about Phil.)*

Freddie smiled. *(You've still got it, you old fox — the Freddie Factor!)*

CHAPTER 28

Merle pulled the Jeep into the Quarry Market shopping center and looked for a parking space in front of the James Avery jewelry store. The Quarry had indeed once been a real stone quarry. Merle remembered when all of the area now occupied by swanky stores, expensive condominiums, fancy restaurants, and a golf course, used to be known as Cementville. It was the location of Alamo Cement Company and its adjoining company-built community for workers and their families throughout most of the twentieth century. By the nineteen-eighties, the cement plant property had become completely surrounded by city development. The plant moved far north of San Antonio and the land was converted to an upscale living, shopping, dining, and entertainment venue. But when Merle was in high school during the fifties, the hilly dirt roads around the perimeter of Cementville were prime parking and making-out locations, frequented especially by Alamo Heights students because the area was close, convenient, very private, and seldom patrolled by the Alamo Heights police. *(OMG! That night after high school graduation – in the back of John's family station wagon. And the navy polka dot silk dress, the one with the low, low-cut front and floppy white organza collar – well, I forgot about the seam allowance when I stitched the collar on, didn't I? And sandals with no hose, really daring in those days. That was the night I found out how sensitive my nipples are. OMG!)*

Hoping to console herself over Phil's exit from her life, Merle was pursuing women's perennial cure for the blues: shopping. Now focused on selecting her consolation prize, Merle entered the soft, quiet atmosphere of the James Avery jewelry store and began to look at selections of gold and silver rings, earrings, charms, necklaces, and bracelets, many of them religious in theme, all beautifully and tastefully exhibited in exquisitely lit display cases. Merle absentmindedly fingered her own gold loop earrings as she recalled John had bought them here. *(Well . . . not here, here – at the store in Kerrville – the only one back then, on our first anniversary.)*

James Avery, a Texas Hill Country artist and craftsman, had recognized a need early on for classy religious jewelry. His home-based craft shop, started in the fifties, now had stores in several states. In San Antonio, James Avery designs had long been *de rigueur* for baptisms, confirmations and first communions, bar mitzvahs, *quinceañeras*, and graduations. So popular were his Christian-themed pieces, that a local Episcopal priest once published an article titled "By their James Avery Jewelry, Shall Ye Know Them."

Today, however, Merle chose one of the secular designs – a pair of hammered gold loops, glitzier than the ones she wore all the time, but classic nonetheless. And expensive – at least on a school teacher's salary. But she really needed consoling, right? She decided to wear them home, asking the clerk to put her old ones into the monogrammed bag and fancy box that come with all James Avery purchases. *(And yes, I know, if I lose one, I can buy a single replacement as long as the design is still in production.)* She checked her reflection in the sun visor mirror, once she was back in the Jeep. *(Ah, ha . . . they light up my face.*

I needed that!) She smiled. *(Oops, need to bleach the teeth! You add one new thing and everything else starts to look old and shabby! Well . . . if I would stop smoking, that would help considerably.)*

Saturday nite/SA

Bought new earrings today. Now if I can just find that perfect lipstick that will change my life, I'll be all set!

Lots of angst over Phil. Some of it actual physical pain, aching and longing. But I guess the bottom line is I'm lucky to be rid of him. I never would have been able to trust him, would I? Wonder how many other randy old gals he was boffing? My, my, he was certainly a busy boy!

Haven't gotten back on eHarmony yet. Not brave enough. Not ready to get my ego bloodied again so soon. Maybe I'll just lay low for a while.

I am so ready for Thanksgiving break! Can't come soon enough for me! I'm exhausted – not sleeping well, lots of dreams and nightmares. School is crazy busy – feel like I'll never catch up. Got a benchmark test coming up soon that the kids aren't ready for.

And I feel crappy. If this were January or February, I would say it's cedar fever. Need to get allergy meds next time I'm out and about. If I get the energy to be out and about . . . right now, it's all I can do to get up and go to school. Going to take the sleep cure tomorrow.

Freddie was scratching himself again. Merle had forgotten to give him his allergy meds, and lately she hadn't been very careful about what snacks she fed him, either. Now as she petted him in her lap, she noticed several red places where he had scratched repeatedly, one was really raw and scabby.

"Aw . . . jeez! I'm sure not a very good mommy, am I? This looks just awful, Freddie. How could I have not noticed?" *(Something else I've let go all to hell!)*

"You've been, ah . . . distracted, Merle. But I would really appreciate a little help here. This itching makes me nervous and twitchy all the time." He began to scratch behind his ear with his hind leg, then began biting himself on the rump in a staccato rhythm.

"Come on, Fred. Let's get you a pill. Don't worry, I'll put it in a piece of cheese. It'll go down real smooth. I promise. You won't even taste it. And some of that stinky ointment Dr. Jen gave us for your hot spots." *(If I can find it. Haven't needed it 'til now!)* Merle headed off to her bathroom to rat around in Freddie's drawer of doggie paraphernalia.

Monday morning – the Monday of the week before Thanksgiving break – Merle woke up feeling like death warmed-over. *(I just can't stay home, however rotten I feel! Nothing is prepared for class – and I've got that stupid benchmark test to do something about. Shit! God, I feel just awful!)* With great effort and determination, she drug herself out of bed and got ready to go to work, cursing herself for having let things slide so badly, and considering again the benefits of retirement. Dressed in the most comfortable pants and sweater she could find, her old brown SAS loafers, and minimal make-up *(Don't want to scare people!),* she took Fred out for a very abbreviated walk. Then she poured her third cup of coffee into her travel mug, picked up her purse, book bag, and keys, and left. *(This is going to take perseverance. I hope I can muster up some.)*

Once at school her auto-pilot took over as she organized review materials for her history classes. The day was both too long and too short. She felt weak, had difficulty breathing well, and was pretty sure she had fever, but there weren't enough minutes to prepare adequately for a substitute. She talked to each of her classes, albeit briefly, about the seriousness of the upcoming exam and hoped they picked up on the urgency she felt. *(I know, I know, my enthusiasm leaves a lot to be desired!)* After working through both her lunch and conference periods, feeling even worse as the day wore on, ignoring her emails, and leaving only the most basic information in her instructions for her substitute, she left just as soon as all the parents cleared out of the parking lot.

Merle drove straight to the emergency medical clinic on Broadway. *(I really must be sick. I absolutely loathe going to the doctor!)* She filled out forms in the waiting room, then was ushered into an exam room. She worried as she waited for the doctor, and shivered. Finally, he arrived, chart in hand, and began asking questions, nodding like he expected her answers. Then he listened to her chest and looked down her throat and into her ears.

"Ms. McKinney, we're going to take some pictures, but I would say you have pneumonia."

Half an hour later, after the X-rays, and back in the exam room, she actually felt relieved. *(So, I had good reason to feel like shit! And it's NOT lung cancer! They can cure pneumonia, right?)* She tried to focus on the young doctor's instructions. *(He looks to be about thirteen. Maybe a seventh grader.)*

"Stay in bed until you're free of fever. I'm prescribing some antibiotics, an inhaler, and a nebulizer. Follow the directions carefully and you should feel better in a few days. But, please take it easy. Plenty of sleep and fluids, OK? Call if you don't start to improve within forty-eight hours. I'll be checking on you, anyway."

Merle walked out of the clinic with a fistful of prescriptions and hoped she could find the energy to drive to Walgreen's. Maybe she could leave them off at the drive-thru and get Peggy to pick them up later. *(Oh, dear. Peggy is going to have a fit about this! She's always on me for not taking care of myself! As if she does any better – but then, she's younger. More wiggle room at her age.)*

That night Merle slept fitfully, even though she had been too groggy to read, and too weak even to hold up the book. Maybe it was the fever. Peggy brought her meds, plus some extra-strength Tylenol, and a plastic container of Michael's chicken and rice with mushrooms that Merle usually loved, but which seemed to her singularly unappetizing tonight. Nor was she the least bit enticed by the tapioca pudding, her all-time favorite comfort food. She kept drifting in and out of dreams, some of them more than a little erotic. Then, there was getting up to go tinkle. What a pain. She was so tired that she could hardly move, much less walk to the bath. But her prescribed intake of fluids, especially tea and diet ginger ale, finally forced her out of bed. *(God, I feel ninety years old! This is really awful. I'm surfing the furniture like an old woman!)*

"Freddie, you may have to walk yourself tonight."

"Not to worry, Merle. Peggy took me out earlier, I'll be OK." (I think.)

"Oh, I think Peggy must have taken you out."

Once again in bed, wrapped around one of her king-size pillows, velour blanket pulled up to her nose, and Freddie curled up on the fuzzy throw rug beside the bed, Merle began to dream . . .

She and Phil were in her bed, sheets and blanket all a tangle, early morning, maybe that first morning. She heard phrases of "I'll be Your Baby Tonight," Linda Ronstadt belting out the ballad and focused on the mockingbird line, then realized that the birds and the sunlight were both part of her dream. Phil was on top of her, stretched out, resting his upper body on his elbows, and looking at her with the sexiest face ever – bedroom eyes, cock-eyed smile with his one dimple, and soft full lips begging to be kissed. His skin felt amazing against hers. *(Isn't it interesting that skin not exposed to light stays smooth and, for the most part, unblemished? Certainly much better shape than the arms and neck. Makes getting naked not quite so scary for an old gal like me!)* She admired his broad shoulders and powerful arms as he lowered his weight onto her totally, his chest resting on hers, her boobs having each slid sideways. *(At least it's more comfortable like this!)* She reveled in the touching and the feeling, the mass of his body and the warmth of his breath. Moving her hands oh-so-slowly, she caressed the backs of his thighs, his bum, and the small of his back, ran her fingertip up his spine. But now the body resting on her seemed to diminish, to become almost skeletal. She could feel his ribs. Without opening her eyes, she felt his hair, wiry and sparse.

"John?" she whispered. He hugged her tight and kissed her neck. Pressed into her more intensely.

"Merle, please believe I'll always love you – only you." She recognized the line. That's what he had said the night they reconciled after the trial separation. She thought she had lost him, and it hurt her terribly to think on it. But then he came back; he wanted her after all. She remembered well that sunny afternoon in the upstairs apartment in Houston's funky Montrose neighborhood. Late sun filtered through hanging plants and dust specs floated in the air. She had been dressed in her weekend hippie costume, soft faded jeans with her ivory crinkle-cotton angel top. They talked all afternoon over a bottle of Zinfandel and she had fucked his brains out that night. She moved back to San Antonio the next week and they never, ever, considered separating again.

Merle woke up weeping, not quite able to remember what had caused it. Just overcome with a pervading sense of sadness. She hugged the pillow and buried her face in it. *(John, what are you doing in my dreams again? God, I don't want to wake up without you.)* Now she recalled that awful feeling she got every morning in the days right after John's death, always just as she became conscious in the early light, it would hit her, that John was dead. Still dead.

She began to dream again. This time about the little white Victorian cottage at Copano Beach and the great blue heron who patrolled the wave-break, the Ghost Heron.

She felt some better when she finally woke up on Tuesday, just after noon. Slowly, shakily, still reaching for support, she stumbled into the kitchen and poured herself an orange juice mixed with ginger ale, which she immediately chug-a-lugged, and then made a second, this one on ice. Now she noticed the blue sticky-note with Fay's handwriting placed almost exactly at eye level, right where she should have seen it immediately before she opened the cabinet to get out a glass. *(Oops, missed that. Hmmm . . . I really am out-of-it!)* She sat down rather suddenly on one of the cane-bottom chairs and read the note from that morning. Fay had brought more food, walked Freddie, and reminded her Grams that she could call or text anytime if she needed anything. And that she would be by again tomorrow. And please get better. Merle peeked at Fred, now peacefully curled up on the sofa in the living room, then put her head down on her folded arms on the kitchen table. Inexplicably, Fay's last sentiment made her start crying again. *(I really need to go back to bed!)*

By Thursday afternoon she was talking on the phone with Doris Luna. "I'm going back to school tomorrow. Last day before Thanksgiving break – gotta go."

"Listen, sweetie, your health comes first. Pneumonia is serious. People die from it all the time. Please be careful. Are you sure you are up to it?"

"Antibiotics are a wonderful thing. I felt absolutely horrible for a couple of days, but much improved now. Even hungry, again." *(And smoking. For about two days there, a cigarette was the last thing on my mind.)*

"Well . . . take it easy – and don't stay 'til dark like you sometimes do, OK?" Doris wasn't convinced.

"There won't be a whole lot of teaching going on. I think I can handle it. Besides, I have a cute tradition that I do – a Thanksgiving lesson I've done every year on the day before Thanksgiving break, uses an actual letter from one of the Pilgrims describing the first Thanksgiving. I could do it in my sleep, but only I can do it. And I certainly don't want to miss Turkey Bowling!"

Freddie perked up. "Turkey bowling?"

Later Merle poured herself into a tub of hot water, slid down low, and soaked. She had been in the same cotton nightgown, fuzzy blue robe, and black leather mules for three days now. Time for a bath and clean clothes. Freddie sat wedged into the corner of the small bath, watching her intently. Every few minutes he came over to the tub and licked her face. *(Glad I didn't feel like using my Noxema. He wouldn't like that at all! Make his mouth pucker, it would – and his little pink tongue curl right up.)* She felt limp when she finally climbed out of the tub, and her skin was rosy from being steamed and soaked, but she was revived enough to put on sweats instead of another nightie. And she moved her nest from the bed to the sofa in the living room. *(Ah, progress!)* Even thought about getting out the blue Bicycle cards to play a hand of Sol, but decided on junk TV instead. Playing cards required manual dexterity, and energy to think.

Freddie barked when the doorbell rang. *(Who on earth . . .?)* She shuffled into the kitchen, bent down and pulled the bar from the sliding door, pushed it open, and stepped out onto the balcony to see who was at the front door. Angel smiled up at her.

"So, you do know how to use a doorbell, after all?" She went downstairs to open up and he handed her a heavy plastic grocery bag. It smelled wonderful.

"*Tamales*? It's a little early, isn't it?"

"Naw, my family likes to beat the rush. These are from *mi tía*, she always makes them at Thanksgiving instead of Christmas. That way the *tamalada* doesn't interrupt our Christmas shopping – or our Christmas beer drinking."

"I see. Makes sense to me."

"My mom told her what a nice lady you are, so she sent these to you. They're *deliciosos*. Trust me, I'm an expert." Angel smiled. His mother had dressed him, again. He looked spiffy in pressed jeans and a short-sleeve oxford cloth shirt, and he smelled good, too, the *tamales* notwithstanding.

"Please thank her for me. I'm really glad to get them. Homemade *tamales* are hard to come by unless you have a connection." *(I guess I have a connection.)*

"Gotta go. Take care, *madrina*. Happy Thanksgiving." And he was gone. Again. *(Seems the men in my life have a habit of appearing and disappearing rather precipitously. Wonder if it's me?)*

Ever since her first taste of authentic, homemade, and handmade *tamales*, Merle had believed that, at least in San Antonio, homemade *tamales* should be one of the protected human rights. Unquestionably necessary for civilized existence. She even suggested that, in divorce cases when one or both of the parties were Hispanic, tamale rights should be mandated in the legal decree. Her favorite flavor was the traditional shredded pork, frequently steamed in pork broth made from the *cabeza*, but she also favored the sweet fruit and nut flavor that some families made especially for Christmas. These smelled like pork.

"Whatcha got in the bag, Merle? Smells fantastic! Can I see, huh? Please? PLEASE?" Freddie was literally bouncing around and between her feet, hardly able to contain himself. Merle placed the fragrant, and somewhat greasy, bag of maybe three dozen *tamales* on the counter, carefully pushing it well back, out of doggie reach, and considered Freddie. It was good to see him perky again. She missed his antics and acrobatics. He seemed to have gone into a funk when she got sick. Sympathetic reaction? Maybe, but he was certainly animated now.

"Tamales are not for doggies, Fred."

"How about Mexican doggies? Mexican doggies eat tamales. Mexican doggies LOVE tamales! I can be Mexican. My great-uncle Julio was a Chihuahua."

CHAPTER 29

Turkey Bowling! The highlight of the last day of school before Thanksgiving break. This dubious tradition took place in middle school hallways, with heavy plastic bowling pins supplied and set by the PE department, and used frozen turkeys in plastic bags to knock them down. When slung with adequate velocity, a twenty-pound Butterball could skate down a well-polished school hallway at astonishing speed. Student fans sat along the sides of the hall, with their backs against the lockers, cheering their favorite teachers as they competed for prizes (frozen turkeys, of course) and trying not to get hit by wayward birds, or flying pins. The yelling was so intense that score-keepers used poster boards and jumbo markers to keep the crowd advised on the progress of the games. There were tournaments erupting in every wing of Lozano Middle School. And then the bell rang. *(Oh, my God. Is it really over?)*

Merle corralled her kids into her classroom to wait for their bus numbers to be announced. After the room had cleared, she put her head down on her folded arms at her desk and wondered if she would ever be able to move again.

She was drifting, thinking about Thanksgiving, and Thanksgivings past. The traditional Texas A&M vs. the University of Texas football game. *(Whatever happened to that? Some kind of conference reorganization jiggery-pokery, as I recall. Gone now. Too bad. Was really a big deal in "the day," as the kids say.)* She remembered one particular

Turkey Day game at Kyle Field in College Station when she had visited John. She stayed – along with three other weekend dates – at the home of a sorority sister who lived in College Station, her father a physics professor at the university. This was in the bad old days when Thanksgiving break consisted of only Thanksgiving Day and the Friday after. It was more like a teaser for Christmas than a real vacation. And there was always an underlying urgency to squeeze in every bit of recreation possible before returning to campus for finals, flat-out, non-stop madness until Christmas. John was a junior, and in the Corps, a Cadet, an Aggie – and proud of it, as only a Texas Aggie could be. They went to the annual Bonfire the night before the game, singing and cheering in the enormous crowd. *(Absolutely awesome. Engineering students constructed it, wedding cake design, using untold numbers of trees stripped like telephone poles, twenty plus feet tall. When they lit it, the roar almost knocked me off my feet. All over now . . . since the '99 disaster. Something else gone forever.)* And afterward, they joined a small, but nevertheless raucous, gathering of John's classmates and their dates in the woods somewhere south of campus, maybe private property, near a creek, lots of beer. Someone had driven to the Panhandle to buy Coors and had several coolers in the back of his pick-up with entire cases iced down. *(Rocky Mountain Champagne, we called it!)*

    The next day they sat with the Corps of Cadets for the big game. Merle wore a bright blue wool suit with navy kid pumps and John bought her a giant mum corsage with ribbons and trinkets hanging almost to the hem of her skirt, white mum with maroon ribbons, A&M's colors. The cowbell jingled when she walked and the giant flower shed spikey white petals when she jumped up and down. *(Can't imagine wearing heels and a suit, for christssake, to a football game! But we did. The end of an age, alas.)* John looked super handsome in his uniform. Tradition was that Aggies kissed their dates every time A&M scored. They won the game. Merle loved it. After the game they had escaped to John's dorm room and locked themselves in, turned off the lights, and made love on his bunk, completely ignoring all the friendly, knowing knocks on the door and suggestive comments from the hallway.

"Ms. McKinney? Are you alright?" The afternoon custodian stood in the classroom door leaning on the tall handle of her hall dust mop. "You don't look so good, *mijita*"

"Oh . . . ah . . . Hi, Oralia. I must have . . . ah . . . dozed off. Oh dear . . . got to go home." Merle looked up, out of focus, her face a little mashed on one side where she had slept on it. *(Did I drool on the desk?)*

"Here, let me help you. You've been sick, haven't you? Let's get your stuff together and I'll help you to your car."

Merle liked Oralia a lot; they went way back, probably fifteen years or more. From the beginning, she had watched over Merle like a *tía*; got her matching blue desks – thirty of them – for her room. While most classrooms had a hodgepodge of old and new, assorted colors and styles, Merle's was the only classroom in the eighth-grade wing that was uniform and all new. *(Don't know who she shortchanged. Don't care. Look nice, don't they? Yes, kids do notice what the room looks like!)* Merle loved the fact that Oralia knew hundreds of Spanish *dichos* – sayings and folk wisdom. Most of them were pretty obscure and quite earthy, but endearing – and funny, clever, both in their content and delivery. Merle and Oralia had spent many an afternoon discussing the finer distinctions of Spanish vocabulary and Oralia patiently explaining the significance of a *dicho* until Merle finally got it. All in Spanish, of course. She made sure Merle got plenty of practice. Oralia spoke beautiful, articulate, old-style Spanish, almost nineteenth century wordings and constructions. Her knowledge of Mexican folklore, customs and traditions was unparalleled. And she loved the music of Augustín Lara almost as much as Merle did. She had spent her childhood in a ranching hamlet in the Sonora Desert of northern Mexico; didn't come to San Antonio until she was a teen. *(Always wanted to see if she would let me write her life's story – would be a real shame to lose all that history. She is so typical of an age – an epoch, really. Someone needs to document it. Another project for when I retire?)*

With Oralia's help, Merle stuffed about a thousand student papers into her book bag, collected a few other items she may – or may not – have needed, put on her jacket, and headed rather unsteadily toward the Jeep, Oralia following behind as though she expected Merle to topple over any second. *(Going straight home. Going straight to BED . . . right after I walk Freddie.)*

Saturday morning was clear, cold, and windy. Dry, brown, oak leaves swirling in the yards and in the street. Merle held the red knotted leash taut as Freddie leaned against its tension and peed on some shrubs. The traffic on Broadway seemed sparse for the first full day of Thanksgiving vacation. The air was fresh and uncharacteristically light. Merle inhaled with a deep sigh. *(Maybe everyone left town? I'm sure going to – but not 'til tomorrow. OMG, a whole week off! I really, really NEED this!)*

"Come on, Fred. Let's take the whole block this morning."

"Well, you certainly perked up, didn't you? Drugs working, are they?"

"I'm sure you can tell that I'm MUCH better. Great, in fact. And we're going to the coast tomorrow. I know you're glad to hear that. We'll have a nice time. A few days to ourselves, we'll go out on the pier. You can chase Copano cottontails. Then the whole tribe arrives on Wednesday evening for marathon cooking and eating. You'll like that, too. Turkey – and everything that goes with it." Merle was on a roll. Freddie stopped listening.

"Turkey, oh boy, turkey. Wait – do I know what that is? Not sure, but sounds wonderful. I can almost smell it now!"

Merle had just finished pulling on a pair of soft, clingy jeans and her cuddly rose sweatshirt. She fluffed her hair, spritzed some Blue Grass down her front, dabbed on some pink lipstick, curled her eyelashes, and the doorbell rang. Startled from his nap in the sun, on the living room carpet, resting on his back with his floppy paws in the air, Freddie sprang into a frenzy, barking furiously. *(What? Not Angel – again?)* She pulled up the safety bar from the sliding glass door and stepped out on the balcony to see who was downstairs. *(Oh SHIT! What now?)*

Phil looked up at Merle and smiled, with his one dimple, beautiful big, brown eyes hidden behind Ray-Bans. *(But I know they're there.)* He waved a book in the air – her book, her copy of *Love in the Time of Cholera.*

Seated at the kitchen table, Phil was telling Merle, in noxious detail, how much he and his new lady friend had enjoyed Marquez's story of enduring passion. Seems they read it aloud to each other on a road trip to northern California. *(Ah, ha! I knew he was a flake!)* Then he moved on to a disgusting description of his new love interest. *(I want to strangle him . . . right now. With my bare hands. I'm gonna leap right over this table and gouge his eyes out. What an asshole!)*

"Phil, I'm really very busy right now packing for the coast." Merle stood up, hoping Phil would get the message and leave soon. "Thanks for returning the book. Glad you liked it. Hope you get around to reading it in Spanish someday."

She walked into the living room, Phil close behind. When she sat on the back of a club chair, sort of leaned on it, waiting for him to go, he moved right in. Now straddling her, he started rubbing her arms and swaying his body from side to side in an old familiar move, making inarticulate cuddly noises. *(What the hell is he doing?)* When he leaned close to her she could smell his freshly washed and ironed cotton sports shirt. It all started to feel sort of comfortable, soothing. *(What the hell am I doing?)*

"Not a good move, Phil. You're quite the temptation, but no." She pushed him away and stood, walked to the sofa and sat down. Phil followed, seating himself opposite her. He noticed the deck of blue Bicycle cards on the coffee table and picked them up, shuffled effortlessly, feathering and fanning. Merle watched with admiration and wondered why they had never played cards. *(He's probably the type who doesn't like to lose. So, just as well we never played.)*

"I fall in love too easily. I'm really sorry I hurt you, Merle." *(Yeah, I'm sorry too.)*

He fanned the cards out, face down, and offered them to her. She chose one and pulled it out. He nodded again and she turned it over on the table.

"Ah, the Queen of Hearts. How about that!" He smiled at her, with his one dimple. *(Yeah, I was YOUR Queen of Hearts! Don't you get it? You fucking idiot!)* "I better go."

At the front door he squeezed her around the shoulders briefly and kissed her on the forehead, then left without another word. Merle stood motionless, staring into the middle distance.

"What the hell just happened?"

Freddie had been keeping a very low profile ever since he realized who the visitor was, and picked up on Merle's distinctly hostile vibes. Now he studied Merle from the top of the stairs.

"Phil didn't even notice me, much less play ball with me like he used to. What's up with that? Sorta makes you wonder, doesn't it?"

"Come on, Twinkletoes, let's get packed." Suddenly Merle was a flurry of activity, sprinting up the stairs two at a time, that is until her hinky knee stopped her. *(Oooff! Ouch.)*

Saturday night late/SA

Phil – of all people – came by today. Thought I was gonna faint. Fortuitously, I had just finished freshening up – looked and smelled great, especially for a recently recovered pneumonia patient. Didn't stop him from telling me all about his new squeeze, tho'. Really wanted to whack him. Ostensibly, he returned my book – Gabriel Garcia Marquez's "Cholera." Went on and on about the beauty of true love and passion. He was so completely seduced by Marquez's romantic hero in the story that he failed to notice that the guy was a pedophile and responsible for his young niece's suicide.

I pulled the Queen of Hearts out of a deck of cards he offered me. Couldn't do that again in a million years! Omen? Of what?

I don't think Freddie likes him anymore.

We're going to the coast tomorrow – right after church. We're all packed. Can't wait – a whole week away. (Retirement is looking better and better all the time.)

"God of our fathers, whose almighty hand . . ." *(dum, ta-da-dum).* Merle listened to the full-bodied sound of the St. David's choir as they processed majestically down the center aisle two-by-two, and the organ pounded away, low notes tickling eardrums and teasing fillings. She found a seat on the left side of the church and squeezed in, inhaling the clean aroma of fresh-cut flowers, and carefully unfolding the kneeler. She quickly dropped into an "Episcopalian squat" (knees braced on the kneeler and butt on the front edge of the pew) for a brief prayer before the Sunday morning service began in earnest. The choir sound surrounded her as they recessed up the side aisles, now in single file, heading toward the balcony choir loft.

"Be thou our ruler, guardian, guide, and stay . . ." *(Well, I sure as hell hope so. Please, Lord, make it be so.)* Merle found the appropriate pages in the *Book of Common Prayer*, marked them with pages from her bulletin inserts, and looked around at the crowded sanctuary. She spotted Alpha Ann with her family on the right side, up near the front. *(My goodness, her older brother is turning into quite the looker! And, wow – that must be the girlfriend from UT. She's a Tri-Delt, I think. What was it Annie said about her? Can't remember.)*

Merle enjoyed the familiar liturgy. It reassured her that she was worshiping a powerful, benevolent, and omnipotent God, within a great historic and sacred tradition. She had read some theology when she was younger, and struggled along and along with some of the dogmas and doctrines, but in the end it seemed to her that many of the details didn't really matter that much. What did matter was that Christianity was a better, happier, more productive way to live, if practiced in the true spirit of Jesus' teachings. *(Yeah, that's the trick, alright, isn't it?)*

Now she focused on the Collect, ". . . we give you thanks for the fruits of the earth in their season and . . . make us, we pray, faithful stewards of your great bounty . . ." *(Yes, I do have a lot to be thankful for. In the big scheme of things, I, too, have been given a Great Bounty. Better be careful what I choose to do with it! A little guidance along these lines would be greatly appreciated, Lord.)*

After communion, blessing, and another Thanksgiving hymn, the service ended and Merle headed for the Jeep, deciding to skip morning coffee in the parish hall, even though she almost always enjoyed it, because she wanted to get the hell out of Dodge and on the road to the coast just as soon as possible. She drove home singing "We gather together to ask the Lord's blessing . . ." to herself.

"OK, Fred. Looks like we're packed. You've been a big help." Merle stood at the top of the stairs, with a big smile on her freckled face, sweaty curls clinging to her neck, and surveyed the heap of suitcases and assorted bags and boxes she had assembled.

"I do what I can, sweetie. Let's get going." The terrier was tracing circles on the living room carpet, just as fast as he could run, long pink tongue hanging out.

"Whoa, slow down. You're going to rip the rug – haven't had your nails clipped recently. Besides, I want to eat some lunch before we head out. Actually, before I try to carry all that stuff to the car." Merle walked into the kitchen, opened the fridge and pulled out the bag of tamales that Angel had given her the day before.

"This looks like a good idea." Merle placed three of the filled and folded corn husks on a paper plate, popped them into the microwave, and then licked the tamale-flavored grease off her fingers. Freddie had stopped dead in his tracks. The delicious smell of tamales hit him hard, olfactory nerves instantly shifting into overdrive. He was transported, mesmerized. Before he knew what he was doing, he had completely forgotten about the coast and was sitting at Merle's feet, frantically begging.

"Please, Merle, just a taste? I'll even speak Spanish, 'tah-mah-lay.' See?" He began making squeaky, whining sounds.

"Stop it, Fred. Here, I'll let you lick a corn husk, OK?" She carefully pulled on the outside edge of a grease-soaked husk and rolled a plump *tamal* out onto the plate, then held the empty husk down for Fred.

Completely overcome by the sensory fireworks going off in his head, Freddie lunged at Merle's hand, clamping her thumb, along with the fragrant tamale wrapper, firmly between his razor-sharp little teeth.

"OUCH. Oh, SHIT! Let go, let go NOW!" Merle tried desperately to get Fred to release his grip. Finally, she whacked him on the nose with a wooden spoon and he let go.

"Oh, NO. Oh, YIKES! Merle, honey, I am SO SORRY!! I didn't mean to – really. I don't know what happened to me. Here, let me lick it."

"Fred, you little monster! BAD DOG! You bit right through my thumbnail. Dammit!" *(Shit . . . hurts. REALLY hurts. And I'm bleeding all over everything!)* Merle stared at her punctured nail, a small tooth-sized hole oozing dark blood. Then she turned her thumb over and found a sizeable gash on the pad, also bleeding. She grabbed a paper towel and wrapped it tightly around her throbbing wound. In the bathroom, after rinsing it completely with cold water, she wrapped it again and ratted around in the cabinet with one hand – the other hand – until she found a dusty bottle of hydrogen peroxide. *(Wonder how old this stuff is? Guess it still works. Hydrogen peroxide doesn't spoil, does it?)* Holding her hand over the sink, she dribbled the clear liquid on her injury, both sides, and watched it erupt into a foam of tiny bubbles. Freddie had followed her into the bath and now sat scrunched into the corner by the toilet, looking devastated.

"Guess you like tamales as much as you like chocolate, huh?"

Freddie slid to a crouch and covered his eyes with his paws. *(Aw . . . jeez. Where did he learn that? That's an Asta move, if I ever saw one. I swear, that dog is prescient.)*

After she bandaged up the disaster, slathering it with Neosporin and placing a small gauze pad under a large Band-Aid, so that she covered the holes on both sides of her thumb. After she grabbed a couple of Tylenol, she got a cold Bohemia out of the fridge and plopped down on the living room sofa. *(Sooner or later, I guess I should take the nail polish off. Eeek, that nail polish remover is gonna smart something awful!)* Freddie had followed her into the living room and sat at her feet, looking as hopeful as he could manage.

"Can I lick your face?" He gingerly placed a paw on her knee.

"Not now, Fred. I've got get over being mad at you first, then you can get in my lap and lick my face."

The little yellow Jeep turned off I-37 onto US 181 toward Corpus Christi and Casa Esperanza. Merle sang to Freddie as he rode shotgun next to her. "We gather together to ask the Lord's blessing . . .'" Merle knew all the verses. One of the seldom-mentioned perks of being an Episcopalian. *(We NEVER sing the short version!)*

Freddie laid his head on the center console, as close as he could get to Merle's lap while she was driving. He knew the limits, had learned them the hard way. Looking up at her as she sang, he pondered her recent mood improvement. And was thankful.

"Freddie, I'm thankful I have you. Part of my own Great Bounty. You're a good dog, in spite of recent events. And you're my favorite companion." She patted his head and rubbed him behind the ears.

"Yikes, Merle, I'm touched. Really, I am. Especially BECAUSE of recent events." Fred sat up and looked out the front window. Late fall wildflowers still dotted the highway shoulders, pretty daisy-like yellow things that Merle couldn't remember the name of. Bright, chilly autumn day in South Texas.

"I'm thankful for you, Merle. Truly. For you ... and streetsnax. Yes, definitely for streetsnax. But mostly for you."

CHAPTER 30

"What a pretty little house!" Merle whipped her yellow Jeep into the driveway, put it in gear, lowered all the windows, and turned off the engine. *(Got to air out. Got to remember to close them tonight.)* Then she sat there considering her beloved retreat. The white frame Victorian cottage with green shutters – real, functional, hurricane shutters – and plenty of gingerbread, sat on a narrow lot facing Pineda Park and Copano Bay beyond, smothered with lush bougainvillea, oleanders, and cannas, all still blooming in the clear fall sunshine. (*Well, not so much lush as overgrown.*) "I do love the colors – don't care if they need trimming." The sight of her beach house always cheered her up. And Lord knows, she needed it. *(My life's been an absolute train wreck!)* Casa Esperanza – Hope's House, House of Hope.

"Let me out, Merle. Smells WONDERFUL! Gotta go check for streetsnax."

Merle got out of the car, Fred fast on her heels, stretched her legs, *(Sit too long in one position and everything freezes up! Oh, ouch!)* then slowly began to unload her extensive cargo, piling items on the front porch first before moving them inside. Freddie had wandered over toward the park and was focused on something in the grassy ditch. Suddenly, he began to screech and jump around. *(What on earth?)* She ran over to him with the red leash in her hand.

"No, NO, Fred! That one's not a streetsnack – at least not yet." A very much alive, and definitely panicked, green frog hopped quickly away, in the zig-zag way of frogs, as fast as his crooked hind legs could propel him. She clipped the leash onto Fred's collar. "At least wait until someone runs over it."

Perversely, thinking about Freddie's streetsnax reminded Merle that she hadn't eaten all day, the tamale lunch having been aborted after Freddie bit her. Now she checked the cottage fridge to see what was available, Freddie observing from under the white enamel-top kitchen table.

"Ah, ha. We have eggs. Always a good sign. Let's see . . . would it still be considered *migas* if I don't have any chips? Maybe not, how about a cheese and veggie omelet?" She busied herself slicing and chopping a rather elderly green bell pepper she had scrounged from the crisper drawer. *(Maybe I should soak it in some ice water? Try to revive it a bit?)* Even though Freddie had mangled her left thumb, not her more essential right thumb, the injury and resulting bandage still made her simple task difficult and awkward, trying as she did to not put any pressure on it. *(Ugh! It's oozing again. And hurts.)* She went into the bath and got two Tylenol out of the medicine cabinet. Washed them down with some fizzy water and sat down a few minutes on a kitchen stool. While the pepper pieces were sizzling in olive oil, she added diced onion and tomatoes *(Glad I picked up some fresh ones at Entrepreneur Corner),* poured in scrambled eggs and sprinkled grated cheese on top. *(Not much, but it'll have to do.)* She shook the empty plastic zipper bag, and thumped it a couple of times, with her uninjured hand. Then she seasoned the mess with salt, coarse-ground black pepper, a little garlic powder, and a few drops of Tabasco, grabbed her favorite spatula, mixed and turned the mixture until it was nicely browned, and slid it onto her plate. Although still pissed at Freddie over the tamale husk disaster, she did fork off a small blob of omelet for him and scraped it into his bowl.

"Yes, Freddie, you'll get the plate to lick when I'm finished. Not now. You can stop whining, please." She sat at the dining room table, Freddie planted expectantly at her feet, and began going through her mail – three days' worth she had collected from her condo mailbox before she left San Antonio, plus the accumulation from her Copano Beach PO box which she had picked up on her way into town. All of it in a heap on the table. She sorted her way through, pitching ads, flyers, "resident," hunting catalogs, and saving a smaller pile to actually look at, maybe even read. Searching for real mail first, she picked up an official-looking envelope, Bexar County District Attorney. *(Aw, shit! What now?)*

Seems the DA was informing her of the upcoming trial, the State of Texas vs. William Russell Epps, on charges of possession and distribution of child pornography. Court date was set for December 27th and she would be called to testify. *(Oh, wonderful! Just what I want to do with my Christmas vacation! Not to mention I'll have to face that creep in court!)*

While she was stewing over the DA's letter, she forgot completely about the cigarette dangling in her fingers. She had been drawing on it furiously, but absentmindedly, and now she had ash all down her front. A large glowing ember was burning its way brightly through her turquoise sweater. Right in the middle, between two rows of cables. Jumping up and brushing off the offending substance, she frightened Freddie who immediately began to bark.

"Crap! Look at that HUGE hole! And this is my favorite sweater! Dammit! DAMMIT!" She stormed into the bedroom and jerked off her top, wadded it up and stuffed it into the garbage, then searched for a replacement.

"Remember, Merle, this is a VACATION!"

"I gotta go sit on the front porch and chill out! With a beer."

By Monday afternoon Merle was into the Thanksgiving spirit full on! She had the Grandmother's Kitchen thing going and the house smelled wonderful, Eagles wailing on the box. Weather clear and cold and bright. When she heard footsteps on the front porch, she wiped her hands on her apron, her 'Buela's old 1940s calico with rick-rack trim apron that she loved to wear in this comfortable, friendly old kitchen, and walked quickly to the door before anyone could ring the bell and set off Freddie. Four Hispanic children of indeterminate age and sex stared at her, bright brown eyes almost visible beneath unruly black hair. One of them produced a piece of paper. Merle noticed a silver Toyota Corolla idling in the street in front of her house, elderly female driver, also Hispanic. *(Wonder what we have here?)*

"What can I do for you ladies . . . and gentlemen?" Shy giggles.

"We're all ladies, 'mam. That is, we're all girls. We're on a scavenger hunt." The tallest one shoved the list toward Merle. "This is Linda, and this is Whitney, and that's Alexa. I'm Marianne." She pointed to each child in order, and then to herself. Merle could see now that all the moppets were indeed female, and unquestionably related. Dressed uniformly in jeans and T-shirts and tennies.

"Who's in the car?" Merle looked toward the street. The lady driver waved.

"Oh, that's our grandmother. She made the list."

"Well, let's ask her to come in. And I'll see what I can do for you." *(Wow, this is certainly different. What a clever idea to keep the kiddies occupied!)* She headed toward the street, leaving the girls to admire and fawn over Freddie, who was loving it. (Doing my cutest doggie act — ever!)

Half an hour later, Herlinda Garcia *(Wonder if Linda was named after her?)* and her four granddaughters sat around Merle's dining room table drinking hot chocolate and eating the oatmeal-raisin cookies Merle had baked that morning. Merle had placed a small box, a square gift box from her Christmas collection, in the middle of the table. It contained an assemblage of small items from the scavenger hunt list – jumbo paperclip, rubber band, matchbook, zip-tie, Christmas card, . . .

"I'm sorry I couldn't find you a hat pin. I really thought I had one." *(And I probably do, just can't find it. I really need to organize my sewing stuff. What a mess that is! Can't find anything!)* Merle winced as she thought about her futile effort to locate the elusive hat pin in the labyrinth of her sewing closet.

A few minutes later, she saw them all off with a smile on her face. *(Nice family.)* The bright, friendly coastal sun had finally done its job. Merle's brain was on pause.

CARLITA KOSTY

Wednesday morning, early/Copano Beach

Checked my kids' benchmark scores online – they're horrible! But, know what? I don't friggin' care! I think I just decided to retire. I'm gonna turn in my keys. And my damn electronic gradebook. Never did like computers much, John notwithstanding.

I'm sitting here at the dining room table drinking coffee – good coffee, too, HEB's Texas Pecan flavor – and looking out at the Bay, and thinking it would be really nice to live here fulltime. I think I could get used to this.

And the birds are lovely.

Just heard the garbage truck dump my bin. There goes my favorite turquoise sweater with the burn hole in it – the evidence of my sin.

Got to see a doctor about my damn knee. Hurts all the time.

Played Sol last nite and won two in a row – blue card rules and all. Some weeks ago I put a dimple on the King of Clubs so he would look like Phil. So, I fixed it – added another dimple to match. Now he looks like Burl Ives with a Prince Valiant hairdo.

"Come on, Fang. Want to go to the store with me?"

"Sure! Shotgun?... Wait, what's this "fang" business? Yikes, I said I was sorry, Merle. It was an accident. REALLY, it was."

"At least I'm laughing about it." Merle said more to herself than to Freddie, as she picked up her purse, sunglasses, car keys, and hat

– always a hat in Copano Beach. *(Keeps the wind from blowing my hair into my eyes. Hmmm . . . something to consider for retirement. Do I really want to have "hat hair" the rest of my life?)* They were off to pick up an egg sandwich she had ordered earlier from the Pelican Sandwich Shop and to get a morning Corpus Christi paper and a pack of cigarettes at the Copano Stop'n'Shop.

After almost missing most of the giant potholes in the caliche and shell parking lot, Merle parked the Jeep, and left Fred with the windows cracked, while she went into the small convenience store. It was dark inside, but several customers made it seem warm and cheerful. Aisles were close and crowded, shelves packed, and prices exorbitant, but there was an astounding selection of chips, colas, beer, and tobacco products.

Merle had just dropped the cigarettes into her purse and was zipping her wallet when a familiar face appeared in her peripheral vision.

"Ah, Freddie's rescuer! Hi, . . . ah, Leroy, is it? Nice to see you!" Merle checked to make sure her ciggies weren't visible in her purse. She turned toward him, looked up and smiled. Then took off her hat and fluffed her hair.

"Yes, yes it is. But, if you don't mind, let's make it Roy." He removed his straw cowboy hat and stood up straight. *(Wow, he's a lot taller than I remember. I like 'em tall.)* Then he looked Merle over just a tiny bit too slowly, and smiled. *(Oh, but I do remember that Robin Williams smile!)* He continued, "Leroy wasn't too bad in Louisiana, but I think Roy is more suitable for Texas. If you know what I mean?" He nodded at her like she should – should know what he meant. She didn't. Hadn't a clue.

"OK, then Roy it is. How you been, Roy?"

"Oh, can't complain. You got a crowd coming for Thanksgiving?"

"Yeah, they'll be in tomorrow night. You?"

"Haven't got much of a family anymore. An old oil field buddy of mine is coming in and we're going up to the Hill Country for a few days. Maybe do a little hunting. So, keep track of that mutt of your's, hear? I won't be around to rescue him for a few days." He grinned, put his hat back on and went about his way, looking for whatever it was he was looking for in the little store.

How long had it been since Leroy (now Roy) Adler found Freddie huddled on his front porch? Merle tried to remember. It was during that awful weekend when the Phil situation was coming all unglued, and she had been so miserable. So miserable and awful to be around, that Fred had escaped, just ran off, then got lost. *(That was Columbus Day weekend, so maybe five or six weeks ago?)* Merle reflected a bit on how her life had changed in those five or six weeks. And then she allowed her brain to expand the examination to the past five or six months. She flinched at that. *(A LOT of water under the bridge. Actually, I'm much improved, I think. But one thing hasn't changed: I still don't have a man.)*

"Hmmm... Freddie, remember that old fisherman who pulled you in out of the rain a few weeks back?"

"Yeah, the one with Cujo chained in his bathroom? Sure, I remember him. He was nice — and his house smelled delicious. But the clawing noises put me off."

"I just saw him again. He's real cute. And I did notice this time – no wedding ring. Plus, he said he didn't have much family, anymore." Merle paused momentarily to ponder on "anymore," and why he might have chosen that particular word.

"Oh, my egg sandwich. Almost forgot." Snapping out of her thoughts and back to reality, she backed the Jeep around, trying as much as possible to avoid the craters, then headed across the highway to the sandwich shop.

"Aw, jeez! Now he's gonna think I'm following him!" Merle pulled into the restaurant parking lot just in time to see Roy disappear inside, through the screen door. "But I've got to get my egg sandwich – can't just leave it. Molly would never speak to me again! And I do enjoy getting special-order sticky buns. Maybe I should call her?" What to do? What to do? Freddie had correctly discerned that her soliloquy was just that, and not directed at him, or at anyone in particular. He curled up on the front seat and worried a small sandbur that was tangled in the fuzz between his toes. Suddenly, inexplicably, Merle felt as though her whole life depended on what she did, right now.

"OK, I'm going in."

Inside the brightly-lit restaurant the atmosphere was casual, but busy. It smelled of hamburgers on the grill and French fries, with an undertone of cinnamon and brown sugar. Several of the picnic-style tables, complete with red-and-white check oilcloth covers, were occupied. One in the corner was overflowing with a large family of tow-headed children who were busying themselves playing with small packets of sugar and sugar substitutes, matching and trading the colors, waiting impatiently for their meal. Merle spotted Roy at the counter, paying for his order. He was dressed in Levis, worn to a patina, and a venerable old plaid flannel shirt, tucked in, and tennies. *(Nice ass.)* He turned around just as she walked up.

"I promise I'm not following you, Roy. It's just that I forgot about my egg sandwich." Merle walked up to him and smiled – the biggest, brightest smile she had mustered up in quite a while. She thought he winked at her. *(But maybe it was just steam from the grill.)*

"Well, I guess I wouldn't mind too much if you were following me." He grinned at her and his pale grey eyes sparkled. An "aw, shucks" moment. "This place seems to be popular – and not just with the tourists. You come here often?"

"Yeah, I don't like cooking for one. Freddie hardly counts. Their stuff is really good – and all homemade." *(Now he knows I live alone, too. At least, if he has any sense, he does.)*

"My grandma used to bring me here. It's been in Copano Beach a really long time."

"If I remember right, you were cooking gumbo when I picked up Freddie. Do you cook often?" That made him smile, then chuckle.

"I do, and quite often. Actually, I'm pretty talented in the kitchen. Come by sometime and I'll prove it to you." *(This time I KNOW he winked. I'm sure of it.)* She giggled a bit. Then bit her tongue. *(This scene is becoming surreal. Out of a movie. Did I miss the first cue?)*

"Love to! I'll bring the beer." *(Let's see if he can suggest a day? Or is this all just polite small talk – and flirting?)*

They left the restaurant together, him opening the door for her, and her thanking him for doing so. As she approached the Jeep and saw Freddie, she had an idea. *(Maybe I can make something happen*

. . .) Fred looked at her somewhat dubiously, trying to figure out what exactly it was that she wanted.

"Run, Freddie. Off you go . . . toward the vacant lot, please, not the highway." She tried to push his butt off the driver's seat. He dug in with his sharp little toenails, curling them like talons.

"No! What's the matter with you, Merle? I'm a GOOD dog." Determined, Merle kept shoving.

"Stop that. Here comes your friend."

Merle turned around to discover Roy walking toward her and Freddie. *(Shit! That didn't work.)* Merle suddenly saw herself as the female lead in a 1940s black-and-white romantic comedy, pulling off improbable antics to attract her man. *(This is crazy – the way I'm acting.)*

"I see your little runaway is behavin' better. You musta' trained him well. Guess he was just scared the other night." Roy reached in and rubbed Freddie behind the ears, let Fred lick his hand. "A runner is usually always a runner. So, this is good." *(Yeah, he behaves when he wants to behave!)*

"Thanks. I've been working with him. We're both slow learners."

"I've got your back, Merle. You can count on me!"

SPANISH WORDS & PHRASES

Abuela, 'Buela – grandmother

Aguas frescas – iced fruit-flavored drinks

Amor – love

Arroz con pollo – chicken and rice

¡Arráncame! – tear from me

Aséquia – aqueduct

Buena suerte – good luck

Cabeza – head

Cabrito – roasted or baked kid

Caca – poop, shit

Café con leche – coffee with milk

Calabaza – squash

Cantina – bar

Chalupa – fried tortilla with refried beans, meat, & vegetables on top

Chica – girl, girlfriend

Chiles rellenos – stuffed peppers

Chili con carne – spicy beef soup

Chili con queso – hot cheese and tomato dip

¡Chinga! – Fuck!

Comadre – literally, one's child's godmother; used for a close female friend

Como – like, as

Conjunto – Mexican western music, (literally "together")

Corrida – ballad

Dichos – sayings, folk wisdom

Eres – you are

Esperanza – hope

Existe – existence

Fajitas – beef strips grilled with onions and tomatoes

Familia – family

Flan, flanes – egg custard with caramel topping

Flauta – chicken filled tortilla fried in oil

Frontera – frontier, border

Guacamole – Mexican avocado dip

Guayabera – men's short sleeve shirt, linen or cotton, usually with tucks and pockets, worn loose

Hada madrina – fairy godmother

Hasta la vista – until I see you

Hecho a mano – handmade

Hola – hello

Huera – blondie, white girl

Huevos rancheros – fried eggs with salsa

Limeños – people from Lima, Peru

Madrina – godmother

Mi, mis, mía/o – my

Migas – scrambled eggs with leftovers, corn chips, and cheese, (literally, "scraps")

Mijito/mijita – my little son/daughter; collectively children

Moco Loco – crazy bugger

Muchísimas gracias – many thanks

Nadie – nobody

Norteamericanos – North Americans

Piñata – paper mâché decorated container holding candies & prizes, animal or other shapes

Pan dulce – sweet bread, traditional Mexican pastries

Pendejo – good-for-nothing, dummy

¿Qué pasa? – what's happening? what's up?

Quiero – I love, I want

Quinceañera – fifteenth birthday celebration, debut

Ranchito – a little ranch or farm

Razón – reason

Raspa – snow cone

Revolución – the 1910-1920 civil war in Mexico

Sala – living room

Santo – carved and painted wood statue of a saint, Jesus, or the Virgin Mary

Santa – holy woman, good-hearted woman

Simpático – charming and agreeable

Tamal – one tamale (meat pie usually made with pork, cornmeal dough, and wrapped in a corn husk)

Tamalada – a tamale making party

Taquería – taco stand, small restaurant

Taquitos – little tacos, breakfast tacos, or small "street" tacos

¡Ten cuidado! – be careful

Tía/tío – aunt, uncle

Tu, te – you, your

Vatos – guys, dudes

Vida – life

Viejita – little old lady

ACKNOWLEDGEMENTS

This book has been a long time coming. My dear friend and critic, Cristina Sumners, was with me at its conception and encouraged me to keep writing when I despaired. I owe her a great debt for believing in me.

I could not have gotten Merle and Freddie's story on paper without the advice and assistance of a great number of people. First, my volunteer readers, who diligently completed their assignments, but also kept contacting me asking if they could show my manuscript to a neighbor, a sister-in-law, a friend, . . . You know who you are, and I thank you from the bottom of my heart.

I do want to recognize two of those readers: Ginny Byrd, who was the first person to see the completed manuscript, and who told me that I had described her teaching experience "exactly!" And Gene Alber who ignored my instructions not to sweat the small stuff and provided me with both an extensive typed critique and an abundance of sticky notes in the manuscript itself.

Very special thanks go to Bill Ingram and Marian Johnson, two grammar gurus who spent many hours going over my manuscript with red pen and excellent expertise. And to my good friend Alma Ortiz who served as my consultant on Spanish language and Mexican-American culture. Early on, I had an idea for my book cover. Artist Tambria Reed somehow managed to interpret that concept and I shall be forever grateful to her for her work on my behalf.

And certainly, I will never be able to thank enough my dear Richard, my mainstay and worst critic, without whose support, advice, and enduring tolerance, this story never would have seen the light of day.